DEADLY CONVICTIONS

PHILIP LUBER

WARNER BOOKS

A Warner Communications Company

The author gratefully acknowledges the following for giving permission to use copyrighted material:
Model Penal Code (page vii): Copyright © 1962 by The American Law Institute. Reprinted with
the permission of The American Law Institute.
Excerpts from the DSM-III (pages 40 and 190): American Psychiatric Association Diagnostic and
Statistical Manual of Mental Disorders, Third Edition, Washington, D.C., APA, 1980.
"I Remember It Well" by Alan Jay Lerner/Frederick Lowe (page 134): Copyright © 1957 & 1958
by Lowel Corporation. Copyright renewed, all rights assigned to Chappell & Co., Inc. International
Copyright Secured. ALL RIGHTS RESERVED. Used by permission.
"April Showers" by B. G. DeSylva and Louis Silvers (page 193): © 1921—Warner Bros. Music.
Copyright renewed; extended term of copyright deriving from Louis Silvers assigned and effective
March 30, 1980 to RANGE ROAD MUSIC INC. and QUARTET MUSIC INC., administered by
HERALD SQUARE MUSIC INC. Used by permission. All rights reserved.

W A Warner Communications Company

Printed in the United States of America
First Printing: June 1986
10 9 8 7 6 5 4 3 2 1

Designed by Giorgetta Bell McRee

Library of Congress Cataloging-in-Publication Data

Luber, Philip.
  Deadly convictions.

  I. Title.
PS3562.U22D4 1986   813'.54   85-43160
ISBN 0-446-51299-0

ACKNOWLEDGMENTS

To my wife, Cynthia Mate.

To my agent, Alice Fried Martell, who believed I could write this book; and to my editor, Nansey Neiman, who showed me how.

To my friends, for their encouragement: Greig Cranna, Lenny and Elizabeth Gibson, David O. Greenleaf, Karen A. Katz, and Chester Swett, Jr.

Special thanks to Leslie Keenan and the rest of the staff at Warner Books.

A person is not criminally responsible for conduct if at the time of such conduct, as a result of mental disease or mental defect, he lacks substantial capacity either to appreciate the criminality (wrongfulness) of his conduct or to conform his conduct to the requirements of the law.

American Law Institute

PART
ONE

It was Christmas Eve, 1982. A light snow was spreading thinly on the city streets.

Cardonick drove his Pinto down the Fairmount Street ramp and onto the Schuylkill Expressway. He scanned the signs: CENTER CITY PHILADEL-PHIA, BEAR LEFT. STADIUMS AND NEW JERSEY, BEAR RIGHT. He checked his watch: *Eight forty-five.* Taillights stretched before him like a string of red beads. He hit cruising speed and melted into the traffic.

His left hand on the steering wheel, Cardonick reached across his body with his right hand and balanced the Ruger Mini-14 rifle on the edge of the half-open car window. The Art Museum loomed in the distance as he fired his first shot. A green Cadillac swerved abruptly in the distance. Acrid gun fumes swirled around him.

The Cadillac regained its bearing. It slowed down as the unseen driver guided it into the breakdown lane. Again Cardonick bore down on the trigger. Again the fumes enveloped him. The bullet danced harmlessly into the night.

Not good enough, you son of a bitch. He rolled the window completely open. Snowflakes filled the Pinto. He grabbed the wheel with his right hand and shifted the weapon to his left one.

His third shot connected. Thirty yards ahead the rear window of a white Chevy shattered. The Chevy accelerated and bore right toward New Jersey. Cardonick followed suit. His Pinto sideswiped a small sedan and sent it hurtling into the guardrail. He saw the flames in his side-view mirror.

William Penn's statue rose on the left from City Hall tower, its copper patina a sickly shade of green. Cardonick squeezed off three rapid shots. A pickup truck two lanes over careened into a foreign compact. The white Chevy jumped wildly across the center rail and landed wheels-up in the lane of oncoming traffic. Brakes squealed like animals in a slaughterhouse.

Cardonick rolled up the car window and boosted the volume of his radio. Bruce Springsteen was singing the old Crystals' version of "Santa Claus Is Coming to Town." The heater's exhaust fan sucked in the gun fumes, mixed them with the warm engine air, and spit them back into the Pinto. The mixture seemed twice as powerful. Cardonick's eyes filled with tears.

He felt as if the shots had displaced some enormous inner pressure and had kept him from bursting apart. He was relieved. He glanced at the license plate on the car in front of him and added the digits left to right, then right to left, then in random order. The sums were identical. He took comfort in the consistency.

The South Philadelphia gasoline refineries passed by on his right. The fetid odor mixed with the gun fumes and the engine heat. He remembered hearing a comedian refer to the refinery smell as "the cosmic fart." He smiled and placed the rifle on the floor.

Flashing blue lights bounced off of his rear- and side-view mirrors. A police car hovered directly behind. A second cruiser came alongside the Pinto and its driver motioned toward the breakdown lane.

Cardonick slowed down. The cruiser alongside him pulled ahead. The Pinto glided into the breakdown lane simultaneously with the two cruisers. Suddenly Cardonick slammed down on the accelerator and angled back sharply into the stream of traffic. A Plymouth banked hard off his front left bumper, twisted perpendicular to the road, and was struck by two other cars from behind.

LAST EXIT BEFORE TOLL BRIDGE TO NEW JERSEY, ½ MILE. The bridge would be blocked by now, he knew. He veered right and took the last Pennsylvania exit from the expressway. He turned left at the end of the ramp, then right one block later, and massive Veterans Stadium loomed in front of him. The Pinto blasted through the steel chain stretched across the parking lot entrance.

He heard the pop of an unseen pistol. The bullet sheared off his radio antenna and pierced the windshield. His cheek stung as if a wet towel were snapping against it. Tiny circles of blood splattered onto the side window.

Cardonick aimed full-throttle toward the stadium. Six or seven cruisers materialized magically and interposed themselves between the

Pinto and its target. He dropped to the floor, steadying the wheel with his left hand and depressing the gas pedal with his right. He tasted the mixture of sweat and blood as it rolled down his cheek and past his lips.

He heard one shot, then another, then several more. His tires exploded and the Pinto jerked unevenly across the asphalt. Cardonick was thrown against the car door, and it sprang open. His head and shoulders stretched into the darkness. Snow particles lashed against his forehead like so many tiny whips.

He closed his eyes as the car sputtered quickly to a halt. When he opened them he was staring into the barrel of a pistol. The hand holding the gun was shaking nervously, its finger rubbing against the trigger. "Go ahead," murmured Cardonick. "Kill me, I want you to."

Driving to work late Christmas Eve, Detective Captain Stanley Schacter listened to his favorite Willie Nelson cassette. Nearly forty years earlier Schacter had spent six months of his Air Force duty stationed outside of San Antonio, the only time in his life he spent more than two weeks away from Philadelphia. He carried back from Texas a fondness for enchiladas, huevos rancheros, Lone Star beer, and country music. And he vowed never again to leave his hometown.

Schacter was not a demonstrative man, and he seldom thought about or used the word *love*, but he loved Philadelphia: the even-handed symmetry of its streets, the green acres of its city parks, the aroma of soft pretzels and minute-steaks. And he loved the fierce loyalties it inspired. People who moved to Philadelphia stayed there, and those who moved away still considered it their home.

Like most of its natives, Schacter knew that the city of Philadelphia does not actually exist as a distinct entity; it lives only as a figment of some cartographer's imagination. Philadelphia is really a collection of neighborhoods, and these neighborhoods are like little cities unto themselves—each with its own beliefs, customs, and spirit. He was fond of recalling the days when *American Bandstand* originated from Philadelphia and Dick Clark used to pass his microphone to the kids in the studio. When they introduced themselves, it was "Suzie from West Philly" and "Jimmy from Germantown" and "Kathy from the Northeast." That was the Philadelphia—those were the Philadelphias—that Schacter knew.

Detective Captain Schacter had worked every Christmas Eve of his thirty-four years on the police force. First it was a function of his lack of seniority. Then it became a matter of interest. Ultimately—and he would never say this out loud to anyone—it became his way of returning something to the city that raised him and to the men who worked for him. *Someone like Rienzi would never understand that,* he thought.

Inside the station Lieutenant Rienzi watched the late-night news. The weatherman was predicting that the snow would fall until early morning. All over Philadelphia, Rienzi mused, snow-removal workers would need to choose between holiday pay rates and spending Christmas morning with their families. Rienzi, a bachelor and a miscreant, sniggered at the thought.

Detective Captain Schacter arrived for work promptly at 11:30 P.M. He riffled through the evening arrest reports on his way upstairs to his office. *Four disorderly persons, three B & E's, two armed assaults...* "And a partridge in a pear tree," he said to no one in particular when he reached the second-floor landing.

The rim of his expensive meerschaum smacked against the handrail at the top of the stairs. The damp, half-smoked tobacco tumbled through his fingers and halfway down the staircase. *Damn,* he thought, and reached down to clean the mess. Just as his fingers reached out to touch the tobacco, a heavy black boot stomped onto the debris.

"Helps it grow," said Lieutenant Rienzi as he ground the heel of his boot against the threadbare carpet.

Startled, Schacter dropped his papers to the floor.

The younger detective smiled widely and chuckled. The fluorescent light bounced off a gold-panelled artificial incisor. "Merry Christmas, Captain."

Schacter picked up the arrest reports and headed toward his office without responding. Rienzi followed him.

"Did you listen to the news on your way in to work?"

"The news?"

"I just wondered if you heard, Captain. We have a real hot one tonight. A guy named Gordon Cardonick. Drove down the Schuylkill Expressway, pulled out a Ruger Mini-14, started shooting into the other cars."

Schacter leafed through the arrest reports again and found no mention of any shootings.

"I have them right here, Captain. I knew you would want to see them as soon as you arrived."

Schacter read Rienzi's papers. He grunted, whistled low, and grunted

6

again. *Three dead, five nearly dead, enough twisted sheet metal to shingle a small house...* "Good God, we'll have to print more warrants to handle all of this."

Rienzi laughed broadly. "Absolutely. We have a little bit of everything on this one. Manslaughter, or maybe even murder charges. Vehicular homicide, driving to endanger, assault and battery with a dangerous weapon, leaving the scene of an accident. We even have him for trespassing. You name it, we've got it. And just in time for the late news. The guy on Channel Six called him the Christmas Eve Sniper. Pretty catchy, if you ask me."

Schacter was unprepared for this. Christmas Eve was usually a time-out period from the more gruesome aspects of police work. He learned from the incident report that one of the murder victims was a little girl; she died in her father's arms as police rushed to her aid. For a moment he thought about his own grandchild. He looked up at Rienzi. The lieutenant stood before a mirror combing his mustache and whistling, apparently unaffected by the horror of the sniping incident.

The captain sighed as he finished reading the reports on Cardonick. "Is he going to live?"

"Sir?"

"It says here he was shot."

"Just a flesh wound. They're patching him up right now. I left instructions to have him brought up here when they finish."

"Uh-huh. Do we know anything about this man, Lieutenant?"

"He's white. Twenty-six years old. We're checking for a past arrest record. Lives in Oxford Circle, up in the Northeast, according to the address in his wallet. I called Central Office and they're sending someone in that area to check it out."

Schacter pulled a plug of tobacco from the tin and crumbled it into the bowl. He sucked on the unlit pipe and stared at the arrest reports. He was drawn over and over to the final paragraph. *When the subject was pulled from his car, he yelled, "Go ahead, kill me, I want you to." On the way to the station he kept asking us when we were going to kill him.*

"That's all for now, Rienzi. Let me know when they bring the sniper upstairs."

Denise put little Jennifer to bed, locked the doors and windows, took the phone off the hook, and drew a warm bath for herself. Jennifer was more stubborn than usual, but less so than expected for Christmas Eve.

"Will Daddy come see us tomorrow?" she had asked as Denise tucked her in.

"I don't know," Denise had said. "I hope so."

I hope not, she thought moments later.

Denise swished water along the length of the tub. A tiny wave crested at her feet and reverberated, smaller now, toward her shoulders. A sand candle reflected off the porcelain and tile and cloaked the room in magenta.

She wondered if six-and-a-half-year-old Jennifer still believed in Santa Claus. When Denise was a child she thought that Santa, the Tooth Fairy, and a whole host of others came into her room each night. They had the prescience to know exactly when she would open her eyes, and they would disappear just before that moment. She used to try to fool them. She would lift her eyelids very slowly—just enough to move them, but not enough to open them. Then she would relax the muscles and pretend to let her lids fall shut. Suddenly she would spring them open and try to catch one of her silent visitors. She never caught them. Soon she stopped trying. Eventually she stopped believing.

Up on the skylight the snow was falling more heavily than before. Midnight neared, and Elvis sang about a blue Christmas. She realized— and the unwelcome thought made her shiver—that this was her first Christmas Eve alone. First she had her family, and then she had Gordon. She wondered if he was thinking of her tonight.

Officer Guerra parked his cruiser in the middle of the block. He had lived in Philadelphia for five years, and still the Oxford Circle row houses reminded him of waiters in a Chinese restaurant. *Maybe the natives can tell them apart, but I sure as hell can't.* He was unfamiliar with Souder Street. By parking in the middle, he assured himself of having to walk no more than a half block. *Unless I'm on the wrong goddamn block, that is.* His flashlight guided him to number 7062.

The doorbell rang just as Denise was wrapping herself in her robe. She pulled it tight around herself and dashed downstairs. She placed the phone back on the hook. She was startled to see a policeman through the peephole. "Yes?"

"Police, ma'am."

"Yes? What is it?"

Guerra hesitated. Some people would open the door when they saw him. Most would open once he identified himself. Very few required further persuasion. "Does Gordon Cardonick live here?" he called through the door.

Yes... no... I don't know. Lost for an answer, Denise swung open the door. "I'm Mrs. Cardonick. Gordon isn't living here right now. Is there something I can do for you?" The phone rang. "Just a minute, I'll be right with you." *Who would be calling so late at night?*

"Denise?"

No, Mother, it's Dinah Shore. "Hello, Mother."

"Oh, God, Denise. I knew something like this would happen. It's so horrible. Does Jenny know yet?"

How many times have I asked you not to call her Jenny? "Mother, what are you talking about?" She realized that her mother was crying; she looked through the open door at the policeman, and she began to quake. *Oh, dear Jesus, it's Gordon. He's dead, he's dead.*

The phone fell from her hand. She heard her mother calling. The room began to spin around her. Officer Guerra caught her just before she hit the floor.

"Hear ye, hear ye," intoned the bailiff. "Superior Court of Philadelphia, December 28, 1982, now in session, the Honorable Raymond T. Gleason presiding. All rise."

Judge Gleason waddled through the archway separating the courtroom from his chambers. His robe, custom-fit to accommodate his girth and short stature, stretched almost to the floor. Hidden in its folds was three days' worth of mustard stains from soft pretzels.

The judge wrapped his gnarled fingers around his gavel. The courtroom was packed with reporters and observers. *These insanity trials always draw a good crowd,* Gleason mused. He glanced toward the bosomy redhead in the front row of the jury. She was sporting another new Christmas outfit. This one came to a tight tuck underneath her breasts, lifting them into midair where they hung poised like giant birds.

Judge Gleason studied the defendant. Her baggy blue polyester suit and ruby red lipstick highlighted the chalky whiteness of her skin. She stared blankly at the courtroom wall. Gleason wondered what she'd looked like when she punctured her victim's heart with a letter opener.

The judge addressed her attorney. "Mr. Lehman," he said, "the Commonwealth rested yesterday. Is the defense ready to proceed?"

Lehman stood. "We are, Your Honor. The defense calls Dr. Thomas Whitney."

Whitney took the witness stand and was sworn in by the bailiff. He glanced at the message carved on the inside of the stand. Scrawled years earlier by an unknown commentator, its presence was known to everyone except the judge. He read: *Judge Gleason blows horses for beer money.* It made Whitney feel sorry for the judge, even though he knew firsthand how insensitive and uncaring Gleason could be.

Whitney was not an unhandsome man, although his modesty led him to dwell upon his imperfections: the tiny roll of stomach fat, imperceptible to the observer; the unevenly graying temples; the ragged sprinkling of hair across his chest; and the faint scars on his neck left by a childhood encounter with a barbed wire fence during a New England thunderstorm.

Others—his students, patients, and colleagues in Philadelphia's psychiatric community—were kinder in their assessment of him. They would comment on his eyes, where decades of gentle smiling had pressed crow's feet onto a relatively uncreased face. His teeth, straight and white, reflected forty-seven years of non-indulgence: no smoking, few sweets, and very little alcohol. (He hated it when people remarked upon his teeth; it made him feel as though he were a show horse.)

Most of all, people admired his ability to set others at ease. Whether in the examining room, the lecture hall, or the courtroom (where he often testified as an expert on mental illness), Dr. Thomas Whitney's prepossessing manner quickly won trust from his audience.

He was a highly respected forensic psychiatrist, and he cut an imposing figure on the witness stand. His appearance as well as his testimony bore the quiet stamp of a man who polished his shoes twice weekly and who arranged the items in his kitchen cupboard from left to right according to size. He inherited his sense of order and propriety from his deceased father, a Boston Brahmin lawyer who'd been fond of reciting from Ecclesiastes: "To every thing there is a season, and a time to every purpose under the heaven."

Defense Attorney Lehman rose and walked toward Whitney. The attorney rubbed his hand across his lacquered hair and surreptitiously wiped the excess pomade on the inside of his jacket pocket. "Would you please tell the court your current occupation and position?"

"I'm the director of forensic evaluation at the Littleton State Hospital, and adjunct professor of law and psychiatry at Benjamin Franklin University."

"Now, Dr. Whitney," said Lehman, "please describe your training and experience."

"...Harvard graduate, 1957..."

It was Michael Andrews blowing his head off right in front of me...

"...then Harvard Medical School..."

His father sold chemicals to pharmaceutical firms and he used to bring materials home and teach Michael how to perform experiments.

Michael and I were fifteen that Patriots Day morning when we rode our bikes down to the North Bridge. He wanted to demonstrate an experiment for me. We parked our bikes in the woods and slid down the bank to the Concord River.

"... residency in psychiatry at Massachusetts General Hospital beginning in 1961...."

They were getting ready to reenact the Battle of Concord. People in Minuteman costumes were ready across the river with their muskets. Coming up behind us was a group of men dressed up like British redcoats. "Get ready, Thomas," Michael said. "Here comes my own little version of the shot heard 'round the world.

"The powder in this vial is potassium permanganate," he told me. "It's an oxidizing agent. And this is phosphorus," he said as he pulled a second vial out of his jacket. "It ignites if it's exposed to the air." He placed the yellow chunk of solid chemical on the riverbank and sprinkled the powder over it.

We waited and waited and nothing happened. The Minutemen were heading toward the far side of the bridge. The British were closing in behind us. Michael dropped one of his vials and leaned over to pick it up. Just then the phosphorus and permanganate exploded with a loud crack and a blinding white flash.

When I opened my eyes I was sprawled on the ground. The British were scattering in every direction. I heard a moan and a gurgling noise next to me. Michael's arms were jerking wildly in the air. There was a hole where his face should have been.

Blood was pouring out like it would never end. I wrapped myself around him and tried to stop it. "Someone get a doctor! Where's the fucking doctor!" I could feel his heart beat and then I could feel it not beating. He died right in my arms. It took them forever to peel me off him. That's when I decided to be a doctor.

Judge Gleason waited impatiently for the conclusion of Whitney's narrative. The judge had heard it all before. Once, years earlier, he had prevented a jury from hearing Whitney's qualifications. The judge, always antagonistic toward psychiatrists, had stated condescendingly that "we are all aware of Dr. Whitney's background. We won't make him convince us that he's qualified to testify in this matter." The jury's guilty verdict was appealed. The Pennsylvania Supreme Court ruled in favor of the defense, citing the prejudicial effect of Gleason's refusal to let the jurors listen to Whitney's qualifications. A new trial was ordered and the defendant was acquitted by the second jury. *The bastard never lets me forget that,* thought Gleason. *Every time he gives this speech it gets longer and longer and . . .*

Whitney noticed that the redhead was staring at him. She opened her mouth slightly and moistened her upper lip with her tongue. Embarrassed, he dropped his eyes and turned away.

"I was an army lieutenant from 1964 until 1966. I was a staff psychiatrist in the Philippines. This was during the time of the American troop buildup in South Vietnam."

They brought Corporal Redgate in from Saigon for observation. He'd been arrested for raping and killing a twelve-year-old village girl. The rape was so brutal that her labia minora were sheared off and buried inside her. He strangled her, strapped her to a post, and left her to rot in the rice paddies. They traced him from a clump of his hair they found when they pried open her stiff, dead fingers.

"I specialized in the diagnosis and treatment of men who suffered from combat-related psychiatric trauma."

Redgate had no signs of mental illness, but he did have a long history of violence and antisocial behavior. He got off on an insanity plea. The chief psychiatrist testified at the court-martial. He said: "Anybody who would do something like this has to be crazy." I was disgusted. It was either quit medicine or become a forensic psychiatrist.

"Beginning in 1966, I investigated child abuse cases for the Pennsylvania Department of Social Services.

"From 1969 to 1979 I was a professor at both the Law and Medical Schools of Franklin University. I was also a consultant at Littleton State Hospital, where I conducted pretrial psychiatric evaluations of persons charged with major crimes of violence.

"I became Littleton's director of forensic evaluation in 1979, and became an adjunct professor at Franklin University."

Lehman walked toward the witness stand. "Doctor, how many evaluations have you conducted of defendants in murder cases?"

"I've examined approximately two hundred accused murderers."

"Your Honor," Lehman said, "the defense moves to have the court accept Dr. Whitney as an expert witness."

"Mr. Tortelli, does the Commonwealth wish to be heard?" asked the judge. District Attorney Tortelli, an unctuous, sweaty little man, shook his head and shrugged his shoulders in resignation. "Very well. You may proceed with your direct examination, Mr. Lehman."

Whitney outlined the results of his criminal responsibility evaluation of the defendant. He recapitulated the unchallenged facts of the case: she did, indeed, kill her former employer in full view of seven witnesses. Whitney summarized her long history of mental illness and stated that, on the date in question, the defendant was acutely psychotic and grossly out of contact with reality.

"Doctor," said Lehman as he stroked his hair again, "in your opinion, was the defendant mentally capable of forming criminal intent? Did she realize—could she have realized—that she was committing a criminal act?"

Whitney paused. The room was still and all eyes were upon him. "Definitely not. Her acute psychosis—her delusions and hallucinations—made her unable to appreciate the true meaning of her actions. She was unable to understand the difference between right and wrong. In my opinion she absolutely could not realize that she was actually committing criminal murder."

"And, therefore, your recommendation to this court would be what, Doctor?"

Whitney looked at the woman. She appeared emotionless—almost lifeless—and lost in a private world. But Whitney knew the inner terrors she experienced, and he pitied her. He said: "I recommend that she be found not criminally responsible for her actions. That she be found not guilty by reason of insanity."

Tortelli's pencil point broke as he scribbled notes feverishly. Judge Gleason sighed. *I knew it,* he thought with resignation and mild disgust.

The defense rested after Tortelli's feeble cross-examination of Whitney. Closing arguments were presented. Tortelli asked for a conviction on the charge of first-degree murder, and Lehman argued that his client should be found not guilty by reason of insanity. The judge delivered his charge to the jury and court was adjourned.

As Whitney gathered his coat and papers to leave, the bailiff approached him. "Dr. Whitney, the judge wants to speak with you." The bailiff escorted him to the judge's chambers.

The ancient steam heater filled the room with an oppressive dampness. Large drops of water collected on the inside of the windows, obfuscating the view of Broad Street five stories below. Law books lined the long rows of floor-to-ceiling bookcases, and thick layers of dust peeked over their bindings. A half-eaten soft pretzel grew hard and stale on the corner of Gleason's desk. A toilet flushed, the bathroom door opened, and the judge stepped through as he zippered his fly shut.

"Ah, Tommy. Come in, come in. Something to drink?"

14

"Too early in the day for me, Judge," replied Whitney.

Gleason always called Whitney by that name. No one else—not even his mother—ever called him Tommy. Although Gleason's ostensible motivation was to be friendly and familiar, Whitney knew that the real intent was to demean. Whitney knew this, Gleason knew that Whitney knew, and Whitney knew that Gleason knew he knew. They had been through this many times before.

Gleason turned away, poured Scotch and water into a glass, and stirred the mixture with his index finger. "Looks like you made quite a friend in there, Tommy."

"Friend?"

"The red-haired girl with the large chest. Front row of the jury." The judge licked his mixing finger and sat at his desk. "Don't tell me you didn't notice her."

Whitney forced a respectful smile onto his face. His conversations with Gleason always made him angry, but he remained his usual cordial self. The psychiatrist conjured up an image of himself on trial. *How do you plead to the charge of assault and battery with a dangerous pretzel?* the bailiff would inquire. *Not guilty by reason of insanity,* Whitney would reply.

Gleason began to laugh for no apparent reason. His drink slipped through his stubby fingers and spilled across the desk. "Shit, goddamnitall!" He blotted the liquid with the morning *Inquirer.*

"Why did you want to see me, Judge?"

"Ah, yes, yes." Gleason smacked his palms together. "I just wanted to tell you about some business I sent your way earlier today."

"Business?"

"Come, come, Tommy. Don't you read the newspapers? Gordon Cardonick, the maniac who did those shootings on the expressway. He had a pretrial hearing this morning and his attorney asked me to order a criminal responsibility evaluation. He's on his way to Littleton right now."

"So?"

Gleason leaned back in his chair. He swung his legs up and rested them on top of the soggy *Inquirer.* "I just wanted to make sure you knew that I'm the judge of record on this case. I'll be waiting for you on this one, Tommy, just in case you try to get this guy off, too." The judge smiled. "It was good speaking with you, Doctor."

The psychiatrist grabbed his briefcase and headed toward the door. Gleason stood and called after him. "Wait." Whitney stopped and looked back over his shoulder. "Whitney, do me a favor. Do yourself a favor. Do the whole goddamn Commonwealth a favor. Don't assign this evaluation to yourself. Let somebody else handle it. You must be getting tired of our little posttrial chats. I know I am."

The men glowered at each other for several seconds, the disdain in each one's eyes feeding the contempt in the other's. Whitney opened the door and walked out.

Whitney heard Gleason's door slam shut as he headed toward the elevator. By the time he reached the courthouse lobby, he'd decided to assign himself the case of the Christmas Eve Sniper.

3

Littleton Institute for the Criminally Insane used to be a hellhole. Situated on the outskirts of Philadelphia, it had been used as a warehouse for storing violent psychotics, retarded delinquents, and other grossly intractable misfits and outcasts. It had been run by incompetent administrators who hired incompetent doctors, and patients were locked away for years without any official review.

In 1961 Dr. Percy Osborne, a young psychiatrist who was expert in the use of new antipsychotic medications, came to Littleton. The medicines he used revolutionized psychiatry. Patients spent less time in hospitals and more time in their communities, and Pennsylvania began to discharge patients from its state hospital system.

There was, however, still a core of chronically violent patients unsuited for release into the community who needed treatment in a maximum-security setting. Thus they were transferred to Littleton. In keeping with the therapeutic spirit of the times, the institute was renamed Littleton State Hospital. It became an evaluation and treatment facility for chronically violent patients, as well as for inmates who have mental breakdowns in prison, and for those persons found criminally insane.

"Let's go, faggot! Move it!" The burly state trooper reached into the rear of the police cruiser, clamped his hand around the prisoner's neck, and yanked him out. "I said move it," he shouted as his cargo tumbled into a heap on the gravel driveway.

The prisoner rolled onto his knees. He tried to pull himself upright but his handcuffs and leg-irons hampered movement. He balanced himself on his left foot; his right leg buckled underneath him. He shifted his weight to the right foot; his left side crumpled and he crashed into the pebbles again. The heat from his flushed cheeks melted the coating of ice on the driveway. He could smell the idling motor's exhaust.

The state trooper straddled his quarry and chuckled. "Hey, faggot, need some help?" He grabbed the man's collar and jerked him to his feet. The prisoner teetered for a moment on his chained legs and then fell across the bumper of the cruiser.

The prisoner heard the trooper's laughter and felt the hands closing like a vise around his shoulders. Just then a voice boomed from the building ten yards away. "Hey, you! That's enough! Get your hands off him!"

The trooper murmured an obscenity and relaxed his grip. The prisoner turned in the direction of the voice and saw a short, fat man in a prison guard uniform standing in the doorway. Two larger guards stood behind him. The trooper grabbed the prisoner's arm and escorted him toward the door; he halted five feet from the fat man and smiled.

The fat man glanced at the prisoner's contorted face and knew that the trooper's fingers were crushing his arm. He looked up at the younger, larger man and returned his smile. Suddenly he darted forward with his pudgy thumb and forefinger, jamming them into the fleshy area of the trooper's palm. The fat man slowly rotated his own wrist until the trooper's hand detached itself from the prisoner's arm. Still smiling, the fat man kept twisting while the trooper's arm began to spasm. The trooper stumbled backward into a bank of dirty snow.

The prisoner stood and watched as the guards laughed at the trooper. He read the sign above the door:

Patient Admitting Area

Transporting officers must holster all firearms.

Percy Osborne, M.D.

Superintendent, Littleton State Hospital

The fat man bent down and reached inside the stunned trooper's coat. He removed a sheaf of papers and quickly thumbed through them. "Arrest warrants, a court order for an evaluation—all right, get up. Everything looks in order. Get out of here."

The fat man ordered the other guards to unlock the prisoner's leg-irons. The trooper, faint and ashen-faced, wobbled toward his cruiser as the fat man led the prisoner into the Admissions Building.

A barren corridor stretched before them. Lining both sides were massive steel doors, each with a tiny Plexiglas window and a flap that could be opened from the corridor at mealtime.

The fat man and his cohorts led the prisoner down the corridor. Most of the metal doors were clamped shut; beside each one was a small stack of clothing and a pair of shoes. The prisoner peered past the open doors. Behind them were cells that measured no more than seven feet square. Each one contained nothing but a sheetless mattress and a hole in the floor. The paint on the walls was cracked and peeling. A small, heavily barred window occupied the topmost portion of each cell's back wall. The entire corridor reeked of urine and disinfectant.

"Hey, Fatso," screamed the man in the first cell. "Who's your new fucking friend, you motherfucker! Get me the fuck out of here! I wanna see a fucking doctor, you fucking asshole!"

"I see we have The Screamer back again," said the fat man.

The Screamer continued his harangue as they made their way down the corridor. The three guards guided the prisoner into the interview room, removed his handcuffs, and sat him at a desk.

"I'm Captain Orris," the fat man stated as he took a seat on the opposite side of the desk. The other guards watched from across the room. "I'm the chief prison guard here in the Admissions Building. You look familiar. Ever been here before?"

The prisoner, his head bowed, nodded weakly.

"What's your name?" asked Orris.

The prisoner made no response. He sat shivering with his head bowed. The fat man sighed and looked once more at the papers he had taken from the trooper's coat.

"Cardonick? Or is that Candonick? I can't tell if this is an 'r' or an 'n.' Which is it?"

The prisoner continued to sit silently. Orris slammed his open hand against the desktop. "Damn it, you! I asked you what your name is!"

The prisoner flinched and made brief eye contact with his interrogator. He bowed his head again and answered meekly, "Cardonick."

"Okay, Cardonick. That's a lot better. We oughta get things straight before we go any further. I stopped that trooper from bothering you because that's my job, and because as near as I could tell there wasn't no reason for him to do that. But if you step out of line, we can get real unfriendly here, too. Understand?"

Cardonick nodded.

"Good," said Orris. He looked more closely at the prisoner. He estimated him to be about five foot ten, one hundred forty or forty-five pounds. His tousled, shoulder-length hair had been shaved near the right ear, revealing a clotting wound. He sat hunched and cowering like a small animal.

Cardonick, thought Orris. *Cardonick. Damn, that sounds familiar.* He read through the arrest warrants, whistling softly as he realized the extent of the charges that had been brought against the man across from him. Suddenly he remembered: *Gordon Cardonick. The Christmas Eve Sniper. Well, well. I'll be damned.*

"The nurse will be here in a while to check you over," he continued, "and then one of the psychiatrists will interview you. If you don't give us no trouble, tomorrow you'll get moved to the Evaluation Building."

The two younger guards led Cardonick to an open cell and asked him to disrobe. They told him to bend over and spread his buttocks, and they checked for contraband with a flashlight. "Hey, you fuckheads," yelled The Screamer from the end of the corridor. "You think we keep guns and knives up our fucking assholes?"

They moved Cardonick into the cell and slammed the door shut.

Denise felt out of place as she glanced around the waiting room. Twenty or thirty people sat in groups of two and three. She appeared to be the only solitary person waiting to enter Littleton's visiting room.

Out of the corner of her eye she could see the prison guard at the reception desk staring at her. She knew the look very well. So often men would gaze leeringly at her legs, or her chest, or her buttocks, or her perfectly formed nose, or her loosely curled long blonde hair. She knew that if she stared back at him the guard would hurriedly pull his eyes away. But she was too tired and depressed to care.

Denise shifted in her seat and looked up at the woman walking toward her. The woman carried a notepad and pen; a puffed-out vinyl handbag hung from her shoulder. Wire-rimmed glasses with lightly tinted lenses rested on the front of the woman's nose. She pushed them back toward the bridge, but within seconds they slipped back down again.

"Excuse me. Are you Mrs. Cardonick?"

"Yes, I am," replied Denise.

"Oh, good. The guard at the desk couldn't remember for sure. A lot of people visit Littleton between Christmas and New Year's. Sometimes it's a little difficult to keep track. May I have your full name, please?"

"Denise. Denise Susan Cardonick."

The woman adjusted her glasses and scribbled on her pad. "Your husband was admitted about twenty minutes ago. One of the doctors will examine him soon and then you'll be allowed to see him."

Denise shifted excitedly in her seat. "Have you seen him? They wouldn't let me talk to him at the courthouse." Her purse fell to the floor. She scooped its spilled contents into her hands and dropped them back in the purse. She sat upright and ran her hands over her hair and shoulders, primping herself for her visit. "How is he? Are you a nurse?"

The woman smiled. "No, I don't work here. I'm a reporter for the *Philadelphia Inquirer*. My name is Selma Aaron."

The color drained from Denise's face. She bit down on her lip and tried to recall what she'd been saying and doing while the woman had been watching.

"I'd like to talk with you for a few minutes, Denise. May I call you Denise?"

"No. I mean, yes. I mean, I don't know if this is right. I don't have anything to say, and..." She thought about the television reports and newspaper photos she'd been keeping from Jennifer. Tears filled her eyes as she wondered how she might break the news to her daughter.

"Here, have some of my Kleenex," offered the reporter.

"Thank you, Miss...uh..."

"Aaron. Selma Aaron. Please, call me Selma."

Denise dabbed her eyes with the tissue.

"I'm sure these past few days have been rough for you," continued the reporter. "I want people to read your side of the story. You can tell them what Gordon is really like, why things fell apart between the two of you—yes, I know about your separation—what effect the breakup had on you and on him. People want to understand what happened."

Denise squeezed the tissue into a small ball. She looked around for a wastebasket; finding none, she tucked the wad into her purse. "How can I make people understand when I don't even understand it myself?"

The reporter sat next to her. "There must be a reason for all of this. I talked to one of the arresting officers. He says your husband asked the police to kill him." She adjusted her glasses once more. "Did you know that? Has your husband ever tried to kill himself? Do you think your recent breakup had anything to do with him getting so depressed?"

Denise spread her hand across her lap to flatten the wrinkles in her expensive imported skirt. It was a Christmas present from Gordon; she had admired it in Wanamaker's window since September. When he gave it to her she became angry—angry that he would try to buy her affection that way, and angry that he would waste so much money when they were having trouble paying Jennifer's medical bills. Now she felt guilty for having yelled at him so. She hoped he would like the way it looked on her.

She turned toward the reporter. "Please. I can't talk to you. I'm sorry, really I am. If I thought it would do any good, I'd talk to you all day. But right now I just want to be alone."

The reporter sighed, adjusted her glasses, and stood up. "Have you ever visited Littleton before?"

"No."

"Well, it's a crazy place, I can tell you that. The doctors complain that it's too much like a prison and the guards complain that it's too much like a hospital. Maybe you'd like me to tell you some more about the place."

Denise looked at the floor and numbly shook her head.

"Here, take my card. If you change your mind about talking, give me a call." The reporter walked to the front desk and began talking to the guard.

Denise rubbed the base of her ring finger. She'd removed her wedding band when she and Gordon separated, but the skin on her finger remained red and unnaturally smooth even now, two months later. She wondered if the mark would ever fade away. She knew that her hurt and anger would not. She rubbed her tongue over her chipped rear molar and thought about the beatings...

Denise looked up at the prison guard bending down to catch her attention. "Please come with me, Mrs. Cardonick," he said.

Selma Aaron watched Denise primp herself nervously once more. Denise followed the guard into a small anteroom. Moments later she emerged, tears streaming down her cheeks, and bolted out the front door into the late December chill. Selma called after her but Denise didn't respond. The reporter asked the guard a few questions, dashed into the foyer, and telephoned the *Inquirer* city room.

"Hello, Harry? It's Selma. Put a hold on that story I phoned in earlier—I've got a new lead-in... Harry, I don't give a good goddamn. Set the page all over again. This is a hot exclusive. Take this down: 'Gordon Cardonick, the so-called Christmas Eve Sniper, attempted suicide shortly after his admission to Littleton State Hospital this afternoon. Cardonick, charged with fatally shooting three motorists on the Schuylkill Expressway, was sent to Littleton for pretrial psychiatric testing. He used chunks of peeling paint to cut his wrists in his cell in the Admissions Building at that hospital. Although doctors believe his injuries are not serious, they have transferred him for emergency care to County General Hospital.'" She hesitated for a moment. "New paragraph: 'Cardonick's estranged wife, Denise, was at Littleton waiting to see her husband when she learned of his suicide attempt. She appeared shaken but would not comment...'"

Stanley Schacter identified himself at the gate and pulled his Plymouth into the sports arena's VIP parking lot. The area was reserved for the well-connected, for friends and family of management, and for the athletes. The special pass he'd wangled was one of the few perks he indulged in as a detective captain.

When he stepped out of his car, he heard a gruff voice behind him. "Hey, pal, you can't park in this lot! Move it!"

Schacter whirled around, prepared to pull rank on whoever was yelling at him, and saw Thomas Whitney.

Whitney laughed heartily. "I got you that time, didn't I, Stan?"

Schacter pretended to look dismayed. "I don't know about you, Thomas. For a famous psychiatrist, you're a pretty sick man."

The two friends laughed, shook hands, and walked together into the basketball game.

They had met sixteen years earlier, on Labor Day weekend, 1966. Schacter was only a forty-four-year-old lieutenant detective back then. Driving home that night he answered a call on his police radio. Headquarters wondered if he would mind stopping in Chestnut Hill on his way home to Mount Airy. A doctor's home office had been burglarized, and the Chestnut Hill precinct was low on detectives because of the holiday. Schacter obliged as he always did.

A real estate agent's "Sold" sign stood near the curb at the address Schacter took from the dispatcher. The house was shielded by ancient oaks and thickly grown shrubbery and wasn't visible from the street. Manicured hedges lined the long, winding driveway that led to a three-story stone house atop a knoll overlooking a gazebo and a small duck pond. This was Chestnut Hill: Philadelphia's last patrician bastion. A patrol car, its door open and radio squawking, sat in the macadam circle at the driveway's end.

A police officer was interviewing the victim when Schacter entered the ransacked office. "Lieutenant," said the officer, "this is Dr. Whitney. He says he got home about twenty minutes ago, came in through the garage entrance, then heard a noise coming from the office. I guess he scared the burglar away. It looks like the guy came in through that window over there, and then got out by knocking down this door."

Schacter surveyed the scene for a few minutes. Whitney was tall and thin, and his trim beard gave him the appearance of a young college professor. Schacter was taken aback by the doctor's youthfulness. He estimated Whitney's age—correctly—at thirty-one.

"Obviously," Schacter said to the uniformed officer, "this was done by an amateur." He kicked his way through the mess and leaned against the windowsill on the far side of the room.

The officer appeared bewildered. "How can you tell, sir?"

Schacter grinned. "Take a look at the doctor's desk over there." The bottom drawer was still open, its contents half emptied onto the floor.

"Yes. So?"

The detective lieutenant grunted. "The top three drawers are shut. The thief worked his way through the dresser from top to bottom, the way an average person might do." Schacter strolled across the room to demonstrate. "That means he opened the top drawer first." Schacter did likewise. "Then, in order to get into the second drawer, he shut the top drawer." He continued the demonstration. "He repeated this pattern with drawers two and three, finally reaching the bottom drawer which, of course, he wouldn't bother to close when he was finished."

The patrolman stared at the desk. "I still don't get it," he said.

"An intruder wants to get in and out as fast as he can," Schacter explained as he pushed shut the bottom desk drawer. "This is how an experienced burglar would do it." He went through the desk again, starting with the bottom drawer this time, and leaving each drawer open as he moved toward the top. "When you do it that way, you save the time it takes to close each drawer. And this is the way the desk would look if the person who broke in knew what the hell he was doing: all four drawers still open."

The young doctor rubbed his hand along the top of the desk and sighed.

The patrolman, flushed and fidgeting, turned away from the other two men and scribbled in his notepad. Schacter sensed the man's embarrassment and tried to bolster him. "You did good work, son. You can tell your captain I said so. No, I'll tell him myself. Officer Keller, isn't it?"

"Yes, sir." The officer was still nervous. "How did you know that?"

Schacter smiled. "Your name tag, son." He tapped the man's chest, and all three laughed. "I'll finish up here. You can go back to the station and make your report." The officer stuffed his notepad into his shirt pocket and left through the battered doorway.

"So, you said your name is Whitney, didn't you, Doctor?"

"Yes. Thomas Whitney."

"What kind of doctor are you?"

"Pardon?"

"I mean, are you a baby doctor, or an eye doctor, or what? Do you keep drugs here? A lot of the time neighborhood kids will break into a doctor's office looking for drugs."

"Oh, I see. I'm a psychiatrist."

Schacter grunted.

"But I don't have any drugs in my office. In fact, I don't have much of anything in here. As you can see, I'm barely moved in. I just came to Philadelphia a couple of weeks ago."

Schacter noted the man's broad New England accent. It hinted of Back Bay drawing rooms and summers on Nantucket. The detective gazed around the room. He walked over to the window and studied the pattern of broken glass underneath it. "Did they get anything, Doctor?"

"Nothing of value, as far as I can tell. I'm glad they didn't take my balls."

"Huh?"

Whitney blushed under the detective's harsh gaze. "Over there," he said, pointing to the bookshelf. "My collection of baseballs. Some of them are over forty years old."

Schacter walked to the shelf. He bent over and examined the glass-enclosed balls. The ink on them had begun to fade, but he had no trouble making out the autographs: *Jimmie Foxx. Ted Williams. Johnny Pesky. Bobby Doerr.*

Schacter stood up and smiled at the younger man. "You must be a Red Sox fan."

Whitney returned the detective's smile. "All my life," he replied.

"Now, me, I've always been a Phillies fan. I guess that stamps me as some kind of psycho-neurotic, huh?"

They talked about burglary and baseball for a half hour. That was the beginning of their association, a friendship that had touched upon their personal and professional lives for sixteen years.

Whitney had decided to move to Philadelphia very suddenly. After his discharge from the army the previous January, he had returned to his mother's estate in Concord, Massachusetts, and taken a part-time position at one of the town's private prep schools. The relaxed pace of Concord was a relief after so many months of pressured duty in the Philippines.

In February of that year he began dating Allison Tremblay, whom he'd known since childhood. Like Whitney, she came from a long line of Yankee traders, bankers, and lawyers. She was "of fine New England stock," Whitney's father would have said. Whitney's parents had always assumed that he would marry someone like Allison.

Whitney had spent a large portion of his young adulthood trying to disprove that assumption. He'd taken up with a variety of women, no one for more than a few months at a time. None of them had the background or bearing that would earn the approval of Whitney's parents. And that suited Whitney quite well.

But his army experience had left him lonely and weary, and he longed for some semblance of regularity in his life. What his relationship with Allison Tremblay lacked in excitement it made up for in comfort and security.

And so Whitney and Allison were married in April of 1966. They purchased a renovated farmhouse in nearby Carlisle. By June of that year Whitney was a father-to-be.

By July he was a widower.

The fire began in the middle of a dry summer morning. By the time Whitney returned home for lunch the farmhouse was completely gutted. Allison had been napping in the den; the fire had started in the nearby laundry room. "She never had a chance," a fireman told him as they stood in front of the rubble. "These old homes go up so damn fast."

The fire chief couldn't say for sure what had caused the blaze. "Maybe the wiring was bad," he said. "Or maybe your wife forgot to shut the iron off. You'd be surprised how often people do that."

No, thought Whitney, *I wouldn't be surprised.* It was something he

27

often neglected to do, and Allison had gently scolded him more than once for his forgetfulness. He'd been in a hurry that morning. He couldn't recall whether he'd even used the iron, let alone decide whether he'd remembered to turn it off.

He tried to convince himself that Allison's death wasn't his fault, but it didn't work. He kept his self-blame and guilt secret, holding it inside where it festered like an infected wound.

Whitney had to get away. He learned of an opening with Philadelphia's Department of Social Services, applied for it, and was hired almost immediately. And so, scant weeks after the fire, he was living three hundred and fifty miles away in Chestnut Hill.

Whitney certainly didn't need his salary. He would have been financially secure for the rest of his life without work, thanks to the trust fund bequeathed him by his father, and his inheritance of Allison's share of the Tremblay fortune. But he definitely needed to work. He needed to lose himself in others' lives so he could forget his own loneliness and guilt. He rededicated himself to psychiatry, and he used his profession as an escape, as a shield against the pain of his losses.

In his new job, Whitney evaluated abusive parents and made recommendations for treatment or, in some cases, for removing the children from their homes. His work with violent families often brought him into contact with Detective Stanley Schacter, and they became close friends.

Whitney left the Department of Social Services after three years. He was tired of seeing so much suffering and being so powerless to stop it. The clincher came when a six-year-old girl disappeared. Whitney had evaluated her family months earlier for DSS and had recommended foster placement for the girl, but her father had hired a lawyer to delay matters. And although the girl never reappeared and her body was never found, Whitney was certain she'd been killed by her father. "I don't think I can take this job anymore," he complained to Schacter after the young girl disappeared. "The court is too damned slow, and the DSS lawyers just don't give a shit."

In 1969 Whitney was appointed assistant professor of law and psychiatry at Franklin University. He seemed born to the role of university professor. His courses were always packed full of eager medical students or admiring would-be lawyers. He published in the proper journals. His comprehensive treatise on the insanity defense was published in the *Virginia Law Review*. He became one of the few non-attorneys to garner a Distinguished Achievement citation from the

American Bar Association. The university gave him early tenure at the joint request of the deans of the two professional schools.

Shortly after he began teaching at Franklin, Whitney met Percy Osborne, a Main Line psychiatrist fifteen years his senior. Osborne had been the superintendent at Littleton State Hospital for five or six years. Osborne certainly didn't need to work for the state; well known for his pioneer work with antipsychotic medications, he could have had his pick of tenured positions at prestigious colleges or private psychiatric hospitals. Indeed, Osborne really didn't need to work at all; old money coursed through both sides of his genealogy, funneling its way through generations of frugal forebears into Osborne's portfolio. Osborne worked for a combination of reasons: a fear of boredom, a sense of *noblesse oblige,* and a Quaker ethic that proscribed self-indulgence.

Whitney, of course, understood Osborne's reasons very well. Whitney's father had volunteered his time as an unpaid trustee to various Brahmin organizations. His mother still served on the governing boards of the Boston Symphony Orchestra and the New England Antiquarian Society. All of her charitable efforts, though, were restricted to the upper class. "Let the Democrats take care of the poor," she often quoted her late husband. Whitney inherited their spirit of social involvement, if not their allegiance to class differences. It was this spirit that had led him initially to work for the Department of Social Services. And it was this spirit that led him to accept Percy Osborne's request to serve as a consultant at Littleton State Hospital.

Whitney remained on the Littleton consulting staff throughout his Franklin years. He conducted pretrial psychiatric evaluations of violent, disturbed men and women. His clinical experiences there offered an excitement he couldn't find by treating bored Chestnut Hill matrons in his private practice. It wasn't the fear of external danger that made his work exciting. Rather, it was the inner stirrings, triggered by the violence of its patients, that made Littleton so stimulating to Whitney. For every sexual or aggressive wish he ever had, there was a Littleton patient who had acted upon the same fantasy.

Whitney's work at Littleton enriched his teaching and his professional writing. It provided him with anecdotes which he could use to regale an audience of students or colleagues, and it served as a springboard for his own national prominence.

He came to the public eye early in his career. The week after Whitney received tenure a challenger for a Congressional seat in

Connecticut was gunned down outside his home. The perpetrator was a college dropout who had tried, unsuccessfully, to join the staff of the candidate's opponent. The assassination was seen by most observers as a crazed man's twisted attempt to curry the incumbent's favor. An insanity plea was entered, and an insanity verdict was expected. But the prosecuting federal attorney had worked as a Philadelphia assistant district attorney. He knew Whitney from the psychiatrist's work at Littleton, and he remembered losing a case in which Whitney testified for the defense. The federal attorney hired Whitney to evaluate the assassin, and the psychiatrist's testimony was instrumental in securing a guilty verdict. It was the first of many times that Whitney was a participant at controversial criminal proceedings.

In the spring of 1979, as Whitney was ending his tenth year at Franklin, Osborne invited him to a fateful meeting in the superintendent's office. "So, Thomas," began Osborne, "tell me what you have planned for the fall."

Whitney was flattered by the older man's interest. For the first six years of their association he had addressed or referred to the man only as "Dr. Osborne." He still felt disrespectful using the man's first name, even though Osborne had implored him to do so.

"Well, sir, I mean, Percy, the same as usual. I'm teaching the same courses I taught this year, may have time for one or two private forensic cases out-of-state, then there's—"

Osborne interrupted. "Were you planning to stay on here as a consultant, Thomas?" Whitney had seldom seen the man appear so stern and preoccupied. He wondered for a moment if he had done something wrong.

"Well," Whitney continued, "I certainly hope you'll . . ."

Osborne lowered his eyes and began to fumble aimlessly through a stack of papers as he spoke. "Thomas, I want you to come to work here."

"Well, so do I, sir."

"Call me Percy." He looked up at Whitney. "No, I don't think you understand. I want you to come on board here as director of forensic evaluation."

"But there is no such . . . I thought you . . ."

"I know, I know." Osborne stood up and looked out the window behind his desk. "I've controlled everything here for almost twenty years. There's never even been a director of forensic evaluation until now."

"Then why . . ."

Osborne turned back to face Whitney. He leaned against the windowsill and suddenly appeared old and bent. "I'll be sixty next month, Thomas. And this job has taken its toll. I don't know how much longer I'll be here . . . at Littleton, that is. I want to pull back on some of my responsibilities, maybe do a little writing, maybe . . ."

Osborne looked down at the floor. His shoulders sagged and his breathing grew heavy. After long moments of palpable silence he sat down, placed one leg on his desk, and stretched his arms out behind his head.

"The way I figure it, Thomas, the job would demand three to four days per week. You could probably stay on at Franklin in an adjunct position, perhaps teach one course each semester or supervise some residents. Might make it more difficult to find time for private work, though."

"What about Ralph Malzone?" asked Whitney.

"Ralph Malzone? What about him?"

"He's been working at Littleton full-time for six or seven years now. Don't you think he might want the job?"

Osborne frowned. "In his better moments, which are few and far between, Ralph is aware of his limitations—of which there are many." He noticed Whitney shifting in his chair. "You may feel uncomfortable hearing me speak bluntly, but you should know where things stand. After all, he'll be working for you if you take the job. Ralph can manage the trivial cases, but he can't handle the big ones. He can't grasp subtlety, he's like Jell-O on the witness stand, and he can't stay objective. Besides," Osborne continued slowly, "we have to take the long view. We have to consider who would be best suited for my job when I step down. The governor will probably let me nominate my own successor."

Whitney avoided Osborne's direct gaze. He felt himself blushing.

Osborne leaned forward and clasped his hands on the desk. "So," he said, smiling, "I'm offering you the opportunity you've always wanted. A chance to work longer hours under greater pressure for less pay. What do you say? I guess you'd like to think about it for a week or two?"

Behind the older man's smile Whitney thought he saw a look of forlornness. He remembered a moment many years earlier when he visited his father in the hospital a few days before the elder Whitney's death. *"Thomas,"* said his father, *"I want you to promise me you'll end*

31

this indecisiveness about entering medical school. And for God's sake, Thomas, think about what you're doing before you decide to marry that Jewish girl, what's her name—'' His father bore then the same look that Osborne had now. And although Whitney had already decided tentatively to break off his engagement and to enter medical school, he refused to promise his father anything. He had always regretted this, for it was their last conversation.

"No," Whitney heard himself saying now. Osborne sighed. "I mean, no, I don't think I need that much time." His own voice sounded far away to him. "Unless I tell you tomorrow that I've changed my mind, let's say I'll take the job."

He didn't change his mind. For over three years he'd been Littleton's director of forensic evaluation. Osborne was older, whiter, and thinner. Whitney didn't know if he wanted to become the next superintendent, but he did know the offer would be forthcoming.

Throughout everything—his early DSS struggles, his halcyon days at Franklin, his stewardship-in-waiting at Littleton—he remained friendly with Stanley Schacter. On occasion Whitney asked the detective to deliver a guest lecture for one of his classes. Sometimes the doctor would find one of Schacter's police reports in the file of a Littleton patient. He often thought that the detective would have made a fine psychiatrist. He mentioned that to Schacter the night the older man received his promotion to captain. "You know," Schacter responded with atypical lyricism, "we're not very different in what we do, Thomas. You may see me as a stationhouse doctor. Well, I've always thought of you as a detective of the soul."

The 76ers were in fine form tonight, the last home game of 1982. Dr. J. poured in one thunderous slam-dunk after another, and each time the rafters shook as the P.A. announcer bellowed, *"E-r-r-r-v-v-i-i-n-n-g!"* Schacter sat quietly. He was not the demonstrative sort when things went well, although he never hesitated to pound his fist against his chair when the team played poorly.

Whitney usually seemed to enjoy the games, no matter how well they were played, no matter who won. But tonight he was uncommonly quiet. Schacter guessed at the cause. "I hear you had another run-in with our judicial friend."

Whitney was staring at the scoreboard with the dull intensity of a man in a daze. Schacter nudged his shoulder.

"Pardon? Did you say something?"

"Judge Gleason. I hear you had one of your famous meetings with him yesterday."

"Oh, him. I try to forget about those meetings. How did you know?"

"He called me after you left. Wanted to make sure the police report on the sniper got sent up to Littleton. I interrogated that guy, did you know that? He's a real odd bird. Anyway, Gleason was having a shit fit. What did you say to him?"

Whitney shrugged his shoulders and looked around aimlessly. The crowd stood to applaud a play on the court, surrounding the two seated men like four walls.

"Thomas?"

Whitney reached into his tweed jacket. "This arrived in today's mail," he said as he passed the folded note paper to Schacter. Crooked trails of dried blood lined the margins.

> *Dear Thomas,*
> *The game begins in earnest.*
> *The stakes are very high.*
> *Please notify your loved ones.*
> *Will they miss you when you die?*

Schacter grunted heavily. "Goddamn. I thought we had finally scared this guy off."

Schacter kept the letters in a dog-eared manila folder in his bottom desk drawer, stuck behind a can of Coke and a month-old Tastykake Chocolate Junior. He opened the folder and inserted the latest letter.

Whitney had shown the first letter to Schacter more than a year earlier. Now the detective took it from the folder and read it once more.

> *November 30, 1981*
>
> *Dear Dr. Whitney:*
>   *Today is Winston Churchill's birthday. He would have been 107. He once said to a drinking companion who had nine children, "I like my cigar, too, but I take it out once in a while."*
>   *I wanted to break the ice with a bit of humor, because I have something quite serious to say.*
>   *I'm gravely concerned for your welfare, Dr. Whitney. Did you know that the suicide rate among psychiatrists is several times the national average?*
>   *Sincerely,*
>   *The Phoenix (can you guess who?)*

A second letter arrived three weeks after the first one. Whitney turned it over to Schacter.

December 19, 1981

Dear Dr. Whitney:

I hope you receive this note before you leave for your conference in Barbados—and how did I know about your trip, you wonder? (I'm reminded of the story about the fellow who bragged about his new ladyfriend from the Caribbean. "Jamaica?" someone asked him. "Not yet," he replied, "but I'm trying like hell.")

I do hope your trip rejuvenates you. You've been looking a bit peaked lately. When was the last time you had a checkup? (I'm reminded of the story about the movie queen's visit to her gynecologist. "Have you had a checkup in the past two years?" the doctor asked. "No," she said, "but I've had three Hungarians, two Italians, and a Pole.")

Seriously, Dr. Whitney, do take care of yourself. You're not getting any younger, and bachelors die earlier (or so say the actuarial tables). How old are you now, anyway? Aha—it took you a few seconds to recall, didn't it? A sure sign of cortical atrophy!

Let me refresh your memory. You were born in Boston on July 4, 1935. (That makes you forty-six, in case you hadn't figured it out yet.) You grew up on your family's Concord estate. You were an only child. The world seemed to revolve around you. And then, when you were six or seven, you discovered that those wonderful fireworks displays every year on your birthday didn't have a damn thing to do with you. It's been downhill ever since.

How did you get those little scars on your neck? A suicide attempt? No, you would never try to do away with yourself in such a crude manner, would you, Thomas—may I call you Thomas? A dozen Seconals followed by a carafe of Dom Perignon, perhaps, or a kamikaze run down the slopes of Killington. But a cold razor across the Adam's apple? No, you must have had an accident.

And accidents will happen, even to the best of us. Pity the poor surgeon. His hand slips, his patient dies, everyone in the operating room knows about it. Better to be a psychiatrist: the failures are much more private.

I wonder, then, why psychiatrists have such a high suicide rate?

Oh, you're right, I'm repeating myself—I mentioned that in my first letter. But it's been on my mind lately, because I am so terribly worried about you. Do take care of yourself, Thomas.
        Sincerely,
        The Phoenix (are you still guessing?)

Schacter remembered how frightened Whitney had felt that someone whom he didn't know (or did he?) would express this gratuitous concern about his welfare. "My father used to paraphrase something Thoreau wrote: 'If you see a stranger coming up your front path to do something good for you, get your butt out the back door as fast as you can.' I get suspicious when somebody takes such an unsolicited interest in my well-being. There's no telling what's hiding underneath. You've heard the expression 'killing him with kindness,' haven't you? And these letters—all this talk of accidents and suicide. I think the writer wants to kill me, Stan."

The letters bore Philadelphia postmarks. Each message was neatly printed. Schacter had the paper checked for fingerprints; none were clearly discernible (other than Whitney's). The two men were still puzzling over the situation when the third letter arrived at Whitney's home.

January 1, 1982

Dear Thomas,
    Happy New Year!!
    I'm reminded of the story about the naive young groom who didn't know anything about sex. On the first night of his honeymoon his bride waited longingly in bed. "Maybe you can find someone to give you lessons," she said sarcastically when it became clear that he couldn't satisfy her.
    "Good idea," the stupid fellow replied. He went down to the hotel lobby and persuaded a sailor to come back with him to the room. The sailor got undressed and headed toward the bed, but first he took a knife and scratched a line on the floor in front of the groom. "Step over that line," said the sailor, "and you're a dead man." Then he made ferocious love to the bride for an hour and a half.
    No sooner had the sailor left when the groom broke into hysterical laughter. "What the hell's so funny?" asked his wife. "Don't you understand what just happened here?"
    "I sure do. I stepped over the line three times and he didn't even see me."

And so we step over the line into 1982. Do you make New Year's resolutions, Thomas? Do you have any vices? Any excesses? Any lines you cross when no one else is around? I don't think you smoke—I've never seen you do it, anyway. Of course, I've never seen you piss, shit, or fuck, but I assume you do at least one or two of those things.

I'll think of you often during the coming year. And I know you'll be thinking about me.

Sincerely,

The Phoenix (you may as well stop guessing)

"It's gotten to the point where I dread opening my mail," Whitney said when he brought that third letter to Schacter.

"Have you ever been to Arizona?" asked the detective.

"Excuse me?"

"Maybe it's someone you met there, and that's why he signs his name as 'Phoenix.'"

Whitney smiled. "The phoenix is a bird. A mythical bird, actually. According to Egyptian mythology, it lived alone in the desert for hundreds of years, consumed itself in fire, and then rose up from the ashes to begin another life. This may be the letter writer's way of telling me that getting rid of him won't be easy, that he's indestructible. Anyway, what makes you so sure the letters weren't written by a woman?"

"It's got to be a man. All of his jokes put women down in a sick, sexual way. A woman wouldn't tell jokes like that. And the latest one—the story about the newlyweds and the sailor—gets violent as well. He sounds like someone who treats women as objects, someone who could hurt them if he didn't get his way with them."

Whitney pondered the detective's statement for several minutes. "I think it's someone who knows me," he said. "Some of the information he used could have come from a third source. But the scars on my neck—I think he must have seen them in person."

Schacter grunted and rubbed his chin. "Whoever he is, he seems bright enough. Uses big words, nothing spelled wrong as far as I can tell. 'Cortical atrophy'—what's that, something from medicine? Maybe he knows something about your profession. Anyway, he knows how to turn a phrase." He grunted once more. "All right," he continued, "let's assume it's a man, and let's assume it's someone who's met you. Any ideas who it could be?"

"Hell, Stan. I've been asking myself that question for weeks. I've thought about my Franklin colleagues, the Littleton staff, friends and acquaintances. I guess a lot would be capable, but none seem likely."

"How about this comment about doctors who make mistakes? Maybe he's one of your patients, or a former patient. Maybe even a patient's jealous husband—don't women sometimes fall in love with their psychiatrists?"

Whitney sighed. "Sure, it's natural for a patient to think she—or he—is in love with me. But just as often they hate me for the psychological pain that being in therapy causes."

"Like shooting the messenger that brings the bad news?"

"Something like that. It's hard being despised by someone whom you've tried to help. And if it is a patient or a patient's spouse I'm in a real bind, because the rule of patient-doctor privacy prevents me from giving you their names. But whoever it is, he's definitely escalating his attack. He's gone on a first-name basis with me. His language is getting vulgar. His humor is more vicious. Now he's even commenting—crudely, of course—on my bodily functions."

"Escalating," Schacter repeated. He sucked on his unlit pipe and flicked one of the letters with his thumb. "Let's say this guy is pretty smart, manipulative—maybe even sociopathic, angry as hell at women—and let's say that things escalate over time with him until he acts violently. Sounds a lot like a rapist to me."

Whitney blanched. "Damn, I hope not. They scare me more than most killers I've met. Murder is usually a simple crime of violence. Rape is much more complicated."

"There's a saying that's popular these days, Thomas. 'Rape is a crime of violence, not sex.'"

"That's wrong, though," Whitney responded. "It's a crime of violence *and* sex."

Schacter puffed on his pipe and pondered his friend's predicament. "I want a list of every accused rapist you've evaluated at Littleton. He's daring us to catch him. But you know, Thomas, I have a feeling our friend isn't as smart as he thinks he is."

"Oh?"

"Look here, in his first letter. 'I like my cigar, too, but I take it out once in a while.'"

"What about it?"

"I may not know my Churchill, but I certainly know my Marx."

"Karl Marx smoked a cigar?" asked Whitney.

38

•

Schacter smiled. "Not Karl Marx—Groucho Marx. That's his line."

No letters arrived during the next three months. During the hiatus Whitney and Schacter studied the doctor's list. In his dozen-plus years as a forensic psychiatrist, he'd evaluated over one hundred accused rapists, most of them at Littleton. Whitney had recommended that most of them be found responsible for their actions. A few, he believed, were legally insane when they committed their crimes.

"Perhaps our friend is angry because of some mistake he thinks you made. Would that help narrow down the list?"

"Not really," replied Whitney. "Some criminals start out hoping for an NGRI—'not guilty by reason of insanity.' They see it as a way of beating the system. But people who get found NGRI of violent crimes usually get committed to mental hospitals for longer than the sentence they could have received. A lot of them wind up wishing they had pleaded guilty."

Schacter grunted and furrowed his brow. "So he could be either someone who was hoping for an NGRI and didn't get one, or someone who got one and wishes he didn't."

"Exactly."

"Terrific," said the detective sarcastically. "In other words, it could be anyone on the list."

"If he's on the list at all."

Schacter flipped his fingers through the letters. "I'm no doctor, but this guy doesn't sound crazy to me. Let's forget about the ones who got found NGRI. We'll look for someone who tried to plead insanity, but who ultimately got found guilty."

Each week Whitney brought Schacter several patient records from the Littleton files. In late March, a few days after Whitney delivered the final stack of records, he received a call from Schacter. "Thomas, I think we may have our man. Does the name George Castell ring a bell?"

"No, I'm afraid not. Don't forget, Stan, I've examined hundreds, maybe thousands, of patients over the years."

"Well, let me tell you what I've learned from reading his record."

Castell was sent to Littleton for a pretrial evaluation in 1978. He was accused of committing three West Philadelphia rapes over a fourteen-month period. He abducted his victims at knife-point in parking lots. He blindfolded them, took them to his apartment, and sexually assaulted them. He then returned them to their cars.

One of his victims, Sheila Pressman, removed a heart-shaped ring from her finger and surreptitiously placed it between Castell's mattress and box spring. When Castell was arrested two months later on drug charges, the police found Sheila's ring. It was the first solid link between Castell and the rapes.

As the case against him grew, Castell and his attorney realized that it would be ludicrous, and that he would receive a longer sentence, if he pleaded not guilty. At the request of his attorney, Castell was evaluated by a court-affiliated doctor on the day of his arraignment. The doctor, a third-year psychiatric resident with no forensic experience, stated in his report:

> In my opinion, Mr. Castell suffers from a mental disorder best characterized as an Atypical Impulse Control Disorder. According to the American Psychiatric Association, the essential features of an impulse control disorder are: "a failure to resist an impulse or temptation to perform some act that is harmful to the individual or others," and "an experience of pleasure, gratification, or release at the time of the act."
>
> It is true that the term "impulse control disorder" is usually reserved for conditions such as pathological gambling; kleptomania; pyromania; or unpredictable, explosive outbursts. However, Mr. Castell's repeated pattern of releasing pent-up sexual energy by acting violently toward others appears to fall (atypically) within this general category.
>
> There appears to be a cause-and-effect relationship between Mr. Castell's psychiatric condition and his criminal actions. His behavior at the time of the offenses was very much a product of his Atypical Impulse Control Disorder.

The doctor stopped short of suggesting that the defendant's behavior was beyond his conscious control. Nevertheless Castell's attorney saw an opening—admittedly minuscule—for an insanity defense.

The district attorney, too, saw this opening. Anxious to undercut the defense, he asked the judge to send Castell to Littleton for a criminal responsibility evaluation. Castell was examined by Whitney, who was then on Littleton's consulting staff. Whitney wrote:

> Mr. Castell freely admits his involvement in the sexual assaults. Thus there are three questions to be addressed: (1) Was the defendant mentally ill when the crimes occurred? (2) Was he psychologically capable of understanding right from wrong? (3) Was he mentally capable of controlling his behavior?

There is no evidence to suggest that Mr. Castell has ever suffered from a major mental disorder. He has never experienced hallucinations or delusional beliefs. He has never endured a depression so severe that it clouded his ability to perceive reality. He has never had a period of uncontrollable mania.

We must distinguish between a so-called "irresistible impulse" and an impulse that is intentionally not resisted. Mr. Castell's crimes were not conducted on the spur of the moment. He successfully executed a complex series of actions. He planned his movements carefully and tried to avoid detection.

In my opinion Mr. Castell was in full control of his mental faculties and his behavior when the assaults occurred. There were no impairments in his ability to perceive, comprehend, or interpret reality. He was not acting under the belief that he was being controlled by demons, God, alien forces, or other external agents.

Mr. Castell is not mentally ill, nor does he suffer from any intellectual, cognitive, or organic defects that would render him unable to understand or control his behavior. I recommend that the court find Mr. Castell criminally responsible for his behavior on the dates in question.

"He plea-bargained when he got back to court," Schacter reported. "In exchange for a guilty plea on one count—the Pressman assault—the D.A. dropped the other two rape charges. I spoke with the public defender who handled Castell's case. He says it was your report that clinched things against his client. He told Castell that no jury would find him NGRI after hearing you testify. That's when they decided to plead out."

"I think I remember him now," said Whitney. "He was a pretty clever guy. I guess he could be the letter writer. Is he still in prison?"

"His lawyer wasn't sure. Castell made some threats after the trial about suing him for misrepresentation. Nothing ever came of it, but it was the end of their association. But—get this—the lawyer says Castell might have become eligible for parole last October or November—just before you received that first letter."

A few days later Schacter called again. "Meet me at Jimmy's Bar after work. We've got something to celebrate."

Castell was dead. He had been denied parole the first week of November, and in early February he was stabbed to death by another prisoner over a gambling debt. "When he missed parole he probably remembered that it was your report that sealed his fate. Without it he might have had a chance for an NGRI and he might have been released earlier. Anyway, I guess we know now why you haven't gotten any more letters recently."

Whitney frowned. "I guess I feel a little guilty."

"Guilty? What the hell for?"

"I've wanted this guy dead for months. So now I guess I feel as though that wish magically killed him. It's difficult coming to grips with your own murderous impulses."

Schacter grunted. "You think too goddamn much, Thomas."

Two weeks afterward Whitney walked into Schacter's office and dropped an envelope on the detective's desk. "Dead men don't write letters," he said.

Schacter read:

April 11, 1982

Dear Thomas,

Happy Easter!

A psychiatrist interviewed three patients to determine whether they were well enough for discharge from a mental hospital. "Whoever answers this next question correctly will be allowed to go home," he said. "Tell me: What is the meaning of Easter?"

Said the first patient: "Easter is when we dress up in costumes and go out trick or treating." He was sent back to his ward.

Said the second patient: "Easter is when that funny little man in a red uniform jumps down the chimney with presents for everyone." He, too, was excused from the examination room.

The third patient thought for several moments. "Easter," he said, "commemorates the resurrection of our Lord, Jesus Christ. He was crucified on Good Friday, and on Easter morning he rolled back the rock in front of his cave, stepped outside, and then . . ."

"Yes?"

". . . and then . . . and then . . ."

"Yes? Yes?"

". . . and then he saw his shadow, went back inside, and we had six more fucking weeks of winter."

So here I am, Thomas, metaphorically back from the dead. Were you afraid I'd forgotten about you? I could never do that, not after all that we've been through together. I look at our relationship as I would a marriage: together until death do us part.

Doctors always seem so in control of themselves, so sure of the power they wield over others. No wonder their patients often look upon them as if they were God. I wonder, then: What is it like for a doctor to contemplate his own death?

Personally, I've always felt that doctors—you psychiatrists in particular—carry too much of a burden. Society asks too much of you. With the flick of a fountain pen you can put someone in the hospital, and with another flick you can return freedom to him. Or say the word and one person gets excused for his crime; say a different word and another person wastes away in prison. Too much power for one person to have. Too much responsibility. Too much stress, strain, and aggravation. No wonder so many psychiatrists end their own lives.

So—how are you feeling, my friend?

The Phoenix

The detective grunted. "I guess it wasn't Castell after all." He pondered the letter. "I do have another idea, though."

Whitney tossed his hands into the air with a desperate sigh.

"No, really, Thomas, hear me out. If this is being done by someone who knows you, I think we can at least stop him from writing to you again. I want you to tell everyone you know about the letters."

"You want me to . . . what?"

"Everyone. But tell them that you think you may be able to figure out who the writer is. Say that if the police can identify the owner of a partial fingerprint they picked up, they'll issue a warrant for the person's arrest."

"I don't get it."

"Our friend hasn't given us a hell of a lot to go on. But if he thinks that maybe he's slipped up, left a fingerprint or some other clue, then he'll probably be afraid to write to you again. I want you to work the story into the next conversation you have with every friend or colleague. Try to create the impression that you're taking each person into your confidence, as if you're saying, 'But I don't suspect you.' Because this plan will only work if each person feels that he isn't under suspicion yet, but that he might be if he slips up once more."

Whitney insisted on not telling his private patients. He said he had always followed the traditional psychiatric practice of retaining a therapeutic neutrality—almost an anonymity—with them. Telling them about the letters would intrude too much on that practice and would interfere thereafter with therapy. Instead he placed the letters in a stack on his office desk where they could be seen by his patients, topped by a piece of Schacter's police stationery with a handwritten note that proclaimed, "Case solved!"

The letters stopped. "It's a relief, of course," said Whitney. "But I don't like thinking that the letters came from someone I still have contact with, and that I may never know for sure who that person was."

That was almost nine months ago, Schacter realized. Like the bird for whom the writer had named himself, Whitney's nemesis had risen once more. There was no end. The torment continued.

Schacter reached into his desk drawer and unwrapped the month-old Chocolate Junior. He remembered the company's logo from his childhood: "Tastykake—The cake that made mother stop baking." In the intervening years the price had quadrupled, the size had shrunk, and the creamy chocolate filling between the two sponge-cake layers had nearly disappeared. The product remained indigenous to Philadelphia, though, which was a matter of civic pride to Schacter. This particular cake still had some resiliency. *Probably safe to eat it,* he thought.

He looked again at the report he had just received from the police lab. The dried red liquid on the latest mystery letter was definitely human blood. Schacter glanced at the envelope once more. There was no need to take the letter out, though. He had already memorized its message.

> *The game begins in earnest.*
> *The stakes are very high.*
> *Please notify your loved ones.*
> *Will they miss you when you die?*

When Dr. Anna Roth awoke that morning her whole body was shaking. First she noticed her feet. They were kicking the covers from underneath like twin volcanoes in the first stages of eruption. The tremors traveled up her legs and across her torso. They coursed entirely through her. Even her teeth were chattering.

Earthquake! Percy never told me that Pennsylvania has earthquakes! But the bed itself was still. The windows didn't rattle. A quick survey of the room revealed nothing overturned. *Not an earthquake,* she thought.

The heat. She wondered if the furnace in the apartment building had malfunctioned during the frigid December night. But the quiet hiss of steam from the corner radiator ruled out that possibility. *Not the heat,* she thought.

Her body calmed. She sat up slowly. Everything appeared in order. She stood up. She was halfway across the room when she remembered the dream. Her body began to shake once more. The walls of the room seemed to recede several yards and then rush in on her. She leaned against the dresser for support.

In her dream Anna was a teenager once again. She was standing at her mother's side near the train tracks, just as she had done forty years earlier. A light drizzle fell. Water rolled off the soldiers' helmets like quicksilver. The crowd of villagers was packed tightly around her. Then there was a voice: *Alle Juden mussen ihre Sachen abgeben und sollen links eine Reihe machen! Schnell! Einsteigen! (All Jews must surrender their belongings and form a line on the left! Quickly! Step into the boxcar!)* She stood on her toes to see who had issued the command. Although

45

everything else about the scene was just as she remembered it, the voice had an unmistakable New England accent. She stood on her toes until they ached.

Suddenly she was a ballerina whirling on her toes in an elegant pirouette. The crowd disappeared. A single soldier stood with his back toward her. He didn't speak, but Anna knew that the voice was his. He clapped his hands slowly. At first he seemed to be applauding her. Then Anna realized he was gesturing her—commanding her— to continue. She was tired; she ached; she wanted to stop. Still the soldier clapped. She struggled toward him, hoping to glimpse her tormentor's face. *If only he would see me,* she thought, *he might take pity on me and let me stop.* But no matter which way she turned—and even though the soldier didn't appear to move—she could see only his back.

The rainfall intensified. The soldier's body disappeared, leaving only his clapping hands suspended in midair. Anna looked down at her own hands; they were the fifty-seven-year-old hands of her adult self. She saw the tattooed serial number on her wrist turn to fresh blood. She held her wrist out in the rain to wash the numbers away, but the cuts were fresh, and the numbers kept reappearing no matter how much blood the rain swept away.

Now her legs were crossed at the ankles; her arms were stretched out at her sides. Blood poured from her hands and feet. She was crucified to the barbed wire of Auschwitz. A dozen soldiers stood in a semicircle below her, all of them with their backs toward her, clapping in slow unison. *Do not forgive them, Lord,* she said, *for they know what they do.*

The dream was still on her mind as she pulled into her parking space at Littleton. She still found it odd to be driving to work, even though it had been more than a year since Percy Osborne coaxed her out of her Manhattan practice.

She didn't require much coaxing, actually. They were talking over lunch at the Psychoanalytic Society Annual Meeting. She turned to her old friend and said, "I believe I've passed my usefulness as an analyst. My patients have begun to bore me. Their midlife crises, the existential *angst*—they seem so drab and uninteresting that I have difficulty remembering them. Last week I almost called one of them by another's name." Osborne was picking aimlessly at his salad. "And," Anna continued with a smile, "I don't believe you've heard a word I've been saying."

Osborne looked up at last. "Hmm? Oh, I'm sorry." He paused in silence for several moments. "Anna," said Osborne, "I'm retiring soon. I have cancer."

"Percy . . ." Her own troubles paled by comparison. She felt ashamed.

"No, it's all right. I'm surprised I even told you. The only others who know are my wife and my oldest son. Anyway, I've already cut back on my work load at the hospital. I began doing that about two years ago, when I found out. Thomas Whitney—you met him a few years ago when you visited me at Littleton—has taken over many of my old duties. And I think he'll do a fine job in my position when I retire. I surely would feel a lot better, though," Osborne continued with a gentle sparkle in his eyes, "if Whitney had someone like you for guidance. An older and wiser head, as it were."

And so Anna Roth came to Littleton as the director of one of its wards. "Many of the patients on that ward were found NGRI," Osborne told her. "Not guilty by reason of insanity."

Not guilty by reason of insanity. The concept seemed an anomaly of logic. *How can you acknowledge that somebody did something, and then say they are not responsible for the deed?* It chafed against her sense of order, her raw wounds from Auschwitz, her bitterness toward the ones who denied or escaped responsibility for those horrors.

After the war Anna wrote a book about her concentration camp experiences. Entitled *Chaos, Cruelty, and Redemption,* it began:

> The first step toward psychological redemption is the acknowledgment of personal responsibility. A man says, "I was only following orders," and in so doing he strips away another shred of his own humanity. A woman professes, "We were ignorant, we did not know, we are not to blame," and thus avoids the self-examination that would set her spirit free.

Anna Roth grew to loathe the insanity defense. *How can we help someone come to terms with his own cruelty if we first tell him that he is not guilty of that cruelty?*

For Anna, Jimmy Bree was a perfect case in point. He was a chronically mentally ill young man who had lived all of his life in the sheltered environment of his mother's home. He remained there long after his father died and his siblings moved away. His mother was the central force in his world; as such, she also became the prime focus of his delusions and hallucinations. When he stopped taking his antipsychotic medication, she threatened to have him committed to a mental hospital. He became paranoid, believed the medicine was poison, thought she was hiding it in his food, and decided that she must be an agent of the archangel Lucifer.

Jimmy Bree killed his mother. He stabbed her with such incredible ferocity that the chef's knife pierced entirely through her and stuck an inch into the kitchen floor. The police report included the final entry Hannah Bree made in her diary: *Jimmy—no Thorazine all week—curtains for me.*

He was sent to Littleton for a pretrial evaluation. Thomas Whitney recommended that he be found not criminally responsible. The young man was transferred to Dr. Roth's building to await trial. He became hyper-religious. He wanted to be punished. He begged Anna to help him find the strength to plead guilty to the murder charge, but in the end he surrendered to his attorney's wish to enter an insanity plea.

The day after Jimmy Bree was found NGRI he tried to hang himself. "I don't understand it," he cried to Anna Roth when she spoke with him on the emergency ward. "I killed my mother, I killed her, I know I did, and now they tell me I'm not guilty."

In the eight months since that day Jimmy Bree had remained completely mute. It was as if he were inflicting punishment on himself to compensate for the court's decision to absolve him of responsibility.

Anna looked into his room when she arrived on the ward. He was oblivious of her. His attention was riveted to a tiny eight-legged predaceous playmate.

Spider, spider, crawl inside her.

Jimmy Bree watched the spider slowly weave its way down the left leg of his state-issued trousers. It crawled along the main seam, burrowed down into the cuff, and finally reappeared and perched itself on the upturned bottom of Jimmy's pants leg. It stood there motionless for several moments.

Take a life, make a life. Undo what thou hast done—I command thee! Jesus of Mary. Peter, Paul, and Mary. Peter Paul Mounds ... chocolate-covered coconut. Coo-coo nut. I'm a coo-coo nut.

Jimmy took a cigarette paper from his shirt pocket and gently slipped it underneath the spider. He placed his cargo onto the floor and smiled, satisfied, as the spider crawled off the paper and escaped.

NGRI.

No Girls Reside Inside.

She lied, she lied, she died, she died.
NGRI.

Anna glanced at Jimmy Bree's toiletries shelf. A pencil was standing point-down, stuck deeply into a lump of wet tissue paper. He did this quite often. It reminded Anna of the police report: *Suspect's mother was stretched out on her back in pool of blood. One gust of air came from her mouth and then she stopped breathing. CPR was attempted with negative results. An eight-inch knife was stuck all the way through her stomach and into the floor, pinning her there.*

The first anniversary of the killing was near. Anna worried that Jimmy might again become acutely suicidal. "You've killed him," she had shouted at Whitney when she stormed into his office the day after Jimmy attempted suicide. "You've killed Jimmy Bree."

"What the devil are you talking about, Anna? I've just come from the emergency ward. They tell me he'll recover without any complications."

"His body is still alive," she continued, "but his spirit is dead." Her hand was shaking and her voice cracked. "Punishment was his only hope of survival. You've taken that away from him by telling him he's not responsible for what he did."

Whitney sighed deeply. He looked directly into her eyes. "Anna," he said softly, "the war is over. Some people were punished. Others went scot-free. Let it go, Anna. There's nothing you can do to change the past."

"How dare you!" She wouldn't have believed herself capable of it; she had never struck another person in her adult life. But she extended her right arm toward Whitney in a backhand motion, her knuckles glancing off his cheekbone. The pain shot through her entire arm and Whitney fell from his chair.

Sweat beads poured into her eyes, stinging them and rendering her sightless for an instant. When she opened them Whitney was propping himself up against the wall of his office. She turned hastily to leave. "Bravo," she heard him say as she fled. He clapped his hands slowly three times.

Whitney and the feelings he evoked in her remained a bane in Anna Roth's daily life at Littleton. She wished she could be rid of him. She loathed thinking about the day—soon to come, no doubt—when Percy Osborne would relinquish his position to the New Englander. If only Whitney wasn't at Littleton, she was sure she could get the hospital's priorities straightened out about insanity and capability.

She thought about all of this as she glanced at the morning paper in her office. CHRISTMAS EVE SNIPER RECOVERING FROM SUICIDE ATTEMPT, read the headline. *More work for Thomas Whitney,* thought Anna. *Why won't he face up to the harm he's causing?*

It struck her. *He wouldn't face up,* she thought. *The soldier in my dream. The one with the accent who kept clapping.* Suddenly her legs ached as if she'd been dancing for days.

Ralph Malzone looked out the window of his Center City apartment on New Year's morning. The week-old snow had turned beige from trolley exhaust. Little piles of dog turds dotted the snow like sprinkles on an ice cream cone.

He reread the article near the back of the local news section.

SNIPER RETURNS TO LITTLETON
by Selma Aaron

December 31—Gordon Cardonick, the so-called Christmas Eve Sniper, was returned to Littleton State Hospital today under heavy security. Cardonick, 26, had been treated at County General Hospital for superficial wounds suffered during a suicide attempt at Littleton three days ago.

Cardonick will undergo psychiatric testing in connection with the Christ-mas Eve shooting deaths of three motorists on the Schuylkill Expressway. He pleaded not guilty at his arraignment on December 28 and is expected to raise insanity as a defense against the charges.

Dr. Ralph Malzone, Assistant Director of Forensic Evaluation, stated that the psychiatric tests are expected to take a month to complete.

He liked seeing his name in the paper; it happened so rarely. He seldom got to evaluate patients who'd committed high-visibility crimes. *Another starring role for Thomas Whitney,* he thought. *Damn him. God, goddamn him.*

Malzone had worked at Littleton ever since he finished his psychiatric residency in 1973. There was little prestige associated with working there. Everyone knew that Littleton's psychiatric staff, with the exception of Osborne, Whitney, and Anna Roth, was composed of unextraordinary doctors. "Oh, how interesting!" people said when they met him and heard where he worked. Then they would turn away as if prolonged contact with him might prove injurious to their health.

He'd spent his first four years at Littleton writing medication orders, dictating progress notes, and running an occasional psychotherapy group for chronic, regressed patients. Then his successful treatment of a difficult patient promised to boost his career. The woman had a long history of violent outbursts. She seemed unlikely ever to leave Littleton for a less secure setting. Malzone carefully reevaluated her and prescribed a medication regimen that kept her assault-free for several months.

That case brought Malzone to the favorable notice of Percy Osborne. The superintendent, who spent much of his time administering the Forensic Evaluation Building, transferred Malzone there and worked closely with him. It was widely known that Osborne hoped to relinquish some of those forensic duties. Malzone fancied himself the superintendent's protégé and imagined that eventually he would be placed in charge of the Evaluation Building.

But he was passed over for that promotion. The job went to Whitney instead, and the last three years at Littleton had been hellish for Malzone. Whitney held a tight rein over forensic assignments. He kept the most challenging and controversial cases for himself, and he gave Malzone the most inconsequential cases. Malzone became bored and frustrated with his job. His chagrin played itself out in verbal duels with his wife and son. Everything seemed to have fallen apart during the past year, and Jeanette had finally filed for a divorce.

Since the separation his jealousy of Whitney had bubbled to the surface, so much so that he was often unable to stomach the thought of going to work. He began to dip into his several-hundred-hour reserve of sick time (he'd never before used even a day's worth). Indeed, he felt sick: sick with the loss of his family, his envy of others (especially Whitney), and the painful realization that, at best, his life would never be anything more than ordinary.

He heard glockenspiel music. By now, he knew, there were thousands of people lining Broad Street to watch the Mummers and the New Year's Day parade. Malzone poured Scotch into a glass and tried not to think about Whitney.

Whitney sat in his office in Littleton's Forensic Evaluation Building. With a yellow pad of legal paper balanced on his knee, he planned the first lecture for the spring semester course he would be teaching at the law school. He wrote:

Some are born mad, some achieve madness, and some have madness thrust upon them.

That isn't quite what Shakespeare wrote, but it's not too far from the truth.

Your syllabus says that this course is called "Mental Illness and the Law." In the next few classes, we'll be defining mental illness and talking about its causes. For now, let me just say that some people are born mad—or at least half-mad. It's in their genes and it's in their blood. You'll be reading in this week's assignment about neurotransmitters, the dopamine hypothesis, and the biological treatment of mental illness.

And some people achieve madness on their own, usually by misusing drugs or alcohol.

Malzone entered the office without knocking. "I got Gordon Cardonick's chart for you out of the record room, Thomas. Was there anything else you wanted me to do?"

"The new psychiatric residents from the medical school are coming today, Ralph. They'll spend the morning with Dr. Osborne, and they have their first supervision seminar with me at three o'clock. I'd appreciate it if you would give them a tour of the Forensic Building sometime after lunch."

Whitney counted on Malzone to keep track of case assignments, evaluation deadlines, staff meetings—in short, to do the things one might normally expect an administrative assistant to do. At times he felt guilty for relegating Malzone to such pedestrian chores. But then, after all, Malzone was only a pedestrian psychiatrist.

Whitney dismissed Malzone and returned to his notepad:

> But what about that last group of people—the ones who have madness thrust upon them? I'll be talking to you about some people whose life stories may give you nightmares. The insane arsonist whose mother used to chain him to the cellar floor and make him eat Alpo from a dog bowl. The psychotic teenage killer who was raped repeatedly by his own father from the time he was six years old until the time of the murder. And when you hear these stories you'll wonder, as you lie awake at night, if madness might not have been thrust upon you, too, under similar circumstances.

He put down his pen and buzzed his secretary on the intercom. "Set up an appointment with Gordon Cardonick in the early afternoon, please. Two o'clock would be fine."

Whitney hadn't read the man's chart, because he preferred his initial impressions of patients to be unsullied by preconceptions. If he liked a patient at the outset—or if he hated, feared, or pitied him—Whitney wanted that first burst of feeling to derive from something he experienced himself, and not from something he read or heard from someone else. He put Cardonick's file aside.

At around two o'clock Cardonick was escorted to Whitney's office by two burly prison guards. "You want us to stay in here with you while you talk to him, Doc?"

"No, thank you. That won't be necessary."

"Yeah, okay. Just whistle if you need us. We'll be out here." They shut the office door behind themselves.

The patient stood absolutely still for several seconds. His eyes darted back and forth as they took in every square inch of territory. Finally they came to rest on Whitney, locking on the psychiatrist with a cold and empty stare. He said nothing.

Whitney felt uncomfortable underneath the man's intense gaze. He noticed the crusty scabs along his right cheekbone. "Please have a seat, Mr. Cardonick."

Cardonick took the chair farthest from Whitney's desk. His facial expression was wooden. His eyes remained fixed rigidly on his questioner.

"Mr. Cardonick, I'm Dr. Whitney. I'd like to talk with you for a little while, if I may."

Cardonick stared without speaking.

Each patient presented a unique challenge, and Whitney wondered how he could best set this one at ease. He smiled tentatively at Cardonick. Some patients—the more paranoid ones—found friendliness more frightening than coldness, though, and Whitney tried to keep his smile formal and polite.

"Do you understand why you're at Littleton State Hospital, Mr. Cardonick?"

Cardonick's lips moved imperceptibly, as if he were a ventriloquist sending his words through some unseen dummy. "The judge sent me here."

"Mm-hmm. And why was that?"

"They say I killed someone." His voice sounded empty. He appeared devoid of any feeling.

"I see. Well, I'm a psychiatrist. The court has asked me to examine you and to write a report. So I'll be meeting with you a few times, asking you a lot of questions about yourself, testing your mind to see how it's functioning, things like that."

Cardonick snickered softly; it was the first overt sign of any emotion. He looked at the heavy glass ashtray on the table next to his chair.

Whitney followed the patient's glance. He opened his desk drawer and took out the pack of Marlboros he kept handy for just such occasions. "Would you like a cigarette?"

It all happened quickly—so quickly that Whitney later compared the scene to a movie that had been run through a projector at triple speed. Cardonick snapped his eyes back toward the doctor. He jumped to his feet. "It was you. It was you, you cocksucker. And now you want to poison *me*, too." He palmed the ashtray as if it were a discus and hurled it toward Whitney. The doctor ducked and the ashtray shattered against the wall, a tiny shard slicing the bridge of Whitney's nose.

Whitney threw himself to the floor behind his desk. He heard the sounds of fists upon flesh and of moans and whimpers. When he stood the two prison guards were dragging Cardonick by his hair and shirt. "I meant to tell you, Doc," said one of the guards as they struggled with the patient. "He's got this thing about cigarettes."

Neither Whitney nor the guards noticed the smug expression on Cardonick's face as he was led out of the office.

"Such are the occasional perils of working at Littleton," said Whitney as he rubbed the Band-Aid on his nose. The four psychiatric residents from Franklin Medical School listened attentively. "The people are wild and dangerous." He paused for effect. "And the patients can be pretty rough, too." The residents laughed. Whitney recalled for an instant the time Anna Roth struck him in her rage after Jimmy Bree's attempted suicide.

"As I was saying," he continued, "'insanity' isn't a medical term. It's a legal concept. Only a judge or jury can call someone insane—can say that, because of his mental state, he isn't guilty of committing a crime. You'll each be assigned to do an evaluation next week. It'll be your job as a forensic psychiatrist-in-training to advise the court, to give an expert opinion on criminal responsibility."

"Suppose someone admits to doing the crime," said one of the residents. "Mental illness or not, how can that person be considered not guilty when he's just told you he did it?"

"Good question, George. Let's suppose I'm charged with murdering a colleague." He wished immediately that he had chosen another example. "In order for the state to get me convicted it has to satisfy three conditions. First, it has to show that a killing actually took place. They'll have a hell of a time convicting me, for instance, if they can't produce the dead body. We'll call this the Jimmy Hoffa theory of jurisprudence." The residents chuckled.

"Second," continued Whitney, "the state has to prove that it was me—not you, you, or you—who did the killing. Finally, the state has to prove I had *mens rea*. That's a Latin phrase. It means 'guilty mind.' In our society, we only punish people for *criminal* behavior. The state has to prove that the defendant had criminal intention, that he had a guilty mind. If a two-year-old kills his sister with a rock, he wouldn't be convicted of murder, because no court would find him capable of forming criminal intent. And so it is with the insanity defense. There's a long Anglo-American tradition of excusing someone from blame, of not finding him *criminally* responsible, if his action was a direct product of a mental illness."

Whitney glanced at his pile of papers. Cardonick's folder was on top of the stack. He wondered what he would find when he read its contents. He could count on the fingers of one hand the number of times he had been assaulted at Littleton; patients usually reserved that sort of behavior for one another or the guards. And he couldn't recall anyone ever having used a weapon before (if an ashtray could be counted as a weapon).

"Well, that's enough for one day. I'll hand out your first case assignments tomorrow. Good day, gentlemen."

Malzone walked into the room as the residents were filing out. "Thomas, I just heard about the fracas with the sniper. Are you all right?"

He sensed the disingenuousness of Malzone's concern. "I'm fine, Ralph. Thanks for asking." He gathered his stack of papers and headed toward the exit.

9

The telephone rang moments after Whitney arrived home. He picked up the receiver before the fourth ring, signaling his answering service that he was home and would take the call himself.

"Is this Dr. Whitney?" It was a woman with a strident voice and a thick local accent. He didn't recognize her.

"Who is this, please?"

"Dr. Whitney?"

"Yes?"

"Dr. Whitney, this is Selma Aaron from the *Philadelphia Inquirer*. I'd like to ask you some questions about Gordon Cardonick."

Whitney had brought Cardonick's record home. There were two charts, one from each of the man's admissions to Littleton. Whitney glanced at them while he spoke. "I'm sorry, miss. I'm not able to give interviews about my work. I'm sorry, but I hope you understand."

"I see. So you are going to be the doctor evaluating him, then?"

She had already divined, from one innocent comment, more than he cared to reveal. He shifted in his seat and fiddled with the telephone cord. "I'm afraid I can't comment any further, miss."

"Have you read the police report yet?"

Whitney didn't respond. He couldn't think of anything to say, and yet it was an anathema to him to hang up on anyone. He hated being rude.

"Do you plan to interview his wife, Doctor?"

"I'm sorry, miss. I really must go now. Good-bye."

Moments later his phone rang again. He tried to disguise the anger in his voice when he answered it.

"Hello? Is that you, Thomas? It's your mother."

He didn't know what annoyed him more: her failure to recognize his voice or her assumption that he needed help identifying hers. "Hello, Mother. I tried calling you over the weekend to wish you a Happy New Year, but there was no answer." He wondered if he would ever be able to begin a conversation with her without sounding so guilt-ridden.

"Oh, I decided to close up the city house and spend the holidays at the country farm."

Patricia Alden Whitney divided her time among three homes in an orderly and predictable fashion. The spring and fall were spent at the main estate in Concord. It was the house Thomas grew up in, the home she shared with her husband for twenty-four years until he succumbed to cancer in 1957. She still referred to it as a country farm even though Concord had long since turned suburban and the land had not been farmed for nearly a century.

The summer found her on East Haven Island, twelve miles by ferry off the Maine coast. Her architect grandfather had designed much of the island's village area, multiplying the already substantial Alden family fortune in the process. Thirty years ago she and her husband had bought two hundred acres of waterfront land and an eighteenth-century house, and she renovated several smaller structures as summer quarters for other members of the family.

Winter was a time for husbanding resources and, for the past two decades, she had spent December through February in her Back Bay town house, close to the conveniences of the city.

The moves were quite regular: on March first she would go out to Concord, on June first up to Maine, on September first back to Concord, and on December first to Boston. Maria, her cook and companion, supervised the moves with a Yankee circumspection learned from years at the side of Patricia Whitney.

"Really? What made you change your schedule like that, Mother?"

"Oh, I don't know. Your Aunt Jane and I were breakfasting at the Copley Plaza last week, and I suddenly decided that I'd had enough of the city for this year. I decided to come out here for some peace and quiet. I sat by the window and watched people cross-country-ski out in the back field. It's been years since I've done that. Do you still have your skis, Thomas?"

They had fought terribly after his father died; Whitney wanted to take the man's skis, but his mother insisted that they remain in Concord. He was angry that she didn't remember. "I never did have skis of my own, Mother. And I haven't gone skiing since Father died."

"Oh, I see. Well, the snow is really quite lovely here this year. Your Aunt Jane was always a marvelous skier. Did I tell you that I saw her recently?"

She was repeating herself. He castigated himself for his petulant tone. He wanted to say something tender, to let her know how much he worried about her growing old, to apologize for failing to give her the grandchildren she still harbored a secret wish for.

He had to give her credit; she seldom raised that topic directly. Perhaps she could sense his painful memories of Allison, pregnant and trapped in that burning farmhouse. But Whitney knew of his mother's concern. Patricia Alden Whitney's portion of the Alden generation-skipping trust had but one generation left. She had no other children. Were Whitney to remain childless, the money would revert to her sister's two sons. They were horrid, squat creatures with no social breeding who had already spent much of their own inheritances on racehorses and young girls. It galled her, Whitney knew, to countenance her share of the family wealth being squandered in such a fashion.

"Yes," he said, "it's been snowing a lot in Philadelphia, too." It was the best he could do. Their conversations always seemed to dwindle down to the small-talk details of the weather.

"Yes. Well, Thomas, I must go now."

She was a frugal woman, her considerable wealth to the contrary. She always left a tip of twelve-and-a-half percent—no more, no less—and she always sat with a stopwatch when she made long-distance calls. Whitney wondered what the stopwatch was reading at that moment.

"Good-bye, Mother. I'll call you soon. And say hello for me to Aunt Jane if you speak with her in the meanwhile."

"Oh, yes. Did I mention that we had breakfast together last week? Well, good-bye, Thomas."

Talking to her on the phone was like shaking hands with someone who wore gloves. You could gauge the person's strength, but it was difficult to sense the texture or warmth.

Whitney picked up Cardonick's folder and walked into the kitchen. He filled a stoneware mug three-quarters of the way with tap water, draped a camomile tea bag over its side, and placed it in the microwave oven. He set the timer for precisely two minutes and ten seconds and spread the papers from Cardonick's first chart across the antique oak kitchen table.

Cardonick's first admission to Littleton State Hospital occurred almost exactly two years earlier, a week before Christmas in 1980. On that occasion he was sent to Littleton from Holmesboro State Prison where he was serving a two-year sentence for assault and battery. According to the terse note from the Holmesboro psychiatrist:

Since beginning his prison sentence three months ago, this inmate has become increasingly paranoid, agitated, and withdrawn. Yesterday he refused to come out of his cell for breakfast. He threw a bucket of urine at a guard and was placed in lockup. This morning he set his mattress on fire. When guards attempted to remove him from the cell he held them at bay with a razor blade. He could not be calmed and the guards had to use tear gas to enter the cell and extinguish the fire. On interview this morning he impressed as bizarre and manneristic and may have been hallucinating. Eye contact was poor, affect was inappropriate, concentration and memory functions appeared impaired. Complained of loss of appetite and sleeping difficulty. Spoke in vague terms about guards taunting him over the intercom at night. Is impulsive and erratic, possibly psychotic, not able to tolerate prison. Refer to Littleton State Hospital for complete psychiatric evaluation.

Cardonick came to Littleton's Building One, the unit that houses prison inmates, and was evaluated by Dr. Adrienne Gillespie. She stated that he was suffering from a paranoid psychotic reaction, and she speculated that the condition may have resulted from the ingestion of illicit drugs in prison. She agreed with the referring psychiatrist that Cardonick was not then psychologically capable of serving his sentence in prison, and she recommended he be committed to Littleton for treatment. There was a commitment hearing in Littleton District Court. Cardonick didn't contest the doctor's recommendation—doing time at Littleton certainly seemed preferable to staying in prison—and he was committed.

Whitney found little additional information in the record of Cardonick's first Littleton admission. He wasn't surprised. Littleton's records reflected the patchwork quality of its psychiatric treatment. There were too many patients and too few doctors, and other than dispensing medication treatment was limited. Problem patients—the ones who became violent—had many entries in their charts. But most of the patients took medicine willingly and seldom had outbursts, and the documentation in their records was meager.

Cardonick had been prescribed Haldol, an antipsychotic drug with sedating effects, upon admission, and the medicine had been discontinued after a month. He remained nonpsychotic for the bulk of his first admission to Littleton. There was a short discharge summary: he was paroled in September of 1981, nine months after arriving at Littleton, having served half of his two-year sentence. He was released with a recommendation that he seek outpatient counseling.

In the back pages of the chart from that first admission, amidst various court-related forms and writs, Whitney found a copy of the assault and battery warrant. The victim was the patient's wife, Denise Cardonick.

The chart from Cardonick's second admission—barely a week old— was already thicker than the first chart. The police report ran several pages, with detailed descriptions of damages, and statements from a score of victims and witnesses. There were nineteen warrants: three counts of first-degree murder; twelve counts of assault and battery with a dangerous weapon; and one each for driving to endanger, leaving the scene of an accident, unlicensed possession of a firearm, and trespassing. Whitney, like Schacter before him, was struck by the arresting officer's statement: *When the subject was pulled from his car, he yelled, "Go ahead, kill me, I want you to." On way to the station he kept asking us when we were going to kill him.*

There was a handwritten note from Schacter: "The subject was interviewed after he got medical care for a superficial gunshot wound on his upper right cheek. He acknowledged receiving a Miranda warning. Lt. Rienzi reread his rights to him just to be sure. The subject refused to speak without an attorney present. He claims to be indigent and says he'll need a public defender. Interview terminated."

Whitney turned to an entry entitled *Interview w/Denise Cardonick, defendant's wife.* According to the information scribbled by the interviewing police officer, Denise and Gordon Cardonick had been separated for two months. "Six-year-old daughter lives with her. Says no idea where defendant lives last two months. Maybe couch in music studio—he is musician. Says defendant known for violent outbursts. Past arrests for receiving stolen property, asslt. & bat. on wife. Also history of alcohol, drug use, odd behavior."

Whitney made an entry on his notepad: *Arrange for interview with Denise Cardonick.*

Whitney sat by the wood-burning stove in his kitchen and looked out at the bright, frigid morning. The previous day's sunshine had melted the top layer of snow, and the overnight freeze had created a thin mirrorlike coating of ice.

He wrote:

Monday, January 10

Dear Peter,

Thank you for your thoughtful Christmas gift. I'm happy to add Dr. Bowlby's latest volume to my library.

Thank you also for your kind sentiments, though I fear you underestimate your own achievements. Your internship at Massachusetts General has very little to do with my letter of recommendation, and everything to do with your excellent record here at Franklin Medical School. But I'm glad that you like it in Boston, and pleased to have contributed in some small way.

With fondest wishes for the New Year, I am

Yours truly,
Thomas Whitney

His list of thank-you notes got longer every Christmas. The number of former students swelled each year, and many of them remembered him on the holiday with gifts and kind thoughts. Whitney had a natural-born teacher's greatest quality: a knack for making each student feel uniquely appreciated and cared for.

63

Whitney ate a light breakfast and left for Littleton. His first appointment was set for nine o'clock. He arrived at the Forensic Evaluation Building at a quarter before. Carla, his secretary, hadn't arrived yet. Whitney pulled his mail out of the pigeonhole receptacle above Carla's desk and turned toward his office.

Then he saw her.

Later he realized that she had sandy blonde hair that hung in layers of soft curls halfway down her back. Later he saw the tawny skin and the slender limbs, and the angled features that lent a touch of toughness to her. But at first all he could see were her eyes.

He was hard-pressed to identify their color. They seemed hazel, then blue, then green. She stayed seated; he stood his ground. But her eyes hurtled toward him, her pupils growing wide as if to surround him and draw him in. Meanwhile the rest of the room seemed to recede from him, like a scene viewed through reversed binoculars. He spied the trace of a tear in the corner of one eye.

". . . said that your secretary would be here soon. He said I could wait here for you. I hope you don't mind."

How long had she been speaking? "I'm sorry. What was that?"

She smoothed the wrinkles in her long skirt and brushed a strand of hair off her face. "I'm Denise, Denise Cardonick. Dr. Malzone—I think that was his name—he said I could wait here for you. I guess I'm early. Should I come back in fifteen minutes?"

There was the faintest bit of rasp in her voice. The corridor lights seemed to flicker when she spoke. "Hmm? Oh, no, not at all. Just give me a few minutes to call my phone, uh, phone my call." He ducked inside his office before she could answer.

He shut the door behind him. His body was cold; his face was hot. He imagined that she could see him through the door as he leaned there for support, so piercing were her eyes.

His intercom rang. "Dr. Whitney?"

"Yes, Carla."

"Oh, good. I figured you must be in there when I saw your door closed. Can I get you some coffee?"

"No, thank you, Carla."

"Oh. Well, your nine o'clock is here. Mrs. Cardonick. Should I send her in?"

Whitney glanced around his office. It reflected the quality of Littleton's janitorial service. The wastebasket brimmed with the previous week's trash and the ashtrays were still full. "No, I'll come out for her when I'm ready."

He moved about the office, straightening, emptying, rubbing dust off his desk with Kleenex. When he was finished he opened his door. "Mrs. Cardonick?"

Denise set down the six-month-old office copy of *Time*. She pulled the ends of her woolen shawl across her chest and stood to greet him. She seemed to glide across the reception area. Whitney closed the door and showed her to the seat nearest his desk.

"Thank you for asking me to come." Her voice wavered. "I've been afraid to talk to people. And then you called, and I figured . . . if you can't trust a psychiatrist, who can you trust?"

He noticed that she wasn't wearing a wedding ring.

"I haven't seen much of Gordon lately," she rattled on. "We separated a couple of months ago. I never thought it would have such an effect on him." She reached for the tissue box on Whitney's desk. "If it wasn't so horrible—all those innocent people—I'd almost feel good that it had an effect on him at all."

She blew her nose. It was raw; she had cried often of late. "I'm sorry," she said.

He saw a tiny drop of mucus spill along her upper lip. He found it quite endearing. If only he could reach out and pat her face dry . . . "That's all right, really. If you'd rather come back some other time—"

"Oh, God, no! When you called me last week I wanted to come in right away. You sounded so nice on the phone."

He blushed.

"Oh, God, I'm sorry. That sounds horrible, doesn't it. But everyone else has been so unfriendly. Reporters telephone at all hours. People call and then hang up. I won't even let my daughter leave the house. We're like prisoners." She breathed deeply.

Whitney settled back into his leather chair. He propped his legal pad against one knee and rested his elbow on the other. He tried to appear relaxed, concerned, thoughtful. He had never seen anyone as beautiful as the woman sitting across from him.

Her face turned red as her tears continued to well up. Her blush took the winter chill out of the poorly heated office. Whitney imagined he could see a wave of warm air rise off her, cross the space between them, and come to rest on his cheek.

He began to take notes . . .

* * *

If the weather hadn't turned sour that February morning in 1974, she might never have met him.

Denise sat alone in the school lunchroom. Usually she went across the street to Buzzy's Burgers with her friends. But it was raining, and she had no umbrella, and, besides, she needed the time to prepare for her Music Appreciation exam that afternoon.

"So, you gonna eat the rest of your french fries, or what?"

The boy looked familiar. Wasn't he the one who signed his name as "Dick Hurtz" at study hall? (The students wrote their names on a seating chart on the first day of study hall. At the next meeting the proctor called out the names they had signed. "Dick Hurtz" she called once, twice, then a third time. "Who's Dick Hurtz?" she finally shouted. "Mine does" came a reply from the back of the auditorium. Denise had to ask someone to explain the joke to her.)

"You gonna eat them, or can I have them?"

She could have told him to go away. She could have told him to keep his long, skinny fingers off her food. She could have told him to shave off the scraggly little beard he was trying to grow and leave her alone. But she was depressed by the rain, she didn't feel like studying, and she was grateful for the company.

"Sure, I mean, no, you can have them, I guess. They're cold, anyway."

He snagged a handful of her fries and sat down uninvited. He stared at her chest. "You must be a junior," he said.

"Huh?" She looked down at her blouse.

"Your book. The Music Appreciation class, right? I took it last year when I was a junior. What's your name?"

"Huh?"

"Your name. You got one, don't you?"

"Oh, right. Denise. Denise Boudreau."

The stranger twirled the last limp synthetic potato between his fingers. "Denise." He smiled. "That's a nice name. Listen, you want to know the questions on the music test?"

"Do I . . . what?"

"The questions. On the music test. I got them right here." He tapped the breast pocket of his leather vest.

"Where did you . . . Did you steal them?"

She pulled away from him ever so slightly. He saw her shocked expression. "No, of course not," he protested. "Do I look like the kind of guy who would do something like that?"

"Well, no. I mean, I don't know. Who are you?"

"Look, Denise. He asks the same questions every February. I wrote them down after last year's test because I knew the guy is too lazy to make up new questions every year. And here I am, willing to give them to you for free."

"Just like that."

"Sure, just like that."

She opened her book and pretended to study it. "No, thanks."

He sighed. "Okay. Look. Everyone else has already bought a copy. You don't take it, you're screwed. Old man Hartwell marks on a curve. You get eighty percent right and you can still flunk if everyone else gets ninety or a hundred percent." He dropped the list of questions beside her and began to walk away. "Oh, one more thing, Denise."

She didn't look up. "What!"

"You're holding your book upside-down. Keep that up and you'll really need those questions."

She turned the book right-side-up and slammed it down on the table. The stranger laughed as he headed toward the exit.

Her friend Carol walked up to her. "I didn't know you were friends with him, Denise."

"I don't even know him," she said, angry and embarrassed at the same time. "Who is he?"

"His name is Gordon Cardonick, and he's no good. C'mon, we'll be late for music class. You know what I heard? I heard half the class has a copy of the questions already."

Denise crumpled Gordon's list into a ball and threw it away. She followed Carol down the hall.

Gordon was waiting for her after school. She pretended not to see him, but he followed her across the street to Buzzy's. "I owe you some french fries," he said as he sat down at the counter next to her. "So, how was the test?"

"The questions were pretty hard." She sneered. "But I guess you know that already, don't you?"

"Yeah, I guess so. How did you make out?"

"I did okay." She smiled in spite of herself. "Music is my favorite subject. I sing soprano in the school choir."

"No kidding?" It was the first time he appeared almost as interested in her as he was in himself. "I sing, too. And I play piano. I've got a band. The Keystones. Maybe you've heard of us."

She shook her head. "Uh-uh."

He frowned. "Yeah, well, we may be playing your junior prom in a few months. Say, you wanna come hear us rehearse? I'm on my way there right now."

"No."

"No?" He was incredulous.

"No," she repeated.

"Why not?"

"Because first of all, I don't even know you. And as far as I can tell, you're an egomaniac. And besides, I'm engaged."

"Engaged, huh?" His nose wriggled as if he had just sensed an unpleasant odor. "Well, maybe some other time."

"I doubt it." She looked away from him and ordered a soda from the woman behind the counter.

He turned his attention to the slender brunette at a nearby table. "Hey, Belinda," he yelled to her. "You wanna come to rehearsal with me? I'm leaving now."

The girl's face lit up. "Yeah, sure, Gordon. Let's go."

"Be right with you, baby." He leaned over and whispered into Denise's ear. "My name is Gordon," he said. "Gordon Cardonick." His tongue glanced off the inside of her ear—was it an accident?—and sent a chill into her.

Carol sat down next to her after Gordon left. "Well, Denise, that's quite a trick."

"Huh?"

"I heard you say you're engaged. That's quite a trick for someone who has to beg her parents for permission to go on dates."

"I just said that to get rid of him."

"Maybe. Then again, maybe you were hoping it would get him interested in you." Carol laughed. "I'd like to see the expression on your father's face if you tried to bring Gordon Cardonick home."

"My mother says any friend of mine is welcome in our home," Denise replied defensively.

"Yeah, sure. And we both know what a tower of strength she is."

"Shut up, Carol."

Denise detested the way her mother never stood up for herself. Ethel Boudreau had moved directly from her parents' home into marriage at age nineteen. Denise's mother made no decisions, took no initiatives, formed no opinions—did absolutely nothing—without checking first for her husband's approval.

George Boudreau ruled the family with an iron fist. He was never known to tolerate dissension, change an opinion, or admit fault. "As long as you're living in my house," he would tell his three daughters, "you'll do things my way." It was little wonder that Denise's sisters had rebelled.

Jill, eight years older than Denise, left home at age sixteen. Denise remembered shivering in the basement, hiding underneath the stairway, and listening to the battle raging upstairs between her father and Jill. "Just try it, you son of a bitch," her sister said. "Try and stop me and I'll tell everyone about you. Everyone—including Neesey." Neesey was Denise's nickname. Denise never knew for certain—never really wanted to know—what Jill was referring to that night.

Mona, the middle daughter, had experimented with nearly every drug known to man. Her father kicked her out of the house when she was seventeen. She moved in with her maternal grandmother, a kindly woman with none of the steeliness required for managing her new charge. Mona's personality changed like the weather to match those of the men in her life. When she dated a political activist from the University of Pennsylvania she grew her hair long, smoked marijuana, went braless, and talked incessantly about the Third World. When she took up with a biker she cut her hair short and tinted it red, drank beer, and wore chain bracelets and push-up bras without cups.

George and Ethel Boudreau resolved that Denise would never go the way of their two older daughters. And so they held even more tightly to her reins, pulling back on her whenever she showed an inclination toward independent motion.

Denise resented her parents' restrictiveness, but she was too frightened to challenge them. And so she became "the good one"—the child who studied hard and dated very little (and then only with boys who met with her father's approval).

In April of her junior year, Denise's high school class went for an overnight trip to New York City. The trip was organized by her history teacher, and provisions were made for close and careful supervision. Her father wouldn't allow her to go. "I know what happens on those trips," he said with the conviction of someone who believes everyone is trying to get away with as much as possible. "Sex, drugs, and all sorts of goings-on."

Even after her teacher tried to intercede on her behalf, Denise's father refused to give permission. And so Denise was forced to stay behind, relegated to being baby-sat in the sophomore class along with the two other juniors who couldn't go to New York.

She was sitting alone in Buzzy's Burgers that afternoon. All her friends were in New York. Gordon asked her to go with him to his band's rehearsal. He had invited her two or three times since their meeting a couple of months earlier, and she had always refused. But this time was different. *What the hell,* she thought. *Where does being good get you?*

She began to attend his rehearsals regularly. Gordon wasn't particularly nice to her. He was bossy, conceited, and short-tempered, but she was a little bit in awe of him. He seemed strong where she was weak, confident where she was full of confusion and self-doubt.

"I think he's just trying to get into your pants, Denise," said Carol. "Boys like Gordon like the challenge of making it with a virgin, and you have virgin written all over you."

"Yeah, well, maybe you just have a dirty mind. Maybe he's just looking for a friend."

But Denise sensed that Carol was right. A few days later, Gordon invited her to his house after school. He lived with his aunt and uncle, both of whom worked during the day. He tried to get her into bed, first with logic, then with liquor, then with physical force. She fought him off and ran home.

Her father, who had stayed home from work that day with a hangover, bristled at her disheveled appearance. He slapped her across the face, accused her of all sorts of sexual and personal outrages, and banished her to her room.

Denise cried for an hour, then for another hour, and then she could cry no more. When she went downstairs her father cursed her and yelled at her, but somehow she had lost the capacity to feel frightened or hurt by him. She felt numb.

Denise and her parents ate dinner in silence. George Boudreau consumed three beers with his meal, then left for a local tavern to continue drinking. Denise's mother retired to the den to watch a rerun of *I Love Lucy.* And Denise walked back to Gordon's house.

"Take me someplace," she said to the surprised young man. "Anywhere, I don't care. Just get me away from here."

Gordon drove to a golf course in Jenkintown. They stretched out on a blanket underneath a quarter-moon. He undressed himself, then her, and they made love. She wanted desperately to feel close to him, but Gordon puffed and panted on top of her obliviously. Denise wrapped her calves around him, pulling him in as close and as deep as she could. When it was over she wanted to cry, but she had no tears left.

Gordon graduated in June. The band began playing regularly at a Center City bar, and Denise often stayed there with them until the early hours of the morning.

Being with Gordon somehow gave her the courage to challenge her father, and the battle lines were drawn. George Boudreau threatened repeatedly to throw her out of the house if she didn't obey him, and Denise became increasingly defiant. History—her sisters' history—seemed to be repeating itself.

In the middle of Denise's senior year the Keystones were booked into a series of clubs in New Jersey and Maryland. Denise couldn't bear the thought of being left behind. She told her mother of her plans.

"And what am I supposed to do?" asked Ethel Boudreau. "Just stand by and let you drop out of school and ruin your life?"

"Oh, Mother . . ."

"'Oh, Mother' my ass, little girl." Denise was unaccustomed to hearing such language from her mother. "Let's see what your father says about this." She walked to the bottom of the steps and called upstairs to her husband. "George! George, come down here! Your daughter wants to throw her life away!"

Denise's father stumbled down the stairs, tucking his shirt into his pants along the way. "For Chrissake, Ethel. What is it now?"

"Tell him! Tell him, Denise!"

Denise backed away until the kitchen table was directly between her father and herself; there was no telling how he might react. "I'm leaving, Daddy. I'm going with Gordon."

His eyes grew narrow. His ears twitched. Denise watched a vein bulge on his neck. "The hell you are," he said.

Her voice quivered. "I'm eighteen now, Daddy. You can't stop me."

"Oh no? Watch me."

She'd always been so shy and obedient. But now, as Boudreau slowly circled the table toward her, Denise circled in the same direction, matching the man's pace in order to keep the table between them. He switched direction, then varied his pace, then switched direction again and again. She countered every move.

He stopped moving. They stared at each other across the table. Suddenly he lunged out at her. She slammed her hip against the side of the table, digging the opposite edge into her father's crotch. He doubled over, cursing. Ethel gasped as Denise grabbed her coat and ran out the front door.

The band was managed by a friend of Gordon's who went by the sobriquet of Fat Willie. He hired her as the band's traveling secretary. Denise and a pockmarked teenaged boy named Jinx were responsible for setting up the band's equipment before shows, running for meals, driving the bus Willie had rented for the group, and checking everyone in and out of the cheap motels.

She always had her own motel room on the Keystones' tour. Gordon's ground rules were unstated but clear: Denise was to have no claim on him, but she was to be available to him whenever he wanted her. Sometimes Gordon asked her to stay with him; sometimes he occupied himself with the lascivious attentions of one or more of the groupies.

Denise told herself that her jealousy of those girls was a sign of immaturity, of weakness, of old-fashioned prudishness she'd learned from her parents and that she was trying to conquer. She was still a novice at lovemaking. She enjoyed the closeness of making love, but her excitement came mainly from the thought that she was wanted, and hardly at all from the act itself.

One night Gordon asked her to pick up two pizzas and a six-pack on her way to his room. Jinx helped her carry the food. Denise thanked the boy with a kiss on his forehead just as Gordon opened the door. After Jinx left, Gordon grabbed her by the arm and flung her across the room onto one of the pizzas; melted mozzarella cheese squished out the side of the box and clung to her blouse and jeans.

"So, did you fuck him?" His nostrils flared and his face grew purple. She'd never seen Gordon like this, and yet it seemed oddly familiar.

"Did I . . . what?"

"You fucked him, didn't you? Admit it." He pulled on her blouse until the buttons popped. He grasped the front of her bra and twisted it; the clasp dug into her back.

"Gordon, I love you!" She'd never said that to him before.

"Cunt!" He pushed her facedown onto the bed and yanked her jeans and panties down to her knees. He straddled her and began slapping her bare rear with a rolled-up *TV Guide*. "Well, did you?"

She squirmed underneath him. "Oww! No, you know I didn't. Stop, please!"

He kept smacking her. "Admit it. You fucked him. Admit it."

"No." The more she wriggled, the faster he hit her.

"Liar! Tell me."

"No." He was inside her now, still hitting her bottom. She was

72

surprised by her own wetness. Her wriggling became purposeful and rhythmic.

"Bitch!"

"No."

He dropped the *TV Guide* and began smacking her with his open palm in time with her undulations. "This is your last chance. Did you fuck him?"

"Yes!" she screamed as she began to buck frantically. "I did," she lied. "I fucked him just like I'm fucking you now. Fuck me, Gordon. Fuck me!" *Finally,* she thought. *Finally.*

When it was over Gordon lifted her tenderly and carried her into the bathroom. He laid her down in the tub, filled it with warm water, and ran a soft sponge up and down her body. "Damn," he said, "you're fantastic."

"I can't believe I told you all that," she said.

Whitney looked at his watch. More than an hour had passed; it felt like ten minutes. He glanced at his pad and discovered that, somewhere in the middle of her story, he'd stopped taking notes.

He felt like a man at the end of a long dream. He hovered for an instant between the dream and reality. Carla sounded Whitney's intercom, abruptly ending his reverie. He felt like a scuba diver who'd been rushed to the surface too quickly.

"Dr. Whitney?"

"Uh...yes, Carla."

"Dr. Malzone is here to see you."

"I'll be with him in a minute."

Denise stood up. "Oh, my. I've taken up so much of your time. You wanted to know about Gordon, and here I've spent all this time talking about myself. I'm sorry."

"No, it's all right, really." Whitney sprang to his feet, knocking his pad to the floor. He felt vaguely guilty, as if he'd been caught imagining something he had no business thinking about. "All of this is very important. The more information I get, the more thorough my evaluation of your husband will be." The word *husband* stuck in his throat.

"Would you consider coming back again next Monday?" asked Whitney. "This has been very useful to me. I hate to inconvenience you, but—"

"I'd love to come back." She hesitated. "I mean, you're very easy to talk to."

He scribbled on his pad. "This is my number at the hospital here, in case you need to, uh, change your appointment." He handed the paper to her.

"Thank you, Dr. Whitney." Denise folded the paper into fourths and placed it in her purse. She turned quickly, her long skirt whirling about her in delicate disarray.

Malzone watched her as she passed him in the open door. He studied her inch by inch, like an approving buyer at a cattle auction. When he faced Whitney the older man was still watching Denise as she disappeared down the hall.

T he clock on the wall outside Anna Roth's office had never worked properly. When she first came to Littleton the clock was losing a minute each hour, and the daily time loss had increased over the years. Now, although the second hand continued its regular sweep around the dial, the minute and hour hands remained stationary. Well-meaning visitors, fooled by the moving second hand into thinking that the clock worked reliably, would often reset it. The new time would remain frozen in place until the next uninformed visitor intervened.

Anna resisted all efforts to get rid of the clock. It seemed a perfect allegory for life at Littleton State Hospital. There was the constant activity one might expect at an institution for severely disturbed and dangerous patients. But there was also a peculiar stasis to the place: many patients never improved markedly; the brick-and-cinder-block construction lent an oppressive sterility and sameness to the squat buildings; and the crises of shortages, breakdowns, and employee burnout recurred with depressing regularity.

Anna went to the nurses station to write medication orders. The patients were crammed into the small day room. The television was tuned to a show called *First Month*, a summary of the most important Philadelphia news stories of 1982.

A new patient occupied a post in the middle of the day room. He was dressed neatly in gray institutional slacks, and he was meticulously groomed. The young man stood at rigid attention, turning forty-five degrees at regular ten-second intervals. Each time he turned he made a guttural clicking noise deep in his throat.

I am Camera Man, he told himself. *Focus and shoot. Wide-angle photo: patients gathered in day room before lunch.*

Click.

Long shot, telephoto lens: doctor and nurse conspiring in soundproof room. Photo will reveal all.

Click.

Close-up, zoom in and focus: Jimmy Bree and his invisible companions. The plotting continues.

Click.

Special effect, still photo of television screen: broken bodies and battered machines. Now appearing at Littleton State Hospital: the Christmas Eve Sniper.

Click.

Click.

Click.

Anna Roth watched him from the glassed-in nurses station. "I see we have a new patient."

"Yes, Doctor," replied Nurse Ellen Tellmark. "He was arrested for creating a disturbance on a bus in Doylestown. Then he punched the policeman who came to arrest him. He wouldn't cooperate with Dr. Malzone's evaluation of him, so I guess he'll be found incompetent to stand trial. He's pretty paranoid, if you ask me."

The patient wheeled around and stared at the nurses station. His eyes and Anna's locked together. She imagined darts of light shooting toward her.

"What is his name?"

"Karatzis. Marcus Karatzis."

Click. He dropped his focus on Anna and turned forty-five degrees to his right.

Anna uncapped her fountain pen and went to work on the medication order sheets. "What medication is Mr. Karatzis taking?"

Ellen rolled her eyes toward the ceiling. "He's on a Malzone. Here, maybe you can make some sense out of it." She handed the patient's medication sheet to Anna.

The phrase "on a Malzone" was a derisive term coined by one of Littleton's nurses. It referred to Ralph Malzone's reputation for ordering bizarre combinations and dosages of medicines for his patients. When a patient was transferred from the Forensic Evaluation Building, Anna routinely reviewed the man's medication order. Often a change was required to bring the patient's treatment regimen within the bounds of standard psychiatric practice.

Anna surveyed the four dozen blue vinyl notebooks in the nurses station, one for each patient on the ward. A majority of the patients had been found not guilty of a serious crime by reason of insanity.

"In the old days," Percy Osborne had told her when he hired her, "a patient who was found NGRI could wind up committed to Littleton for the remainder of his life without ever being reviewed in court."

Anna knew this was true. She'd seen a court order written in the early 1960s that remanded a patient to Littleton "until such time as the doctors determine that he is no longer mentally ill and a danger to society."

"It was really quite criminal in its own right," Osborne had said. "The courts ceded an enormous amount of power to psychiatrists, and there wasn't even a judicial review process. There were many abuses, cases in which patients were incarcerated for periods far longer than necessary. After all, why take the chance of releasing a dangerous patient—and possibly damaging your reputation—when society is giving you a green light to keep any patient locked up for as long as you wish?"

Around 1970 Osborne lobbied for an overhaul of Pennsylvania's mental health laws. The state legislature passed a bill that mandated regular judicial reviews of all committed patients. At each review the Commonwealth was required to prove that a patient still needed involuntary hospitalization for the treatment of mental illness. If the evidence, usually a doctor's opinion, failed to convince a judge that the patient needed further hospital treatment, that patient was released from Littleton immediately.

Thus each patient on her unit was entitled to a new commitment hearing at least once each year. And Anna Roth was responsible for deciding whether to ask the court to recommit them.

Anna finished writing the medication orders. She checked her watch and realized she was due in the Administration Building for her weekly meeting with Osborne. She tucked Marcus Karatzis' chart under her arm and returned to her office down the hall. She placed the chart on top of her briefcase—she wanted to remember to take it home—and bundled up for the short walk to the superintendent's office.

Osborne was waiting for her. After some small talk he made the announcement that Anna had hoped would never come. "I wanted you to be the first to know, Anna. I've submitted my resignation to the governor."

"Percy! Just like that?"

"Not so fast—you're not getting rid of me that quickly," he joked. "The resignation takes effect at the end of June. Until then, you'll just have to put up with me."

He held his hand out toward her. She clasped it in hers and instinctively drew it toward her face. She kissed it and let her tears trickle down upon it.

"I'm going to tell Thomas Whitney tomorrow. I want to recommend him to the governor as the new superintendent. But first I need to know: Do you think you could work with him?"

She stared at the floor.

"I know the two of you have had your differences," he continued. "I'm old, but I'm not blind."

Osborne walked toward the window and looked out across the hospital grounds. "This place was a hellhole when I came here, Anna. I'd like to think I've made things better. And I want to leave it to someone who'll care for it. I just hope he's willing to take it."

Her friend sounded like a man writing his last will and testament. She couldn't refuse his wish. "I think Whitney will make a very good superintendent, Percy."

She slept fitfully that night. She dreamed she was at a zoo. The day was bright and hot, and there were no other visitors. She stood in front of a cage that was set off at a distance from all the other cages.

Marcus Karatzis stood on the other side of the bars. He held a camera at his waist. He advanced the film, clicked off a shot, advanced the film again, clicked off another shot, and so on. The flash exploded in her face each time he took a picture. He never held the camera to his eyes. He stared at Anna with the blank, mechanical intensity of an early-morning television test pattern.

Anna tried to back away from the bars. She could sense her legs in motion, and she could feel the ground passing below her feet, and yet she remained stationary. She couldn't tell where the walls of the cage were. *I am in a cage*, she thought, and she was terrified. *I'm old, but I'm not blind. I am in a cage.* The flash from Karatzis' camera exploded once more, blinding her.

She awoke with a start and switched on her lamp. She noticed Karatzis' chart—she had reviewed it before she went to sleep—and was filled with a sense of total, sudden understanding. She grabbed a pen and recorded her insights in bold letters on the front of his chart. Satisfied, she fell back into a heavy sleep.

The words stared back at her when she awoke in the morning:

One camera plus the person who has it are able to read everything that is written down.

Two cameras plus the person who has them are able to read another person's mind.

Three cameras plus the person who has them are able to make another person bleed.

She felt as though a thousand hidden eyes were watching her.

12

Whitney telephoned Stanley Schacter. "I've been going over the police report on Gordon Cardonick. I remember a couple of weeks ago at the basketball game, you told me you thought he was...what was it you said? 'A real odd bird'?"

"That sounds right," the detective said.

"I was hoping you could give me more details about the shootings. What do all the charges refer to?"

Schacter laughed. "What's the matter, Thomas? Don't you read the newspapers anymore?"

"Not when I'm in the middle of an evaluation." He thought about the reporter who called him at home to talk about Cardonick. "I don't trust them. I'd rather get the story first from you."

Schacter inspected his copy of the police report. "Well, where would you like to start?"

"Tell me about the three murder charges."

"Those are the people he shot to death. One of them died from the bullet wound. The other two, we can't be sure whether they died from the bullets or from the crashes when their cars went out of control. Six of one, half a dozen of the other, I guess. The shooting was the real cause in each case, any way you look at it, so we went for first-degree murder."

"What can you tell me about the victims?"

"Well, the first one was a little girl, ten years old. Daughter of a preacher from South Philadelphia. A real Bible-thumper, that guy. Calls himself Reverend Isaac. He's got a local Sunday morning radio show, real popular in the black neighborhoods. I listened in last week out of curiosity. You know the type: 'Send your dollars to Jesus, in care of me at this station.'

"Anyway, Reverend Isaac was driving his Cadillac—you should have seen that car, Thomas—I think I could live in it if I had to. Anyway, he was driving, and his daughter Sarah was sleeping in the backseat. Cardonick's first shot—the first one we know about, anyway—cut through the trunk of the Cadillac and struck the girl in the neck. She bled to death from the carotid artery."

Whitney's own neck twinged slightly. "What about her father? Was he hurt?"

"No. Pretty shook up. Didn't stop him from doing his radio show, though."

"Uh-huh. What about the others?"

"Well, the other two were shot a little farther down the expressway, closer to the oil refineries. Both of them were hit at around the same time. Cardonick must have fired off a volley of shots. Both of them crashed pretty bad after they were hit. One was driving a pickup truck. Joseph Pulaski, forty-five years old. Came from South River, New Jersey, small town up near New Brunswick. The other one was a student at the University of Pennsylvania. He was Elliot Sharman, from Darien, Connecticut."

Whitney finished one legal pad and pulled out another one. "What about all these charges of assault and battery with a dangerous weapon?"

"There were twelve of them. One guy driving in the opposite direction was grazed by a bullet. And when Cardonick was racing down the road he struck three cars that had a total of eleven people in them."

"You mean, the weapon in eleven of those charges was his car?"

"You got it. Hey, you never know what to expect in a case like this. We figure, throw on every charge you can think of. Give the D.A. some cards to play with when it comes to plea-bargaining. That's why we added the motor vehicle charges—driving to endanger, leaving the scene of an accident."

"You also booked him for the unlicensed use of a firearm."

"Yes," said the detective. "The Ruger Mini-14 rifle he used belongs to his uncle. Cardonick moved in with his aunt and uncle after his wife kicked him out a couple of months ago. The uncle says he didn't know Cardonick had taken the gun."

Whitney turned to the last arrest warrant in Cardonick's court papers. "There's a trespassing charge here, Stan. What the hell is that?"

"Aha! He drove through a chained-off entrance to the ballpark. Now *that* really pissed me off."

Both men laughed.

"What was it about Cardonick that made him seem so odd?"

Schacter paused. Whitney could hear him lighting his pipe. "Well, first of all, there's that stuff he said when he was arrested. I guess you read that in the report. Brinkley, the officer who captured him, said Cardonick really seemed to think he was going to be killed.

"Second, there's the way he behaved when I interviewed him. Maybe I should say tried to interview him, since he pretty much refused to talk without a lawyer present. His eyes kept darting around, like he was looking for something or seeing things in the air. And he had this weird smile the whole time, even though at one point he began to cry a little. I wondered if he was high on something.

"Third—and I'm not sure if this was written up in the report you have, because it happened the next day—he did something in his cell that I still don't understand. He took off his clothes and tied them to the bars in the shape of a cross. Go figure that one out."

Whitney stopped writing and rested the end of his pen against his chin. He frowned. "What do you think, Stan? What does all of this mean? Why did he kill those people?"

Schacter grunted. "Hell, I don't know. If you ask me, he's just some fucked-up, crazy guy, probably pretty depressed, who decided to go out in a blaze of glory. The victims were just in the wrong place at the wrong time."

Whitney sighed. "Expanded suicide," he mumbled.

"Huh?"

"Expanded suicide. That's what we call it when a person gets so depressed he wants to kill himself, but so angry that he has to take some of the world with him first. We often see the syndrome in family violence. A man loses his job and gets depressed, then gets angry at his family because they're depending on him to support him. So he kills his wife or kids and then kills himself. And if you add psychosis to the depression and anger, you can get something really bizarre. Like the Jonestown Massacre, or maybe—"

"The Christmas Eve Sniper," said Schacter.

"The Christmas Eve Sniper," repeated Whitney. "For now, it's as good an explanation as any."

* * *

No one had ever accused Whitney of being hopelessly romantic.

His instinct for dissecting relationships served him well. It kept him from surrendering to the pull of his emotions, and that was the stock-in-trade of a good psychiatrist. Yet sometimes he yearned to be rid of it. "For God's sake, Thomas," a ladyfriend once said as she walked out his door for the last time, "it doesn't take much courage to analyze something to death. It takes more courage to make a leap of faith."

But he wasn't much of a leaper. And so, by Sunday night, he had managed to forget much about his first meeting with Denise. True, he remembered the way she looked and the things she said. He even remembered how struck he had been by her ingenuous manner. But that first rush of feeling, the surge that took his breath away and left him feeling weak all over—to the extent that he remembered it, he was inclined to ascribe it to the weather, fatigue, or indigestion.

He was already in bed when the phone rang. His lamp and radio were still on, but he was half asleep. The ringing jolted him awake. He quickly sat upright, cleared his throat, and reached for the phone.

"Yes? Hello?" His voice sounded small and twisted, like that of someone who had just inhaled helium. He told himself he should have let his answering service take the call.

The caller was silent for a moment. When she spoke, it was with the reluctant tremulousness of someone who feared she might be intruding.

"Hello? Dr. Whitney?"

"This is he."

"Dr. Whitney, this is Denise Cardonick."

He felt his pulse quicken. He wanted to believe it was a parasympathetic nervous system response to the suddenness of his awakening.

"Dr. Whitney?" she repeated after several seconds of silence.

"Yes, hello, Mrs. Cardonick. How can I help you?" How unnatural those words sounded to him. But there was something about her, something he couldn't quite describe, that made him want to help her. She'd seemed so open and yet so frightened and vulnerable when he met her. It was a beguiling combination.

"I . . . I looked your number up in the phone book. I hope you don't mind me calling you at home."

She sounded nervous and unsure of herself. She said she would be unable to meet with Whitney the next day. She said something about a baby-sitter or car problems or someone being sick. Whitney couldn't quite follow her. She wanted to know if she could reschedule her second appointment with him. He suggested that they meet the following day.

"Oh, thank you very much. That's Tuesday, January eighteenth. And I'm sorry if I bothered you and Mrs. Whitney... if you're married, that is."

"No, I'm not—" He stopped himself. He wondered why he found himself on the verge of revealing his marital status to her. "I'm not bothered at all, Mrs. Cardonick. I'll see you on Tuesday. Good night."

"Good night, Dr. Whitney."

He placed the phone back in its cradle and frowned. For the first time he realized how much he'd been looking forward to seeing her again. There was something so familiar about her, something that filled Whitney with a longing he'd first felt nearly three decades earlier...

It was the summer he turned eighteen, his family's first summer on East Haven. The previous year his father had purchased a two-hundred-acre waterfront estate on the small island off the Maine coast; it was his way of celebrating Eisenhower's election and the Republicans' return to power.

Whitney had never seen any place that beautiful. He swam out to a tiny island each afternoon and basked in the sun. Every evening he would watch the sun's last rays bounce off the masts of the large tourist sailboats ("cattleboats" they were called derisively by year-round island-ers) as they cut across the channel between East Haven and the neighboring islands.

His father hired a widower from the mainland to care for the grounds. Charles Dietz moved into a small building that in decades past had served as the estate's carriage house. He brought with him his daughter Marlene. None of the Whitneys—nor anyone else, for that matter—saw much of Marlene. The carriage house was on the remote rear corner of the estate, and she never seemed to stray far from it. And Whitney's parents had instructed him to allow the groundskeeper and his daughter their privacy.

One day in July, when the air was uncommonly damp and chilly, even for Maine, Whitney succumbed to his curiosity and took a late morning walk back toward the carriage house.

He found her sitting on a knoll overlooking a meadow. She'd wrapped a blanket completely around herself to ward off the cold. All he could see was her face and the jet-black hair that flowed in soft curls down to her waist. She looked to be about his age. He hadn't expected her to be so pretty.

"Oh, excuse me," he said. "I didn't know anybody was here."

She didn't give away anything with her expression. He couldn't tell whether she was pleased or annoyed that he had found her. "You one of the rich folks?" she asked.

"Huh?"

"The rich folks," she repeated. Her voice was soft and her eyes were as dark as her hair. "My daddy, he works for some rich folks. They live over by the water. You one of them?"

"Uh, yes, that is, if you mean your father is Mr. Dietz."

She studied his face. "You must be the boy."

"Huh?"

"Ain't you their boy? The one who just had his birthday? Must be. You ain't old enough to be Mr. Whitney."

"Uh-huh. I mean, yes, I'm Thomas. Thomas Whitney."

"I'm Marlene." She turned back toward the meadow and closed her eyes. The wind swirled through her hair and whipped it across her face.

She opened her eyes several seconds later. "You still here?"

He felt ashamed of himself. "I'm sorry." He turned to leave.

She called after him a few moments later. "Hey, boy. You can sit here with me a couple of minutes if you want. Wind feels good today."

They sat together for a little while. At noon he got up to leave. "I told a couple of the guys I'd meet them in town for lunch. Hey," he said, pretending that the thought was unrehearsed, "do you want to come?"

"No. Thanks. Think I'll sit here for a spell. What're you doing tomorrow?"

"I'll probably go bike riding in the morning," he replied. "Would you like to come?"

"No, but if you want to pass by here again, I guess that would be okay."

"Yeah. Well, maybe I'll be seeing you. So long."

"You be talking to my father later?"

"Yeah, I guess so."

"Well, if I was you I wouldn't say nothing about visiting me. He don't like me associating with boys."

The cold spell wouldn't break, and Whitney came back the next day and the next day and the day after that. She was always waiting for him when he arrived, sitting on the knoll, wrapped in her blanket.

He never stayed very long; she never said very much. But he felt quite close to her. He was entranced by her mixture of coarseness and beauty and fragility. She reminded him of a sparrow whose wounded wings wouldn't allow her to fly.

On the fifth day, the clouds broke early in the morning. Whitney packed some sandwiches and took two bicycles to the carriage house. She was sitting on the knoll, still covered by her blanket.

"I thought we could have a picnic on the beach a couple miles up the island," he said.

"I can't go with you, Thomas." She was frightened. He hadn't seen that look on her face before.

"Why not?" His feelings were hurt. "Your father won't be back all day. I heard my mother say so. He took the ferry to Rockland to get some tractor parts."

The harder he tried to convince her, the more strident her refusal became. He left angrily, without saying good-bye.

The next day he learned her secret. He got to the knoll before her. He looked toward the carriage house and watched her approach. She was crawling toward the knoll. Her arms did all the work. Her legs trailed behind like inert chunks of flesh; they were like dead lumps tacked onto a live body, hanging there for no particular reason.

Oh God, he thought. *Polio.*

She continued crawling until she saw him. She gave out a tiny yelp, then turned and tried to crawl away.

"Marlene! Wait!" He ran to her, fell to his knees, and kissed her on the forehead. He cradled her in his arms for several minutes. Words failed him.

"Oh, Thomas, please don't leave me."

She rolled on top of him and ran her hands inside his shirt. It made him shiver. She kissed him hard on the mouth, sucking the air out of him until he felt dizzy.

Every morning thereafter, as soon as Whitney saw Charles Dietz arrive for work, he would walk toward the water, then slip into the woods and head back across the estate to the carriage house. When he was with Marlene he felt as though they were alone in the world. He pretended the summer would never end.

One mid-August morning the groundskeeper arrived at the main house with two small satchels. He was quitting two weeks early, he explained. He was sorry for the suddenness, and he hoped that it wouldn't be too much of an inconvenience, but he was leaving on the morning ferry.

"It's my daughter," he told Mrs. Whitney. "Something ain't right with her, ever since that cold spell we had a few weeks back." He shot an angry glance at the boy, then turned back toward Mrs. Whitney. "I guess this was too much for her, what with her mother dying just last year. She wants to go back home."

Liar, thought Whitney. He bolted out the door and ran toward the carriage house. He didn't know what he would do once he got there, but surely he and Marlene would find a way to stay together.

The carriage house was empty. He ran out to the road and headed toward the island's dock area a mile and a half away. He got there just in time to see the ferry pull away. Charles Dietz was standing on the deck, his back toward East Haven. His daughter was hidden from view.

"Marlene, wait," Whitney screamed, but the words were swallowed by the noise from the ferry and the whistling of the wind.

He entered Harvard a few weeks later and plunged into his classes with the single-mindedness of someone who had much to forget. And gradually the Cambridge autumn—sailboats on the Charles River, study-dates with Radcliffe girls—wiped away his sadness.

Marlene telephoned him in November. She'd left her father and was working as a bank teller in Augusta. She wanted very much to visit Whitney.

They sat together in the coffee shop of the Parker House, where, his fertile imagination having abandoned him temporarily, they had registered as Mr. and Mrs. Smith. Whitney wondered what he'd ever seen in her. Her shyness, her unpolished ways, even her handicap—all of the things that once had attracted him to her were now symbols of the differences and distance between them.

She called a couple of times more during his freshman year; he didn't call back. Whitney never saw her again.

It was the pattern of his life: he was forever drawn to the fragile and the wounded, the abused and the unfortunate. They touched him in ways no one else could. But a little closeness was a dangerous thing. The frailties that he found attractive in a particular woman were always the same weaknesses that ultimately repelled him. In every beginning were the seeds of the inevitable end.

Whitney thought of all this as he lay awake after Denise Cardonick's call. When he was in the middle of a case, he usually hoped it would be completed as quickly as possible. But now he thought about Denise, and he found himself wishing that Cardonick's evaluation could go on and on.

*   *   *

Malzone had no practical purpose for examining Gordon Cardonick's chart. He did it anyway.

He told himself that, as assistant director of forensic evaluation, he had a duty to remain *au courant* on all of the patients on the ward. But he was only interested in the case because it belonged to Whitney. Malzone always read the charts of Whitney's patients, just in case Whitney made a mistake he could take advantage of.

Malzone read the psychiatric note that Dr. Pellman wrote on the admissions ward after a cursory fifteen-minute exam.

December 28, 1982. Twenty-six-year-old white male, admitted this date for criminal responsibility evaluation on several charges of murder and assault. Patient appeared mute. Body was tense, tremors noted. Either unwilling or unable to cooperate with the interview. Had bizarre grin, clearly inappropriate to the gravity of his situation. Eye contact was fixed, facial expression somewhat wooden. Appeared to be responding to internal stimuli—possible hallucinations.

In my opinion, patient is acutely psychotic. In order to improve his condition I placed him on Haldol, 5 mg., p.o., b.i.d.

Shortly after that interview Cardonick used slivers of peeling paint to slice open his wrists. He was transferred to County General Hospital for medical care. A psychiatrist there recorded her observations:

Mr. Cardonick is manifesting vegetative signs of a major depression: he complains of a diminished appetite with a recent weight loss of ten pounds. He has been experiencing insomnia and early morning awakening for the past several weeks. He suffers also from anhedonia and fatigue. There is notable psychomotor retardation which at times verges on catatonia.

The patient has recurrent thoughts of death and suicide. He claims his daughter was recently killed by toxic vapors and he believes that someone poisoned her. He vacillates between wanting to kill himself out of grief and wanting revenge for her murder.

This belief about his daughter's death is delusional, but he cannot be dissuaded from it.

Impression: Mr. Cardonick is severely depressed and delusional. The mood disturbance appears to be the primary problem, and his delusional and disorganized thinking is probably a secondary complication of his depression.

Recommendation: Continue Haldol for his psychotic symptomatology. Also add Elavil, 50 mg., t.i.d., for his depression. Gradually increase the Elavil to a therapeutic dosage.

He returned to Littleton three days later and was placed on the Evaluation Unit. Shortly after he arrived there he got into an unprovoked fracas with another patient. Cardonick lunged at the man and tried to pry a cigarette out of his mouth. "Murderer!" cried Cardonick. "I'll kill you!" He was subdued quickly by three prison guards.

Malzone's heart was beating a little faster when he finished reading Cardonick's chart. *This guy is nuts*, he thought. No doubt Cardonick would plead insanity, and everything Malzone had read in the chart suggested that the defense would succeed. Whitney would make head-lines with his testimony, and his reputation would spread even further.

Malzone had a terrible headache.

Whitney and Cardonick sat on opposite sides of the table in the Secure Interview Room. A pane of shatterproof glass stood between them. The glass ran from the ceiling to the floor and from wall to wall, bisecting the entire room. Two microphones dangled from the ceiling, one on either side of the glass. Each microphone picked up the conversation from one side of the room and relayed it through a speaker to the opposite side.

Whitney seldom used the Secure Interview Room for his examinations. He felt uneasy in its harsh atmosphere. But the ashtray incident had left him more unsettled than he cared to admit, and he wasn't taking any chances with Cardonick this time around.

"Good morning. I'm Dr. Whitney. We met last week."

Cardonick extended his right hand until it bumped against the glass partition. He jiggled it up and down in a pantomime of a handshake. There was a comic flavor to the act, but there was an edge of bizarreness in it, and a wild look behind the man's smile.

"Do you remember me, Mr. Cardonick?"

The patient stared back at him without speaking.

Whitney couldn't read anything in Cardonick's expression. "Well?" said the psychiatrist. "Do you remember me?"

"I remember Mama," he replied, and he hummed a few notes from the theme song of that old television program.

"I see." Whitney began to take notes.

Cardonick's voice was flat and dull. "Remember the Alamo. Remember the Maine. Remember to brush after every meal."

Whitney continued to transcribe Cardonick's remarks. From the corner of his eye he could see the patient watching every move he made.

Cardonick extended his hands, palms toward the floor, as if he were delivering a benediction. "Spilliniforous millenitudes of plasmatic obviarity."

He's playing with me, feeling me out, thought Whitney. A lot of patients did that at first. He looked directly at Cardonick and spoke in a firm but cordial tone. "I don't understand your answer. Do you remember meeting me last week?"

The patient leaned forward and studied Whitney's face through the glass partition. "I remember you. You offered me a cigarette."

"Yes, that's right. And you apparently thought that I was trying to kill you."

Cardonick smiled as if he were musing upon some private joke. "The Surgeon General has determined that smoking is dangerous to your health."

"Yes, well, there seemed to be a little more to it than that. You became quite upset."

Cardonick turned away from Whitney's gaze. "I tend to get sick," he mumbled. "Sick in the head. That's why they send people here, right? Littleton. Littleton State Hospital." He laughed. "Littleton Shittleton. It's a little ton of shit."

Whitney always paid attention to a patient's opening remarks. He wondered: *Why, from the entire universe of possible statements, did he choose to begin the way he did?*

"When I asked you if you remembered me, you said that you remembered Mama. What do you remember?"

The smile vanished from Cardonick's face. He blinked rapidly and took a sudden quick breath. "She died." Cardonick's voice sounded dead itself.

"I see. How old were you?"

"Thirteen."

Whitney saw a trace of a tear in the corner of Cardonick's left eye. "That must have been very sad for you. How did she die?"

"You know." Cardonick peered directly at the psychiatrist. Whitney felt frightened. He couldn't explain why.

"No, I'm sorry. I don't know. Can you tell me?"

"My father killed her."

Whitney grimaced. "Oh, my. That's terrible. Were you with her when it happened?"

Cardonick dropped his eyes. "Yes."

"And were you hurt, too?"

"Huh?" Cardonick looked as if he were watching a movie parading across the glass partition. Whitney wondered if the patient was hallucinating.

"Were you hurt? Did your father try to hurt you, too?"

Cardonick laughed bitterly. "Always."

"Can you tell me about it?"

The patient laughed again. "He'd beat the shit out of you if you ate too fast. He'd beat the shit out of you if you ate too slow. Or if you talked too loud. Or if you didn't talk loud enough. If you cried when he hit you, he told you to act like a man and he hit you until you stopped crying."

Seldom did Whitney stumble into such a highly charged area so early in an interview. He wished he could sweep it aside for the moment. But the matter was out in the open already, and there was no way he could pretend to ignore it.

"How was she killed?" Whitney wondered if Cardonick's mother had been shot to death, if the Christmas Eve killings represented a crazed reenactment of the trauma of her death.

"How should I know?" replied the patient in a tone of voice that asked to be left alone. His face became rigid. He closed his eyes. He pressed his hands against his ears.

"But you were there," said Whitney. "You saw what happened."

Cardonick's voice became strident. "No. Nobody was with her. She was alone. My father was in jail."

"You mean he was arrested after he killed her?"

"No. My father was arrested before she died. He was in the jail. She was all alone when she died."

"I don't understand. You say your father killed her, and that you were there. But then you say she was alone when it happened."

Cardonick leaned forward very slowly, his eyes still closed. His forehead crashed against the shatterproof glass. Whitney thought the man had fainted, but then Cardonick slammed his head against the partition again and again. The blows jolted the glass and the table.

Whitney pressed the button on his side of the table. A buzzer rang in the guard area just beyond the Secure Interview Room. A guard entered Cardonick's side of the room, recognized the urgency of the situation, and called for additional help. Within seconds two more guards came to help restrain the patient and lead him out of the Secure Interview Room.

Whitney remained behind to finish writing notes about the interview. Two things were certain: First, an understanding of Cardonick's history would be crucial. Second, the patient was not currently able to provide reliable information himself.

When Whitney entered the nursing area to return the patient's chart, Cardonick was sitting at a desk in the corridor. He was playing cards with one of the guards who had restrained him just a few minutes earlier.

"I assumed he'd be placed in a seclusion room," Whitney said to the nurse on duty.

"No," she replied. "Gordon calmed down as soon as he got back to the ward."

"Oh." Whitney was puzzled by the patient's sudden recovery.

"And then the guard offered to play a game of gin with him. Gordon really likes to play games."

Whitney watched the card game, unnoticed by the patient. The guard studied his hand and tried to decide what to discard. Cardonick waited patiently, humming a tune—it sounded like the theme song from *I Remember Mama*—and fanning the cards in his hand. *Gordon really likes to play games.*

The guard finally made up his mind and discarded the three of diamonds. "Gin," said Cardonick as he spread his cards faceup on the desk.

"Shit!" The guard slapped his cards down in disgust. "Deal 'em, asshole."

One of the other guards walked by them. "Hey, Frank. Did you lose again to this head case?"

"Yeah, well, maybe he is a fucking head case. And maybe I'm the fucking pope, too."

Cardonick smiled broadly. He gathered up the deck of cards and began to shuffle. Then he realized that he was being observed. He shot a glance at Whitney so vicious and piercing that it sent a chill through him.

14

"Say hello to the nice doctor, Jennifer."

Denise pointed her daughter toward Whitney and gently tapped the back of her shoulder. The little girl dropped her head to her chest and buried her face in the folds of her mother's skirt.

"Hello, Jennifer. How are you today?"

She peeked toward him from the corner of her eye, then turned away once more. The behavior would have seemed cute in a younger child. But Jennifer was almost seven, and Whitney wondered if her shyness was born from something more sinister or sad.

"She's afraid of doctors," explained Denise. "Jennifer, this is a doctor for Mommy. See, I brought your picture books for you to look at while I talk to the doctor."

The little girl had her mother's thick blonde curls and finely chiseled features. She wore heavy glasses that made her blue eyes seem twice as large.

Denise turned toward Carla. "Can she wait out here? She won't be any problem, I promise."

The secretary put down her pastry. "Jennifer," she cooed with her eyes opened wide like an owl. "Look what I have for you!" She pulled a Hershey bar out of her desk and slowly unwrapped it. Jennifer reached for it tentatively. Carla swooped the child into her arms and placed her in her lap. "We'll be just fine, Mrs. Cardonick. Won't we, Jennifer?"

Whitney escorted Denise into his office and shut the door.

"She cried all morning. Whenever I keep her home from school she thinks she's going to the doctor or the hospital. Do you have children, Doctor?"

"Excuse me?" Her directness startled him.

"I was thinking that you'd make a really good father. You'd know how to be patient with kids."

"Thank you." He cleared his throat and readied his notepad to cover his uneasiness.

Denise noticed the record album leaning against the psychiatrist's bookcase. "I see you have one of the Keystones' records."

"Yes. I was curious after our last meeting." He felt mildly embarrassed at the admission. "I borrowed this from a colleague—from his daughter, actually. She said it was the group's first album, but I notice that your husband doesn't play on it."

"No," replied Denise. "He left the band before they became famous."

"I see."

She gazed at the record and frowned, then looked back at Whitney. "You know," she continued, "I was afraid you wouldn't want to see me again. I thought you might be disgusted with me after our last meeting."

Whitney thought back to the motel scene she had described. He imagined her coated with pizza sauce and mozzarella cheese as Cardonick beat and mounted her.

"But I thought you should know about that night," Denise continued, "because that was the first clue I had that Gordon could become violent."

Whitney began to scribble notes while she spoke.

"This may sound crazy to you, Doctor, but I really fell in love with Gordon that night." She clasped her hands together tightly. "But I think a part of me began to hate him, too."

It was the first time she had ever given herself to anyone so completely.

She was angry at Gordon for degrading her. And her own participation in the tawdry scene disgusted her. But more than anything else, she felt completely overcome by sexual fever.

When Gordon pressed himself on her that night—as he slapped her and forced her to make up lies about being unfaithful to him—something clicked inside of her. She learned a horrible secret about herself, and it was like crossing a chasm on a tiny cable that snapped behind her. There was no turning back.

The secret was this: She thrived on pain. From that night onward, the more Gordon hurt her, the more she was drawn to him. It wasn't as though she were a glutton for pure physical pain. Rather, she hungered for the psychological control he loved to wield over her.

He was always testing the limits of that hunger. Soon he grew bored with repeating that first scene of domination. One night he brought her back to his room after the band finished playing. He asked her if she was prepared to prove her love for him.

"You know I am," she replied.

He dialed the front desk. "Hey, Gina? This is Gordon Cardonick... Yeah, I got the note you left backstage. Yeah, I'm glad you liked the show... Listen, you sound nice. Can you get someone to relieve you for a little while?"

He undressed Denise and guided her toward the closet. He put a chair into the closet and commanded her to sit. He tied her to the chair with towels and wrapped one around her mouth.

"Just watch and listen," he said. "No matter what happens, stay there and don't make a sound."

Gordon left the door cracked open. She could peer out into the dimly lit room, but she was invisible in the darkness of the closet.

Five minutes later the desk clerk was at Gordon's door. "I gotta be back there real soon," she said as she pulled at his belt buckle. She hiked her skirt above her hips and peeled off her panties. In a flash the two of them were pounding at each other on the motel room floor, inches away from the captive audience in the closet.

Denise grew limp as she watched them. Sweat poured off her own body as it began to twitch involuntarily to the rhythm of the couple on the other side of the door. She bit down on the towel around her mouth to keep from moaning.

When it was over, the desk clerk smoothed her clothing and ran a comb through her hair. "Thanks, babe," she said, and she left as quickly as she had come.

Denise pushed Gordon to the floor when he untied her. She bit down hard on his shoulder, straddled him, and shoved him inside of her. She imagined herself as a racehorse sprinting for the wire. And when she crossed the finish line she watched the sweat from her breasts drip onto his chest. "I love you," she said, and collapsed into his arms.

"That first tour lasted about two months," Denise continued as she searched through her handbag. "I wrote all the dates down in case you needed them. Ah, here they are. We came back to Philadelphia in March of 1975."

"What happened then?" asked Whitney.

"Well, for a little while things were pretty good. Willie, the Keystones' manager, was booking the band into a bunch of places in New England for the spring and summer. He figured they were a couple of steps away from getting a record contract, maybe even getting a gig as the opening act on a national tour."

"And you and Gordon?"

"We moved in with his Aunt Sarah and Uncle Ted. They were pretty nice to us. They even let us stay in the same room without hassling us." She chuckled. "My parents would have had a fit if I tried to do that in their house."

"What about your parents?"

"I went over there a couple of times, usually when only my mother was home. They were pretty cold to me. They had a good reason to be that way, I guess. They thought I was turning out like my sisters after all. They didn't want to have anything to do with Gordon. Maybe they figured if they ignored him he'd go away."

Denise rolled the strap of her handbag between her fingers and looked out the window behind Whitney's desk. Several moments passed.

"Anyway," she resumed with a sigh, "we stayed with his aunt and uncle for a couple of months. They were Gordon's legal guardians when he was younger. Did you know that? You should talk with them if you want to know about his childhood. Gordon's mother died when he was thirteen, and his father abandoned him around the same time. So Gordon's Aunt Sarah—his mother's older sister—took him in. Here, I wrote down their names and telephone number."

Whitney took the paper from her.

"You know, those couple of months were probably the most normal ones Gordon and I ever had together. Nothing real crazy, no drugs, no weird scenes. That stuff didn't start again until we went back on the road in June."

"What about the other band members? You haven't told me anything about them yet. Why did your husband leave the Keystones?"

Denise folded and unfolded her piece of paper several times. She rested the back of her head against her chair and closed her eyes. She let out a long, slow breath.

*   *   *

Gordon played piano in the high school orchestra. His Aunt Sarah encouraged his musical pursuits, and she rented the storeroom behind the Keystone Drugstore so he could practice without distractions.

Early in his junior year Gordon invited Solly Levin to improvise with him in the storeroom. Solly was a transfer student from New York. He and his mother had moved to Northeast Philadelphia a year earlier after his father ran away to Miami with a manicurist. "My old man was always an asshole," he once told Gordon. "His cuticles were his only strong quality."

Solly played electric bass. He was tall and excruciatingly thin, with arrow-straight hair that came to his shoulders. No matter how rapidly his hands moved up and down the instrument, he always stood rock-still when he played, and his pasty skin and vacant stare gave him a ghostlike appearance.

Solly introduced Gordon to Paul Garber, the rotund son of an alcoholic librarian and an accountant under investigation for tax fraud. Paul had mastered the art of abusing his own body. He overate, overdrank, and oversmoked. His two-pack-a-day habit made his voice click and scratch like metal scraping against metal. Paul brought the same untethered intensity to his drumming. He attacked his snares like some mesomorphic demon.

The foursome was completed with the addition of Curtis Miller. Curt was the fair-haired boy of the junior class. He was a straight-A student, although he never needed to study very hard. He was soft-spoken and handsome, free of arrogance and guile. Curt played guitar and shared the vocals with Gordon.

Willie Finkleman—Fat Willie—was a pharmacist's son. He used to come out to the storeroom to smoke marijuana and listen to the band. Willie began working for his father after he was expelled from high school for selling amphetamines to the football players. No doubt he ingested a fair amount of them himself; he always moved and spoke like a windmill in a hurricane, and he never seemed to require much sleep, but for some reason he stayed fat.

"Hey, call me Fat Willie. So, what do you guys need? Uppers? Downers? Something to calm you down? Something to pick you up? Hey, c'mon, my father owns this place. Drugs run in the family. You guys got a name for yourselves yet? I know—we'll call you the Keystones, after the store. The old man'll get a kick out of it. So, you want to make some money? Next week, my cousin's wedding. She just announced it last week. No time to make any plans. She got herself knocked up. A real shit-for-brains. She thought she couldn't get pregnant if she laid on top. Hey, how about some rubbers? We got your lubricated, we got your nonlubricated, we got your lambskin, your latex, your wax paper and a rubber band—no, no, just kidding. A guy came in yesterday and bought a dozen Trojans. 'That'll be three bucks,' I tell him, 'and fifteen cents for the tax.' 'Tacks?' he says. 'I thought you rolled these damn things on.' "

So Willie became the band's manager. Gordon had his reservations, because Willie's presence interfered with his role as group leader. But there was no arguing with success. By the middle of the band members' senior year, near the end of 1973, the Keystones were playing regularly at school dances and neighborhood functions. Shortly after graduation they moved on to local clubs and bars. And by the end of 1974, during Denise's senior year, they were on tour in New Jersey and Maryland.

Gordon's falling out with Willie and the Keystones occurred during the 1975 summer tour of New England. The more successful the band became, the more Willie kept Gordon in the background. "Gordy, Gordy," he said, "those songs you've been writing—much too depressing. For Simon and Garfunkel, sure, but not for a rock band. Hey, listen, I know you started the group, and I know Curt was the last to join. But don't forget he's the main man on stage. The thirteen-year-old girls like him—just a touch of sex, nothing so heavy that their mothers won't let them buy tickets or records. But, hey, all for one and one for all, right? We still split the money five ways even, one share for each of us. After expenses, of course."

Gordon was miserable in the peripheral role he'd been assigned. He became increasingly argumentative with the other members, especially Curt. He began to spend most of his time and money on alcohol and cocaine. One night in Hyannis he showed up so high that Jinx had to disconnect the keyboard amplifier to keep people from hearing how badly he was playing. A few nights later he arrived for a party in Willie's room with the fourteen-year-old daughter of a Boston town official. Gordon had pumped her full of beer and had her blouse unbuttoned before Willie realized what was happening. The manager pulled the girl away and packed her into a cab. "Cardonick, are you nuts or something? You want us all to wind up with statutory rape charges?"

Solly was elected to bring the news to Gordon in early July. "They thought you might take it better from me, seeing as how you've known me the longest. I'm sorry, man, but you're out. We all feel that way. Willie says we can hire someone to play keyboards for the rest of the summer, then we hold tryouts for a new member. Hey, man, I'm really sorry."

Denise left with Gordon. There was never any doubt that she would, even though Willie offered to let her stay on with the band until the end of the summer. "He needs me now," was all she could reply. "He really needs me."

They returned to Philadelphia and moved back in with Gordon's aunt and uncle. Gordon worked sporadically as a studio musician. Denise took a job with the Center City law firm of Jason, Jason, Wright. She became a junior secretary to the elder Mr. Jason, a silver-haired and mild-mannered man with impeccable habits.

Denise and Gordon married in mid-August after they learned she was pregnant. Denise's parents agreed to a cease-fire. She was negotiating from a position of strength this time: George and Louise Boudreau were finally going to be grandparents, and they had to accept the reality of Gordon as a son-in-law.

Denise's parents and Gordon's aunt and uncle cosigned a mortgage agreement and gave the couple the down payment for a row house in Northeast Philadelphia. The two-story home was five blocks away from Denise's parents, and she had remained there ever since.

Gordon and Denise were listening to the radio while they decorated their Christmas tree that year. "We continue our countdown of hits with a Philadelphia band that took its name from the drugstore where they used to practice. Just over a year ago the boys were playing for fifty dollars a night at a high school junior prom. Now they're performing their own brand of blue-eyed soul all across the country on a tour with the Thaxton Brothers. They're making their first appearance this week on *America Pop Twenty-Five* with a song written by band member Curtis Miller. Here they are with the number sixteen record in the nation, the Keystones and 'Fast Lane.'"

Gordon threw an ornament to the floor and stormed out of the house. When he returned two hours later he reeked of alcohol. "Bitch!" he screamed as he grabbed a knife and twisted Denise's arm behind her back. "I oughta cut the fucking thing out of you." He pushed her aside and passed out on the floor.

He sank into a serious depression during the next two months. He didn't look for work. He fell asleep early each night and got up after Denise left for work. When she came home in the evenings she would find him still in his bathrobe, unshaven and unwashed. He talked elliptically of suicide. Denise did her best to show him how much she loved him, but Gordon knew that he'd begun to need her much more than she needed him. He felt like a cripple leaning on her for support. And like all cripples, he began to hate his crutch as much as he depended upon it.

Denise confided in Mr. Jason about Gordon's inability to work. She didn't provide him with the details, and she assured him that it was a temporary problem, but she told him she would be grateful for any overtime work he could assign to her. In early February 1976 she began working late several times each week. She was six-and-a-half months' pregnant, and she was anxious to earn as much as possible before going on maternity leave.

One evening Gordon showed up unexpectedly at Denise's office. He stood in the corridor and watched her through the glass door. She sat at her desk crying. Mr. Jason stood behind her with a consoling arm draped around her shoulder.

Gordon shoved open the door and advanced upon them. "Get your coat," he commanded.

"But, Gordon—"

"Get your goddamn coat!" His eyes were wide and glazed, but he was completely sober. Denise rushed to the closet for her coat.

He turned toward Mr. Jason. "And you. I know what you're up to. Stay the fuck away from my wife. I'm warning you."

He grabbed Denise by the arm and rushed her toward the elevator. He slapped her repeatedly about the shoulders and face on their way to the lobby and out to the car. "Say good-bye to your precious Mr. Jason. This was your last day working for him."

They headed toward home at breakneck speed. Denise was too busy fending off his blows to see what happened next. Gordon lost control of the car on the Schuylkill Expressway and plowed it into a guardrail. They were pinned inside for several minutes. Rescue workers pried them loose and whisked them away in separate ambulances.

"That was a close call," said the emergency room internist as he patched up Gordon's superficial wounds.

"My wife. Where is she?"

The attending nurse hesitated before answering. "She's in the maternity operating room. The trauma of the accident induced premature labor."

"Is she all right?"

The nurse and internist looked at each other; neither spoke.

"My wife! Is she going to be all right?"

"Yes, yes," the internist replied with a mixture of sadness and impatience. "She's all right. You're both very lucky, you know. But..." The doctor turned his eyes away. "I'm not so sure we can say the same about your baby. We may not be able to save her."

"Her lungs suffered the most damage. Broncho-pulmonary...Can you believe I've forgotten the last word?"

"Dysplasia?" offered Whitney.

"That's it," said Denise. "Broncho-pulmonary dysplasia. When Jennifer was born she had a lot of difficulty breathing. Respiratory distress syndrome, that's what they called it."

"It's quite common with premature births."

"Uh-huh, that's what they told me. Anyway, they put her on a respirator to force oxygen into her. She was in really bad shape. They had to pump the oxygen into her lungs under very high pressure, and that's what caused the broncho-pulmonary dysplasia. She still has attacks two or three times a year. It's like she can't get enough air inside of her. A cold can bring it on. Sometimes it comes when she's upset about something. We have to put her on oxygen at home, and a couple of times she's had to go in the hospital."

"That must be very frightening."

"I'll say—for her and for us. She has problems with her eyes, too, because of the respirator. Something about the blood vessels in her eyes getting thicker than normal. I forget what the doctor called it."

Whitney smiled. "They probably have a funny-sounding name for that, too."

"Probably." She returned his smile.

Denise fell silent. She glanced toward the office door. "I guess Jennifer and your secretary are getting along all right."

"I'm sure they are."

Denise stared at the door for several moments. "You know, sometimes I feel like the world is conspiring against me. All of those hassles with my parents, then my problems with Gordon, then my baby's illness, and now this."

Whitney poured two cups of ice water from the pitcher on his desk. He offered her one. She drained it instantly. He saw the tiny blonde hairs on her arm, the curve of her torso as it peeked between the buttons of her blouse. Most women her age bored him, their sensuality dulled by their callowness. Denise was an exception.

"I guess things weren't very good between Gordon and me, even at the beginning. I lied to myself for a long time. It's funny what you can convince yourself to believe if you try hard enough. But after Jennifer was born I couldn't fool myself any more."

"And yet you stayed with him."

She sighed. "For Jennifer's sake, at least that's what I thought. He really does love her, you know. It just about kills him every time she has another attack."

"Was that the only reason you stayed?" For the first time, Whitney felt as though he were intruding.

Denise shrugged her shoulders. "I don't know. Sometimes I think it all depends on what you get used to. My father was very strict with me. He had his reasons, I guess. And Gordon—well, I've told you how he was with me."

She stared at Whitney intently. "But . . . you know," she continued, "when a man is nice to me, I figure he must be mistaking me for someone else."

Whitney wondered if she was talking about him.

"There was this boy I dated just before I met Gordon. His name was Rollie Plotkin. Rollie was a college student, a few years older than me. He was going to be a doctor, and he was so nice to me. My parents liked him, and he wanted to marry me. But I felt like some impostor when I was with him, like he wasn't seeing the real me, or else he wouldn't be so interested in me. So I broke up with him, because I figured sooner or later he'd get wise and break up with me. Sometimes I wonder what would have happened if I stayed with him." She laughed sadly. "Can you picture that? Me, a doctor's wife?"

"What made you finally decide to leave Gordon?"

Denise laughed bitterly. "Finally? I wonder. I tried before, you know. It's strange. Whenever I try to split up with Gordon, he winds up at Littleton State Hospital."

"You must be referring to his assault and battery charge."

"Yes. Two and a half years ago."

Enough was enough. She was tired of the abuse, the drugs, the philandering, the alcohol, the incurable and irrational jealousy. Thanks to a recent promotion from Mr. Jason, she was even making enough money now. She would try to make do without him.

She asked him to leave; he refused. She offered to move out; he threatened her.

"Tell him you'll get a restraining order preventing him from coming into the house unless he leaves voluntarily," advised Mr. Jason.

"On what grounds?"

"My dear," the old man replied, "surely all of your suffering counts for something. After all, I know something about judges. And what about his arrest last year? What was it, receiving stolen property?"

"Yes."

"Well, suspended sentence or not, it's *prima facie* evidence of his questionable character. A judge will be quite conservative when a four-year-old child is involved. He'll issue a temporary restraining order, and that will strengthen your hand if you decide to sue for divorce and custody. So tell him you'll get that order if he doesn't move out."

Denise was surprised by Gordon's calmness when she announced her ultimatum. A restraining order wouldn't be necessary, he assured her, now that he realized how much she wanted a trial separation. Anyway, he stated, some time apart might help their marriage in the long run. She agreed, in part to hasten his departure, but also in part because she wanted to believe it.

Gordon called his aunt to tell her what had happened. He asked if he could live at her house for the time being. "She was pretty upset," he reported to Denise as he packed a suitcase. "You know how fond of you she is. Say, how about if I take Jennifer with me, just for tonight. It might make Aunt Sarah feel better."

That was the last she saw of her daughter for two weeks. Gordon never arrived at his aunt's house that night. He embarked on an odyssey to parts unknown. Denise received one postcard from Virginia and another from Georgia. Some nights he would call her and plead tearfully for another chance. Other nights he would threaten to stay in another state and get custody of Jennifer unless she took him back. Mr. Jason counseled her to bring kidnapping charges, but she was afraid that doing so would make Gordon even more desperate.

Gordon was obviously drunk when he called her on the last night in July. Denise could hear Jennifer crying for her in the background. "I just called to say good-bye, honey." He broke into uncontrolled sobbing. "It's no good. I can't make it without you, and you won't let me make it with you."

"Gordon, let me talk to my baby!"

"It'll all be over soon. She won't suffer, I promise. One bullet, straight through her sweet little heart, and then one for me."

"Gordon, no! Listen to me!" She was screaming. She forced herself to speak calmly. "Darling, I miss you. I want you back so badly. Please hurry. I'm dying here without the two of you."

Denise hung up without waiting for his reply. She hoped she had said enough. She called Mr. Jason and told him frantically what had transpired. "Stay there," he said. "There's no telling what he'll do if he comes back and you're not there. I'll call the police and ask them to send someone to protect you."

Gordon appeared moments later; he must have called her from the pay phone down the block. She knew she should remain calm until the police arrived, but the tension had pushed her beyond the breaking point.

"You son of a bitch!" she screamed as soon as he opened the door. "Get out! Get out and never come back!"

She held on to Jennifer firmly and shoved Gordon outside. She locked the door and cowered with her daughter in the corner of the room.

Metal hinges and chunks of wood shot across the room as Gordon threw himself through the door. He was dazed for an instant. Denise grabbed Jennifer and dashed into the street.

Gordon caught up with her and threw her up against the fender of a parked car. "Cunt! You lying, fucking cunt!" She saw the silhouette of his fist as it passed back and forth between her eyes and a nearby streetlamp. She felt it pounding against her body.

A siren and the screeching of brakes from a police cruiser pierced the night.

"He pleaded guilty to assault and battery, and the D.A. agreed not to bring kidnapping charges. It seemed fair to me at the time. It still does."

"According to the information in his record," said Whitney, "your husband served a year of his sentence. Three months in prison, nine months at Littleton, and then he left here on parole."

"That's right. He got out in September 1981, and he was on parole for one year. It just ended a few months ago."

The door to Whitney's office flew open. Jennifer was covered with cookie crumbs and chocolate smears. "Mommy, I wanna go home."

"In a minute, sweetheart. Mommy is almost finished." She took the little girl back to Carla and returned to the office. She walked slowly around the room as she spoke.

"After hearing all of that, you're going to think this next part sounds crazy," Denise continued, "but I went back to him when he got out of Littleton."

Whitney felt suddenly sad.

"When he called me that night to say he couldn't make it with me or without me, I guess I felt that way, too, after he went to prison. When he was locked up it was safe to be with him again. I'd visit and we'd talk, and it was like all the bad feelings faded after a while. He asked me for another chance, and I said yes."

She sat down and pressed hard against her eyelids with the heels of her palms. "Things were a little better for about a year. But then his parole ended, and I guess he didn't have to worry about being hauled back to prison on parole violation. Things became just as ugly as before. It was giving Jennifer attacks. So I got a two-month restraining order late in October, and I told him I was filing for divorce. I took Jennifer over to his aunt's house a couple of times so Gordon could see her. He kept trying to get me to change my mind. Who knows, maybe he would have eventually."

"He didn't threaten you?"

"No. I think he was too depressed. We did have one argument on the phone. It was the day before Christmas, the last time I talked to him before... right before the incident. I told him I was trying to get an extension on the restraining order. We started yelling at each other. Jennifer was in the room with me, and she started to gasp for air the way she does when an attack is about to start. 'Now look what you've done,' I said to him, and then I hung up."

"I know this has been a difficult time for both of you," Whitney said. "Thank you for letting me come here to talk with you."

The sniper's aunt and uncle sat on the sofa in their living room. Tears ran down Sarah Cardonick's cheeks as she blew her nose in an embroidered handkerchief. Theodore Cardonick held his wife's hand firmly in his own. "We just want to do anything we can to help, Doctor," he said.

It was uncommon for Whitney to make home visits. But Gordon Cardonick was an uncommon case. Sarah Cardonick was reluctant to meet with Whitney. He'd heard it in her voice when he tried to make an appointment over the phone. And so the psychiatrist had suggested he come to their house; he was afraid they'd cancel any appointment he might make with them at Littleton.

"If I'm going to understand what happened, and what led your nephew to do . . . what he did, I need to learn about his past. And he isn't well enough to give me an accurate history himself. That's why I asked you to meet with me."

Sarah sighed. "We're the only family he has left, except for Denise and Jennifer, of course."

"Is it true that his mother is deceased?"

"Yes," Sarah replied, her eyes growing moist once more. "Valerie, my younger sister. And his father is as good as dead. We haven't heard from that bastard—excuse me, Doctor—we haven't heard from him in years, since Valerie . . . since just after . . . after she killed . . ."

Sarah grabbed her head with both hands and closed her eyes in anguish.

Theodore Cardonick broke the embarrassing silence. "Would you care to see Gordon's old room, Doctor?"

The three of them walked upstairs to a small room at the rear of the row house. The walls of the room were decorated with huge posters of odd-looking musicians: a guitar player with green hair, a fat drummer wearing a skeleton costume, a group dressed in red standing amid flames.

Theodore Cardonick offered a chair to Whitney and then sat on the edge of the bed. "It's stayed the same in here ever since Gordon moved out, eight or nine years ago. We talked about converting it into a study, but we never did get around to it."

"That picture is more recent, of course," Sarah said as she sat next to her husband. She pointed to a photo of Cardonick and Denise and their daughter Jennifer.

Thinking about Denise with the sniper made Whitney sad. "Please," he said, changing the subject, "tell me about your sister, Gordon's mother."

Sarah smiled weakly. "She was four years younger than me. I loved Valerie, Doctor. She was so sick as a little girl, and we all worried about her so much. . ."

Valerie was a delicate child, wary of leaving her mother's side. She would dissolve into tears at the slightest frustration. Her peers made fun of her awkward ways, and that pushed her even further into her shell. And even though she blossomed into a strikingly pretty teenager, she had few girlfriends and no boyfriends.

Playing piano was her one interest. She was accepted by the Jefferson School of Music during her senior year in high school, but she never enrolled. A few days after her high school graduation, in June of 1955, she met Richard Green. Within a month they were married.

"We were shocked, all of us," said Sarah. "It happened so quickly. One day she was an eighteen-year-old recluse. The next day she had a husband."

"Why do you think she did it?" asked Whitney.

"I really don't know." She sighed and squeezed her crumpled handkerchief. "He was the first man who ever expressed any interest in her. Maybe she was afraid she'd never get another chance."

Whatever her sister's motives were for getting married, Sarah was sure of one thing: Richard Green was a horrible choice. He dominated

Valerie in every conceivable way. He was fired from job after job. He was a drunkard, a liar, a gambler, and a cheat.

The Greens moved to Logan, a run-down section on the edge of the North Philadelphia ghetto. The initial glow of married life faded quickly. Sometimes several days would elapse with nary a civil word, nor any word, passing between them. Richard would occasionally leave home for days at a time.

Less than a year after their wedding, in May of 1956, Valerie gave birth to Gordon, their only child. She was nineteen years old.

"Valerie became seriously depressed right after Gordon was born. She had to be hospitalized for a few weeks. And that was only the first time. She was in and out of the hospital eight, maybe nine times between 1956 and her death in 1969. The doctors said she was manic-depressive."

"Sometimes her doctor put her into the hospital because she was depressed," said Theodore Cardonick. "Other times she'd get agitated and paranoid and think people were out to get her. Once the police took her to the hospital after she went into Gimbel's and spent an hour trying on the same two pairs of shoes, over and over. Another time they picked her up for walking down the middle of Broad Street, shouting about Jesus."

Valerie's depressions, her friendlessness, her fearfulness, the loveless wasteland that was her marriage—all of this caused her to lean on young Gordon for the support and affection she couldn't get from her husband.

"She and Gordon were close," Sarah said.

"Too damn close, if you want my opinion," said her husband. "Valerie was always playing with Gordon's hair, patting his bottom, rubbing his shoulders, whispering baby-talk into his ear—even when he was nine or ten. Once around that time we went to see her, and I found the two of them napping together in bed, rolled up in an embrace. It made me sick to my stomach. No wonder he had so many problems in school."

The boy was bright, but his performance in elementary school was poor. He was moody, petulant, and given to unpredictable outbursts. He was a constant discipline problem: he set fires in the school lavatory, tormented neighbors' pets, and stole from other children. Twice he attacked classmates for no reason.

"Valerie couldn't bear to punish Gordon," Sarah said. "She blamed the other schoolchildren for the trouble he caused. In her eyes Gordon could do no wrong."

"What about his father?" asked Whitney. "What did he have to say about all of this?"

Theodore Cardonick laughed sardonically. "Richard Green was a rotten son of a bitch. We didn't find out until 1969 just how rotten he really was."

In the fall of that year Gordon began junior high school. He was suspended almost immediately for truancy. When he returned to school he was covered with bruises which, according to a note from Valerie, resulted from a fall. But Gordon confided to a school counselor that the bruises were caused by one of his father's frequent beatings.

The counselor alerted the Department of Social Services. After an investigation, Richard Green was indicted on three counts of assault and battery. He pleaded guilty to one count; the others were dropped in return for his pledge not to contact Gordon without DSS approval. In December of 1969 he began serving a two-year prison sentence.

The DSS psychiatrist assigned to the case recommended that the state take temporary custody of Gordon. The psychiatrist stated that Valerie Green's instability and her failure to report her husband's abusiveness raised serious questions about her fitness as a parent. The thirteen-year-old boy was placed in a temporary foster home.

Two days later, on December 23, 1969, Valerie closed herself in her garage, surrounded herself with snapshots of her son, and started the engine of her car.

"She was supposed to spend Christmas with us," Sarah said. "We didn't want her to be alone. When we got there to pick her up we found her chain-locked to the bumper of her car. She was naked. Her eyes were wide open. I remember standing over her, screaming at her, trying to tug her off the bumper, slapping her to wake her up. But we were too late."

"Carbon monoxide poisoning," said Theodore Cardonick.

"She used a bicycle lock," continued Sarah. "She chained herself to the car and threw the key across the garage. I guess she was afraid she'd change her mind otherwise."

"She did change her mind at the last minute," said Theodore. "Her wrists were rubbed raw as if she had tried to wriggle free. But the key was out of her reach."

"Ironic, isn't it?" said Sarah. "The one time my sister actually succeeds at a plan, it kills her." She began to sob softly.

"That must have been very hard for all of you," Whitney said.

Sarah clenched her fists and glared at him. "You goddamn psychiatrists! Who are you to say someone isn't fit to raise her own flesh and blood? Who made you God? Tell me, who made you God?"

Sarah buried her head in her husband's chest. He rocked her and soothed her as she cried. "Please forgive her, Doctor. She's been through an awful lot on account of that boy."

Sarah and Theodore Cardonick were unable to have children of their own. After Valerie Green died, they petitioned the court for custody of Gordon. The DSS approved of them, and the boy moved into their Northeast Philadelphia home.

Richard Green didn't fight this arrangement. He was glad to be free from the responsibility of being a parent. He moved out of state after receiving parole the following year and disappeared from Gordon's life forever.

The junior high years were relatively stable ones for Gordon. His grades were good. There was no delinquent behavior. In 1971, on his own initiative, he changed his name to Gordon Cardonick.

His grades slipped again in high school. His attendance was erratic. In his junior year he began to experiment with alcohol and a variety of drugs, a pattern that continued into his adult life.

"Gordon played piano in the high school orchestra," continued Sarah. "It was the only thing that pulled him through those years. I hate to think what would have become of him otherwise. His music teacher said he had exceptional talent. He reminded me of his mother, the way she was going to study music until she ran off to marry that . . . that man."

Theodore Cardonick sighed. "Gordon didn't take school very seriously. We considered it a minor miracle that he stayed with it long enough to graduate."

"He couldn't wait to be done with it," agreed Sarah. "He wanted to get out on the road with that rock 'n' roll band of his. I don't know, Doctor. Somewhere along the line we lost him. There were all his problems in school, then later on there were his arrests and the difficulties with Denise."

Whitney glanced at the picture of Denise.

Theodore Cardonick continued. "My wife and I were pleased when he married Denise. We thought things were finally starting to work out for him. They didn't, of course, but I guess you know all about that. Denise told us she's been meeting with you."

"We've talked, yes," replied Whitney. He was anxious to avoid talking about those meetings. "You said something about Gordon being arrested before?"

Sarah placed her handkerchief in her lap. "Just after Jennifer was born, Gordon was arrested for possession of cocaine. The charges were dropped, though. Insufficient evidence, something like that. About a year later he was convicted of stealing equipment from a recording studio where he was working. He was put on probation. The first time he went to prison was a couple of years ago, after he was convicted of assaulting Denise."

"He managed to stay out of trouble after he got out on parole last year," continued Theodore Cardonick. "Then a few weeks before this past Christmas, Denise's boss had him arrested for making verbal threats. I posted bail, and he was supposed to go on trial the last week of December. Then Gordon got arrested for the shootings, and the man decided not to press the verbal threats charge."

"He just couldn't make anything work out for himself," said Sarah. "Jobs, his marriage, being a father. And he drank a lot, and I suspect he was involved with drugs, too."

"Did he ever seek professional help?" asked Whitney.

"Not on his own," she replied. "Ted and I took him to a hospital emergency room once. I guess it was in 1978. Gordon had a fight with Denise and came to our house to spend the night. The next day he was walking around in a stupor, and we found a bottle of sleeping pills near his bed."

"The psychiatrist at the hospital told us Gordon was seriously depressed," said her husband.

"Brilliant," Sarah said sarcastically. "Doctors are great for telling you the obvious, but what else have they ever done for him?" She stared at Whitney angrily.

"Now, Sarah," chided Theodore. "Gordon never even gave the hospital a chance to help him. He left the next day, signed himself out, even though they told him they thought he should stay for more treatment."

"I know, I know," she sighed.

"Maybe we didn't do enough to get help for him. I keep telling myself I should have done more. I knew Gordon was getting sick again right before the shootings."

"We both knew," Sarah said. "Gordon came to live with us after Denise got the restraining order against him in October. He spent most of his time in his room. He wasn't working, wasn't even looking for work. He wasn't doing much of anything except sleeping. He hardly ever shaved, didn't eat much, some days he wouldn't even get dressed."

"He seemed pretty confused," said Theodore Cardonick. "It was almost like living with a zombie."

"One night," she continued, "I heard him talking out loud in his room. It was frightening. At first it sounded like he was laughing and talking to Jennifer, and then it sounded like he was crying and talking to his dead mother.

"He kept calling Denise on the phone, trying to get her to take him back. He called her office one day in early December. Her boss answered her phone. Gordon started shouting at him, threatening to kill him. He said something like 'I know you're the one who's behind all this.' The man had Gordon charged with making threats, like Ted told you.

"We made an appointment for Gordon with a counselor at the community mental health center, but Gordon wouldn't go there. Then we had our family doctor over to the house. Gordon refused to be examined, but the doctor was concerned about him and recommended a psychiatrist. And he said that if Gordon wouldn't go for help that we should see the psychiatrist ourselves and get him committed on an emergency basis."

"And did you do that?" asked Whitney.

Sarah breathed deeply. "No. Gordon finally began to come around a little bit the week before Christmas. He started eating and he spent some time downstairs watching the football games. He went out by himself a few evenings that week. He still seemed depressed, but at least he was starting to take care of himself again."

"What do you remember about December twenty-fourth, the day of the shootings?" asked Whitney.

Sarah sighed. "He seemed happy that morning. He said that the restraining order was almost expired and that he was going to talk to Denise."

"He was sure he could get back together with her," said Theodore Cardonick. "I told him not to expect too much, but he didn't want to hear what I was saying."

"Gordon wasn't here when we got home that evening. Ted and I figured he was taking gifts to Denise and Jennifer. Then around ten o'clock the police came to the house. That's when we learned about the shootings."

Now it was Theodore Cardonick who appeared to be on the verge of crying. "As soon as they told us what had happened," he said, "I thought about my rifle. I ran down to the basement where I keep it, and it was gone." His wife touched his hand, and his tears began to flow. "Damn it. It was my goddamn gun that killed those people, Doctor. It was my goddamn gun."

Whitney watched in silent sadness as the couple tried in vain to comfort each other. And as they cried together on the edge of their nephew's bed, Sarah Cardonick's angry words reverberated in Whitney's mind.

Who made you God? Tell me, who made you God?

J*anuary 16, 1983*

Dear Thomas,

The rearranged letters of Spiro Agnew's name spell "grow a penis."

The rearranged letters of Ronald Reagan's name spell "an oral danger."

And the rearranged letters of your name—Thomas Alden Whitney —spell "amen in thy slow death."

Speaking of death: A man died and entered heaven. On his first day there his guardian angel gave him a tour. The angel pointed out all of the local sights: the meditation gallery, the wing fitting room, the harp repair factory.

At noon, the angel took the newcomer to Heaven's Cafeteria. They walked to the end of the line, picked up trays and silverware, and waited patiently for their turn at the food.

Suddenly all eyes turned and every voice hushed as a tall, barrel-chested man plowed his way through the swinging door and into the cafeteria. He was of indeterminate age, deeply tanned, with flowing silver hair and a full beard. The tall man elbowed everyone else aside, pushed his way to the front of the line, and slammed his tray down in front of the hot lunches.

"Holy smoke!" exclaimed the newcomer. "Who in heaven's name is that?"

"Oh, that's just God," replied the angel. "Sometimes he likes to play doctor."

I hope you'll forgive all this talk of death, but it's been very much on my mind. And if you can't share your thoughts and feelings with your favorite doctor in the whole world, then things are in a sorry state, indeed.

I feel as though every letter brings us closer and closer to each other.

AMEN IN THY SLOW DEATH.

Your friend,
The Phoenix

wo weeks had passed since Whitney's second interview with Cardonick. According to the nurses and guards who knew the patient, he'd been quiet and manageable in the interim. So Whitney decided to use his office instead of the Secure Interview Room for the third meeting. He left his door cracked open, though, so the guard outside could hear if any disturbance developed.

Cardonick still moved and talked slowly, as if concentration required a great deal of effort. But he was neatly groomed, and he was dressed in freshly pressed jeans, a clean sweatshirt, and Nike athletic shoes. He seemed more aware of his surroundings than he had been during the earlier interviews. Whitney commented to him on his apparent improvement.

"Yeah," replied Cardonick, "well, I'm just trying to get along."

"How have you been feeling?"

"Pretty messed up. The reality of things is beginning to hit me, if you know what I mean."

"Please, go on."

Cardonick hesitated for a moment. "Well, when I first got here I felt like I was losing my mind, like I was in a dream, and maybe I would wake up and things would be back to normal. But I couldn't wake up. I'll tell you, it scared the living shit out of me."

"And now?"

"And now . . . well, I still get a little confused sometimes, but my thinking feels more normal, more under control. But I've never felt as depressed as I do now."

"Maybe you have something worth feeling depressed about."

Cardonick appeared puzzled. "What do you mean?"

"I understand that you've been having family troubles lately."

The patient frowned. "Family troubles. Huh, that's a funny way to put it."

"I see. Tell me, how would you describe it?"

Cardonick looked past Whitney as if he were watching a faraway scene. "I'd say I lost the only thing that mattered to me," he said bitterly. "I'd say my life is a complete washout. I'd say my fucking life is as good as over. There—is that what you wanted to hear?"

"I'm interested in hearing whatever you're willing to tell me about these last few months."

And so Cardonick talked about the unsteady life he'd led since the end of his parole the previous September. He talked about the fights with Denise, Jennifer's illness, his failure to find work, his inability to cope with his responsibilities as a husband and a father.

"Everything was starting to fall apart. And then in October Denise asked me to leave." He sighed. "I couldn't believe it. Maybe I just didn't want to believe it. I felt like the whole world was against me. I thought someone had to be turning Denise against me, too. Maybe her boss, maybe her mother, maybe the police—hell, I didn't know who to trust or who my enemies were."

"And you were living with your aunt and uncle during this time?"

"I moved back with them after Denise kicked me out. But to be honest, Doctor, I don't remember very much about those two months. I wasn't interested in doing anything or going anywhere. The whole time seems like one long blur."

"I see." Whitney leafed through the notes from his interview with Sarah and Theodore Cardonick. "Your aunt told me that you were starting to feel a little better a few days before you were arrested."

"Yeah, that's the funny thing. I really did think things were beginning to look up. I bought a bike for Jennifer for Christmas, and Denise was going to let me bring it after I put it together. And I just knew things were going to work out after all. She was going to take me back, and everything was going to be fine. After two months of not giving a shit whether I lived or died, all of a sudden I was full of energy and happy, really happy."

"Is that how you were feeling the day before Christmas?"

Cardonick leaned back in his chair. "The day before Christmas," he said. "Doctor, did you ever feel like you could see things before they happen? I know that sounds crazy. But it's like a cloud vaporizes—a cloud that's hung over you so long you'd forgotten it was there—and suddenly you see things clearly for the first time. Do you know what I mean?"

Whitney turned to a fresh piece of notepaper. "What happened that day, Mr. Cardonick?"

The patient placed his hands behind his head, gazed toward the ceiling, and took a deep breath. "It all seems so strange now, so unbelievable, but . . . when I woke up that morning I knew immediately that it would be a really important day. It was like God wanted me to understand something, but I didn't know what. All day long I had this feeling that something was going to happen but I didn't know what it was supposed to be. I was waiting to find out. I kept thinking about Jesus, about a prayer my mother taught me when I was little. I've never paid too much attention to religion, but I felt very holy that day.

"I tried to keep busy by putting Jennifer's bike together. But my mind kept wandering and I couldn't get it done right. I still felt like I was waiting for something important to happen. Then, all of a sudden, I wondered if I was going to die."

"How did you feel? Was it a frightening thought, or a comforting one?"

"That's exactly it," Cardonick said. "Maybe you do understand what I mean. Maybe it's not so crazy after all. But here I was thinking that perhaps I was supposed to die, and yet it didn't scare me in the least. I felt like I finally understood some secret that had been hidden right in front of me all of the time. Like God was revealing things to me, and all I had to do was make myself ready to receive his message.

"Around five o'clock I was in the cellar, still trying to put the bike together. My hand slipped on the screwdriver and I cut a gash in my palm. And it was really weird, but the instant I saw my blood I had this sense of total peace, complete understanding. It was like the feeling you get when you're high on acid, when you think you see the grand scheme of things, how you fit in with the rest of the world, the rest of the whole fucking universe.

"I started sucking the blood from my palm. I was aware of the slightest little sensation, every little change. Each time I sucked a little blood out of the cut I felt my whole body go weak. And when I swallowed it I could feel myself getting strong again. It kept going like that—weak, strong, suck, swallow, weak, strong, suck, swallow—until the bleeding ended.

"When the blood stopped I was calm. I kept thinking about Denise and how much I loved her. It was beautiful. I sat there on the floor for what seemed like a really long time. I closed my eyes and thought about her, and just then the telephone rang. It was Denise. I thought it was some kind of sign, her calling me in the moment that I was thinking about her.

"She was upset about something. I was having a hard time understanding her. I asked her if I could bring presents to the house the next day, Christmas morning. She sounded frightened, started yelling at me, told me to stay away from the house. Jennifer was crying, too. I could hear her in the background. I got really worried.

"Denise got hysterical. She said Jennifer was having an attack, that she couldn't breathe right. I could tell from Denise's voice that she was really afraid. Then she hung up.

"I felt cold, so cold inside. And then I realized: Denise and Jennifer were in danger. Her call was a signal. The cold feeling was a sign. Someone was threatening her. She was disguising her message in case they were listening, and that's why she sounded so confused. But I recognized it in her voice, and I knew I had to protect her. I had to go to her."

"Why didn't you just call the police if you thought she was in danger?"

"Ha. That's a laugh. Cops hate me. They always have. They'd never try to help me. Besides, for all I knew they were behind the whole thing, trying to destroy me by destroying Denise and Jennifer. I couldn't go to them. It was up to me to do something to save my family.

"I looked around the cellar and I saw my uncle's rifle. I guess it had been there the whole time, but that was the first I noticed it. I thought it was another sign—my uncle was trying to help me, but he couldn't do anything directly for fear that they might get him, too. So he left the rifle where I would see it at the right time.

"I took the rifle and some ammunition. My hand started to bleed again. I sucked it as hard as I could to make myself strong. It felt like ice. I looked in the mirror as I put my coat on. I could see right through myself. My ears started to hurt, like I could hear Denise screaming for her life.

"The house was dark when I got there. I let myself in the back door and climbed up the cellar stairs into the kitchen. She wasn't there, but I could still hear her screaming.

"I looked out the front window. A car drove by, and I thought it must be the person who wanted to kill my family. I ran out to my car and drove down the street, but he was gone.

"I kept driving around the neighborhood. I lost track of the time. The snow was falling. It looked just like the night Jennifer was born. Everything felt so fucking cold.

"I was thinking about Jennifer's breathing attack, wondering what had caused it, when I started to cry. All of a sudden I started to choke, just like Jennifer does when she has an attack. I thought I was dying.

"I was on the expressway by then. I didn't know how I got there. Something must have pulled me there. I heard a voice, a woman's voice, saying, 'The air—beware. The air—beware.' And then I finally understood. The message I had been waiting for. It was the cars. Those goddamn, fucking cars—spitting out all that ugly exhaust, that goddamn poison. They were killing Jennifer. They were killing me. I knew I had to put a stop to it. For a second I thought the world was ending, and I thought about shooting myself rather than watching it happen.

"The next thing I remember I was driving near the oil refineries. The rifle felt hot in my hand. I realized I must have shot it, and I wondered if I had killed myself and if I was a ghost driving down the road.

"A cop pulled up beside me. He was waving to me, like he was trying to let me know that everything was going to be all right now. I relaxed a little. Then a second cruiser showed up, and one of the bastards tried to force me off the road. The cold feeling came back. I kept thinking, 'They know what's going on. They're part of it.' I tried to get away from them, but they surrounded me and shot me. I was sure they were going to kill me, and that they were putting it off as a kind of mental torture. I asked them to get it over with, but they didn't, of course.

"It was all so fucking scary. Even worse than the first time I cracked up in 1980, the first time I came to Littleton."

Cardonick had become increasingly agitated during his description of that day's events. He now sank back into his chair, completely spent. A faint smile crept across his lips. "What else would you like to know, Doctor?"

Whitney was tempted to ask Cardonick about all of the things that had transpired since his arrest: his suicide attempt, his delusions about Jennifer being dead, his assaultiveness during their first meeting. But his evaluation only needed to focus on Cardonick's state of mind at the time of the shootings.

"Actually," replied Whitney, "I think you've already told me all I need to know."

"Well, I just hope it was good enough."

"Yes, you were very helpful."

Almost too damn helpful, thought Whitney. Rarely had the psychiatrist heard a patient articulate so clearly the experience of going mad. What was it the nurse had said? *Gordon really likes to play games.* For a few moments, Whitney wondered if Cardonick had been playing a game with him. Perhaps Cardonick was a shill, a confederate of someone studying psychiatrists at state hospitals, someone testing Whitney's ability to discriminate between malingering and real mental illness.

Whitney dismissed the thought. *Now who's getting paranoid?* he asked himself.

"I'll have the guard escort you back to your ward now. I do have one last question, though."

"Yes, Doctor?"

"Most patients ask me questions. 'How long will I be in the hospital?' 'What are you going to tell the judge in your report?' Things like that. But you haven't asked anything at all. Why is that?"

Cardonick stood. "Because frankly, Doctor, it doesn't matter to me. You can do anything you want with me, because unless you can get my wife to come back to me, I really don't care."

Cardonick walked toward the door. He stopped and turned to face Whitney. "By the way, Doctor. I think I owe you an apology."

"Oh?"

"For throwing that ashtray at you. I was having crazy ideas about cigarettes when I first got here. I thought people who smoked were trying to poison the air, trying to make my daughter have attacks. When you offered me a cigarette, I thought you were one of them."

"I see."

Cardonick smiled weakly. "But I'm doing much better now. I guess you can tell, huh?"

18

The neighborhoods of Philadelphia fan out like spokes from the hub of the Center City area. The North Philadelphia neighborhood is on the innermost section of one of those spokes. When Schacter was growing up there it was filled with middle-class Jewish merchants. Now it suffers from years of white flight and urban corrosion.

Farther north and west is Germantown, a tarnished remnant of a brighter era. A hundred years ago it was a long carriage ride from Philadelphia proper, and was home for landed gentry and others who lived off the city's vitality but away from its dirt and noise. Now it too is ghettolike with its plywood windows and sheet-metal doors. Once-elegant mansions lay in disrepair, divided long ago into ratty apartments for Bohemian types and the working poor. Schacter's younger daughter lived there when she was a student at Temple University. She showed him the chipped porcelain commode in her bathroom. "Just think," she told him, sighing sadly for what once had been. "John Greenleaf Whittier once took a crap in this toilet."

Mt. Airy is the next stop on the spoke extending northwest from Center City. Stanley and Katherine Schacter had lived there for thirty-five years, watching its character change slowly but inexorably. It had turned into a buffer zone between the creeping decay of Germantown and the affluence of Chestnut Hill, where Schacter's friend Whitney lived. Mt. Airy is a mixture of white and black; young and old; people on the way up, and people who would always struggle just to stay even.

*   *   *

Schacter's wife Katherine wanted things to go without a hitch when she entertained, even when the only guest was an old family friend like Thomas Whitney. She discovered at the last minute that she lacked two things crucial for the Sunday brunch she was preparing, and so Schacter was sent into the early winter morning to buy the missing items. Tiny drops of frozen rain whipped by a strong northeast wind cut into his face like dozens of cold, sharp needles.

Thank heaven for 7-11, he thought as he walked back home. The convenience store was always open, even on Sunday mornings, and it was only a block from his house. Otherwise he would've had to drive two miles to the nearest twenty-four-hour supermarket. Katherine would have insisted.

She was upstairs when he returned. "Did you get the cream cheese?" she yelled to him.

"Uh-huh," he yelled back.

"Good. Thomas likes cream cheese with his bagel and lox. Is it Philadelphia Brand?"

"Is it... I don't... wait a minute." Schacter looked in the bag he was carrying. "Yeah. Philadelphia Brand Cream Cheese by Kraft."

"Good. How about the Sunday *New York Times?* Did you get that?"

"No. It's late today. The clerk said it's late everywhere, so I figured it wouldn't do any good to look for it anyplace else." It was a lie. He'd forgotten to buy the paper. But it was a lie he could live with, considering the weather.

"Darn," said Katherine as she walked downstairs. "Oh well. I guess we'll have to make do with just the *Inquirer*. Thomas will be disappointed."

Katherine always made a fuss over Whitney. It had been like that for sixteen years, ever since the first time he visited the Schacters. Their oldest daughter was twenty-one and unmarried back then. Katherine used to draw Whitney's attention to the girl's fine qualities and comment on what a good wife she would make some lucky man. It didn't seem to bother Katherine that Whitney was ten years older than the girl or that he wasn't Jewish.

Schacter was thankful that Whitney had never taken Katherine's bait. He would've hated to gain a son-in-law and lose a friend.

He went upstairs to shave. When he returned downstairs, Katherine and Whitney were sitting and drinking coffee in the den.

"Stanley," she said, "I was just telling Thomas I hope he'll stay to watch the football game with us after brunch."

Schacter reached for one of his pipes and filled it with tobacco. "Yeah, what do you say, Thomas? The Eagles are playing the Redskins today. Should be a good game."

"I'm afraid not, Stan. I need to take care of some paperwork I brought home with me."

"Well, you two men can work this out. I need to finish preparing our meal. Stanley, don't take no for an answer."

Katherine was always glad to see Whitney. He could set anyone at ease, friend or stranger, almost instantly. Katherine's other friends often asked about him, even though they'd met him only briefly at one of the Schacters' parties. People could talk to him once and feel as though they'd known him for years. Actually, he seldom revealed much about himself to them. But his way of making others feel safe enough to talk about themselves made Whitney stand out in their memories.

Schacter looked at his watch after Katherine departed for the kitchen. "Hey! I almost forgot what time it is." He turned on the radio. "You should find this very interesting, Thomas."

"What's that, Stan?"

"Sssh!" Schacter fiddled with the radio dial.

A rich baritone voice pierced through the static on the radio. "Courage," the man said. "We're talking about courage. It takes courage to listen to Jesus, to take Him into your heart. It takes courage to accept and forgive your enemies."

"Stanley," chided Whitney, "have you been born again behind my back?"

Schacter lit his pipe. "We're listening to Reverend Isaac. I told you about him before, remember?"

"Reverend Isaac?"

"Uh-huh. Isaac Hopkins. The father of the little girl who was killed by the Christmas Eve Sniper."

The radio voice continued. "It takes courage to dwell in the castle of His mercy and His everlasting love." Muffled choruses of "amen" punctuated the speaker's sentences.

"Why are we listening to this?" asked Whitney.

Schacter shrugged his shoulders. "I don't know. Curiosity, I guess. When I met him during my investigation, I couldn't decide whether he was a charlatan. I've been listening on and off, trying to make up my mind, just to tie up loose ends."

Schacter remembered the preacher as a tall man, well built, with coal-black skin, massive hands, and wide eyes. There was a predictable sameness to most of Reverend Isaac's radio sermons. This one today was different, though. There were no theatrical vocal crescendos, no fist-pounding on the podium, no pleas for listeners' dollars in order to continue the ministry and spread God's word. The voice was quiet and sad this Sunday morning.

"Brothers and sisters," said the preacher. "I believe. I believe my daughter is happy today. I believe she is with her Heavenly Father and that she has found her peace with Him. I believe He has forgiven her for any sins she committed in her short life on earth. And I believe my daughter has forgiven Gordon Cardonick."

The chorus of voices transformed into a sea of silence.

"Brothers and sisters, pray with me now. Let us pray for the Heavenly spirit of my daughter. And let us pray for Gordon Cardonick, that his sickness may be healed, that his soul may be cleansed, that his heart shall open up to the Lord and let Him in. Let us pray."

There was total quiet on the airwaves. Even the static seemed to recede. Schacter felt a sudden chill sweep through him. "Well," said the detective. "It sounds like the good reverend wants to do your job for you."

"Pardon?"

"Apparently he's already made up his mind about Cardonick. What were his words? 'Pray that his sickness may be healed.' Reverend Isaac thinks the guy is nuts."

"That's the common perception, though, isn't it? That someone would have to be insane to do what Cardonick did?"

"Hey—I'm just the cop in this case. You're the doctor. You tell me. Just between us, is Cardonick crazy?"

Whitney paused for a moment. "Well, he's certainly no paragon of mental health. Even when he's functioning at his highest level, he's what we psychiatrists refer to as a hoafug."

"A ho—a what?"

"A hoafug. A Hell of a Fucked-Up Guy." Whitney smiled. "It's against the law for anyone other than a doctor to make that diagnosis."

"Sure. I can't wait to hear you say that in court."

"However, he's not crazy," continued Whitney. "Not in the usual sense of the word. He's not a chronic mental patient, doesn't suffer from schizophrenia, for instance. But if you're asking me if he was psychotic—if he was crazy—on Christmas Eve, then I think the answer is yes."

126

"Are you saying this is a case of temporary insanity?"

"Well, that's not a phrase I'm particularly fond of. But yes, you could call it that."

Schacter grunted and relit his pipe. "So. I assume you're recommending that he be found not guilty by reason of insanity?"

"Yes, I am. NGRI. In fact, that's the paperwork I referred to earlier. I have to get my report off to the judge."

"Well, it's like I said at the very beginning. He's a real odd bird."

"I'll say," agreed Whitney. "I usually feel at least a little sympathy for NGRI patients, no matter how horrible their crimes were. They're sick. They need help. And I'm a doctor."

"And in this case?"

Whitney shook his head. "Nothing. I just can't make any connection with him. There's something missing in his makeup. He comes across as cold and calculating, even through all the craziness." He laughed. "In fact, when I was meeting with him, I almost thought he was faking the whole damn thing."

"I don't think so," said Schacter.

"Neither do I. Who said all mental patients have to be sympathetic characters? Besides, everything points in the direction of an NGRI. His story, the background I got from his aunt and uncle and from his wife—she's the lucky one, let me tell you."

"His wife?"

"Yes. Just before Cardonick shot his victims, he went looking for her with a rifle. He thought God was sending him messages, telling him that it was his day to die. And he told himself he had to protect his wife. You see, he had suddenly gotten the idea that she was in grave danger, that someone was going to harm her—a delusion that reflected his own feelings about their separation. Luckily for her, she wasn't home when he got there. If she had been, I'm sure he would have wound up killing her—maybe their daughter, too—and then himself."

Schacter whistled through his teeth as he let out a deep breath.

Katherine poked her head into the den. "You boys can come in anytime now. Brunch is on the table. Well, Thomas. Are you staying for the football game?"

"I'm still trying to convince him, dear. We'll be there in a minute." Schacter turned to Whitney after Katherine left. "Actually, you'd be doing me a favor by staying. If you don't, Katherine will make me take her and her elderly sister out to dinner. Sister Sally is getting soft upstairs." Schacter pointed to his head. "She tends to stick herself in the chin with her fork and to dab her mouth with the edge of the tablecloth. It's very depressing. I really don't feel like dealing with it today."

"I thought Katherine was an only child," said Whitney.

"She is," laughed Schacter. "She is. Stay anyway, okay?" He slapped his friend on the back and guided him into the dining room.

Judge Gleason didn't like the way Cardonick's trial was shaping up.

The defendant was pleading insanity, and the prosecution wasn't trying very hard to undercut that defense. Apparently the district attorney was content to have Cardonick committed to Littleton—the usual outcome of a successful insanity defense in a murder trial. But that wasn't good enough for Gleason. The judge didn't want some doctor five or ten years later pronouncing Cardonick cured and recommending his release. He wanted Cardonick locked away in prison for good.

It was obvious to the judge that Fuller Bloomberg, Cardonick's court-appointed defense attorney, had spent many hours preparing the case. A recent law school graduate, Bloomberg still held a belief peculiar to the species of young public defenders: that even the most wretched client was entitled to a full and fair defense.

The lawyer paced methodically in front of the witness stand. He'd already gotten testimony from Denise and from Cardonick's aunt and uncle about his behavior around the time of the shootings. And Denise's employer, Mr. Jason, had testified about the irrational threats Cardonick made against him a couple of weeks before Christmas Eve.

Thomas Whitney, Bloomberg's final witness, was testifying. He'd already outlined Cardonick's life history. "In my opinion," Whitney concluded, "on the night in question Mr. Cardonick was suffering from something we call a major depression with mood-congruent psychotic features."

"Is that a generally recognized psychiatric diagnosis, Doctor?"

"Yes. It's listed in the American Psychiatric Association's Diagnostic Manual. It's one of many mood disorders we've been able to identify in psychiatric patients."

"In layman's terms, Doctor, could you describe the defendant's condition on that night?"

Whitney turned toward the jurors. "He had a mental breakdown—he'd been building up to it for a couple of months, actually—and he lost contact with reality. He was severely depressed. In fact, I think he's been clinically depressed for much of his adult life. And on Christmas Eve he experienced a psychotic break. He had delusions, hallucinations, and he was clinically paranoid."

Gleason glanced at the jury box. All eyes and ears were tuned to the witness stand. It reminded the judge of the television commercial for a famous stockbroker: *When Dr. Thomas Whitney talks, people listen.*

Bloomberg leaned against the railing in front of the jury box. He was looking toward the jurors while he directed his question to Whitney. "What caused this condition, Doctor?"

Whitney spoke calmly and slowly, like a professor explaining a lesson to his students. As usual, Whitney was having a mesmerizing effect on the jurors. Cardonick was going to get off, thought the judge, and there wasn't a damn thing he could do to stop it.

"From several sources," said Whitney, "we have a consistent description of a man who was seriously depressed for at least two months prior to the killings. His wife had left him, his daughter was seriously ill, he couldn't find work.

"And Christmastime, a difficult period for many people, was especially rough for Mr. Cardonick. December twenty-third was the anniversary of his mother's suicide. And Christmastime was also the anniversary of his earlier psychotic break with reality, the one that led to his first Littleton State Hospital admission in 1980.

"The final blow was the call he received from his wife on December twenty-fourth. She told him she was getting an extension of the restraining order she had taken out against him. His daughter had another attack of her illness, and his wife blamed him for causing it.

"Mr. Cardonick began to hallucinate. He heard his wife's voice screaming in agony. He thought he could see through himself. He had delusions about poisons in the air, about the end of the world, about the death of himself and his loved ones. His ability to reason deteriorated. When his wife called shortly after he had been thinking about her, he believed that his thoughts had somehow magically caused her to call. Later, when a car drove by just as he was worrying about his family's safety, he reasoned that there was a connection between the car and the danger he thought his family was in.

"He felt drawn to the Schuylkill Expressway by some unusual force. This happened in the midst of his extreme concern about his daughter's breathing problem. He thought something or someone was killing her, and he wanted to find the culprit responsible for her condition. But *he* was the person responsible. *He* was the one who had caused the automobile accident—on that same stretch of highway—that caused her premature birth and, indirectly, her chronic pulmonary condition.

"In that moment he suffered a total break with reality. He confused himself with his daughter, believed she was dying, and feared that he would die. He expanded this to include the end of the world, thought that everyone around him was an enemy, and then he struck out in rapid horror."

Gleason watched in dismay as each and every juror focused intently on Whitney.

"Doctor, in your opinion, on Christmas Eve of 1982, was the defendant psychologically capable of forming criminal intentions? Did he understand right from wrong, and did he know that he was committing a crime?"

Gleason stared at Cardonick; the young man was grinning oddly.

The psychiatrist continued: "Right and wrong, good and bad, legal and illegal—he was too psychotic to consider any of those things. His mental illness caused him to be completely out of control."

"Mr. Bloomberg, is the defense ready to present its closing argument?"

"We are, Your Honor."

"Very well. Please proceed."

Bloomberg walked slowly toward the jury box. "Ladies and gentlemen," he began, "in a little while you'll retire to the jury room and attempt to reach a verdict. Before you leave, the judge will deliver some instructions to you. He'll tell you that two conditions must be satisfied in order to convict my client of murder and the other charges against him.

"First, you must agree on certain facts. You must believe that three people were, indeed, shot to death last Christmas Eve, and that my client was the person who pulled the trigger.

"Second, you must believe that my client actually intended to commit a crime. You must find *beyond a reasonable doubt* that he had the mental ability to know he was doing something wrong, that he was mentally able to control his behavior. The judge will tell you that if you have a reasonable doubt—*any* reasonable question in your mind—that Mr. Cardonick was able to understand the criminal wrongfulness of his actions, then you must find him not guilty by reason of insanity.

"The defense has never contested the first of those two conditions. We agree that Mr. Cardonick killed three people that night." Bloomberg glanced toward the prosecuting attorney. "The Commonwealth has provided you with witness statements, ballistics reports, and police testimony, and we do not challenge that evidence.

"But the defense contends that no *crime* was committed that night. Because in order for a man to be guilty of a *crime,* he must have the ability to know right from wrong. He must choose—of his own free will—to do wrong."

The young public defender walked back and forth in front of the jury box. He spoke entirely without notes, a tactic he obviously hoped would make him appear honest and sincere.

"If a man buys a gun, puts on a mask, waits for darkness, holds up a liquor store, and shoots the clerk to death, the law says you should find that man guilty of murder, because he has chosen to do something he knows is criminally wrong.

"But if a two-year-old child pulls the trigger of a gun he finds in a playground, you wouldn't convict him of murder, because a tiny child is mentally incapable of distinguishing between right and wrong."

With a sweeping gesture of his hand, Bloomberg drew the jury's attention to Cardonick. "And that is the crucial element of this case. The law protects the mentally handicapped just as it protects children. You can't punish someone like a criminal—can't find him guilty of a crime—if he is mentally unable to form the intention of doing something wrong."

Bloomberg leaned against the front railing of the jury box. He looked directly at each juror in succession as he continued his remarks.

"Ladies and gentlemen, my client, Gordon Cardonick, was seriously mentally ill on the night in question. You've heard about his family history, the serious mental illness suffered by his mother. And Dr. Whitney testified that my client probably inherited a biological weakness for mental illness from her.

"And look at the childhood this man endured, this man who started out fragile, with an inherited tendency to develop mental illness. Consider the beatings he suffered at the hands of his sadistic and vicious father. Consider the suicide of the mother he loved so much. Is it any wonder, then, that long before the events of Christmas Eve, he had turned into such an unstable person? Is it any wonder that Mr. Cardonick had a lifelong pattern of psychological disturbance, of emotional immaturity, impulsive aggression, drug dependence, unstable relationships, erratic performance in school and work? In many ways, he was a disaster waiting to happen."

The lawyer, one hand still grasping the jury box railing, turned and pointed toward Cardonick.

"Ladies and gentlemen, can you really believe that the events of Christmas Eve were the actions of a sane man? Can you really believe that he knew what he was doing, that he was in touch with reality, that he understood right from wrong and the consequences of his behavior?"

Bloomberg returned to the defense table and stood next to Cardonick.

"Ladies and gentlemen, Mr. Cardonick needs treatment in a hospital, maybe several years' worth. But he shouldn't be thrown in prison like a criminal. I ask you to find him not guilty by reason of insanity."

Whitney hummed the tune for the seven hundredth time. It had been running through his head for two weeks. It wasn't particularly pretty. He didn't even like it. And for the life of him, he couldn't remember more than two words. But he couldn't shake it:

> De-de-de-dum,
> De-de-de-dum.
> De-de-de-dum,
> De-de-de-dum.
> Ah, yes!
> Da-da-da-da, de-da.

Whitney had the notion—he couldn't say why—that it meant something terribly important.

He was sitting alone in the poorly lit chamber. Gleason always kept him waiting for a few minutes. No matter how quickly or slowly he might answer the judge's call (once he even stalled for fifteen minutes just to test the hypothesis), Whitney would find himself waiting. It made him feel like a servant. He hated it.

"Ah, Tommy. There you are." Gleason tossed his robe toward the clothes tree. He missed his mark; he left the robe in a heap on the floor. "Care for a drink?"

"No, thank you, Judge."

Gleason wiped the rim of a glass against his shirt sleeve. "I sent out for an early dinner for the jury. This is one case they wouldn't want to start deliberating on an empty stomach." He poured the glass full of bourbon. "Oh, by the way. Congratulations!"

"Congratulations?"

"Your new job, Tommy. I hear you're going to become Littleton's new superintendent in June."

"Yes."

"Hmm. I guess we won't be seeing very much of you in these parts. Pity. Well, congratulations again."

"Thank you. " He felt uneasy accepting compliments from Gleason, like a condemned man thanking his executioner for a last cigarette and a blindfold. Whitney hummed the mystery tune absentmindedly as Gleason downed his drink.

"Maurice Chevalier!" exclaimed Gleason as he smacked his lips.

"Excuse me?"

"Maurice Chevalier. Wasn't that one of his songs? Let me see, now, don't tell me." Gleason hummed the tune out loud. "Yeah, that's right. He sang it with some old broad, what was her name? Hermione Gingold? They alternated lines, first him, then her: 'We met at nine. We met at eight. I was on time. No, you were late. Ah, yes! I remember it well."

Whitney shrugged his shoulders. He didn't recall ever having heard the song.

"It was from a movie," the judge continued. "Some damn musical. Don't tell me, what the hell was it . . ." He pondered a moment. "I've got it. *Gigi*."

"*Gigi?*"

"*Gigi*," repeated Gleason. "Louis Jourdan runs around all over Paris, making an ass out of himself over Leslie Caron. That's her name in the movie, Gigi."

"I see." It didn't ring a bell. Whitney was disappointed.

The judge leaned back in his chair and propped his feet on the desktop. His eyes narrowed and the disingenuous smile faded quickly from his face. "So, Tommy, you just couldn't resist it, could you?"

"Resist it?"

"This goddamn case. Cardonick. You just had to do it yourself, didn't you?"

Whitney stood and walked toward the window. "Someone had to

evaluate him, Judge. You signed the court order yourself. I don't know what you want me to say."

He pounded his fist on the desk. Some of the bourbon jumped out of its glass. "Say!" His speech was slightly slurred. "I don't want you to say a damn thing. You've already said enough. I've been listening to this insanity crap all morning."

Whitney gazed out at Broad Street and wondered why he'd been so fixated on the tune for the previous two weeks. He didn't have a clue.

Several minutes passed. Gleason regained his composure. "So, Tommy, how do you think it'll turn out. Guilty or NGRI?"

"I don't know, Judge." Whitney yawned.

"Damn it. How can you be so indifferent toward all this?"

"It was just another evaluation, Judge. That's all." He could still picture Denise sitting in the last row of the courtroom. "I give an opinion, the jury decides. I hope the guy gets a fair hearing, and I hope they agree with my conclusions. But I don't have an emotional stake in it, not in a personal sense. No more than a radiologist cares for a person he's just taken X rays of for the first and only time."

"Just like that. Someone kills three people—you saw that minister in there, the little girl's father—and the killer may go scot-free, and you don't give a shit."

"Well, you can commit him to Littleton, Judge. You know that."

"Big deal. Fifteen years ago I could toss a guy like this in Littleton and forget about him. Nowadays, ever since your buddy Osborne got the legislature to pass the Mental Health Law, it's six months in the hospital, and then he gets a brand-new commitment hearing. And every year after that the state has to prove all over again that he's still mentally ill and still dangerous. When the state can't prove it anymore, he walks."

Whitney knew it was senseless to argue. He stood silently in the glare of Gleason's eyes.

"Just another case, you said."

"That's right, Judge."

"You're a disinterested party, a scientist, an unbiased observer."

"Something like that."

Gleason smiled. "Well, I saw the way you kept looking at Cardonick's wife. Nothing disinterested in that, I'd say. I'm surprised you aren't humming 'Thank Heaven for Little Girls.' That's from Gigi, too."

There was a knock at the chamber door. Whitney was grateful for the interruption. "Your Honor," said the bailiff, "the jury is returning. They've reached a verdict."

"Already?" responded the judge. "Holy shit."

INSANITY VERDICT FOR XMAS EVE SNIPER
by Selma Aaron

February 18 — Gordon Cardonick, the so-called Christmas Eve Sniper, was found not guilty by reason of insanity this afternoon in Philadelphia Superior Court. Cardonick, 26, faced murder and assault charges in connection with a shooting spree on the Schuylkill Expressway last December.

The jury required less than an hour to reach its verdict. Afterward Cardonick's attorney, Fuller Bloomberg, stated, "The jury did the right thing. This man is really sick. He needs treatment, not prison."

Most of the afternoon was spent on the testimony and cross-examination of Dr. Thomas Whitney, the principal defense witness. Dr. Whitney, a psychiatrist at Littleton State Hospital, stated that Cardonick was suffering from a severe depression and that he was insane at the time of the shootings. District Attorney Anthony Tortelli's rigorous cross-examination failed to sway Dr. Whitney from his position.

Earlier in the day the defense presented testimony from Cardonick's estranged wife and from the aunt and uncle he was living with when the killings occurred. They stated that shortly after he and his wife separated last October, Cardonick became withdrawn, suspicious, bizarre, and suicidal.

Cardonick was found not guilty by reason of insanity on three counts of first-degree murder and twelve counts of assault and battery with a dangerous weapon. Also disposed of were charges of trespassing, possession of an unlicensed weapon, leaving the scene of an accident, and dangerous driving.

Judge Raymond T. Gleason accepted the jury's verdict and committed Cardonick to the maximum-security Littleton State Hospital for six months, the maximum period provided by Commonwealth law. Cardonick will be entitled to a new commitment hearing at the end of that time.

20

Anna Roth stayed near the rear of the large group as it crossed Littleton's main yard. Whitney walked ahead, his hands gesturing as he lectured to the staff around him. Several people were jostling one another for positions near him. It reminded Anna of pictures she'd seen of a film star being trailed by his entourage.

It was nine o'clock on the last Monday morning in February, time for monthly Grand Rounds, and Whitney was conducting them for the first time. Osborne had given him that responsibility a few weeks earlier when he announced that Whitney would soon succeed him as superintendent.

Usually Anna arrived at the hospital later in the day, but Whitney had extended her a personal invitation to join Grand Rounds. Ever since the day she slapped Whitney, he'd been especially solicitous toward her. She'd forced herself to be civil in return, but it took an enormous amount of energy, and the effort was only marginally successful.

Whitney led the group into Building One, the ward that housed men who'd come to Littleton from prison. The chief nurse described a problem the staff was having with its newest patient, Willard Delahunt. He'd begun serving a prison sentence a month earlier. The man had been refusing to bathe in prison, and he repeatedly assaulted guards and inmates there for no apparent reason. He'd already begun repeating the pattern at Littleton.

"He hasn't bathed here at all?" Whitney asked.

"No," replied the nurse. "Sometimes we get men who won't shower with the other patients, so we let them get up earlier to take a private shower. He won't even do that. But we're more concerned about his assaultiveness."

Whitney asked the nurse and one of the guards to accompany him into the specially constructed interview room. The rest of the group sat behind a two-way mirror so they could observe the examination.

Once inside the room, Whitney positioned a chair next to the door. He directed the nurse and guard to the other side of the room. "I'll sit over here with you," he said. "When I meet with an assaultive patient for the first time, I prefer letting him sit closest to the door."

"But, Doc," said the guard, "isn't it better for you to sit by the door in case he comes after you?"

Whitney smiled. "He's more likely to attack if he thinks *I'm* coming after *him*. I don't want him to feel trapped. If he's near the door, it may help him feel less frightened."

Delahunt was escorted to the room. Whitney introduced himself and invited the man to sit near the door. The patient was short and thin, and he sat rigidly with his arms folded tightly against his chest. He kept tapping his feet nervously against the floor.

"Mr. Delahunt, I understand from the staff that showers are something of a problem for you."

The man's eyes darted back and forth between Whitney, the nurse, and the guard. "No, sir," he stated in a dull voice. "No problem, sir."

"Well, I understand that you've eliminated showers from your routine."

"Yes, sir. I don't want my skinnections to get wet."

Whitney raised his eyebrows. "I see. Why is that?"

The man grimaced. "Because of the light."

"The light?"

"The bathroom light," said Delahunt. "I can't get my skinnections wet under the light."

"What happens if they get wet under the light?"

"They become visible. Then everyone can see them."

"I see. Tell me, how long have you had these skinnections?"

"I don't know. Three weeks, maybe four weeks."

"And have you ever had them before?"

"Yes."

"When was that?"

"The last time I was in jail. A few years ago."

"I see." Whitney pondered for a moment. "You say your skinnections are invisible?"

"Yes, sir."

"But surely some people must know you have them."

The patient's eyes narrowed and he clasped his arms against his body more tightly. "Some," he said.

"Men and women, or just men?" asked Whitney.

"Just men. Just certain men. They step on my skinnections."

"And what happens when they step on your skinnections?"

"It makes me fall over."

"I see. You lose your balance. It must be frightening when that happens."

The patient tapped his feet more quickly. He didn't respond.

"When those men make you lose your balance by stepping on your skinnections, which way do you fall?"

"Huh?"

"Do you fall away from the men, or do you fall toward them?"

"Toward them," he said without hesitation.

"And that is why you've been hitting so many people?"

The man raised his voice. "They had it coming. They tried to hurt me by stepping on my skinnections."

"I see. Thank you." With the patient sitting before him, Whitney turned to the nurse and the guard. "It's very important for Mr. Delahunt to take care of his skinnections until they go away. This is what we need to do.

"First, let him take a shower with the lights out. That way his skinnections won't become visible. But under no circumstances should he be forced to shower, even in the dark, if he doesn't want to."

The patient stopped tapping his feet. "Second," continued Whitney, "give him extra underclothing, as much as he wants, every morning. That way he can stay more covered up, and people won't be able to step on his skinnections so easily.

"Third, I want everyone to address him by his last name only." He turned again to face the patient. "And you, Mr. Delahunt, I want you to call everyone here, including the other patients, by their last names.

"Follow these directions for the next month, and I believe Mr. Delahunt's skinnections will fade away. And that should cut down on the number of fights he gets into."

The patient appeared less anxious. He was ushered out of the room, and Whitney and the others rejoined the rest of the staff.

"Now," said Whitney, "are there any questions?"

The occupational therapist raised her hand. "Dr. Whitney, maybe this is a silly question, but what in the world are skinnections?"

Whitney laughed good-naturedly. "No, I don't think you're being silly at all. What we have here is a classical case of paranoia." He glanced toward Anna. "Dr. Roth, you're our expert on paranoid disorders. Would you care to comment?"

Anna hesitated. Was he trying to catch her off guard, to embarrass her in front of the others? "Dr. Whitney is correct," she said. "This case illustrates the typical homosexual aspect described by Freud in his famous report on Shreber. The patient uses repression and projection to deal with his latent homosexual conflicts."

Anna saw the confused look on the other faces. Whitney smiled briefly. *He's laughing at me*, she thought. *The bastard is laughing at me.*

"Simply stated," Whitney said, "this is how it works. He's unconsciously attracted to another man. His unconscious says, 'I love him.' But this is an unacceptable idea, so he turns it around and imagines that the other person is trying to seduce *him*. And then he attacks that other person. He thinks he's using justifiable force to combat someone else's evil intentions. But it's all delusional, of course."

The occupational therapist spoke again. "But what about the skinnections?"

"Frankly," said Whitney, "I can't say for sure what they are. It's a word he made up in his psychosis. It probably stands for 'skin extensions' or 'skin connections.' He panics in the shower, standing there naked with other men. He doesn't want his homosexual desires to 'become visible.' And out in the yard, when he's attracted to the other men, he imagines *they're* pulling *him* toward them by stepping on the skinnections. He's interpreting everything in a delusional way because he can't come to grips with his own feelings.

"The problem is, he feels very vulnerable when he gets locked up in close quarters with so many men. That's why he gets these skinnections in jail. So everyone should call him by his last name, and let him wear extra underwear. He needs to feel a little more distance from people. Otherwise he'll think they're seducing him, and he'll attack. Hopefully, after he feels a little less threatened, he'll become less delusional."

Moments later the crowd dispersed. Anna turned to leave, but Whitney caught up to her and touched her softly on her arm. "Thank you for coming today, Anna. I really value your help."

"Don't patronize me," she hissed as she pushed his hand away.

"But Anna—"

"Don't ever patronize me again!"

*   *   *

140

Anna and Nurse Ellen Tellmark completed their first interview with the new patient on the NGRI unit. They watched Cardonick walk down the hall as if he didn't have a care in the world.

The nurse closed Cardonick's chart and placed it in the designated slot beside her desk. "I guess if I were in his position, I'd be pretty happy, too."

Anna was still watching the patient. "I'm sorry, what was that?"

"I said he must be pretty relieved to be here, considering where he could have wound up. It says in the paper he could have gotten three consecutive life sentences in prison. Plus fifty years on top of that. If he'd been found guilty, that is."

"Yes," replied the psychiatrist. "If."

"I never could understand that at all."

"I know. It should be 'guilty but insane' instead of 'not guilty by reason of insanity.'" It was an issue she and Whitney would never be able to agree on.

"No, no. I mean, I never could understand what they mean by 'consecutive life sentences.' I mean, how would you like to be someone's cell-mate while he was serving the second life sentence?" She held her nose. "Phew!"

Anna laughed softly. She rubbed the ragged numbers imprinted on her wrist. Sometimes she felt as though Littleton were her second life sentence.

Cardonick returned to the room he was sharing with three other patients. The other men were outside in the yard. His property had just been sent to the ward from the Evaluation Building. He began unpacking the small carton: toiletries, two harmonicas, a drawing his daughter had sent to him, and a faded photograph in its tarnished frame.

He remembered that day in family court many years earlier. He was just thirteen and his father had been sentenced to prison for beating him senseless. The psychiatrist from the Department of Social Services told the judge that the boy's home was too unstable for him. Young Gordon was at risk for grave permanent psychological damage, said the doctor, and it was recommended that the DSS be given custody of him. The judge so ordered.

The boy was escorted from the hearing room by a court officer. The frail woman in the first row moaned and shrieked. She ran to the boy's side and pressed the photograph into his hand. Later in the week her dead body was discovered chained to her car in a fume-filled garage.

Cardonick had framed the photo, and he'd kept it with him ever since. Now he placed it on the shelf next to the bed that had been assigned to him. He read its inscription. *I love you. Remember me always.*

He thought, *Fucking psychiatrists. They're all the same.*

He walked to the laundry room to get clean bedclothes. When he returned to his room an elderly patient was tossing the photograph between his hands and smiling. "Hey, man," said the patient, "who's this fine-lookin' bitch?"

Cardonick pounced on the man in a frenzy, screaming, "That's my mother, you cocksucker!" and ramming the man's head against the wall again and again.

The older man's tongue folded back into his throat, and he went into convulsions. Cardonick continued to pummel the man's torso.

Alerted by the commotion, three guards pulled Cardonick off his victim, spun him around, and whisked him into a seclusion room.

When he was released from the room two hours later, Cardonick approached the man he'd beaten. "If you ever touch that picture again," he hissed in the man's ear, "I'll kill you."

PART TWO

T he sun was setting in the west, a half-moon visible in the eastern sky. A heavy July haze hung over Veterans Stadium as Schacter and Whitney walked across the parking lot.

"Say, Stan, isn't this where Gordon Cardonick was captured last Christmas Eve?"

"Out that way, toward the centerfield side of the ballpark. How's he doing, anyway? Doesn't his commitment period end soon?"

Whitney performed the calculation mentally. "It expires in about six weeks, around the middle of August."

"Then what?"

"Well, he's on a ward for men who get found NGRI, so he's under the care of Dr. Roth, the psychiatrist who administers that ward. I assume she's going to recommend recommitment, but I haven't looked into the situation lately. You know, Stan, it's been almost five months since his trial, and I still get mail about that case. Some of it's pretty nasty."

Schacter grunted. "Well, I guess the only people who'd bother writing to a total stranger are the ones who are pissed off about something."

"Probably," said Whitney. "Which reminds me. I received another one of these yesterday. Thought you should take a look at it."

Schacter recognized the handwriting on the envelope. He read:

July 4, 1983

Dear Thomas,

THE DEADLY CONVICTION:
A BIRTHDAY POEM FOR THE NEW SUPERINTENDENT

Nobody is perfect or even comes close
Although some people think that they may be
So listen my children and you shall hear
Of the future late Thomas A. Whitney

There are sins of commission, mistakes of omission
And many a wrongful prediction
But if you should think that you're free from me now—
That's your deadliest Deadly Conviction.

Many happy returns!
A.I.T.S.D. (AMEN IN THY SLOW DEATH.)

> *Your friend,*
> *The Phoenix*

Schacter grunted. "Any ideas yet on who could be sending these?" Whitney shook his head.

They made their way through the turnstile. Whitney bought a program and Schacter purchased a beer for himself and a Coke for his friend.

Schacter paused in his tracks and glanced around at the massive steel and concrete structure. "I just can't warm up to this place," he said. "It's nothing like the old ballpark, Connie Mack Stadium. This place just looks so damn sterile. And that plastic crap they play on these days—give me grass anytime."

Schacter handed the letter back to Whitney. "I'm sorry about all of this, Thomas."

"I know. It's not your fault, Stan." Whitney forced himself to smile. "Come on, old man," he chided. "Let's get to our seats before the seventh inning stretch."

22

Shortly before noon Whitney walked into a self-service cafeteria near the corner of Broad and Chestnut Streets. It was nearly empty when he arrived, but the workers from nearby Center City office buildings quickly filled it at the lunch hour. He buried his face in the morning paper.

It was a chance meeting, or at least he thought it was. Later it would occur to him that he knew where she worked, and that it wouldn't have been difficult to guess where she ate lunch. (*The unconscious works in strange and wondrous ways,* he would think.) But at the time it seemed entirely coincidental that he should run into her there.

"Excuse me, sir," she said. "Would you pass me the salt?"

He reached for the condiment tray. When he was younger he enjoyed being called "sir." But now he hated it. It made him feel old, especially when it came from someone as young and beautiful as—

"Oh! Dr. Whitney."

He fumbled with the tray nervously. "Hello, Mrs. Cardonick." Suddenly he became self-conscious about his appearance. He tugged on the collar of his shirt and brushed back a strand of hair that had fallen across his forehead.

"It's so nice to see you again," she said. Her genial manner was more that of a forgotten friend than of someone he had known only in his professional capacity.

Whitney, like most in his line of work, had a standing rule about chance meetings with patients: he kept them as innocuous as possible and terminated them as quickly as he could. Otherwise they would render the treatment needlessly, perhaps hopelessly impaired. But

Denise wasn't his patient. Nor was her husband, for that matter; Whitney's evaluation of Gordon Cardonick had been a one-time matter.

"You know," said Denise, "I've thought about you a lot since we had our meetings in February. You made it easier for me to get through a very difficult time."

"Only doing my job." He smiled and looked away. He'd never been able to accept a compliment without feeling slightly embarrassed.

"Maybe," she said. "But, just the same, thanks. I almost called you once just to say that. But I felt strange, like that was against the rules or something." She laughed. "I've heard you psychiatrists can be funny that way. I thought you might even hang up on me."

"I see," he said.

"Would you?"

"Excuse me?" he said.

"If I called you, would you hang up?"

He sensed a certain coquettishness in her manner. "Do I seem like someone who would?"

"Now, isn't that just like a psychiatrist," she laughed. "Answer a question with a question. All right, I'll let you off the hook on that one."

They finished their meals and left the cafeteria together. "Which way are you walking?" she asked.

"That way," he said, pointing west down Chestnut Street.

"Me, too. We can walk together."

He could have sworn the law office where she worked was in a northerly direction, farther up Broad Street. "Oh, I just remembered. I need to attend to some business this way." He pointed east.

She frowned. "What a shame. Well, it was very nice seeing you again."

He headed east, not because he didn't want to walk with her, but because he was frightened of how much he wanted to.

There was an occasional rumble of static on the telephone line. Each time he heard it Whitney imagined waves breaking over the cables stretching from Rockland to East Haven across the bottom of Penobscot Bay.

"Hello, Mother. How are you?"

"Thomas! What a lovely surprise. So good to hear from you."

"How are things in Maine, Mother?"

148

"Marvelous, Thomas. Simply marvelous. The summer people have all arrived. I had lunch with the Putnams the other day. They asked to be remembered to you, of course. And your Aunt Jane is coming up next week to spend the month in one of the guest houses."

They talked idly for a few minutes more. It was his obligatory monthly call.

"Mother, by any chance have you checked up on the carriage house?"

"For goodness' sake, Thomas. I never go all the way back there, you know that. The building's been boarded up for almost twenty years now, ever since you stopped coming up regularly. Whatever made you ask about it?"

He thought about Marlene Dietz, about the summer he turned eighteen, and he felt very old. "Oh, I don't know, Mother. Nothing really, I guess."

"Yes, well, remember now. You promised to come up around Labor Day weekend to help close the place for the winter."

"I know, Mother. I won't forget. Good-bye. And send my love to Aunt Jane."

"Ah, yes, Aunt Jane. She'll be coming up for a visit next week."

"Yes, I know. Good-bye, now."

"Good-bye, Thomas."

He held on to the receiver after she hung up. He closed his eyes and listened to the static. In his mind he could still see Marlene's ferry pushing off from the dock on East Haven Island.

23

Malzone felt as though he were spending half of his waking hours writing letters.

He was overjoyed when Whitney was appointed to the superintendent position. Malzone had been passed by once before—in favor of Whitney—for the position as director of forensic evaluation. He believed it couldn't happen again.

He was wrong.

Whitney turned the director's position over to Manuel Guadalupe, a Mexican-born psychologist—*a goddamn psychologist*—who had just completed his postdoctoral training. "I'm really going to need your help, Ralph," Whitney had said. "We're creating a new position. I'd like you to become Littleton's first deputy superintendent."

The job sounded more prestigious than it was. Each morning he met with Whitney to review the scheduled events of the day. Then Whitney would hand him a folder of paperwork and say, "Take care of these for me, would you, Ralph?" More often than not Malzone's work was an exercise in triviality. He felt, once again, as though he were little more than a glorified chief secretary.

The first matter in his folder this particular morning was a letter written in the jagged cursive style of an elderly man with a chronic psychomotor tremor. It was addressed to the man who'd been replaced as superintendent in 1961 by Percy Osborne:

150

July 7, 1983
Samuel Carvel
Littleton Institute for the Criminally Insane
Littleton, Pennsylvania

Dear Sir:
I request that you send me written confirmation that I was incarcerated at the Institute for the Criminally Insane from November 1959 until January 1962.

And that you recognized that I was completely sane and that I was the victim of false imprisonment.

And that I was being secretly openly electronically monitored by a number of electronic medical scientist doctor federal investigators who in 1983 continue to monitor me.

And that you heard by ear the electronic buzz noise of the secret activity of the electronic medical scientist doctor federal investigators.

I need this information for a lawsuit I am filing against the electronic medical scientist doctor federal investigators.

Very truly yours,
Chester A. Hickey
Rolling Hill Nursing Home
Kerryville, Pennsylvania

Malzone rolled the letter into a tight ball and threw it toward the wastebasket in the corner of his cramped office. The paper wad ricocheted off the front rim and fell to the floor. He left it there and turned to the next item. It was a letter to Whitney from the Pennsylvania commissioner of human services.

Dear Dr. Whitney:
The Governor has instructed me personally to investigate this matter (see enclosure) and to report my findings to him.
Please submit a memo to me on this case.

Malzone read the enclosure.

Dear Mr. Governor:
My name is Frederick T. Osterman. I am serving a state prison sentence for armed robbery. In April of this year I was

taken from prison and unjustly committed to Building One at Littleton State Hospital.

I am writing concerning the substandard medical care I am receiving at that hospital. I am in desperate need of assistance. My left knee suffers from a serious gunshot wound. I have gone untreated for the entire length of my stay at Littleton.

In addition to my severe pain there is the risk of serious infection. Furthermore, I have difficulty walking. When the inmates from Building One are told to line up, I frequently arrive late. Consequently I am often disciplined unfairly for a condition that is beyond my control.

My condition is quite visible to the naked eye. I would be grateful if you would instruct the staff of Littleton State Hospital to attend immediately to my medical needs.

Malzone spent the next two hours reading the patient's chart, interviewing him, and talking with the staff of Building One. He drafted his reply.

Dear Mr. Commissioner:

The Superintendent has instructed me personally to investigate this matter and to report my findings to you.

Mr. Osterman is a twenty-six-year-old man with a history of multiple hospitalizations for psychiatric disorders.

On April 11, 1983, he was transferred from prison to Littleton State Hospital. He appeared acutely confused and complained that he had a "bullet from God" embedded in his knee. He did present with significant redness of his patellar (kneecap) area.

Five days later he was seen ambulating across the yard on his hands and knees. Several notes in his chart indicate that he "walks around like a horse."

Mr. Osterman steadfastly refuses to take the antipsychotic medication that has been prescribed for him. Thus he is correct in stating that "I have gone untreated for the entire length of my stay at Littleton."

Upon examination by myself on this date, Mr. Osterman appeared grossly disorganized and incoherent (his well-worded letter to the Governor notwithstanding).

*When asked if he would consent to be interviewed, he stated:
"The incitedment of the resilient as the side of response has
long been realized as the contradiction of the reality, related
to the cimchinual of captivity. The allowance is mobile. The
exposition of idealisms and the revelation of wholesomeness of
the validity, I'd be most cooperative."*

*When I asked him how long he had been at Littleton State
Hospital, he replied: "Since the invasion of trenology."*

*He described the circumstances of his admission thusly: "Being
entwoned, trabounded, engaged, and woven of the movements
against reality. That's like going to dams and sandies in one
ballestrian response. I hope they get the shrong back and keep
it in the well a long time."*

*According to staff on his ward, in recent weeks he has
suffered from a notable exacerbation of his religious delusions,
paranoid fears, and auditory hallucinations that revolve around
his loud conversations with God and the devil.*

*A complete set of medical tests has been completed. Our
diagnosis is patellar bursitis, most likely caused by incessant
praying on his knees.*

Malzone gave his work to Whitney's secretary for transcription. One
of these days, he thought, *I'll tell him what he can do with his letters.* He
decided he'd earned a prolonged lunch break.

H er voice was sweet and warm over the telephone. "You told me you wouldn't hang up on me," she said.

"Pardon me?" replied Whitney.

"That day I bumped into you at the cafeteria in Center City," said Denise. "I told you I'd been thinking of calling you, and you said you wouldn't hang up on me."

"Oh, right. Of course not. How can I help you?"

She sighed. "I'm confused about Gordon. I've been visiting him at the hospital, and he really seems different. I mean, he really seems to care about me now, more than he ever did before. I just don't know what to do—don't know if I should keep seeing him, keep getting closer to him. Or if I should try to go out with other men. I haven't been doing that, you know."

"Doing what?"

"I haven't been going out with other men."

"I see." He was embarrassed to hear this, although he wasn't sure why.

"Anyway," she continued, "I was wondering if I could see you sometime—anytime—tomorrow. I was planning on coming out to Littleton to visit Gordon, and if it wouldn't be too much trouble..."

"No, no trouble at all. I'd be happy to talk with you. Shall we say two o'clock?"

"Thank you, Doctor. I'll see you then. Good-bye."

Whitney wrote her name in his appointment book in large, red letters, then circled it a half dozen times.

* * *

"I thought you'd want to know about this right away, Doc."

"Yes, thank you," replied Whitney. "Sit down, Bob. Please."

Robert Blodgett, chief guard at Littleton State Hospital, chomped down on his unlit Parodi. Blodgett always had one of the crooked little cigars in his mouth, but Whitney had never seen him actually light and smoke one.

"All right, Bob. Run the whole thing by me. When did this fellow show up?"

"About forty minutes ago. Teddy Green, one of the guards in the visitors' area, recognized him and thought it was pretty odd for him to be here. Teddy decided to check it out with me to see if we should let him in. And then I realized who it was he wanted to visit, and I put two and two together, and I figured I'd better clear it with you before I let him see the patient."

"Has he ever tried to visit anyone at Littleton before?"

Blodgett sucked on the end of his cigar. "Not to my knowledge, Doc."

Whitney drummed his fingers along the arm of his chair. "What's he like?"

"Well, he was none too pleased when I wouldn't let him see the patient right away, I can tell you that. He was a little scary, too. Had this real intense look on his face and said something about the Governor hearing about it. I couldn't quite catch what he said."

"Where is he now?"

"I had him wait with your receptionist. Thought you might want to talk to him yourself. Here, he brought this with him. Says he received it last week."

Whitney read the handwritten letter.

July 2

Dear Reverend Isaac,

Thank you for your prayers. Thank you for your forgiveness.

One of my friends here told me I should listen to your broadcast. At first I was frightened when I heard you speak my name. I thought my illness was returning and that voices were communicating with me over the radio. But my friend tells me that you have been praying for me regularly. I don't know how I can ever repay you.

When I first got here I was filled with hatred. I felt tormented and abused by the universe. I had no faith. I cursed the day I was born and the God who had allowed me to suffer so. Often I felt like killing the guards who watched over me and the doctors who were keeping me here. I felt especially murderous toward the other patients. But I didn't know why.

They assigned me to a job cleaning the bathroom on my ward. Many of the patients are too mentally ill to understand what they are doing. Frequently one finds human waste on the floor. One man sometimes crawls around like a dog and drinks water out of the toilet bowl. Toilets get stuffed to overflowing with thick balls of used bathroom tissue. And if we use up the week's allotment of toilet paper too soon—a not infrequent occurrence—some patients use towels and underwear to wipe themselves, then toss them on the bathroom floor.

I found the job totally disgusting.

Then one afternoon I was cleaning a toilet, repulsed by the filth around me, bemoaning the fact that the path of my life had culminated in that place. I heard a man in the next stall. He was talking to himself. I recognized the voice. Perhaps you have heard of him: his name is Bunker Tomlinson, and, at the time, he was awaiting trial for raping three little girls. (He left here recently, got convicted, and is doing a very long sentence in prison.) Everyone on the ward hated him.

Anyway, as I sat there hating Tomlinson, hating Littleton, hating each and every person responsible for putting me here, I realized that Tomlinson was crying and praying. He was asking the Lord to forgive him. Then he was silent. I heard a gurgling sound. Suddenly I felt like I was choking. There was a painful tightening around my throat, like something was pressing in on it from all sides. I felt dizzy. I stumbled out of my stall and knocked open the door of Tomlinson's stall. His shoelaces were wrapped around his neck and he was hanging from the crossbar on top of the stall. His legs and arms were thrashing wildly.

He looked so weak and helpless. For a moment I stood there, paralyzed from fear. And then I realized why I had hated him, why I had hated all of the patients: they reminded me of my own despicable self.

I crouched underneath Tomlinson and then stood up. I supported the weight of his body with my head and shoulders so the pressure on his neck would ease. My forehead felt wet and hot: urine was dripping down his pants leg. I didn't care. I managed to untie the shoelaces from the crossbar. I don't know how long it took. I did all of this without thinking. Surely the Lord was guiding me.

We tumbled together to the floor. Tomlinson gasped for air for several moments. Then we prayed together.

I know now that I had no cause to despise my own life or have contempt for others. Each life, no matter how short or small, was created by God and put here to serve His purpose.

If I had never been born, Bunker Tomlinson would be dead and your lovely little girl would still be alive. I do not pretend to understand how all of this computes in the Lord's cosmic calculus. I pray He will help me find the answer.

I earn $1.50 per day doing my janitorial job. It now seems like God's blessing, and I would like to use the money for God's work. Please accept the enclosed donation for your church.

Again, thank you for your prayers. They make me strong. Perhaps one day you can forgive me enough to pray with me at Littleton.

Yours in faith,
Gordon Cardonick

Whitney frowned as he replaced the letter in its envelope. "What do you think, Bob?"

"Gee, Doc. I know this guy Cardonick was found NGRI, but that sure sounds like a con talking to me."

"What do you mean?"

"I can't put my finger on it, but I think that whole letter is just one long piece of bull. I haven't met this Cardonick, but already I don't like him."

"Yes," the superintendent replied. Whitney could develop some degree of rapport, however tentative or minuscule, with nearly any patient he evaluated. Usually only the most incoherent schizophrenics and malevolent psychopaths could squelch his natural inclination to feel sympathetic. Cardonick had managed to squelch that inclination.

Blodgett led the visitor into Whitney's office. "Dr. Thomas Whitney, this is—"

"Dr. Whitney! This is an unexpected pleasure." The preacher beamed from ear to ear. His large, jagged teeth looked snow-white against his very black skin. "I'm Isaac Hopkins." With two gigantic strides he had crossed the office and was pumping Whitney's hand before the doctor realized what was happening.

"Hello, Mr. Hopkins."

"Please, Doctor, it's Isaac, or Reverend Isaac, whichever you prefer."

"Yes, well, Mr. Hopkins, I understand you'd like to meet with Gordon Cardonick."

"As I was telling this gentleman over here," continued Reverend Isaac as he gestured toward Blodgett, "the good Lord can still surprise me. If you had told me last week that I'd be sitting here today, I...well, I'm sure you understand."

The man's pupils were so wide they appeared to dominate his entire face. His eyes were trained on Whitney's. They didn't move away, even for a moment. It gave his countenance an eerie, transfixing quality.

"Yes, I think I do," said Whitney. "It must have been awful to lose your daughter to such a horribly senseless act."

The preacher spread his palms upward. "I try not to judge what is and what isn't senseless." He gestured toward the ceiling with his head, but he never took his eyes off Whitney. "I let Him be the arbiter of everything."

"I see. Well, please don't take offense, but I wonder if you've really thought this through completely. It hasn't been all that long since...since your terrible loss. And Mr. Cardonick was the cause, even if he was insane at the time. Are you sure you want to rip open those wounds all over again?"

Blodgett listened carefully. He had another concern entirely: He didn't want an ugly scene in the visiting area. For all he knew Reverend Isaac wanted some sort of confrontation. Perhaps he even intended to attack Cardonick. Anything was possible (although the preacher had been searched and had passed through a metal detector as all visitors did).

Reverend Isaac stared intensely at the superintendent. "Dr. Whitney, I didn't ask to have my daughter taken from me. I didn't ask to have Mr. Cardonick write to me. Something greater than either of us has brought me here. I truly believe that. 'Forgive thine enemies.' The Lord is testing me to see if I'm a worthy shepherd of His flock. Please," he said, his voice suddenly dropping to a whisper, "let me forgive my enemy."

They sat in silence for several moments. Whitney escorted him to the door. "If you'll be good enough to wait in the reception area, I'll contact Mr. Cardonick's doctor to discuss the matter with her. We wouldn't want to create a situation that the patient might not be capable of withstanding."

"I understand, Doctor. Thank you." The preacher left the room.

Whitney turned to Blodgett. "Well, Bob? What do you think?"

The chief guard whistled softly between his front teeth. "It gives me the creeps, Doc. Guys like this—these true believers—I just have a hard time dealing with them, that's all. They give me the willies."

"I know what you mean," said Whitney. "A few years ago I read about a fundamentalist minister who had his own Bible college somewhere in the Midwest. As you might imagine, it was a very conservative place. He was especially outspoken about the evils of premarital sex and the sinfulness of homosexuality. He had very strict regulations about the mingling of male and female students. Then one day he performed the marriage ceremony for two of his prize pupils. On the wedding night the bride confessed to her husband that the minister had been sharing her bed for two months. And then the groom confessed that the minister had been sharing *his* bed for two *years*."

"I guess it takes all kinds," said Blodgett. "So what are you going to do? Do you want me to let this guy in to see Cardonick?"

"The way I see it, Bob, we really don't have a choice. I share your uneasiness. But I can just see the headlines—and believe me, people like this always know how to get headlines. 'Doctor Prevents Patient from Seeing Minister.' 'Mission of Forgiveness Foiled by Mental Hospital.' Publicity like that could really disrupt treatment for the other patients and would give us a lot of unnecessary public relations problems. Now, if Dr. Roth tells me that Mr. Cardonick can't tolerate such a visit, then I'll certainly keep Reverend Isaac out as long as I can. I don't think she'll say that, but not for the same reasons I've just described."

Whitney was right about Anna Roth, of course. "You know how I feel about such things," she lectured him over the phone. "People are responsible for the choices they make." She seemed to lean hard on the word *responsible*. "If Mr. Cardonick wishes to receive the visit, and if Mr. Blodgett has no objections for reasons of security, then I have no right to intercede. Perhaps I might feel differently if Mr. Cardonick were severely psychotic, but he's not."

"Oh?"

"No, his psychotic symptoms responded quite well to treatment. In fact, he's been off all medication for many weeks now."

"I see. Thank you." He hung up. *Damn.* Whitney looked at the other man. "Well, Bob. Looks like Reverend Isaac Hopkins gets to pray with the man who killed his little girl."

Chief Guard Blodgett escorted Reverend Isaac to the visitors' room. Whitney had instructed Blodgett to monitor the visit personally and to report back to him.

"Do you pray, Mr. Blodgett?" the self-styled clergyman asked as they walked briskly through the hall.

The guard chomped on his unlit cigar. "Excuse me?" he replied.

"I just thought that you might want to join Mr. Cardonick and myself in prayer."

They reached the visitors' room. Blodgett halted outside the door. "No, I don't think so, Reverend." He smiled, then added, "I make it a habit never to drink or pray on work time."

"Yes, I understand." Reverend Isaac's deeply set eyes were piercing. He opened his suit jacket and produced a small pamphlet. "I'd be pleased if you'd accept this prayer booklet. I wrote it myself. We send it to people who make donations to our radio crusade."

Blodgett pocketed the pamphlet without looking at it. He held the door open and the two men entered the room.

A long screen barrier ran from wall to wall, bisecting the room. Each side of the room had its own entrance. A few patients were sitting at small tables on one side of the screen. Their visitors sat at tables opposite them. Two guards sat on the patients' side of the room. They were available in case of a disturbance, but otherwise keeping an unobtrusive presence, reading newspapers.

The chief guard showed Reverend Isaac to a seat. Then he exited the room and returned through the entrance on the patients' side. Blodgett relieved one of his underlings—much to that guard's surprise—and waited for Cardonick to appear.

One of the patients in the room stood and moved toward the exit. The man had the gait of a chronic patient: a slow, rigid shuffle, with his arms straight and motionless. His facial expression was wooden. He stared straight ahead, barely blinking, as if his brain had been switched off. Blodgett thought there was something missing in the man, something quintessentially human: the ability to form an emotional connection with other humans.

The patient walked stiffly through the door, almost getting bowled over by Cardonick striding through the door.

Cardonick looked around the room, humming softly to himself as he surveyed the scene. Blodgett saw Reverend Isaac stiffen slightly and push his chair a few inches farther away from the screen.

Cardonick came to the empty chair opposite Reverend Isaac. The visitor stood to greet him, and the two men stared at each other for a moment without speaking. "Reverend Isaac, I'm honored to see you." Cardonick smiled. "You'll have to excuse me for not shaking your hand," he said as he gestured toward the dividing screen.

The two men sat simultaneously. Reverend Isaac fumbled nervously inside his suit jacket and produced one of his prayer booklets. He looked past Cardonick at the chief guard. "Mr. Blodgett, would you lend your booklet to Gordon so we can pray together?"

"That isn't necessary," Cardonick told his visitor. He reached around to his rear pants pocket. "I have my own copy right here."

Reverend Isaac flipped quickly through the pages of his booklet. "Page twelve. Let us pray. 'Dear Lord, help me to fulfill your commandments here on earth . . .'"

Blodgett listened as the two men read together. Reverend Isaac spoke in a tremulous whisper; Cardonick's tones were full and steady. After they were finished, the clergyman bowed his head and sighed.

"I listen to your radio program every Sunday," Cardonick said. "I've even gotten a group of patients together, and we pray with you every week. I tell them that prayer is the most powerful medicine they can take." He smiled. "Thank you for coming, Reverend. I can't begin to tell you how much it means to me."

Reverend Isaac sat upright and spoke directly to Cardonick for the first time. "It's I who should thank you, Gordon. You've invited me here to pass the Lord's greatest test of me."

"I know it's too much to ask for your forgiveness, Reverend. But I want you to know how sorry I am for what I've done. Mental illness is an awful thing, a horrible thing, but seeing you here gives me faith that I'm gonna beat it." He leaned toward the clergyman and placed his palm against the screen. "Yes, I'm gonna beat this thing, and sooner than any doctor would have thought."

Reverend Isaac sat upright and placed his own hand against the screen, opposite Cardonick's. The clergyman buried his face in his other hand and began to weep. Cardonick smiled as if he hadn't a care in the world.

It was the hottest day of the year,
and none of the buildings at Littleton State Hospital were air-conditioned.
A small window fan stirred the humid air in Whitney's office. His radio
was set to an easy-listening station; a newscaster reported that the high
demand for power was causing brownouts in several Delaware Valley
communities.

Perspiration seeped through Whitney's shirt, sticking him to the back
of his swivel chair. Periodic blasts of air from the fan cooled his
perspiration and sent a shiver through him.

Denise looked unaffected by the weather. Her blonde hair was set off
by the deep bronze of her suntanned face. A cotton chemise hung
loosely on her slender body. Whenever she leaned forward, Whitney
caught a glimpse of her body through the chemise's armholes.

"I took the day off from work," she said. "Mr. Jason lets me keep a
pretty flexible schedule."

She leaned back in her chair, tightening the fabric of her chemise
against her torso, exposing ever so slightly her supple shape.

"He's been so good to me," she continued. "He's a very nice man.
He's a widower, and his children are all grown, and sometimes I think
he treats me like a daughter. No matter what I go to him with, he takes
it in stride."

Whitney poured two glasses of ice water from a pitcher on his desk.
She reached for one of the glasses and sipped from it. "Thank you for
letting me see you, Doctor. I want to talk to you about Gordon. I have
a lot of questions."

"Yes, of course. Have you spoken to Dr. Roth? Your husband has been under her care since February, and she may be able to answer some of your questions better than I can."

"But you were the doctor who evaluated him. I guess I should have asked these questions back then, but I tried to put it all out of my mind. But Gordon is coming up for recommitment soon, and I've been thinking a lot about what you said at the trial."

"I see." He lifted his glass. The coaster stuck to its bottom. He peeled it off and dropped it back onto his desk.

"I wrote my questions down." She searched through her purse and pulled out a neatly folded piece of paper. "Okay, here it is. 'Major depression with mood-congruent psychotic features.' That's what you called him at the trial."

"That was my diagnosis, yes."

"Tell me, Doctor. Is he going to be insane for the rest of his life?"

Whitney smiled. "Hardly. You see, Mrs. Cardonick, anybody—you, me, your Mr. Jason—anybody can lose his hold on reality if he's put under enough pressure. Each person has his own breaking point. Some people can withstand a lot of stress, others crack more easily. Your husband isn't going to remain chronically psychotic, but he is more susceptible to periodic breakdowns than most folks are."

She frowned. "But that would mean he'll need treatment forever, wouldn't it?"

"Possibly."

"At Littleton?"

"No, I don't think that's very likely. In this sort of case, treatment is usually switched to an outpatient setting, such as a community clinic or a psychiatrist's office, after a period of observation and treatment in the hospital."

"How long do you think Gordon will be hospitalized, Doctor?"

Whitney squirmed in his chair, his discomfort from the heat compounded by his reluctance to speculate about the length of Cardonick's stay at Littleton. "I'm sorry. These things are hard to predict. Dr. Roth might be in a better position to comment about that."

"Oh." She folded her paper and gazed at the ceiling for a moment. "After Gordon leaves the hospital, then what?"

"Excuse me?"

"After Gordon is released from the hospital, whenever that is, what kind of parole will he be on? I mean, what agency watches over him, who does he have to report to?"

"Ah," sighed Whitney, "that's the $64,000 Question."

"I don't understand."

"Parole only applies to people found guilty," the psychiatrist explained. "They get released after serving a portion of their sentences, and then they remain under the court's control—on parole—for the rest of those sentences."

"What about somebody who's found not guilty by reason of insanity?"

"Nothing," said Whitney, a look of mild disgust crossing his face. "When your husband leaves Littleton State Hospital, he's totally free. No conditions of release, no one to check in with, no obligation to remain in treatment. Nothing."

"Oh, my." A look of alarm spread quickly across her face.

"That's why doctors and judges are very conservative with patients like your husband. They'll want to take a long, hard look at him, probably several years' worth, before they take a chance on recommending his release."

Denise looked down at the floor. "That's strange," she mumbled.

"Excuse me?"

"I was just wondering how much of this Gordon knows. He's going to have another hearing next month, and do you know what he thinks? He tells me he'll be getting out soon. And he really seems to believe it."

Whitney couldn't imagine that Anna Roth would recommend Cardonick's release so soon after the killings. And he had even more trouble picturing a judge assenting to such a recommendation. He made a mental note to call Anna and ask her what she was planning to say at Cardonick's recommitment hearing.

Denise walked to the window and looked out across the hospital grounds. "I wonder why he seems so certain that the judge is going to release him. Even I can see that it's impossible."

Whitney couldn't tell whether she was pleased or troubled by the idea of Cardonick being recommitted. "Yes," he agreed, "you're right. Sometimes people fight against depression by developing unrealistic hopes. Perhaps that's what your husband is doing."

Denise held her hands in front of the fan, then turned around to face him. "Do you remember when I told you about Rollie?"

"Rollie?"

"Yeah. Rollie Plotkin, the older boy who dated me before I met Gordon."

Whitney nodded his head.

"Anyway," she continued, "he's Dr. Rollie Plotkin now. I went to his office last week. He's an internist over in Glenside."

"Oh?"

"I haven't seen him in years, since high school, actually. He just moved back to Philadelphia last year after his training."

"He must have been pleased to see you."

"Oh, I didn't see him. I just went to his office. I got there before him on purpose. I spoke to his receptionist, gave her a false name, pretended I wanted to make an appointment for later in the month. She gave me an appointment card, and I dawdled in the waiting area for a few minutes. Then she left her desk for a second and—this is so embarrassing—I sneaked into his private office."

She searched Whitney's face as if she were looking for a clue to his reaction. "Doesn't that sound horrible?" she asked.

He smiled. "Tell me more."

"I sat down in his chair. It was soft, very plush, and it came all the way around me. It felt so nice to be there. I ran my hands along its sides and I looked around the office. I saw all his diplomas. Then I saw a picture of him and his wife with two little boys. They looked very happy together. And I started to cry."

She walked toward him. There were tears in her eyes. "I just wanted . . . I wondered what it would be like to be with someone who cared for me, someone who wanted to make me happy. I don't think I've ever really been happy." She sat down. "I passed his receptionist on my way out, told her I'd taken a wrong turn. I wonder if she saw me crying."

Whitney was moved by her vulnerability. For a moment he wished he could touch her arm, stroke her hair, tell her that she deserved to be as happy as she wanted to be. "Why do you suppose you looked him up after so many years?"

She tried to smile. "I guess because of what Gordon said about getting released real soon. It scared me. But I haven't even gone through with a divorce. I feel like I'm in limbo somewhere, stuck between a dream I can't have and a reality I can't avoid."

"Can't avoid?"

"Gordon. Gordon gets what he wants. I don't know why he wants me, but he does. Maybe I was hoping Rollie would take me away from Gordon. I don't know. I really don't know why I went there."

The whirring of Whitney's window fan was the only sound in the room for a minute or two. Suddenly Denise threw back her head and laughed. "I'm sorry, Doctor. I just realized how funny this is."

"Oh?"

"Well, I told you I was here to ask about Gordon, but I guess I really came to ask you something about myself."

"And what was that?"

She stared earnestly at him. "What do you think I should do, Doctor? Should I wait for Gordon? Is that the best I can hope for?"

Whitney looked at her for a long time. Try as he might, he couldn't entirely avoid her questioning eyes. "You're a fine person," he said. "Any man would be happy to be with you. You just need to decide what *you* want."

Denise nervously twirled one of her blonde locks between her thumb and forefinger. She laughed and cried at the same time. When she stood to leave, she grabbed impulsively for his hand and squeezed it. Whitney neither drew his hand away nor returned the grasp.

"I'm sorry," she said, and she scurried out of the office.

Whitney stood in the doorway and watched her disappear down the corridor. He was thankful his secretary was on a coffee break, so he could watch Denise unobserved.

His hand still felt warm where she had touched it. He imagined himself running after her, reassuring her, circling her with his arms and drawing her body against his. She wouldn't push him away; he was certain of that.

He realized he'd taken two or three steps down the hall. He sighed, then turned back toward his office. Malzone was leaning against the doorjamb, leering after Denise.

"Hey, Thomas—isn't that Gordon Cardonick's wife?"

Whitney nodded.

Malzone smiled slyly, as if he and Whitney were sharing some lascivious secret. "Why, you old devil, you," he said, and he laughed and slapped Whitney firmly on the back.

Whitney stumbled slightly. He regained his balance, then snapped his forearm sharply into Malzone's rib cage. Malzone fell against the wall, his mouth springing open in surprise. "Jesus Christ, Thomas. What the fuck is your problem?"

"*You're* the problem!" growled Whitney. "Keep your filthy thoughts to yourself." He retreated into his office and slammed the door shut.

27

T he five of them were seated at the lopsided table in Building Three's conference room. "Our main order of business today," said Dr. Anna Roth, chairperson of the meeting, "is a review of Gordon Cardonick's progress."

With her were Harvey Ditweiler, a unit caseworker; Frank Stokey, the ward's chief guard; Ellen Tellmark, the head nurse; and psychologist Georgia Day.

Anna shuffled her papers. "As most of you know, Mr. Cardonick's commitment period is coming to an end on August seventeenth. That's about three weeks away. He'll be returning to court at that time. And, of course, I'll be expected to testify at his hearing. The judge will want to know whether I think Mr. Cardonick should be recommitted."

Anna leafed through Cardonick's chart. "When he was admitted to Littleton," she continued, "he was acutely psychotic and severely depressed. But his psychosis was brought under control quickly. He is no longer taking antipsychotic medication. His depression lifted more gradually, and I discontinued his antidepressant medicine as well. As far as I can tell, Mr. Cardonick shows no current signs of psychosis or depression."

"I know this doesn't happen very often," said Ellen, "but we might be talking about a case of temporary insanity."

"Perhaps," continued Anna. "And when it comes to convincing a judge that a patient still requires hospitalization, those are the most difficult cases. Mr. Cardonick may look as if he has recovered, but we can't forget how seriously ill and dangerous he was just a short time ago.

God knows, seven months isn't a very long time. Speaking of God, I understand our friend Mr. Cardonick has found religion."

"Ugh," said Ditweiler. "You mean that radio preacher, Reverend Isaac."

"Yes." Anna sighed. "I find this aspect of the case most worrisome. I'm disturbed by people who think they speak for God. Men have done horrible things in God's name, and without the slightest sense of guilt or shame. When you're following God's orders you can absolve yourself of responsibility for your actions."

"I get it." Ditweiler chuckled. "NGOG."

"Excuse me?"

"Not Guilty by Order of God."

Anna laughed, and everyone else followed suit. "Ms. Day, I understand Mr. Cardonick is in one of your therapy groups. Would you say he's made any progress there?"

"Well, I notice the changes you referred to earlier. About his psychosis and his depression, that is. In his first month in the group he looked like he was in his own little world. He hardly spoke at all, just sat there with a goofy smile on his face. But now he participates regularly, really gets the group going. He's talked a lot about his problems with drugs, spoken a little bit about times in the past when he felt suicidal. He really uses the therapy sessions very well."

Anna often lost her patience with Georgia. The young psychologist tended to get emotionally overinvolved with the patients, especially the less psychotic ones.

"Has he talked at all about his marital problems, or his mother's suicide, or his violent behavior?" asked Anna.

"No," responded Georgia, struggling to justify her position, "but I really do think he's come a long way in a very short time."

An uncomfortable silence hung over the conference table for several moments. Anna checked her watch and motioned toward Stokey. "I'd like to speak with the patient now. Would you have him brought here, please?"

The guard stepped into the hall and bellowed Cardonick's name. After a few seconds the patient appeared. "Get in here. The doctor wants to see you."

Cardonick stepped into the room. He wore expensive running shoes, neatly pressed gray institutional slacks, and a black T-shirt emblazoned with a drawing of a guitar and the words "Keystones, Spring Tour, 1983." His once-long hair was closely cropped and precisely groomed.

He had regained the weight he lost in the months between his separation and the Christmas Eve killings. He appeared calm and alert.

"Good afternoon," said the psychiatrist. "Please, sit down. I believe you know everyone here. How are you today, Mr. Cardonick?"

"Pretty good, Dr. Roth, thank you."

"I haven't spoken with you for about a week. I wonder how you've been doing without your antidepressant medication. How has your sleep been?"

"To be perfectly honest, I can't complain, Doctor."

"You may if you'd like to," she replied pleasantly.

"No, no problems. In fact, I'm sure Mr. Stokey will tell you I sleep too much." He smiled at the guard; Stokey nodded coldly.

"And your appetite? How have you been eating?"

"Again, no problems, Doctor. Or maybe I should say I have the exact opposite problem now." He pinched his small roll of stomach fat and smiled broadly. "Seriously, though, I'm eating fine."

"Very good." She made a short notation in his chart. "Mr. Cardonick, we're meeting here today to review your progress. As you probably know, your commitment will expire in about three weeks."

"Yes, Doctor."

"The court will want to hear from us when the commitment period ends. We'll be asked for a progress report, recommendations, whether further hospitalization is necessary, and so forth."

"Yes, Doctor."

"We'd like to hear from you." She leaned back in her chair and folded her hands in her lap.

A few silent moments passed. "Where do you want me to begin?"

"Wherever you'd like, Mr. Cardonick."

"Well, I've been feeling a lot better ever since I got off the medicine. I'll be frank with you, Doctor. When I first got here I was in pretty bad shape. I really needed the medicine then. But after I got better, well, to be perfectly honest, I think it was slowing me down. Especially the Haldol. I used to have a lot of side effects—stiffness, dry mouth, sometimes my vision was out of focus. That's all better now."

"I see."

"And I got a job in the library. The librarian needed someone who could understand the Dewey Decimal System, keep track of dates, stuff like that. She said she wanted someone who wouldn't flip out on her and get locked up. Someone who wouldn't leave her stranded without help."

"And how has it gone so far?"

"I like it. I'll be frank with you, Doctor. A lot of the patients are too confused to understand how the library works. I really dig helping them out."

His wide smile sent a sharp shiver through Anna, like the static electricity jolt that comes from touching a doorknob on a winter day.

"Anyway," Cardonick continued, "at least it gives me a little pocket money. Not a whole lot. Just two dollars a day. But that's more than most jobs here pay."

"How do you spend the money?"

"I use a little bit for snacks from the canteen. The rest, well, I don't know if you've ever heard of Reverend Isaac. Reverend Isaac Hopkins. He comes here once a week to visit me. I've been donating most of the money to his church in Philadelphia."

"I see. This Reverend Isaac, is he someone you knew before you came to Littleton?" Anna was testing Cardonick to see how he would react to the question.

He looked down at the table. His left ear twitched involuntarily for a moment. "No, I didn't meet him until I came here."

"Oh?"

"No. He was involved . . . he was one . . . his daughter was one of the people involved in the incident. The incident that brought me here."

"You seem to have difficulty talking about it."

"Yeah, well, to be perfectly honest, I'm trying to get over it as best I can, put it all behind me. Reverend Isaac wants me to join his church when I leave here."

"I see. And have you and he discussed when that might be?"

"Can I be frank with you, Doctor?"

"Please."

"I think I'm ready to leave when my commitment expires."

From the corner of her eye Anna saw Stokey and Ditweiler stiffen. Ellen picked at the eraser on her pencil with her fingernail.

Anna maintained a neutral demeanor and probed further. "You must be feeling much better."

"Definitely. I know the judge sent me here for treatment, and now I know just how much I needed it. So I want to thank everyone here for helping me." He smiled once more. Again Anna felt a cold shiver.

"Please, go on."

"But to be perfectly honest, I think I've been doing pretty well. I haven't been in any trouble since February. I've been off medicine for a long time now without any bad results. And I think I've learned how to control myself a little better."

"I see. What plans would you have for yourself if you were to be discharged at the end of this commitment period?"

"Well, I'd like to find a good counselor when I leave here. Someone like Georgia—excuse me—Miss Day. And I'd like to get back together with my wife. I guess that's the most important thing."

"And what does Mrs. Cardonick say about that?"

"To be perfectly honest, I think she's still a little confused."

"Oh?"

"I'll be frank with you, Doctor. I didn't treat her right a lot of the time. And I know she was considering filing for a divorce right before the incident. But she didn't do that. We're still married, and I think that counts for something."

"I hear she's been here to visit you several times."

Cardonick smiled. "Yeah, I guess she hasn't given up on me, not completely, not just yet. The first time she came, I said to her, 'Don't come to see me unless you think there's a chance we might get back together when I get out of here.' That's all I'm looking for, just a chance."

"And suppose she decides instead to go through with the divorce?"

Cardonick sighed. "Jeez, I don't even want to think about it." He smiled at Anna and continued. "Seriously, though, I just want her to be happy. If she wants a divorce, I think we could still be friends. For our daughter's sake, if nothing else."

"How old is your daughter?"

"She turned seven on her last birthday, right around the time of my trial."

"Does she come to see you, too?"

"No, I told Denise not to bring her here."

"Why is that?"

"I don't want her to see her father this way. Denise says this has all been very rough on Jennifer. Daddy gets arrested on Christmas, Daddy gets put away in the hospital on her birthday—it's hard for her to understand."

"And for you?"

"Huh?"

"Looking back on things now, how do *you* understand the fact that you are here?"

Cardonick stared at her blankly for a moment. "You mean the incident? The incident that brought me here?"

"Yes. The killings. I'm talking about the killings, Mr. Cardonick."

A cold look flashed across his face for an instant. He looked down at his hands and folded and unfolded them on the conference table. "It was my mental illness. I know now that I was really mentally ill."

Anna's voice hardened slightly. "There are millions of mentally ill people in the world, Mr. Cardonick. Very few of them kill."

His face flushed and his eyes blinked nervously. He forced a smile. He spoke in carefully controlled tones. "I think I know what you want. You want to see me as a criminal, as a murderer. Look, the jury said I wasn't responsible for what I did. If it wasn't for my mental illness, it wouldn't have happened. The jury understood. Dr. Whitney understood. Even Reverend Isaac understands, and I killed his daughter, for Chrissake. Look, I'm sorry for what I did, for the mess I made of things, but I can't let it ruin the rest of my life. I know I'll never let anything like that happen again. I really believe I can make it now."

Anna turned to her colleagues. "Do any of you have questions for Mr. Cardonick?"

"I have one," said Ellen. "Gordon, I see you have a new Keystones T-shirt. I thought you'd parted ways with them."

Cardonick glanced at the guitar design on the shirt. "Yeah, well, one of my old buddies in the group mailed it to me. He said they were sorry to hear about how bad things had been going for me, even said they'd record a couple of my old songs on their next album. I'll tell you," he said with a laugh, "I can certainly use the royalties."

"Would you consider going back with them if they asked you to?"

"Well, they haven't asked. But to be perfectly honest with you, I think it's more important to spend time around Denise and Jennifer. Living on the road wouldn't be good for me or my family right now."

"Does anyone else have questions?" asked Anna. "No? Thank you for meeting with us, Mr. Cardonick."

"I have a question," said the patient.

"Yes?"

"What are you gonna recommend to the judge?"

"We'll be talking about that after you leave. Mr. Ditweiler will inform you when we've reached a decision on our recommendation."

"You mean you're gonna put it to a vote?"

"I mean we're going to put it to a discussion."

"But you're the one who'll testify in court, right?"

"That's correct."

"So if the bunch of you can't agree, when push comes to shove, it's only your opinion that matters."

"I'm the one who will take an oath to tell the truth as I see it." She stood, cueing Stokey to escort Cardonick out of the room.

Cardonick couldn't suppress a snicker. "Yeah, that's what I thought."

They stared at each other for a long, uncomfortable moment.

"My word," said the psychiatrist after Cardonick had left. "I can't recall the last time someone spent so much energy trying to convince me that he was being 'frank' and 'perfectly honest.'"

"That's for sure," agreed Ellen. "Methinks the patient doth protest too much."

Ditweiler spoke. "I trust him just about as far as I can throw this table."

"And I trust him about as far as I can throw Harvey Ditweiler," said Stokey.

"I think it's obvious," said Anna, "that Mr. Cardonick hasn't really begun to examine the problems he was having that led to his psychotic episode. And he certainly hasn't accepted any responsibility for what he has done. He blames it on mental illness, as if that illness descended on him like a virus over which he had no control. He takes the statement 'not *criminally* responsible' to mean not responsible at all. I believe you all know how I feel about such matters," said the psychiatrist.

She closed Cardonick's folder. "The violent and cruel man is one who has lost contact with his own humanity. He's severed the bond that ties him to others, the lifeline that lets him feel others' pain and sorrow. He can cure himself only by mourning that loss, by grieving for the harm he has caused. It's a very painful cure.

"But when society tells someone he is not guilty by reason of insanity, it encourages him to avoid that painful cure. 'The court told me I wasn't guilty,' he will say, 'so how can you tell me that I was responsible?'"

Anna smiled. "End of lecture, my friends. So. Do I hear any arguments for recommending discharge when I testify in court? Anyone? No, I guess not. We can only hope that, as far as the judge at his hearing is concerned, common sense will prevail in the end. I'll fill out an official request for recommitment and I'll forward it to Superintendent Whitney for his signature. Good afternoon, everyone."

28

Whitney sat in his office at Littleton early in the morning and tried to read a journal article about a new antipsychotic medicine. His mind wandered after every sentence, though, and he kept thinking about the letter he'd received the day before.

He removed the letter from its envelope and reread it.

August 26

Dear Thomas,
A.I.T.S.D.
There's an old story about a merchant who tossed six shekels to a local beggar at the end of every work week. One Friday afternoon he gave the beggar only half the usual amount.

"What is this?" cried the beggar. "Only three shekels?"

"I'm sorry," mumbled the embarrassed merchant, "but my business was very bad this week."

"So? Just because things are bad for you, why should I have to suffer?"

An elderly widow lived in my neighborhood when I was young. She had a very sour disposition, and she never missed an opportunity to scold me or my friends. She'd yell at us for playing too loudly, or for running near her precious flowers, or for doing any of the hundred and one things children sometimes do.

She was a miserable, wretched creature. My mother told me

that the woman had lost her entire family during the war—they were tortured and then butchered by enemy soldiers—and that she'd barely escaped with her own life. I suppose my mother was trying to make me feel sorry for the woman, but that was a stupid thing for her to do. After all, just because things were bad for the widow, why should I have to suffer?

I went to the grocery store one day and I saw a carton of items being prepared for delivery to the widow. I reached into the carton and loosened the lids on all of the jars, and I cut a small hole in her sack of flour. I laughed out loud throughout the day each time I imagined her spilling her goods all over the kitchen.

The next evening I telephoned several pie shops and had one pie from each sent to the widow's address. I lurked in the shadows outside her house and watched the trucks roll up one after another, and one after another they were turned away by my increasingly apoplectic foe.

In the ensuing weeks my attack grew more consistent and more clever. I called the police several times to report all sorts of hideous crimes at the widow's house. I called the fire department, the water department, even the dog catcher.

She never knew that I was the one, and I never discussed my actions with any of my friends. Eventually she died. I was sorry to see her go, because I had enjoyed so much the little games I played at her expense.

Someone—I think it was Edgar Allan Poe—said that vengeance is satisfying only when your victim knows the identity and motivation of his tormentor.

I disagree.

Your friend,
The Phoenix

Whitney's phone began to ring. Carla, his secretary, hadn't arrived yet, and he answered the phone himself.

"Tommy!" cackled the voice on the other end of the line. "How the hell are ya?"

Only one person ever addressed Whitney that way. "Hello, Judge."

Gleason chortled. "Long time, no see, Tommy. Not since you became superintendent. Good friends like us shouldn't go so long without keeping in touch."

Whitney could almost feel the unctuous sarcasm ooze through the telephone line. "What can I do for you, Judge?"

"Ah, that's what I like about you doctors. Always so ready to help. Actually, Tommy, I just called to thank you for your letter."

"My letter?"

"Your request for Gordon Cardonick's recommitment. I'm really looking forward to this hearing. Will you be coming to court to testify?"

"No. The request was actually written by Dr. Anna Roth. She's in charge of his treatment, so she'll be the one appearing at the hearing."

"Pity," sighed Gleason. "I really do miss our little chats. Well, you can tell your Dr. Roth that I'm a little behind, but I should be able to have the hearing sometime after Labor Day."

I've always known you were a little behind, thought Whitney. "I'll tell her, Judge," he said.

Whitney returned the phone to its cradle and tried once more to read the journal article.

Chief Guard Blodgett arrived at 3:00 with the list of the previous day's admissions. "Recognize any of these names, Doc?"

Whitney scanned the list. "No, Bob, I'm afraid not."

"Down there—the third name from the bottom."

Whitney read: *Tomlinson, Bunker. Admitted 8/30/83 from Holmesboro State Prison.*

"Does it ring a bell now? The letter Reverend Isaac brought with him, the one he received from Gordon Cardonick."

"Of course," said Whitney. "The rapist. The one Cardonick saved from suicide."

"Yeah, well, I've been wondering about that. And the more I think about it, the harder it is to believe. When we read Cardonick's letter Bunker Tomlinson had already been discharged, so I never checked it out any further. But now that he's back, how'd you like to make a little visit to the Admissions Building?"

The two of them walked across the hospital grounds to the one-story structure. Whitney rarely went there. The Admissions Building was a throwback to the days before Percy Osborne, an era when treatment clearly took a backseat to containment and punishment throughout the hospital. The other units had long ago evolved into treatment settings, but the Admissions Unit remained the province of the prison guards.

Whitney and Blodgett read the psychiatric note that had been placed in the patient's chart the previous day:

Admitted from Holmesboro Prison where he is serving three concurrent 15-to-25-year rape sentences. According to Holmesboro psychiatrist, patient is at risk in prison population, constant target for assault and threats, with resultant depression and suicidal ideation.

Upon interview today, patient stated he feels much better now that he is at Littleton. Appears fearful of returning to prison. No symptoms of major depression. No delusions or hallucinations. No disturbances of thought, orientation, concentration, or memory.

Diagnostic Impression: Adjustment Disorder with Anxious Mood, already in partial remission. No medication prescribed at this time.

"Sounds like he was rather unpopular in prison," said Whitney.

"Sex offenders have a pretty rough time of it in open population," said the guard. "Other inmates are always trying to give them a taste of their own medicine."

Tomlinson was brought to the interview room. Like all patients on the Admissions Unit, he was permitted to wear only his underclothing. He was stoop-shouldered and unshaven. His weak handshake and weepy face radiated self-pity.

"Mr. Tomlinson, I don't believe we've met. I'm Dr. Whitney, and I'm the superintendent. And this is Mr. Blodgett, the chief guard. We wanted to see how you're feeling today."

The man's eyes flashed back and forth between the two visitors. "I couldn't take it in prison anymore. I cut my wrist. That's why they sent me here." He held out his arm. The marks were fresh, but not serious enough to have required emergency medical attention.

"Have you ever done anything like this before?" asked Whitney.

"Just in prison. You got no idea what it's like, Doctor."

"I see. And what about Littleton? Did you have any problems with depression while you were here the last time?"

"No, I don't think so. I do pretty good here. That's why I wanted to come back."

Blodgett spoke. "Aren't you forgetting something?"

"Aren't I... I don't... what do you mean?"

"We know about the bathroom," continued the guard. "About you and Gordon Cardonick."

Tomlinson's face blanched. "Is that bastard still here?"

"That's a funny way to talk about someone who saved your life," said Blodgett.

"Yeah, right. Is that what you call it?"

"What would you call it?" asked Whitney.

The prisoner's voice quivered. "I sure don't call it saving your life when someone says he'll cut your throat if you don't suck his cock and then threatens to kill you if you tell anyone."

Whitney's stomach turned cold inside. He'd heard enough. He had the man returned to his holding cell.

"Do you believe him?" asked the psychiatrist on their way back to his office.

"Hard to say," replied Blodgett. "Men who commit sex crimes against kids are pretty miserable characters. They ask for a lot of the trouble that comes their way. A guy like this, he'll willingly give blow jobs to a dozen guys in the prison. Then someone he's neglected will force him to do it. He'll forget who he did willingly and who forced him, so he'll complain to the guards about all of them. Then he gets known as a stool pigeon and everyone wants to kick the shit out of him. So he cuts his wrists—gently, of course—and gets sent down here for a breathing spell. Cardonick may have forced him, or maybe not."

"But what about the suicide attempt? Do you believe him when he says it never happened?"

"Well, this guy wants us to think he's suicidal so we'll let him stay here. You wouldn't expect him to deny a real attempt."

"I agree," said the psychiatrist. "Damn. Cardonick must have fabricated the whole thing just for the effect it would have on Reverend Isaac."

"Like I said last time, Doc, he's a con. He's good at it, too. Well, see you later."

Whitney closed the door to his office and sat in his swivel chair. He stretched his hands toward the ceiling and closed his eyes. He thought about Cardonick, about the strange coldness at the core of the man's being. He remembered some of the things other people had said. *He's a con... Gordon really likes to play games... He tells me he'll be getting out soon. He really believes it...*

He didn't like thinking about Cardonick. A sudden wave of weakness washed over him. The words came back again: *He tells me he'll be getting out soon.*

Impossible, thought Whitney. He couldn't imagine Judge Gleason releasing Cardonick, no matter how much progress the patient might appear to have made. And yet Denise had seemed so certain. And what was her reaction? Did the thought please her? Was she frightened? Whitney couldn't tell, and he felt a sudden powerful need to find out.

He reached for his phone and dialed the Center City number he'd written on his appointment book.

"Mr. Jason's office," said the voice on the other end of the line.

"Mrs. Cardonick? This is Dr. Whitney."

"Dr. Whitney? Is that really you?"

"Mrs. Cardonick, I need to talk to you about your husband and his recommitment hearing. Are you free later?"

"Gosh, I'm afraid I can't get away from work today, because..."

"No, no—I mean this evening. I was planning on coming into town anyway." It was a lie. "I'd be happy to meet you at your office. We could talk over dinner. My treat, of course."

"Oh."

The silence seemed to last for hours. He held the telephone tightly against his ear, and he could feel the beat of the blood rushing through the vein in his temple.

"I get off at five o'clock," she said.

29

Whitney saw the look of consternation on Denise's face. No doubt she was confused by the menu, which was written entirely in French. And only his menu listed the prices, so she probably felt awkward, not knowing how expensive an item to order.

"Would you like me to recommend something?" he asked.

She closed her menu and smiled. "I'll let you order for both of us," she replied.

The room was small. There were only four tables, each in its own corner. The guests all spoke in muted tones, lending an extra touch of intimacy to an already elegant setting.

"The maitre d' seemed to know you," said Denise. "Do you come here often?"

"Fairly often. I used to work nearby at the Department of Social Services when I first came to Philadelphia."

"When was that?"

He thought for a moment. "Oh, sixteen... no, almost seventeen years ago."

"Gee, I guess I was in the fourth grade seventeen years ago. I can hardly remember that far back." She wished immediately that she could pull the words back.

"I know what you mean. When I was a little boy, I'd hear my parents mention something that had happened twenty years earlier, and I couldn't imagine what it would be like to have a memory that old. Twenty years seemed like an eternity to me back then. And now," he said with a sad smile, "now I have memories that go back over forty years. And some of them seem like only yesterday."

"Where did you grow up?"

"Massachusetts. Near Boston. But we lived in Paris for about two years when I was young. My father was a lawyer, and his firm had a branch office over there."

"Paris," sighed Denise. She looked at one of the French daguerreotypes on the wall above their table. "I've always wanted to go there."

"It's a beautiful place."

"It always sounded so romantic to me. Walking along the Seine with someone you really love. My sister went there once. Some married man she was dating took her there for a weekend right before he dumped her. Me, I've never been east of Atlantic City."

"We're even," laughed Whitney, "because I've never been to Atlantic City."

"We used to go there every summer. We rented a little house there—in Margate, actually—right near the beach, about a block past the end of the boardwalk. That was back before they had the gambling casinos."

"What did you like most about going there?"

She thought for a moment. "There was an old hotel in Margate. The Elephant Hotel. It was a tiny old hotel from the 1800s, built in the shape of an elephant. I don't know when it stopped operating as a hotel, but when we were girls you could pay a quarter and walk around inside. It reminds me of . . . have you ever been to the Franklin Institute, over on Logan Square?"

Whitney shook his head.

"Well, they have this large-scale model of a human heart there. And you can walk all the way through it, through the ventricles and the . . . what do you call them?"

"Auricles?"

"Yeah, right," she said. "The auricles. You walk through this giant heart, and the walls are soft and warm, and they pump and sound like a heartbeat. Thump-thump, thump-thump, thump-thump. And I always felt safe inside, protected by something that big. I used to get the same feeling inside the Elephant Hotel."

They passed their meal that way, trading stories about their childhoods. Whitney told her about the day his friend killed himself experimenting with chemicals under the North Bridge, and about his own subsequent decision to study medicine. Denise talked about getting splinters from running on the boardwalk, the diving horse at Steel Pier, and being knocked over by waves on the Jersey shore.

"Can I drop you off someplace?" Whitney asked her after dinner.

"I have my car in a lot near my office. You could walk me back there, if it's not too much trouble."

There was a cool breeze in the late-August night when they left the restaurant. They walked close together, never touching, gathering warmth from each other against the chill of the evening. "Back in Massachusetts, you can hear the Canadian geese flying south on a night like this. It's still summer, but if you try hard enough you can feel the autumn edging its way in."

When they reached her building, Denise decided to take the elevator back to her office to pick up a sweater. They parted company in the lobby.

"Have you ever dated the wife of a patient?" she asked as she stepped into the elevator.

The idea seemed foreign to him. "No, of course not."

She smiled. "Until now, you mean." The doors closed behind her.

And then he realized that they hadn't spoken once about Gordon Cardonick. He remembered inviting her to dinner so he could ask her some questions about the man. But, for the life of him, he couldn't recall what it was he had wanted to know.

The following afternoon, Denise arrived at Whitney's office without an appointment. She stumbled across the room, bumped into a chair, and knocked it onto its side.

"Please," she said, "don't say anything. I know what you're thinking. You think I'm drunk, don't you?"

"Are you?" he asked.

She burst into laughter and fell backwards into the chair near his desk. She landed with such force that the chair slid two feet.

"I only had three glasses of wine at lunch. I can handle it."

She resumed laughing. She chuckled and guffawed until the tears started flowing and then, with alarming suddenness, she broke into uncontrolled sobbing.

She reached for the Kleenex on his desk and blew her nose. "I'm sorry. The last thing I wanted was to make a fool of myself."

"You needn't worry about that," he assured her.

Her sobs receded gradually. She smiled wanly as she dabbed her cheeks. "I knew you'd say something like that. You're always so kind to me."

He waited calmly until she regained her poise. "So, why the tears?"

"I don't know," she sighed. "Maybe it's because of last night."

"Last night?"

"Something happened after you walked me back to my office."

She twisted the tissue between her fingers until it fell to the floor in pieces. She knelt on the floor, swept the pieces together, and carried them to the wastebasket. "Sorry," she said.

"That's all right."

She spun around. "Damn you," she shouted. "You're always so sympathetic, so goddamn calm and understanding. Just once I wish you'd stop being so goddamn perfect and treat me like a real person. What do I have to do to get you mad at me?"

"Treating you like a real person means getting mad at you?"

"Aaagh!" She grabbed her long hair with both hands. "There you go again. I can't take it anymore."

But he couldn't be angry with her. The more sad and injured she appeared, the more he was drawn to her.

"I talked to Gordon on the phone this morning," she said after she composed herself. "He's still pressuring me to come back to him. His court hearing is scheduled for next Tuesday."

"I know."

"He still says he has a good chance of being released. What do you think?"

"I think it's extremely unlikely."

"I hope you're right. I may not be strong enough to fight him if he gets out. He has a way of getting what he wants."

She pulled a mirror out of her handbag. "Look at me. I'm a mess." She ran a comb through her hair and wiped off the eyeliner that had run down her cheeks. She sat down and closed her eyes. She tilted sideways, still under the influence of the wine.

"I slept with my boss last night," Denise said. She opened her eyes. "It was the first time since I got married that I've made love to anyone other than Gordon. But when you left me, I felt so lost. I couldn't bear the idea of being alone the rest of the night." She laughed softly. "I almost ran after you, but I was afraid you'd turn me away." She returned the comb to her handbag. "Should I go on?"

"If you wish." Part of him felt compelled to hear the story. The rest of him wanted to run away and hide.

"I went into the office to pick up my sweater. Mr. Jason was sleeping on the sofa in his office. He does that every once in a while ever since his wife died a few years ago. I got undressed, pulled back his sheet, and lay down on top of him." She began to laugh. "That poor, dear man. He felt so guilty when it was over."

"And you?"

She didn't answer.

"Why are you telling me this?" asked Whitney.

She stared at him as if she were memorizing his face. "Because the whole time I was with him, I was thinking of you."

The shrill three o'clock whistle sounded to signal the change of shift for the guards. Whitney was grateful for the momentary distraction.

Denise broke the silence. "Is there any chance?"

Whitney watched the sun as it played on her face. He wished things were different. He wished they'd met in another way, in another place.

He could barely get the words out. "I'm sorry," he said.

Her body grew small and weak, like a sail that had suddenly lost the wind. Neither one could think of anything else to say.

After several minutes, Denise gathered herself together and walked to the door. She turned to face him one last time. "Good-bye, Dr. Whitney . . . Thomas." She turned and walked away.

He watched from his window as she walked slowly across the parking lot. She paused by her car, then turned and strode briskly toward the entrance to the patient visiting area.

A little while later Whitney peered into the main visiting room. Denise was leaning against the screen that separated her from the sinister-looking man on the other side of the table. She had tears in her eyes. Her husband looked through her without expression.

30

Judge Gleason thought: *This is all Thomas Whitney's fault.* Without his testimony at the trial, Cardonick would have been found guilty of murder. And if the jury had convicted Cardonick, the judge would have imposed a life sentence. *And if Cardonick was in prison,* Gleason told himself, *I wouldn't be pissing my time away on this recommitment hearing.*

He listened impatiently to Anna Roth's testimony. Occasionally her accent made her remarks unintelligible, but Gleason didn't ask for clarification. After all, it was such a waste of time. The outcome of Cardonick's hearing—unlike that of his trial—would be decided not by a jury, but by the judge alone. And Gleason had made up his mind long before the hearing even began.

It was his first day back on the Superior Court bench following an end-of-summer vacation in the Poconos. He would've preferred easing into his work more gradually. Indeed, most recommitment hearings were held in Littleton District Court. But a criminal trial judge had the seldom-exercised right to retain jurisdiction. And Gleason had a special interest in presiding over this case: He wanted to guarantee that Gordon Cardonick stayed where he was.

Marvin Pellman, the assistant attorney general representing the Commonwealth, completed his direct examination of Anna Roth. "Your witness, Counselor."

Fuller Bloomberg, assigned once more by the court to represent Cardonick, walked toward the witness stand.

"Dr. Roth, in layman's terms, is it accurate to characterize psychosis as a mental state that is substantially out of contact with reality?"

"I believe that would be accurate."

"And, formal definitions aside, would you agree that people who hear imaginary voices are usually suffering from psychosis?"

"Usually, yes."

"And would you agree that people who have delusions—fantastic beliefs that have absolutely no basis in reality—would you agree that these people are usually suffering from psychosis?"

"Yes, of course."

"How about extreme grandiosity? People who think that they're really Jesus Christ, or Napoleon, or the president—aren't people with that symptom usually suffering from psychosis?"

"Your Honor," said the weary assistant attorney general, "in the interest of concluding this hearing sometime this year, the Commonwealth stipulates that all of these conditions are symptoms of psychosis."

Gleason peered down at the young attorney. "Very well. Get on with it, please, Mr. Bloomberg."

"Yes, Your Honor. Now, Dr. Roth, most psychiatrists would probably agree with you when you say these symptoms are evidence of psychosis. Correct?"

"I believe . . . yes, that is correct." Anna was puzzled. Usually attorneys attacked her credibility by focusing on the *lack* of consensus among psychiatrists regarding symptoms and diagnoses.

"Now, I assume that, in most cases, you are able to tell whether a patient you've examined is currently psychotic."

"Yes, of course. Such things are not difficult for the average psychiatrist."

"I see. Not difficult even for the average psychiatrist. Of course, you're hardly an average psychiatrist, are you? I'd venture to say you're one of the most able psychiatrists in the Commonwealth."

"Your Honor," said Pellman, "can we get on with the business of this hearing?"

"Relax, Mr. Pellman," replied Gleason. "Counsel is merely reminding the court how credible your own witness is. I don't think you should find that objectionable. Please continue, Mr. Bloomberg."

"Dr. Roth, you testified that on both of Mr. Cardonick's admissions to Littleton State Hospital he was psychotic."

"I did."

"And you agree with Dr. Whitney's conclusion that my client was psychotic last Christmas, don't you?"

"I do."

"What about the average psychiatrist, Dr. Roth? Would that so-called average psychiatrist agree that Mr. Cardonick was psychotic last Christmas?"

"I believe so."

Bloomberg leaned against the witness box and stared directly at Anna. "And what about now, Dr. Roth? Would the average psychiatrist conclude that Mr. Cardonick is psychotic today?"

She had intentionally avoided the issue of current psychosis in her direct testimony. She had focused instead on Cardonick's violence, his history of psychosis, and the unresolved conflicts which could again drive him to madness.

"Dr. Roth? Did you hear my question? Let me break it down for you. Is there any evidence that my client is currently hearing things or seeing things—hallucinating?"

"No."

"Or that he has delusions of any sort?"

"No."

"Or that his thinking is illogical, incoherent, or, you should pardon the expression, crazy?"

"Not that I'm aware of."

"Is there any evidence at all that Mr. Cardonick is still out of contact with reality? Are you aware of *any* symptoms—current symptoms, mind you—that the average psychiatrist would label as psychotic?"

"No," she stated softly.

The judge cupped his ear toward her. "I'm sorry, Doctor. What did you say?"

Anna sighed. "No, Your Honor."

Bloomberg continued. "How do you explain this, Dr. Roth? Perhaps the medication he's taking is controlling the symptoms?"

"The patient is not taking any medication," the doctor stated softly.

"Oh. Is he refusing to take his medicine?"

"No. I discontinued his medication."

Bloomberg feigned incredulity. "And why did you do that?"

"Because it was no longer indicated."

" 'No longer indicated.' I *see*. In other words, his psychosis is—what's that expression you doctors use—in complete remission. Or—in everyday language—cured."

"I'm not sure I would use that exact word."

"No," said Bloomberg, smiling as he placed his notepad on his table. "I guess you wouldn't."

Her voice turned loud and harsh, as if she were lecturing the young lawyer. "There is still the matter of the patient's serious personality disorder."

"Ah, yes. Thank you for reminding me, Doctor. Let me check my notes. Yes, here it is. You said 'the underlying Borderline Personality Disorder leaves him with a continual propensity toward psychosis.' Did I get that right?"

"You did."

"But really, Doctor, does anyone know what a Borderline Personality Disorder is? Isn't it true that it didn't even exist as an official psychiatric diagnosis until 1980?"

"I'm not sure of the exact date."

"And isn't there considerable disagreement among psychiatrists as to who has the disorder and who doesn't? Aren't the diagnostic signs a bit, shall we say, imprecise?"

"There is some disagreement, yes, but—"

"Let me read to you some of the things the American Psychiatric Association's official manual says about this imprecisely defined disorder: 'A pattern of unstable and intense interpersonal relationships.' 'Frequent displays of temper.' 'Uncertainty about issues relating to identity, such as long-term goals or career choice.' 'Feelings of emptiness or boredom.' Heck, that could describe half the people in this courtroom. In fact, didn't a recent article in the *Psychoanalytic Quarterly* suggest that at least six former presidents may have had this so-called disorder?"

"Objection, Your Honor. Counsel is drawing conclusions and offering his own opinions."

"Overruled." Gleason enjoyed watching Bloomberg. The young man always prepared more diligently than the average court-appointed attorney. And since the judge had already made up his mind to recommit Cardonick, there was no harm in letting Bloomberg continue his line of questioning. "Please answer the question, Doctor."

"Yes," said Anna. "That is all true."

"And isn't it true that the usual treatment for this disorder—if the disorder does, in fact, exist—is outpatient psychotherapy?"

"In most cases, yes. But not in the case of someone as dangerous as Mr. Cardonick."

"I see. Tell me, has he committed any disciplinary infractions during the past six months?"

"There was an assaultive incident in February." She turned toward the judge. "A very serious incident."

"Yes," said Bloomberg, "but that was the final day of his trial, more than six months ago. And by your own testimony, he was still taking medication. But, tell me, since he was taken off that medication, have there been any assaults? Any threats? Any refusals to cooperate with his treatment program?"

Anna felt humiliated. Lawyers are so skillful at twisting truth into lies, she told herself. "No."

"Thank you, Dr. Roth. No further questions, Your Honor." He returned to his seat beside Cardonick.

Gleason smiled. He was always happy to see a psychiatrist squirm, even one whose recommendations he agreed with. "You may step down now, Doctor. Mr. Pellman, please continue with your presentation."

The assistant attorney general rose. "The Commonwealth rests, Your Honor."

"Mr. Bloomberg, you may proceed on behalf of your client."

The public defender rose again. "Your Honor, as you know, in this type of hearing the Commonwealth must prove beyond a reasonable doubt that the subject is still mentally ill. I respectfully suggest that the Commonwealth has failed to meet its burden of proof. I move that the court dismiss the petition to recommit my client."

Gleason frowned. He called the two attorneys up to his bench. "Is that all you have, son?" he asked Bloomberg. "No witnesses, no other evidence?"

"Judge, we all know my client was a danger to society in the past." He nodded toward Pellman. "But Marvin hasn't presented a shred of evidence to prove that my client is still mentally ill. All we have is this bogus diagnosis of a personality disorder. Hell, Judge, the way these psychiatrists have things set up, everyone I know has a personality disorder. They've got about a dozen of these personality disorders listed in their manual, each one more vague than the next. They have to think of a diagnosis for everyone so they can collect payment from medical insurance companies."

Gleason chuckled. "I admire your attitude, son. But you were willing to rely on psychiatric testimony in order to defend your client in February. And if you think I'm gonna let this bird hit the streets, you're even crazier than he is. I'm denying your motion for dismissal. If you don't have anything else to present, why don't you wrap things up so we can all get out of here a little early?"

"May I have a few minutes to discuss this with Mr. Cardonick?"

Gleason sighed. "If you must."

Bloomberg huddled at the table with his client. Cardonick listened attentively for a few minutes, then replied. Cardonick became more and more animated.

Bloomberg seemed to sink lower and lower in his seat. Suddenly the attorney turned white. "You did *what*?" he asked in tones that could be heard halfway across the courtroom.

Cardonick continued speaking for a few minutes, then wrote something down and handed it to the lawyer.

Suddenly Bloomberg felt too weak to stand. He addressed the judge from his chair. "Your Honor, we request a recess until tomorrow morning."

The judge motioned the attorneys to his bench once more. "This is a joke, isn't it?"

Bloomberg was sweating profusely. His voice wavered and cracked. "Judge, my client has just given me some information that I think is relevant."

"Fine. Good. Terrific. Then let's take care of it now, damn it."

"I need to get some evidence out of my client's safe deposit box when the banks reopen in the morning. And I'd appreciate it if Marvin could accompany me as a representative of the Commonwealth."

Gleason looked at Pellman. "What do you have to say about this?"

Pellman smiled. "The Commonwealth can afford to be generous in this matter, Judge. Especially if Fuller agrees to buy me breakfast."

But Fuller Bloomberg was in no mood to think about eating.

"You've hardly touched your drink." Reporter Selma Aaron watched him twirl his glass for the two hundredth time. "Fuller? Fuller, are you listening to me?"

"Hmm? Oh, I'm sorry, Selma. My mind must be somewhere else."

"Yes, I can see that. Let me tell you, it certainly flatters a lady when her escort pays her this much attention." Her wire-rimmed glasses slid down her nose again. She pushed them back into place.

"I'm sorry." He pretended to be interested in what she was saying. "What were we talking about before my mind wandered?"

"We weren't talking about anything yet. You've been somewhere between this bar and I-don't-know-where ever since we came in here. What did Cardonick say to you, anyway?"

"Cardonick?"

"C'mon, Fuller, don't play dumb. I know you too well. You turned white as a ghost when you and he were talking in the courtroom."

Bloomberg held his finger to his lips. "Sssh. Attorney-client privilege. Especially when talking to reporters." He glanced down at her notepad.

"All right, all right," she said, stuffing the paper into her puffed-out vinyl handbag. "Now, what the hell is going on? Fuller? Fuller, damn it, talk to me!"

After a long silence he said, "I was thinking about my father. He was a big Al Jolson fan. He used to play these scratchy old seventy-eight records when I was a kid. You could barely make out all the words."

"Uh-huh," said the reporter. It was her turn to simulate interest.

"So one day he was playing 'April Showers.' You know the last verse? 'So keep on looking for a bluebird, and listening for his song, whenever April showers come along.'"

"Yeah? So?"

"Well, the first time I heard it—I must have been around six or seven—I thought Jolson was singing 'so keep on looking, Fuller Bloomberg.'"

The reporter began to laugh. Her glasses slid all the way off her nose. She caught them just before they landed in her guacamole.

"No, seriously, I really did. I kept saying, 'He's singing my name, he's singing my name.' And my father said, 'He sure is, son, he sure is.'"

"That's funny."

"Yeah, I guess it is. Anyway, a couple of months later my teacher was singing the song for the class. We were supposed to learn it for an assembly program. And when she sang 'so keep on looking for a bluebird' I jumped up to correct her. All of the kids started laughing, and she started laughing. I kept insisting that it was 'so keep on looking, Fuller Bloomberg,' because I couldn't believe my father would lie to me like that."

"Oh, Fuller. I'm sure he didn't mean anything by it. He was just trying to make you feel special."

"Yeah, I guess so. But that day in school, when I finally figured out what was happening, I felt like an incredible asshole. Like it was the biggest joke in the world. Everyone was in on it—my father, the teacher, my friends. And I was the butt of it."

She watched her friend as he looked away sadly. "Whatever made you think of that story?"

Bloomberg winced. "Come back to the hearing tomorrow, Selma. It's gonna be 'April Showers' all over again."

"I'd like to call Dr. Anna Roth back to the witness stand," said Bloomberg.

Anna walked briskly to the front of the courtroom. She was incensed at having to spend a second day tied up in court on what should have been a routine matter.

Bloomberg sensed the psychiatrist's impatience. "I just have a few more questions for you, Dr. Roth. Yesterday you stated that Mr. Cardonick has a 'propensity toward psychosis.'"

"Yes."

"In other words, even though he is not currently psychotic, his personality is the sort that could easily break down again and lose contact with reality."

"Absolutely."

"And this is much more likely in his case than in your average so-called personality disorder?"

"Yes. And, as we have seen by recent history, this would make him very, very dangerous indeed."

"I see. Well, thank you for that gratuitous remark, Doctor."

Anna bristled.

"Objection."

"Sustained."

Bloomberg continued without missing a beat. "This propensity toward psychosis—you made that statement on the basis of his past psychotic episodes, didn't you, Doctor?"

"Excuse me?"

"Suppose—just suppose—that Mr. Cardonick had never been psychotic in the past. Would you still think that he's at risk to become psychotic in the future?"

"Objection, Your Honor. Hypothetical and irrelevant. Mr. Cardonick was found insane by this very court. Counsel is asking the doctor to speculate about a condition that clearly does not exist."

"If Your Honor will allow me a little leeway," said Bloomberg, "the relevance of the question will become evident."

Gleason frowned. He wanted to finish the hearing as quickly as possible. But he had a grudging admiration for Bloomberg's tenacity. More often than not, the judge was inclined to be lenient with the young public defender. "Objection overruled, for the time being. You may answer the question, Doctor."

"Let me repeat the question," said Bloomberg. "If Mr. Cardonick had never been psychotic before, would you still have the opinion that he has a propensity toward future psychosis?"

"Such a thing is impossible to say."

"Oh?"

"I would have to reexamine the patient."

"I *see*. In other words, you would have to reconsider your opinion. And it's possible you might come to a different conclusion, isn't it?"

"'Possible' is such a broad word—"

Bloomberg bore down on her. "The question can be answered with a yes or no, Doctor. If Mr. Cardonick had never been psychotic, is it *possible* you would change your mind about this so-called propensity toward psychosis?"

Anna paused. She rubbed the liver spots on her hands. "Yes," she said, the anger in her voice barely modulated. "It is possible."

Bloomberg smiled broadly. "Thank you, Dr. Roth. No further questions, Your Honor."

"Mr. Pellman," said the judge, "does the Commonwealth wish to reexamine its witness?"

"No, Your Honor."

"Very well, then. You may step down, Doctor. Do you have anything to present, Mr. Bloomberg?"

"Yes, Your Honor." He turned toward the gallery. "I'd like to call Gordon Cardonick to the witness stand."

Gleason raised his eyebrows. He hadn't expected this. Cardonick hadn't testified at the trial, and he had remained quiet during that trial and this hearing.

"Raise your hand, please," said the bailiff. "Do you swear that the testimony you are about to give is the truth, the whole truth, and nothing but the truth, so help you God?"

"I do."

"Please be seated."

Bloomberg paced back and forth for a moment. He caught Selma Aaron's eye in the reporters' area. Selma had been unable to coax any information out of Bloomberg the previous afternoon in the bar. But she knew that something was dreadfully wrong. Her friend had the disconcerted look of a man who was about to perform a distasteful, but obligatory, duty.

"Mr. Cardonick," began the attorney, "you've heard the testimony about your mental condition on the two occasions you were admitted to Littleton State Hospital."

"Yes, sir."

"Would you tell the court, in your own words, the circumstances of your first admission to Littleton on December 18, 1980."

"Well, I was serving an assault sentence at Holmesboro State Prison, and I ran into some trouble up there."

"What sort of trouble?"

"I used to sell drugs on the street. There was this one particular guy I'd done some deals with. He thought he'd gotten the raw end of one of our, uh, business transactions. Word was out he was gonna have me roughed up in prison. He knew lots of people there, too. It sounded like a serious threat to me."

"So what did you do?"

"I got myself sent to Littleton State Hospital."

"How did you do that?"

"I faked it."

"You did what?"

"I faked it. I pretended to be crazy. Listen, when you've seen as many guys flip out on uppers—amphetamines—as I have, it's a pretty easy thing to fake."

Gleason's fingers tightened involuntarily around his gavel. In the reporters' gallery, Selma felt suddenly flushed.

"Now, Mr. Cardonick, last Christmas Eve you shot three people to death, didn't you?"

"Yes, sir."

Gleason examined Cardonick's eyes for any trace of nervousness or remorse. He saw none.

"And you were admitted to Littleton State Hospital for the second time on December 28, 1982. You were evaluated for criminal responsibility by Dr. Thomas Whitney."

"Yes, sir."

"Dr. Whitney thought that you were legally insane when you killed those people. He said you were mentally ill and that you couldn't really understand what you were doing. I'd like you to tell the court, in your own words, what your mental health was like last Christmas Eve."

"Well, I guess I was a little depressed. My wife had left me. I felt bad about not spending the holiday at home with her and our little girl."

"I see. Well, then, do you think you were mentally ill last Christmas Eve?"

196

"No, sir, I wasn't."

"But weren't you hearing voices?"

"No, sir."

"Didn't you have insane ideas? Didn't you think you were receiving special signs from God?"

"No, sir."

"Didn't you think that your wife and daughter were in danger, that someone wanted to kill them and you had to protect them?"

"No, sir."

"But didn't you think the car fumes on the expressway were choking your daughter to death? Didn't you shoot at the cars in order to save her?"

"No, sir."

"But that's what Dr. Whitney said in his report. And now you're denying it. How do you explain all of this?"

Cardonick looked at Anna Roth. She thought she saw a trace of a smile cross his face.

"Well, Mr. Cardonick?" asked Bloomberg.

"I faked it."

Gleason had heard enough. He commanded the two lawyers to approach the bench. "What the hell are you trying to pull?" he said to Bloomberg. "Do you think I'm an idiot? You can't really believe I'm going to fall for this self-serving bullshit you and your client are trying to peddle. Is this all you have?"

"Judge, I'm just about to offer some physical evidence."

Gleason looked at Pellman. The assistant attorney general shrugged his shoulders. "All right, Counselor. You have about two minutes to straighten this out."

Bloomberg took a small key from his pocket. "Mr. Cardonick, do you recognize this key?"

"Yes, sir. It's the key to my safe deposit box. Number 6935."

"Your Honor," said the young public defender. "In order to save the court's time, I'd like the assistant attorney general to stipulate that the following facts are true.

"First, early this morning Mr. Pellman and I went to the home of Sarah Cardonick, my client's aunt. I told her where to find this key hidden in my client's room, and she brought it to us.

"Second, Mr. Pellman and I went to Northeast Savings and Loan with the key and your court order. We asked to see the records of Mr. Cardonick's safe deposit box.

"Third, the records showed that the box was rented on December 24, 1982, the day of the shootings. The records showed that Mr. Cardonick was the only person authorized to open the box, and that no one else has opened it since that date.

"Fourth, as soon as the bank officer produced the box, I asked Mr. Pellman to tie it shut with string. Neither he nor I opened it to inspect the contents, and he's had it in his possession all morning."

"Well, Mr. Pellman?" asked the judge.

"The Commonwealth so stipulates, Your Honor."

Pellman gave the box to Bloomberg. The public defender carried the box to the bench and laid it before the judge. He handed Gleason a pair of scissors to cut the string.

"Mr. Cardonick," said Bloomberg, "please describe the contents of this box to the court."

"Yes, sir. There's only a couple of things in there. There's the receipt for the box itself. Then there's a large brown envelope, folded over a few times so it would fit."

Gleason removed the envelope from the safe deposit box.

"Inside the envelope is some money. It's all in hundred-dollar bills. It should come to five thousand dollars."

The judge counted the money. "It's all here."

"Mr. Cardonick," said Bloomberg, "would you please tell the court who gave you that money."

"Well, I'm not sure, exactly. I never knew his real name."

"Go on."

"Well, I don't pretend to be proud of this, but that money was a down payment for a hit. I was supposed to kill someone."

Selma began to scribble furiously in her notepad. She looked across the room at Denise. All of the color had drained from the young woman's face.

"You see, after I finished my prison sentence I couldn't find steady work as a musician. A couple of small studio jobs here and there, nothing regular. I had this old charge of stealing studio equipment, and that made most people shy away from hiring me.

"I didn't want my wife to know. I was too proud, I guess, or too stupid. I didn't want to rely on her bringing in all of the money. This guy I met at a party offered to lend me a couple hundred. He said his name was Cazzy. I don't know if that was his first or last name, or a nickname, or maybe even a fake name.

"Anyway, he kept lending me money, a little bit at a time, and after a couple of months, I was almost four thousand bucks in the hole. Then Cazzy cut me off. And I was starting to worry, because Cazzy was getting anxious to see a little good faith payment. I knew he was into dealing drugs in a big way, and I figured, you don't screw around—excuse me—you don't mess around with people like that.

"Then one day, I guess it was around December twentieth, Cazzy said he had a way for me to make good on the debt and earn ten thousand bucks on top of it. He said he wanted me to kill this guy who tried to cheat him in a cocaine deal.

"I was pretty scared, and I told him, no way. So he said, okay, but in that case I want the four thousand you owe me in two days. 'Or else,' he said. He didn't have to tell me what that meant.

"So two days later I gave in. I told him I'd kill the guy. He gave me the down payment on December twenty-fourth, the day before Christmas. Half now, he says, half after the job is done.

"And that night I killed the guy Cazzy told me to kill. His name was Sharman. Elliot Sharman. The other two people, the guy from Jersey and Reverend Isaac's little girl, they were accidents. I was aiming for Sharman, and he was trying to get away from me—"

The judge interrupted Cardonick. "Do you . . . do you realize what you're saying?"

"Yes, sir. It's all true, every word."

Gleason could feel the veins on his squat neck bulging out. "And just why the . . . why do you expect me to believe this story?"

Cardonick pointed to the safe deposit box. "I mentioned that the receipt for the box is in there. Some words and numbers are written on the back side."

The judge read out loud: " 'White Chevy, IPK-258, cone' or something like that."

"That's 'C-O-N-N,' " said Cardonick, "short for Connecticut."

"And what does that mean, Mr. Cardonick?" asked Bloomberg. But the lawyer already knew the answer, for that was what had shocked him at the end of the previous day's court session.

"I recorded that information when I went to the safe deposit box, several hours before the killings. When I shot Sharman he was driving a white Chevy with Connecticut license plate IPK-258, just like Cazzy said he would be."

*   *   *

"I don't believe this!" Gleason was angrier than either Pellman or Bloomberg had ever seen him as he paced back and forth in his chambers.

"I have to go back in there after this recess," the judge continued, "and either let an admitted murderer go free or commit a sane person to a mental hospital. Terrific. Just terrific. This is fucking incredible." He turned on the public defender. "How the hell could you let something like this happen? How could you let him perjure himself like that when he was on trial? All this crap about hallucinations and delusions..."

"He didn't perjure himself at the trial," said Bloomberg. "He never testified. Obviously, he lied to Dr. Whitney."

"There's no law against lying to a psychiatrist, Judge," said Pellman, trying to break the tension in the room. "If there was, half of my friends would be in jail."

Gleason wasn't satisfied. "How could you go for an insanity defense when you knew it was all crap?"

Pellman interceded on behalf of his young colleague. "We both know Fuller better than that, Judge. You didn't know Cardonick was lying before, did you, Fuller?"

Bloomberg sighed. He looked preoccupied. "Of course not."

"No, I guess you didn't," said Gleason, slightly calmer. "Cardonick is going to make us all look like jerk-offs. They still elect their judges in this town, you know. This'll be death for me the next time I run."

"Maybe," said Pellman. "But maybe not. This really falls on Dr. Whitney's doorstep more than yours, Judge. I wonder how the governor will feel when he learns his superintendent can't tell a kook from a cold-blooded murderer."

"Whitney!" exclaimed the judge. "This is all Thomas Whitney's fault." He shouted into his intercom. "Sharon, get me Littleton State Hospital, and tell them I want the superintendent on the phone right now."

Bloomberg unbuttoned and rebuttoned his suit jacket several times. "What are you going to say to him?"

"I'm going to tell him to get his ass down here. I want him in that courtroom when I announce my decision, whatever the hell it is."

The intercom rang. "Judge," squealed the nasal voice on the other end, "the superintendent is on vacation in Maine and won't be available until next week."

"Well, isn't that just great," Gleason said sarcastically. "These fucking psychiatrists. If I've said it once I've said it a million times. We should outlaw the goddamn insanity defense and keep these psychiatrists out of the courtroom."

"One thing's for sure, Judge," said Pellman. "A whole lot of people will agree with you now, especially if Cardonick is released."

Especially if Cardonick is released. The thought suddenly took on new meaning for Gleason. He walked to his window and looked down on the late-afternoon shoppers scurrying along Broad Street. *Then everyone would know.* A thought crossed his mind for perhaps the fiftieth time that day, but this time it elicited a tiny smile from his tight lips. *It's all Thomas Whitney's fault.*

M alzone had never met his pa-
perboy. It was one of those curious rituals that define the impersonality
of city life: the *Inquirer* always arrived outside his apartment door before
he awakened and at the end of every month he found a bill tucked
inside its pages, which he dutifully paid by mail.

But this Thursday morning was different. Malzone had been awake
and waiting for over an hour when he heard the opening of the fire door
at the end of the hallway. His was the fourth apartment from the
fire door. He heard the plop of a paper outside the first apartment, then
five seconds of silence, a second thud (closer this time), more silence, a
third (and even closer) thud, then another short silence.

He swung open his door just as the boy prepared to drop the paper.
Malzone grabbed it from the startled youngster and slammed the door
shut in his face with a mumbled "Thank you."

He'd heard the news almost immediately, of course, the day before.
It had been the lead story on the local newscasts and had even made
the *CBS Evening News with Dan Rather*. Now it stared back at him in
black and white, several column inches descending beneath a bold
front-page headline.

XMAS EVE SNIPER RELEASED
by Selma Aaron

September 7 — Gordon Cardonick, the so-called Christmas Eve Sniper, was discharged from Littleton State Hospital this afternoon, just six and a half months after he was found not guilty by reason of insanity for the

202

shooting deaths of three motorists on the Schuylkill Expressway last December 24.

In dramatic testimony at his recommitment hearing in Philadelphia Superior Court, Cardonick, 27, stated that he was "faking it" when he claimed to be mentally ill at the time of the murders.

The article replayed the details of Anna Roth's testimony, Cardonick's testimony, and the new evidence that Cardonick's attorney introduced. Malzone was particularly excited by the section that detailed the judge's comments.

Judge Gleason reserved his harshest criticism for Dr. Thomas Whitney, Superintendent of Littleton State Hospital. Dr. Whitney's trial testimony played a key role in Cardonick's acquittal last February. "This should prove once and for all that the so-called science of psychiatry is nothing but a hodgepodge of untested theories, peculiar beliefs, and old wives' tales," said the judge. "It's irresponsible witchcraft, plain and simple. And when it leads to situations like this one, it's outright hooliganism."

Dr. Whitney was not available for comment.

Malzone had tried to contact Whitney the evening before, but the phone on the Maine island had been disconnected. The superintendent was expected to arrive at his mother's Massachusetts home in the afternoon; Malzone would try to reach him again. He wished he could've seen the expression on Whitney's face when he heard the news.

He bought the *Philadelphia Daily News* at the corner drugstore. The tabloid was playing the story to the hilt. Its headline, which took up the entire front page, read: SNIPER DUPES DOCS, BEATS THE SYSTEM. There was a sidebar story on Reverend Isaac, who was quoted as saying he was convinced of Cardonick's reformation. Denise Cardonick was pictured locked in an embrace with her husband at the gates of Littleton. A state senator was calling for Whitney's dismissal. Malzone's heart leapt for joy.

When he arrived at Littleton he went to Whitney's empty office, shut the door behind himself, and sat in the swivel chair behind the desk. He twirled around and around like a child on a stool at an ice cream counter.

He tried to prepare himself for the day's events. What would he say to the other staff members? How would he answer the reporters who were sure to call him? He remembered Lyndon Johnson's famous statement after Kennedy's assassination: "All that I have, I would gladly give not to be standing here today . . ." Malzone practiced looking humble and mournful. *That will take some doing,* he thought.

He looked out the window. *Not a bad view. I could get used to this.* He was too lost in idyllic fantasy to hear the office door open.

The voice behind him had a familiar edge of disdain. "Jumping the gun a little bit, aren't you, Ralph?"

Malzone turned around quickly. "Dr. Osborne! What . . . what are you . . ."

"I'm troubleshooting for the governor on this one, Ralph. I'll call for you in your office if I need you."

Detective Captain Schacter was sweating and panting by the time he reached the second floor. It was three days past Labor Day, but the humid Philadelphia summer wouldn't die.

"Good morning, Captain," said Lieutenant Rienzi. A mocking smile danced on his lips. "Looks like your friend Whitney really blew it this time."

Schacter grunted and slammed shut his office door. It was going to be one of those days, he thought. At least he would be rid of Rienzi for a little while. Relief turned to exasperation when he turned to face his unexpected company.

The taller of his two visitors helped himself to an unopened pack of cheese crackers from Schacter's desktop. "Well, well. Hello, Stanley," said Chief Yasgur. "Our friend over here is a little upset about the morning headlines. I thought we should all get together for a little tit-a-tit."

The unctuous little man sitting in the corner raised his hand slightly. "Good morning, Captain," said District Attorney Tortelli.

"Let me guess," said Schacter. "This is about my promotion to deputy commissioner."

Tortelli didn't appreciate Schacter's sarcasm. "No, but keep it up and maybe we'll be talking about your early retirement."

Chief Yasgur laughed out loud. "Relax, Tony," he said to Tortelli. "Stanley here is just making a little joke, aren't you, Stanley? Tony's just a little high-strung today. Hard to blame him, though. I guess this sniper case has made all of us look foolish. All of *you,* I should say."

Tortelli took a deep breath. "Yes. Excuse me, Captain." It was an insincere apology.

"Cardonick is sitting like a pig in shit this morning," said the Chief. "And Tony over here tells me that we can't even touch him."

"Double jeopardy," said the district attorney. "He was NGRI, which for our purposes is just as good—just as bad, I should say—as outright acquittal. You can't bring a man to trial a second time after he's been found not guilty."

"Isn't there anything you can prosecute on?" asked Schacter.

Tortelli shook his head. "If you guys had left off one of the charges—the firearm possession charge, say, or trespassing—we could go back and get him on that. Get him locked up for a little while, anyway. But you already charged him with everything under the sun, and he already got found NGRI on the whole thing. You guys picked a hell of a time to start being thorough, let me tell you."

Schacter didn't like Tortelli. The chubby little man was never shy about making excuses for his own botched prosecution by laying the blame on supposedly poor police work.

"How about perjury?" said Schacter.

"Nice try, Stanley," said Yasgur. "That was my thought, too. But Tony tells me Cardonick never testified at the trial. The only lies were the ones he told Whitney. In fact, get this—Tony isn't even sure he can get hold of the five thousand dollars from Cardonick's safe deposit box. Seems Cardonick turned it over to that ridiculous church—you know, Reverend Isaac. Tony's a little shy about going after it now."

"We may think of something eventually," said Tortelli, "but right now we can't move."

"That's where you come in, Stanley," said the chief.

"Me?"

Tortelli tapped his foot nervously. "We're going to give you a chance to redeem yourself."

Yasgur offered Schacter one of the captain's own crackers. "You've gotta admit the police come out of this looking almost as incompetent as Whitney. Now, speaking for myself, I certainly don't blame you for missing the truth when you investigated the murders. Who could expect you to know Cardonick was actually intending to kill one particular victim, especially when there was no prior relationship between them. But I don't think the mayor's gonna see it the same way." The chief made the sign of the cross when he said the word *mayor.*

Schacter looked back and forth between the two men. "So. What do you want me to do?"

"We want you to get Cardonick," said Yasgur.

"Better yet," said Tortelli, "we want you to get Cazzy. Whoever he is, he sounds like a bigger catch. Maybe you can sweat it out of Cardonick, make some kind of a deal."

"I've done some checking with Ferlinger," said the chief, referring to the head of the city's narcotics squad. "We don't get any kind of a readout on anyone named Cazzy."

"We think the man may have made the name up for Cardonick's benefit," said the district attorney.

Schacter picked up one of his briars and began his daily pipe-cleaning ritual. "Cardonick may have made the name up himself to protect the guy," the detective said. "He says he doesn't know anything about this Cazzy, but why should we start believing him now?"

The chief rubbed his chin. "Hmm. It's a possibility, Stanley. Cardonick may figure he's still entitled to the second half of the hit money. That would be plenty incentive to pretend he can't identify the man."

"We've got two avenues of approach to this guy Cazzy," said Schacter. "One's dead, the other's still alive—Elliot Sharman and Gordon Cardonick. If we check out both connections, maybe we'll figure out where they cross."

The chief and the district attorney stood to leave. Schacter hurried them along by getting up and holding the door open. Yasgur towered over the other two men. He wrapped one arm around Schacter and the other around Tortelli. "Boys, boys," he said with a deep laugh. "All for one and one for all, right?"

Schacter shut the door after them. He heard the chief laughing all the way out of the station house. He reached into his desk and pulled out a bottle of Tylenol. It was already shaping up to be one hell of a day.

Whitney's mother had departed East Haven on Sunday, four days earlier. By now she was settled at the family home in Concord. Whitney would be there by late afternoon. He had a ticket for the noon ferry to the Maine coast, and the Massachusetts town was a three-and-a-half-hour ride from there.

On Labor Day evening a ferocious thunderstorm had struck the island and knocked out the phone. It was due to be shut off anyway, so

206

he didn't bother making a special trip into the small town on Tuesday to report it. Instead he unplugged the television and the radio and spent the rest of his vacation in total, blissful isolation from every other living soul. He couldn't remember the last time he'd felt so relaxed.

Whitney rose early on Thursday, packed his car, secured the house, and started to walk. He paid no particular attention to where he was going.

At first he didn't recognize the abandoned one-story structure. It was overgrown with brush and weeds, and rotting plywood was fastened with rusty nails across its windows and door. Then a chilly wind wrapped around him and pushed him toward the building. The island wind was so unpredictable, he thought. He remembered his first summer on East Haven when, in the middle of July, the wind blew and blew for days on end. But it was always warm with Marlene inside the carriage house.

The carriage house. He rushed up to the decaying building and pried loose the board that blocked the entrance. He thought he heard a high-pitched sound—a mouse, perhaps, or a rat—when he kicked open the door, but all was still when he stepped inside.

There was nothing except an old metal chest and the empty oak frame from the bed they'd shared. Echoes from that long-ago summer seemed to bounce around the room. He remembered how frail she'd looked the first time they made love, how much she'd needed him, how much he'd needed her. He wondered what had become of her and whether those same memories ever crossed her mind.

The drive to the dock took less than five minutes. On the way there he thought about Denise Cardonick.

He drove his car onto the ferry. He was the first one on, which meant he would be the first one off from the opposite end when they reached Rockland. He walked to the front of the boat to watch for whales.

A woman was inspecting the faces of everyone in the small crowd of passengers as if she were looking for someone in particular. Whitney was sure he'd never met her, but there was something familiar about her. Perhaps he'd seen her on an earlier ferry trip, although she certainly didn't look like an islander. She had the frantic energy of a city dweller. She sported an oversize vinyl handbag and glasses that kept sliding halfway down the bridge of her nose.

When she saw him she walked over immediately. "Dr. Whitney?"

"Yes, Miss . . ."

"Aaron. Selma Aaron." She paused to see if he recognized her name. He didn't. "I'm a reporter for the *Philadelphia Inquirer*."

"Oh. Were you visiting the island on vacation?"

"Visiting? Oh, no. I never even set foot on the island. I took the ferry over and stayed on it, because your mother said you would be on the noon ferry."

"I don't understand."

"I didn't want to wait until you got back to Philadelphia, or Concord, or even the other side of this ferry ride. I wanted to be the first one to get your comments."

"My . . . comments?"

She looked at him with puzzlement, and then with incredulity. "Oh, my God!" she said. "You don't know yet, do you?" She thrust a copy of the *Inquirer* into his hand.

He read her story about Cardonick's commitment hearing. When he reached the part about Judge Gleason's diatribe against him, Whitney's face turned pale and his stomach felt as though it had been tied into knots. *No!* he thought. *No, no, no . . .*

The reporter produced a tape recorder and pointed its microphone at Whitney's face. "Doctor, what's your reaction to this latest development in the case of the Christmas Eve Sniper?"

. . . no, no, no . . .

"Doctor? Doctor, do you have any comment?"

. . . no, no, no . . . "Excuse me," he mumbled, brushing against her as he rushed away. The squawking of sea gulls sounded like laughter. Maybe they were laughing at him. Gleason, Cardonick, Malzone, perhaps Anna Roth—they'd all be laughing at him.

He ran toward the rear of the ferry. There was still time, he thought. He would jump to the dock just as the ferry pulled away, leaving the reporter behind him. He would call the ticket office on the mainland and ask them to unload his car. He would take the next ferry to the mainland, walk briskly to his car, and avoid this woman altogether. He would . . .

The ferry pulled away seconds too soon. He leaned over its railing, grabbing for the dock in a foolish and unsuccessful attempt to keep the vessel from departing. The voices of the people on the landing grew fainter and fainter until they were swallowed up by the hum of the ferry's engine and the squawking of sea gulls.

The reporter's microphone was inches away from his face when he turned around. Whitney ducked underneath it and ran back to his car at the front of the ferry. He got inside, shut the windows, and locked all the doors.

The woman knocked on his window for several minutes, the huge rings on her hand cracking against the glass like gunfire.

Whitney buried his face in his hands and stifled a scream.

"**G**ordon is taking our daughter to school. He should be back in a few minutes." Denise eyed the man nervously. "What did you say your name was?"

Standing on the steps outside the front door, his eyes were almost even with hers. "Schacter. Detective Captain Stanley Schacter." He flashed his police identification.

She hesitated for a moment. "I guess you can wait inside if you want. I've got a little time before I leave for work."

Schacter stepped into the living room of the two-story row house. The floor was littered with newspapers and empty cartons. A child's tricycle blocked the passageway into the dining area.

"You'll have to excuse the mess. Gordon just moved back with me and we're still trying to straighten things out. Can I get you some coffee?"

"No, don't go to any trouble."

"It's no trouble, really. I'm making some for myself, anyway."

Denise disappeared into the kitchen. Schacter followed her with his eyes. He wondered what sort of woman would stay with a man like Cardonick.

"Is Gordon in some sort of trouble?" she asked when she returned. "Sugar and cream?"

"No," he replied. "I'll take it black. And no, I just want to talk with him about this and that."

"It's about the things he said in court, isn't it? About the man who gave him that money. Cazzy."

"Yeah, Cazzy. We've been trying to get the goods on Cazzy for a hell of a long time."

"You mean, the police know who Cazzy is?"

"Don't you?" He pretended to be surprised. Cardonick wouldn't be intimidated by his presence, but Denise seemed appropriately nervous. Often an anxious spouse was his best source of information.

"I asked Gordon about it, but he said the less I knew, the safer things would be for me and Jennifer."

"Uh-huh. Well, I guess he's got a lot to be worried about. Cazzy isn't happy about this kind of publicity. It's bad for business."

She bit down on her lower lip. "But I don't understand. If you know who he is..."

"Knowing and proving are two different things," said the captain. "People who meet him have a funny habit of developing temporary amnesia. Like your husband did in court. It's often the first symptom of a fatal disease."

"Fatal..." She pondered his statement.

"Yeah. Amnesia followed by sudden heart failure, caused by a bullet."

She struggled unsuccessfully to keep herself from shaking. Schacter believed she was as ignorant as he was about Cazzy, and for a moment he felt bad for frightening her.

"But you're the police. You're supposed to protect people..."

"Yeah, yeah, I know. Listen, my superiors didn't even want me to come here today. They figure your husband made us look pretty bad, and they'd be just as happy to see Cazzy take care of things. But I thought maybe Gordon and I can work something out. Something that works to our mutual satisfaction. One hand washing the other, so to speak."

The front door swung open. Cardonick was a little heavier than he had been on Christmas Eve, but Schacter recognized him by his cold and vacant eyes.

Denise jumped up. "Honey, this is Captain—"

"I know who you are," hissed Cardonick. "What do you want?"

"I'd like to talk to you—"

"Look, I already told you people. I don't know who Cazzy is. They showed me a bunch of pictures. None of them looked like the man who gave me that money."

"I thought we could go over things from the beginning," said Schacter. "Where you met him, who else was there, things like that."

"Honey," Denise interjected, "he says Cazzy will kill you. They already know who the man is. They just need you to help them prove it."

"Shut up! He's bluffing, can't you tell? Tell her, cop. Tell her you made it all up just to scare her."

"Whether I'm bluffing or not, the fact remains that you have information we need, and we may be able to give you something you want."

"Like what?"

"Oh, like a little protection."

"From what?"

"From Cazzy, maybe. Or from the D.A. He's busting his ass—excuse me, ma'am—to find something to charge you with. He was talking about a federal conspiracy charge. Something about depriving people of their civil rights."

"Huh?"

"By killing them."

"Yeah, well, that shit doesn't scare me. I can protect myself."

"Gordon," she said. "It won't hurt to listen to—"

"Shut up, goddamn it! Hey, cop—you got anything else to say, say it now. Or else you can leave."

Schacter walked to the door. "Well, pal, you can't blame a guy for trying to help out. Wouldn't want your little girl to grow up without a father." He looked at Denise. "And I sure wouldn't want anything to happen to her or your lovely wife."

"Gordon . . ."

"Be quiet," he told Denise. "You—get out of here. You got nothing on me."

"Well, if you change your mind, give me a call. Nice meeting you, Mrs. Cardonick." He left the door open and whistled as he walked down the steps to his car.

Cardonick grabbed Denise's arm and squeezed it. "Don't let me ever catch you talking to him again."

"Ouch! Gordon, you're hurting me."

He relaxed his grip. He smiled sweetly and ran his fingers through her blonde curls. "Sorry, baby. I just don't like to see you upset, that's all. There's nothing to worry about. I have a feeling Cazzy will never bother us again."

Bob Marsella sat alone at his private booth in his Center City restaurant, one of several respectable enterprises he owned. Like the others—the restaurants, bars, car washes, and weight-reducing salons— it was a funnel through which gambling and drug profits could pass and come out clean.

He checked his watch. It was his newest toy, a souvenir from his latest trip to Nassau. Its four buttons, pushed in various combinations, could give him Eastern time, West Coast time, a stopwatch with two lap-time readings, a calendar, and two alarms. "Press all four buttons together," he was fond of saying, "and it jerks you off in three-quarter time."

His guest slithered into the booth. "Sorry to keep you waiting, Bob," said Cardonick. "I had to pay a little visit to my lawyer."

"Ugh. Lawyers. Jewish boys who can't stand the sight of blood. Otherwise, they'd be doctors."

"Yeah, but mine's been doing pretty good for me. I guess you've been reading the papers."

"And watching the TV and listening to the radio. Next thing I know, they'll have Christmas Eve Sniper T-shirts, thermos bottles, and lunch boxes. So—let me look at you. I never expected to see you so soon after you got arrested."

Marsella snapped his fingers. An anorexic-looking waitress with long black hair stepped to the booth. "I'll have another Rob Roy. Gordon? What would you like? My treat, of course."

"Nothing right now, thanks." The waitress left. "Anyway, I had to leave some important papers with my lawyer. Sort of an insurance policy."

"I thought they made safe deposit boxes for that sort of thing." He laughed out loud and slapped Cardonick on the back.

"I've already milked that cow. Besides, I wanted to make sure this policy received special treatment."

"Sounds important. What sort of policy is it?" He took his drink from the waitress.

"I guess you could call it insurance against accidental death. And it involves you."

Marsella paused with the glass halfway between the table and his lips. "Me?"

"I'd love to sit here all day and talk about old times, Bob. But I've got a lot of business to attend to, so I'll get straight to the point. My lawyer has a sealed envelope in his safe, with instructions to give it to the police anytime he hasn't heard from me for three days."

Marsella had nothing in particular against the police. He owned quite a few of them. "So?" He took a sip of his drink.

"So. The letter inside identifies you as Cazzy."

Marsella gulped and choked. He spit the drink out of his mouth and down the sides of his face. "You rotten son of a—" He began to cough and wheeze.

"Now, Bob. Not so loud. People are looking our way."

Marsella wiped his face with a napkin. He glowered at Cardonick. "What do you want?"

Cardonick smiled and spread his hands, palms up, on the table. "I'm a reasonable man, Bob. First of all, like I told the judge, the five thousand was only half of what was due. I want the other half, plus another five thousand for my aggravation."

Marsella was seething. "What else?"

"You know that little bar you have up in the Northeast?"

"What about it?"

"I think it's time you hired a new piano player. Say, three nights a week, Monday through Wednesday. I want you to hire me at three hundred a week—on the books, that is—but I want an extra five hundred every week under the table. Cash. No tax records."

"What else?"

"What else?" repeated Cardonick. "Shucks, Bob. I'm not greedy. I think that should just about do it."

"And if I refuse?"

Cardonick sighed. "I don't think you will. I've done a lot of work for you in the past, Bob. I know where too many of your secrets are buried. You're getting away cheap. But if you do refuse, I just may forget to call my lawyer for a few days. And he'd have to cash in my insurance policy sooner than expected. Now, we can't have that, can we?"

The hourly chime on Marsella's watch sounded.

"Damn," said Cardonick as he tapped his own watch. "What time is it?"

"One o'clock."

"Can you believe it? My watch stopped again. I guess I need a new one."

Cardonick looked at Marsella's wrist and held his hand out. Marsella slowly unbuckled the gold-plated band and relinquished his prize.

"Thanks, Bob. You're a real friend. Well, gotta get a move on." Cardonick stood up and snapped his fingers. The thin waitress reappeared. "I think Mr. Marsella needs another Rob Roy. He seems to have spilled the one you just gave him."

214

*   *   *

Clive Burke answered his intercom. "Mr. Burke? There's a Mr. Smedley here to see you. I told him you were busy, but—"

"No, that's all right. Show him in." *Smedley. What the hell is he doing here?*

Burke stood to greet his unwelcome visitor. "Good afternoon, Mr. Cardonick. I thought I told you never to contact me at the office."

"Yes, I know, Mr. Burke. And I'm truly sorry. But at least I used the name we agreed I should go by."

Burke instinctively closed the expensive drapes on the picture window that overlooked Independence Hall. "Why are you here, Mr. Cardonick?"

"I've just come from my lawyer's office, Mr. Burke. I left some papers with him that I think you'll be interested in hearing about. But let's not be so formal. Please, call me Gordon. And do you mind if I call you Cazzy?"

33

There was a touch of autumn in the New England air when Whitney arrived at his mother's Concord home. The willows arched toward the south, yanked back by the gust of cool Canadian air that had moved in the day before. The half dozen apple trees—planted twenty-seven years earlier by Whitney's father—drooped under the weight of the soon-to-be-harvested fruit.

He pulled into the long private drive and parked outside the service entrance. Hal Goodrow, the caretaker, welcomed him warmly and lifted his suitcase from the car.

Moments later Selma Aaron drove up. Whitney stood next to her car door, blocking it so it wouldn't open. "Miss Aaron, I'm afraid you've been on private property for the past hundred and fifty yards. I'm going to have to ask you to leave."

"Please, Dr. Whitney. Just a few minutes. Don't you want to have any input into the story my paper is printing?"

"Miss Aaron, I never speak to the press about my patients, either before, during, or after their stay at Littleton. And I'll have no comment now."

Hal Goodrow paused at the doorway. "Is there some problem, sir?" he bellowed.

"No, thank you, Hal. Miss Aaron is leaving now, aren't you, Miss Aaron."

Selma pushed her glasses back from the tip of her nose. "If you change your mind, you can reach me at the North Bridge Inn."

"Good day, Miss Aaron." He stood in the driveway until she pulled away.

"Mrs. Whitney is resting at the moment, sir. Shall I take your things up to your room?"

"Yes, Hal. Thank you. And after you've done that, please bolt the gate at the end of the drive."

The caretaker was surprised. He couldn't remember the last time the gate had been closed. "Sir?"

"I don't want any more unexpected visitors."

All the doors and windows were open, creating a cross breeze through the main first-floor hallway. Whitney sat at the small telephone table. He opened the drawer, pulled out the long-distance log, and dutifully recorded his entry: *Date: 9/8/83, To: Philadelphia, From: Thomas.* He couldn't remember which of his parents had initiated the practice. His father, ever the lawyer, accounted for every minute of his time. His mother kept track of every penny.

"Hello?" The voice on the other end of the line was warm and cordial.

"Hello, Katherine. It's Thomas. How are you?"

"Oh." Katherine Schacter, usually a gregarious woman, fell silent for a moment. "You must want to speak with Stanley. Hold on just a minute, please."

It was unlike her, thought Whitney, to sound so formal.

"Thomas! Where the hell have you been? I've been trying to contact you since yesterday afternoon."

"I know, Stan. I just got your message. The phones were knocked out on the island. I only arrived in Concord a few minutes ago. Stan, what the hell is going on?"

The detective confirmed that Cardonick had been released from Littleton.

"What about Anna Roth?" asked Whitney. "You mean to tell me she just let Cardonick go straight out the front door? Didn't she try to hold on to him, file an appeal, do something?"

"She wanted to, believe me. She was very upset. But she said the hospital's attorney overruled her and authorized Cardonick's release. He told her there was nothing he could do after the judge issued the discharge order. I even called the judge myself, but it didn't do any good."

Whitney managed a sarcastic laugh. "I bet Gleason must have felt like crapping himself in court when he heard Cardonick's testimony."

"Actually, Thomas," Schacter said hesitantly, "the judge almost seemed pleased by the way things were going. He said it was all your

217

fault, that now everyone would see for themselves how psychiatrists were screwing up the courts. And I'm afraid that's the way most of the press have been reporting it, too."

Whitney thought about Selma Aaron. She'd followed him in her rented Ford all the way from the dock in Rockland. He'd been reluctant even to stop for lunch lest she pounce on him once again.

"So I'm the heavy in this one," mused Whitney.

"Thomas, I really feel lousy about all of this. I let you down again, just like I did with the Phoenix."

"Why do you say that?"

"Because I never realized there was a connection between Cardonick and Elliot Sharman. If I had discovered it before Cardonick's trial in February, none of this would have happened."

Whitney played nervously with the old-fashioned fabric telephone cord. "What happens now?"

"Well, for the time being, Cardonick is home free. But we're working on it, Thomas, I swear we are. We're gonna get this son of a bitch. I think he lied in court when he said he couldn't identify the guy who paid him to kill Sharman. We're gonna try to figure out who this Cazzy is. Then if we can connect Cazzy with Cardonick, we'll get Cardonick on something. Perjury, obstruction of justice, maybe conspiracy."

Whitney feigned optimism. "I'm sure you'll get him, Stan. He'll have to be as pure as a choirboy now with you on his tail." But he had no faith at all in what he was saying. He wondered if his bogus enthusiasm sounded derisive to Schacter. He hung up with a promise to call immediately on his return to town.

He spent the weekend at the family estate. There were calls from two television stations, *Time*, and the *Boston Globe*. He dropped the messages into the garbage.

Selma Aaron was more tenacious than her media colleagues. She stationed herself outside the estate for several hours at a time. Whitney complained about Selma's presence, but Police Chief Moore could find no legal grounds for removing the reporter, and he was wary of the publicity such a move might cause.

In Sunday's predawn hours Whitney heard sirens. Unable to sleep, he dressed quickly and walked half a mile down the country road in the direction of the commotion.

The Joseph Bunton house was on fire. Built in the mid–seventeenth century, the three-story frame structure was steeped in colonial tradition. It was an official national historic landmark, and now its wide-board floors and priceless contents were transmuting into puffs of smoke.

A small crowd of nearby residents watched quietly as the firemen vainly tried to contain the spreading inferno. One wall after another gave way to the flames. Soon the entire building was engulfed. Smoldering shingles, caught by the wind, flew all around. The air smelled of burning wood.

The flames reminded Whitney of Michael Andrews' fatal chemistry experiment on a long-ago Patriots Day, and of his wife Allison's tragic death.

"How sad," said the young woman at Whitney's side. "It reminds me of the old house my grandmother and grandfather lived in when I was a child. They died within weeks of each other. A month later the house burned to the ground, as if it couldn't bear to go on by itself."

Whitney faced the young woman. Selma Aaron returned his forlorn gaze. In that silent moment it was understood that they were not reporter and doctor, hunter and quarry. They were two tired people, each lost in a private sadness.

"It's like a sand castle," Selma said. "You put so much of yourself into building it, and then it gets washed away in a minute."

"Yes," replied Whitney. "So much can be lost in an instant." Sparks flew high into the air. "So much," he repeated softly.

Osborne looked surprisingly fit. Retirement clearly agreed with him. "Come in, Percy. It's good to see a friendly face."

The older man shook Whitney's outstretched hand. Whitney led him into the den. "Be careful not to trip over my bags. I was too tired to drag them upstairs. I just got back from New England a couple of hours ago."

"Yes, I know. It was good of you to let me come on such short notice. I thought that it would be better to talk in person."

Whitney poured two soft drinks. "I figured whatever I need to know, I'd rather hear it from a friend."

"Thank you, Thomas. I hope you still consider me your friend after you hear what I have to say."

"It's that bad, is it?"

Osborne sighed. "The governor is very upset. When he made you superintendent, he offended some powerful legislators who were supporting their own candidates for the job. Now he sees this negative publicity as a personal political setback."

Whitney tried to inject some humor into the situation. "So he decided to punish you for boosting me by making you come out of retirement?"

Osborne laughed. "It makes you wonder, doesn't it? I've been telling myself that it's because he trusts me after the years I worked for him, but maybe this really is his way of getting back at me. But seriously. Charles Ouimette, that state senator from Allegheny County—you know who I mean, the fat one with the buck teeth. This week he's introducing a bill in the legislature calling for elimination of the insanity defense."

"Predictable."

"It is," agreed Osborne. "But Cardonick's case has generated a lot of unfavorable talk in Harrisburg. The governor has a terrific record on mental health issues, of course, and he's opposed to the bill."

"It sounds like there's a 'but' at the end of that sentence."

The former superintendent looked down at the floor and frowned. "There is. You'll probably be subpoenaed to testify before the legislative committee that will be considering Ouimette's bill. So, although the governor specifically states that he still has complete confidence in you, he wants you to take a leave of absence from Littleton. He doesn't want the controversy surrounding you to interfere with the administration of the hospital."

Whitney laughed bitterly. There was more than a trace of self-pity in his voice. "I wonder why he doesn't just fire me."

Osborne didn't respond. He saw no reason to reveal that this was precisely what the governor originally intended, and that only Osborne's impassioned arguments had garnered Whitney a temporary reprieve.

"Well," sighed Whitney, "at least the hospital will be in good hands. How does it feel to be back?"

"No, Thomas. You don't understand. I'm not . . ."

"Oh." The younger man shrugged his shoulders. "Well, Anna Roth and I have certainly had our differences, but I've never doubted her ability."

Osborne smiled wanly. He shook his head back and forth. "It's not Anna, either. The governor didn't want anyone who'd been touched by the Cardonick case. And it's probably just as well. This whole thing has taken a lot out of her. I worry about her."

"Then who . . ."

"Malzone."

Whitney's mouth dropped open. "You're kidding me!"

"No, I'm afraid not. He has some influential friends in the state capital."

Whitney corrected him. "Friends of his father, you mean."

"I suppose. And I've been instructed to consult with Malzone once a week until things are settled one way or another."

Whitney winced at the words *one way or another.*

"So Littleton won't fall apart," continued Osborne. "Not just yet, anyway. Say what you want to about our governor, but he isn't stupid. Malzone will only be acting superintendent."

"I think the key word there is *acting,* Percy." The two old friends laughed sadly.

LITTLETON STATE HOSPITAL
Ralph T. Malzone, M.D.
~~Assistant~~ Superintendent
Acting

September 12, 1983
The Honorable Charles Ouimette
State Senate Office Building
Harrisburg, Pennsylvania

Dear Senator Ouimette:

Thank you for your kind words of support during our phone conversation this afternoon. I share your concern about the growing misuse of psychiatrists in court matters.

Like you, I favor elimination of the insanity defense in favor of the "guilty but mentally ill" approach. I look forward to testifying in favor of your bill when the Human Services Committee conducts hearings later this month.

> *Sincerely yours,*
> *Ralph Malzone, M.D.*

P.S. My father sends his regards to you and your lovely wife.

Malzone imagined how impressive it would be to see his name on the superintendent's letterhead. It would come in good time, he told himself. Whitney's reputation was skidding, and Malzone intended to do everything he could to hurry it along, even if he had to play up to the loutish state senator from Allegheny County.

He made a mental note to tell Manuel Guadalupe, Whitney's

221

handpicked successor as director of forensic evaluations, that the new acting superintendent would be making the assignments thenceforth.

How wonderful things would be, Malzone told himself, if he could only get Whitney out of his way once and for all.

Schacter stared at him across the table of the small Chestnut Hill bistro. "Thomas, you look absolutely terrible. How much weight have you lost?"

Whitney sighed. "I don't know. Six, maybe seven pounds these last couple of weeks."

The detective grunted. "Well, you look beat to shit, that's for sure. I think this whole thing has really knocked you for a loop."

"My, my, aren't you the clever one." He winced as soon as he said it. "I'm sorry, Stan. I shouldn't be taking it out on you."

Schacter watched as Whitney looked halfheartedly at the menu. His friend looked tired, his face drawn and haggard from lack of sleep. Everything seemed like an incredible effort to him, even the short walk to the restaurant where they now sat.

"I don't suppose you've seen a doctor, have you?" asked Schacter.

Whitney either was ignoring the question or he didn't hear it. "I guess I don't feel much like eating," he said.

"Come on, Thomas. You've got to have something. Some soup, at least." Schacter drained his beer. "Any word from the governor on your returning to work?"

Whitney shook his head.

"Thomas, maybe you should take a vacation. It might do you good to get away from all of this. In the meantime, we're still working on Cardonick. He's contacted several known drug dealers. We don't know what he's setting up, but we're keeping an eye on him. Sooner or later he's bound to do something we can get him for. And then maybe things will get back to normal for you."

Whitney stared out the window without speaking.

"Thomas, are you listening to me at all?"

The psychiatrist pulled an envelope from his pocket. "When it rains, it pours. Take a look at this."

Schacter recognized the printing immediately. "Oh, shit." He read the letter.

September 20, 1983

Dear Thomas,

A psychiatrist was walking across the grounds of Littleton State Hospital one afternoon. Three of his patients were engaged in bizarre activities in the middle of the yard. The first was throwing a series of invisible baseballs. The second was kicking an imaginary football. The third stood with his back to the doctor and cried pitifully.

The psychiatrist was very upset. "If you men can't act normally in the hospital," he said, "how do you expect to take care of yourselves after you're discharged?"

"I'm the greatest pitcher who ever lived," replied the first patient. "When I get out of here the Phillies are going to sign me to a lifetime contract."

"I'm the greatest field-goal kicker who ever lived," said the second patient. "When I get out of here the Eagles are going to sign me to a lifetime contract."

The third patient turned toward the psychiatrist. His zipper was down and his prick was dangling in a jar of cashews. "I'll never get out of here," the man sobbed. "I'm fucking nuts."

Don't be too hard on yourself, Thomas. It's so hard these days to tell who is sane and who is crazy. Everyone is bound to make an occasional mistake. Of course, the families of the sniper's victims may have a thing or two to say about psychiatrists who let people get away with murder. But they have no appreciation for the pressures and uncertainties of the profession. It's enough to drive a person crazy.

Thomas, please forgive me for not writing sooner. I don't have as much time on my hands as you do lately. I understand you've been given an unexpected leave from Littleton, and have taken a vacation from teaching at Franklin University.

It must seem as though you haven't a friend in the world. But

224

don't worry, Thomas. I'm close at hand. I know your every move—who you see, where you go, what you do, think, and feel. I'm with you in your hour of need. I'll stick with you until the very end.

I'm back to stay.

Your faithful friend,
The Phoenix

Schacter reread the letter from Whitney's unknown enemy. "Jesus, as if you didn't have enough troubles."

Whitney smiled weakly. "I've been getting weird phone calls, too. Several times in the past couple of weeks my phone has rung, but when I answered it whoever was on the other end wouldn't say anything. I could tell someone was there, though, and then he'd hang up on me."

"It could be a wrong number, someone who gets embarrassed and hangs up when he hears a strange voice."

"That's what I thought at first. Then yesterday I got a call from a Collings Funeral Home. They wanted to know how they could help me."

"I don't understand."

"I didn't either. The woman from the funeral home informed me that their answering service had received a message from me. Somebody called them and left my number, and said he needed help on planning a funeral. Supposedly someone in my household has a terminal condition and may die any day now."

Schacter pushed his chair back and stood. "I'll be right back. I want to check the phone book to see if this funeral home actually exists."

"Sit down, Stan. I already did that. Then I spent a minute trying to convince her that I hadn't called her, but I don't think she believed me. After I hung up I called back just to verify that her call was genuine. She was very unfriendly the second time we spoke. I couldn't blame her, though. She must have thought I was out of my mind."

Schacter checked his watch. "I need to get to work. I'll call the funeral home later and check this all out. In the meantime, I sure wish you'd give some thought to getting away for a while."

"Sure, Stan," replied Whitney, but his mind seemed miles away already.

Chief Yasgur played with a yo-yo. "They make these damn things out of plastic nowadays," he said as he tried unsuccessfully to work the toy. "Just doesn't have the same feel as the old wooden ones."

District Attorney Tortelli tapped his feet nervously as he sat in Schacter's office. "Well, Captain? What have you got so far?"

"We've drawn a blank on getting someone to identify Cazzy," said Schacter. "Cardonick won't cooperate, and none of the known drug figures go by that name."

Tortelli was impatient. "We knew that three weeks ago."

"Ah, yes," said the detective. "But now for some things you didn't know. Cardonick has been keeping some pretty interesting company during the past few weeks."

Lieutenant Rienzi entered without knocking. "You called for me?"

"Come in, Rienzi. I was just about to tell the chief and the D.A. about Cardonick's recent travels. Maybe you can fill them in."

"Yes, sir." Rienzi placed several pictures on Schacter's desk. "Cardonick has made at least one visit to each of these six people."

He pointed to the first picture. "This one is Robert Marsella. He owns several restaurants and bars, including one where Cardonick plays three nights a week. We've had our eye on him for a long time. We think he's bankrolling some major drug operations. He's short on style, heavy on muscle.

"Over here we have Clive Burke, a tax accountant in Center City. We've never been able to tie him directly to drug traffic, but he handles the accounts of some known dealers, and he knows a lot about laundering money. A very clever man. We think he has some high-up connections with our department, because he always seems to know what's going to happen well ahead of time."

The chief began to cough. The yo-yo fell from his hands and rolled underneath the radiator in the corner of the room.

Rienzi continued with the third picture. "Sherman Farber. Two-time loser. Drugs, gambling, suspected of some prostitution-related offenses.

"Gary Peerow. William Herbert. Paul Melton. More of the same. All six people have direct or reported connections to drug trafficking, and all are known recent associates of Gordon Cardonick."

Tortelli paced back and forth. He addressed Schacter. "Sounds like something is in the wind, some big transaction that involves several large operators, with Cardonick right in the middle."

Schacter smiled. "No, I don't think so. They wouldn't rely on Cardonick to put something like that together, not with all the publicity he's been getting recently. I think he's just trading in on old connections, trying to shake some action loose for himself, and having a hard time getting anyone to deal with him."

"But what about Cazzy? How does he fit in?" asked the district attorney.

Schacter reached for one of his pipes. "The more I think about it, gentlemen, the more I'm convinced Cardonick was lying when he said he couldn't identify Cazzy. His story just doesn't ring true. It's too convenient. I don't buy it."

"Then where does all of this leave us?" asked Tortelli.

"I think one of these six men is the mysterious Cazzy. Obviously, Marsella is the best choice right now, since he's actually hired Cardonick to work for him. If we can connect Marsella or any of the others with Elliot Sharman, then we've got our man. And then we'll have Cardonick for perjury at his commitment hearing."

Tortelli sighed. "It's a shame he didn't testify at his trial and tell the same lies he told Dr. Whitney. Because then we'd have him for perjury at the trial, and the penalty for perjury in murder trials can be life imprisonment." He walked toward the door. "If you need help with anything—warrants, tax records—let my office know." He left without saying good-bye.

Chief Yasgur winked at Schacter and Rienzi. "Good show, fellas." He trailed Tortelli down the hall.

"Lieutenant, have you had any luck locating Marilyn Champeau?"

"I'm working on it. She was on Christmas vacation from the University of Pennsylvania when Sharman was killed. She never came back. Her roommates say she was in too much grief to go on."

"We know that Sharman did have some involvement in selling cocaine," said Schacter. "That much of Cardonick's story checks out. Now if we can only get a fix on Cazzy through Sharman."

"I think this Champeau girl may know something. She had her own apartment, but it looks like she was actually living with Sharman. Her family lives in Manhattan. They say she's visiting friends somewhere in Colorado or California. They've only been marginally cooperative helping us track Marilyn down. They sound frightened."

Schacter smiled. "Good. That may mean she knows something. Something that would put her in danger if the wrong person found out."

"Like a positive ID on Cazzy."

"Exactly." The captain gestured toward his desk. "I'd like to run these pictures by her. That might be the key."

Fuller Bloomberg peered across the desk in his inexpensively furnished law office. "I thought Stanley Schacter was handling Cardonick's case."

"He still is," replied the visitor. "I work under the captain. You can call him to check on that if you want."

The young public defender considered the situation for a moment. "No, I guess that won't be necessary. Besides, whatever it is you want, Lieutenant . . ."

"Rienzi."

". . . Lieutenant Rienzi, I doubt that I have anything new to offer."

"Mr. Bloomberg, we have reason to believe that you possess some physical evidence we've been looking for. Evidence that would enable us to charge Mr. Cardonick with various crimes."

"I don't understand."

"You're not implicated in this, of course. Not right now, anyway," he added with a foreboding tone. "For the moment, we assume that you're an unwitting accomplice, and that you'll want to cooperate with our investigation."

Bloomberg stared at his visitor for several moments. His association with Cardonick had brought him notoriety, the type he could easily live without. But that was in the past. He had broken completely with Cardonick after the recommitment hearing.

"There must be some kind of mistake, Lieutenant."

"Hardly. I'm talking about the envelope."

"The . . . what envelope?" asked Bloomberg.

"That's a very convincing pose, Counselor, but I really don't have time to play that game. Your client told a certain party that he gave you a sealed envelope and asked you to put it in your safe. He told you to give it to the police if three days ever passed without you hearing from him. We'd like to take early delivery of that envelope." He paused briefly. "Now."

The attorney spoke into his intercom. "Melanie, would you come in here, please?"

His receptionist entered the office.

"Melanie, would you please direct Lieutenant Rienzi to my safe?"

"To your . . . But I . . . I'm sorry. You're confusing me. You don't have a safe." The woman turned several shades of red.

Bloomberg beamed. "Thank you, Melanie. That will be all."

The receptionist backed out of the office. Bloomberg wondered if she thought he was daft.

"First of all, Lieutenant Rienzi, as you can obviously see, I don't have a safe. You can search the office yourself if you don't believe me. Furthermore, I'm no longer associated with Gordon Cardonick and have no intention of representing him again." His voice turned high-pitched and loud. "Finally, even if that son of a bitch were still my client, if he had given me this envelope you're looking for, I wouldn't hand it over to you. It would be privileged information, as I'm sure you already know. You can tell Captain Schacter I didn't realize he was in the business of asking lawyers to violate attorney-client confidentiality."

"Let me see if I understand this." Rienzi began to scribble notes in his pad. "You say you never heard about this envelope, and you say Cardonick isn't your client anymore?"

"Bingo."

"Hey, you don't need to be so hostile. The police have responsibilities, too, you know. Or don't you care how many more people get hurt?"

Bloomberg regained his composure. "I'm sorry, Lieutenant. This whole case has been one mess after another. He's a very dangerous man. I hope you find what you're looking for."

•

"Come to think of it, Cardonick didn't mention you by name. He said he gave the envelope to his lawyer, so we just assumed he meant you. Someone else must be handling his affairs now. Do you have any idea who he was referring to?"

"No. I'm sorry."

When he was alone again Bloomberg spoke into his intercom. "Melanie, bring me in some water, would you, please?" He opened his desk and grabbed a vial of extra-strength headache tablets.

Selma Aaron pushed her glasses back from the tip of her nose. Malzone sat on the other side of the superintendent's office, his feet propped up on the corner of the desk.

The reporter had been surprised by his willingness to meet with her. She'd guessed that the Littleton doctors would want to avoid questions about the Cardonick case, but Malzone had given her an appointment without hesitation, and had even called her office twice to confirm it.

She thanked him for allowing her to come, then asked him a few preliminary questions about his professional training and experience. Each time she glanced up from her notebook she saw him staring at her chest. She tried to shield herself with her arms.

"And then you became acting superintendent when Dr. Whitney took his leave of absence," the reporter continued.

"Yes," replied Malzone. "And let me tell you, he's a difficult man to follow. Fortunately, I've got a lot of energy for the job." He smiled at her and winked. "I'm single, you know."

His approach to her was so unsubtle that she felt like laughing out loud. "Dr. Malzone, how could—"

"Please. It's Ralph."

"How could something like this happen? Did you have any idea that Cardonick was only pretending to be insane when Dr. Whitney examined him?"

"No, I can't say that I did. You see, I really didn't know Cardonick at all. Of course, usually I consulted with Dr. Whitney on his difficult cases. We were very close to each other. But I was very busy with my own work when Dr. Whitney evaluated Cardonick, so I never even read his chart until the judge forced us to release him. I blame myself, Selma, I really do."

"Oh?"

"Yes." Malzone sighed. "I keep thinking that if I had consulted with Dr. Whitney, if I had helped with Cardonick's evaluation, then maybe I would have realized that Cardonick was making the whole thing up. The man would be in prison, where he belongs. And Thomas Whitney would be sitting in this office, where he belongs."

Selma scribbled Malzone's statement into her notebook. Her reporter's instinct told her that she probably couldn't believe anything he told her.

"It should never have happened, Miss Aaron," said Anna Roth. "Mr. Cardonick should not have had the option of pleading insanity— even if he actually had been mentally ill at the time of the shootings. Mental illness is no defense for murder. We demean our patients—and ourselves as a society—when we create special excuses just for them."

Selma sensed the strength of the woman's convictions, the intensity of her anger. "And so you disagree with Dr. Whitney's views on the insanity defense," the reporter said.

Anna laughed derisively. "Dr. Whitney." She leaned back in her chair and gazed out her office window, focusing on some point in the distance. "Simply stated, he's evil. He's a dangerous man, a psychopath."

"Who?" asked Selma.

"Who? Why, Gordon Cardonick, of course."

"Oh, of course. For a moment I thought you were talking about Dr. Whitney."

"Young lady," Anna said harshly, "pay attention to me when I speak. I know something about the press, mind you. I know you'd like nothing better than to paint us all as fools or charlatans."

Selma averted her eyes from the woman's unfriendly gaze and tapped the point of her pen against her notepad. "I'm sorry if I upset you, Dr. Roth. I'm just trying to help my readers understand how something like this could have come about."

"Then perhaps you should talk with Dr. Whitney." The woman smiled as if she were basking in some secret triumph.

Selma studied the older woman's face. Neither one of them spoke for several moments. A thought suddenly occurred to the reporter, and just as quickly she began to blurt it out. "You're enjoying this, aren't you, Dr. Roth?"

"I beg your pardon?"

"Dr. Whitney's misfortune. You really revel in it. That's why you agreed to speak with me, isn't it?"

Anna's eyes grew narrow. She stood, leaning against her desk with such force that her knuckles turned white. "How dare you presume to know my thoughts! Get out! Get out of here now!"

Selma paused in the office doorway. "I don't know what you call this game, Doctor," she said, "but you aren't dealing with a full deck."

In her dream that night, Anna sat across a small table from Thomas Whitney. They were playing gin rummy. Anna looked down, and she saw playing cards spread out like a fan in her hands. *They're all hearts,* she thought. *Every one of them is a heart.*

"Look at this, Dr. Whitney." She laid her cards faceup on the table.

"Thank you, Dr. Roth." He picked them up one by one, stuck them into his mouth, and chewed them.

Whitney's chest turned transparent. Anna saw his heart beating. It pumped faster and faster until it burst. He opened his mouth; the playing cards had turned to blood.

The red fluid dribbled out at first, then poured and poured. It cascaded down his face, across the table, over Anna's hands. His blood was hot, and Anna felt as though she were on fire. The blood became an ocean, engulfing her, and she was drowning in the sizzling liquid.

She screamed.

T he small box arrived by special delivery late in the afternoon. A letter attached to it was marked *READ ME FIRST*. Whitney recognized the printing. He trembled as he opened the envelope.

October 7, 1983

Dear Thomas,

A first-time Atlantic City vacationer approached the casino roulette table. "How the hell do you play this game?" he said to himself.

A voice whispered: "Just put all your chips on the red fourteen in the middle of the table."

The man looked in the direction of the voice, but there was no one there. "Who said that?" he asked.

"Shut up. Do you want people to think you're talking to yourself? This is God, you idiot. Just do as I say."

So the man placed his chips on the red fourteen and watched the ball bounce around in the roulette wheel. The croupier shouted "red fourteen," and he shoved several chips in the man's direction.

God's voice came to him again. "Put all your chips on the black twenty-three." The man followed God's command, and a moment later he was inundated by a huge mound of chips.

"Now, put all your chips on the red twelve," whispered God. The man did so, of course, and watched the ball make its journey one more time.

"Black thirty-one," shouted the croupier, and he scooped up all of the man's chips.

"Oops," whispered God. "Sorry—my mistake."

So you see, Thomas. Anyone can make a mistake. We're only human, after all, made in God's image. All of us have the same basic weaknesses and strengths.

I'm reminded of something that happened just the other day. Mickey Mouse went to his lawyer's office to talk about getting a divorce. "But, Mickey," his lawyer exclaimed, "you can't divorce Minnie just because you think she's crazy."

"I didn't say she was crazy," replied Mickey. "I said she was fucking Goofy."

Mickey feels as though his whole world is coming to an end. He doesn't know whom he can trust. I certainly can imagine how he feels—can't you?

Your friend,
The Phoenix

P.S. You can open the box now.

Whitney's hands turned cold and clammy. He felt his stomach wrench as he opened the box. Inside was a short note: *Farewell, cruel world—Mickey.* And underneath—a miniature noose tied tightly around its neck, its glassy eyes opened wide, a tiny rivulet of dried blood curling out of its mouth—was the rigid corpse of a mouse.

38

Fuller Bloomberg was pacing in the visitors' area of the station house when Schacter returned from lunch. "Captain," he said, "I need to talk to you. It's very important."

The detective ushered Bloomberg into his office. "I'm glad you're here, Counselor. I was thinking of giving you a call myself. I'd like to ask you a couple of questions."

"Questions?"

Schacter tapped a bundle of papers on his desk. "These are the transcripts of Gordon Cardonick's trial and hearings. I've been studying the case, trying to find some way of reopening it. Something in the pretrial hearing caught my eye. I passed by it the first time I saw it, but it left an uneasy feeling in my stomach. Kind of like when you leave for vacation, and you know you've forgotten something, but you just can't figure out what it is. Know what I mean?"

"Captain, I really need to talk to you about—"

Schacter turned to a page of the transcript. "Ah. Here it is. It says here that you asked Judge Gleason to send Cardonick to Littleton for a criminal responsibility evaluation."

"Yes? So?"

"Well, it says here... let me quote your exact words. 'Your Honor, the defense requests a pretrial evaluation under Commonwealth Law number 342, section ii. I request that my client be remanded to Littleton State Hospital, and that the court order Dr. Thomas Whitney to conduct such an evaluation.'"

"That sounds right," said Bloomberg.

"You know, Counselor, there are several doctors at Littleton who do those evaluations. Don't you think it's a little strange that you should come up with the idea of asking specifically for Dr. Whitney?"

"I didn't ask for him."

"Huh?"

"I mean, the transcript is accurate. But it was Cardonick's idea. He told me that Whitney was the only psychiatrist he would agree to talk with. I figured he knew Whitney from his previous admission to Littleton, and he seemed pretty frightened and depressed at the time, so I thought it made sense to relay his request to the judge."

"Uh-huh." Schacter stuffed a plug of tobacco into a briar and lit it. "Back in 1969, when he was thirteen, your client—"

Bloomberg corrected him. "My former client."

"Right. Your former client. He was evaluated by a psychiatrist at the Department of Social Services. Did he say anything to you about that?"

"Come on, Captain. You know I can't reveal anything about my conversations with him. They're confidential, even if he's no longer my client. Why do you ask? Do you think it means something?"

"Everything means something. The trick is to figure out what that 'something' is." He didn't tell Bloomberg what he thought that something might be.

Schacter knew that the DSS psychiatrist had advised removing young Gordon Green from his home; that much was contained in the trial transcripts. And shortly after he was taken away the boy's mother had killed herself. Schacter wondered if Cardonick blamed the DSS and the psychiatrist for his mother's death. What if Whitney had been that psychiatrist? What if Cardonick lied to Whitney during the evaluation not just to avoid punishment, but also to damage Whitney's reputation?

It seemed too fantastic to believe. Schacter had considered asking Whitney about it, but he didn't want to bother his already troubled friend with such a wild notion, especially about something so far in the past. So Schacter requested a copy of the 1969 psychiatric report. It wouldn't be available for a few more days, but then he'd find out for himself the name of the doctor who had evaluated the boy.

He grunted and relit his pipe. "What was it you wanted to see me about?"

Bloomberg began to wring his hands. "I had a visit this morning from a Donald Thornwell. He offered me twenty thousand dollars for an envelope that Cardonick supposedly left with me for safekeeping."

Schacter grunted again. "This case keeps getting more and more unusual," he said. "Did you ever see this guy before today?"

"Never," said Bloomberg. "He made the appointment with my secretary yesterday. He said he wanted me to represent his son in a drug case. Said he needed help immediately. But as soon as he arrived, he told me that he really had some other business in mind. Something that would pay very well for only a few minutes of work. And that's when he mentioned the envelope."

"Did he threaten you at any time?"

"No," replied the lawyer, "not exactly. But there was something about him, something in how high-strung he looked, that made me think he might be dangerous. Anyway, as I told you, he offered to pay me twenty thousand dollars in cash if I would open my safe and give him the envelope."

"And what did you say?" asked the detective.

"The same thing that I told your Lieutenant Rienzi when he asked me for the envelope. That I no longer have any dealings with Gordon Cardonick, and that I don't even have a safe. I decided not to lecture him about attorney-client confidentiality. He didn't look like the sort of person who would appreciate that. I wasn't sure Thornwell believed me until I let him search the whole office for a safe."

Schacter glared at the attorney without speaking.

Bloomberg felt uncomfortable under the detective's scrutiny. "What's the matter, Captain? Did I say something wrong?"

"Did you say Lieutenant Rienzi came to your office looking for this same envelope?"

"Yes, but I . . . I thought you knew. He said he works for you."

Schacter was enraged. "He does, but this is the first I've heard of any envelope. And I didn't tell Rienzi to question you. Stay where you are, Counselor. I want to get to the bottom of this right now."

Schacter opened his door and shouted Rienzi's name into the hall. A few minutes later the lieutenant appeared. "You called for me?"

"You're damn right I called for you!" He gestured toward Bloomberg. "What the hell is going on here, Rienzi?"

Bloomberg tried to interrupt. "But, Captain—"

"Quiet!" Schacter shouted at the lawyer. "Lieutenant, suppose you tell me why you're interviewing people about Cardonick without my knowledge? And what's all this about an envelope?"

Bloomberg waved both hands frantically. "Please, Captain. There's been a terrible—"

"I told you to shut up, Counselor! Well, Rienzi? I'm waiting for an explanation!"

238

Rienzi scratched his head. "I'm sorry, sir. I don't understand what you're talking about."

"But, Captain," said Bloomberg. "That's what I'm trying to tell you. This isn't the Lieutenant Rienzi who came to my office. I've never seen this man before in my life."

Schacter gasped. He inadvertently inhaled tobacco smoke and began to cough. "Jesus H. Christ!" He looked at Bloomberg, then at Rienzi, and then once more at Bloomberg. "Gentlemen," he said, "will somebody kindly tell me what the fuck is going on?"

It was very late at night—very
early in the morning, actually—and Whitney still couldn't sleep. He
aimlessly turned the dial of his television. Pickings were slim at that
hour, but on one of the local stations an intense-looking young woman
was interviewing a familiar face.

"Reverend Isaac, you've come under fire recently for your support of
Gordon Cardonick, the man many people refer to as the Christmas Eve
Sniper. How do you answer your critics?"

"Well, Paula, I could bore you with some of the standard Bible
truths. You know which ones I mean. 'Judge not, lest ye be judged.'
'Let he who is without sin cast the first stone.' And so on and so forth.
But the truth of the matter is that I'm helping him for very selfish
reasons."

"What are those reasons, Reverend?"

"This was a test of my faith. I'm sure you remember that Gordon
killed my lovely daughter Sarah, my youngest child. And there was
revenge in my heart at the beginning. I'd be embarrassed to repeat now
some of the thoughts I had and some of the things I contemplated.
Hatred was consuming me like some slow poison. And so I asked the
Lord, 'Lord, how can I rid myself of this poison?' And he showed me
that in order to do that, I had to forgive Gordon for his actions. It was
the Lord's ultimate test of me."

"But what was your reaction when you learned that he wasn't really
insane after all, that he killed with premeditation, that he killed for
money?"

"It may surprise you, but that didn't really alter my outlook on things very much. I understand now that he wasn't legally insane. But I still believe he's a deeply troubled young man, and it's just as important as ever for me to forgive him. In fact, I've had several conversations with Gordon since he rejoined the community, and he's more interested than ever in bringing the Lord into his life."

I'll bet, thought Whitney. He turned the television off, undressed, and tried in vain to fall asleep. A half hour later, just as dawn broke, he dressed and went outside for a walk.

It was ironic: When he was keeping a full schedule—working at Littleton, teaching at Franklin, seeing patients in his office at home—sleep came easily, and he could never seem to get enough. But now that he had time on his hands, he was amazed to discover just how little sleep he really needed.

And he certainly had time on his hands. He was still being paid not to show up at Littleton. He'd asked for a leave of absence from his teaching duties, and he'd referred his few private patients to other doctors. He wasn't sure why he'd divested himself of those responsibilities, nor did he care enough to want to figure it out.

So sleep was something that took very little of his time. Nor was he terribly interested in eating, reading, or seeing friends. He realized, of course, that he was showing many classic signs of serious depression: appetite loss, sleep difficulties, lack of interest, and social isolation. But he really didn't feel all that bad. In fact, he didn't feel much of anything.

The pills certainly helped. He started with the samples he'd received from drug manufacturers, then graduated to writing prescriptions for himself. He'd begun by taking an occasional amphetamine to help him get going in the morning, one or two Valiums during the day to take the edge off his anxiety, and Seconals at night to usher in sleep. Then, excusing his behavior as an exercise in scientific discovery, he began reversing the order of the drugs. Now one pill seemed interchangeable with another, and he spent a great deal of time not feeling anxious, not feeling depressed, not feeling tired, not feeling alert—not feeling anything.

"Yes, sir," said the bartender. "One ginger ale coming right up. Trying to lay off the hard stuff, huh?"

Whitney didn't say anything.

"Hey, let me know if I'm talking too much, huh? Mr. Marsella—he's the owner—he says the trick to being a good bartender is knowing which customers want you to talk and which ones just want to drink and be left alone. I'm still pretty new at this, though." He extended his hand. "Joe's the name."

Whitney shook the man's hand without speaking. He took a sip of the soft drink.

"I just started working here last week," continued the bartender. "You come here often?"

Whitney shook his head. "No, I've never been here before."

"Uh-huh. Well, we got a pretty good collection of miniature liquor bottles in that display case over there. There's a pool table in the back, some video games, too. And the piano player starts work in a few minutes."

"Yes," replied Whitney. "I know all about him."

"Oh. Are you a fan of his?"

Whitney shrugged his shoulders without answering.

"Mr. Marsella sure seems to like him, I can tell you that," continued the bartender. "He's got him playing here Monday through Wednesday, every week. Usually the customers ignore him, the way they do with most piano players. But the ones who listen say he's pretty good."

A barmaid overheard their conversation. "Bullshit," she said under her breath.

"Hey, Bonnie," said the bartender with mock seriousness. "This is a family environment."

"Yeah, right. I'm sure." She bit down on her lip and blushed, then returned to her tables.

The bartender lowered his voice and spoke in a conspiratorial tone. "You should have seen her the other night. Gordon—he's our piano player—Gordon was telling me about this trip he's taking next week to Atlantic City, and Bonnie was standing nearby. Now, Gordon knows she's been trying to get him to notice her ever since he started working here, so he asked her if she wanted to go. Well, she just about jumped out of her skin saying yes. Then she asked him if he really meant it, and Gordon said, 'Sure. My wife and I could really use a baby-sitter.'" The bartender laughed out loud. "I'll tell you, pal. Gordon was lucky he didn't wind up with his head stuffed inside a pitcher of beer. She hasn't said a word to him or me since then. Pretty good, huh?"

"A real scream," Whitney said without expression.

"Hey, here he is now."

There was a smattering of applause from three or four people seated near the spinet piano in the corner. Cardonick sat down and played a

242

couple of chords. "Thank you. Thank you very much." He leaned toward his microphone. "There's an old friend of mine in the audience tonight, a very special friend. I'd like to dedicate this first song to him. It's from *Porgy and Bess*, and it tells us that things aren't always what they seem. It's called 'It Ain't Necessarily So.'"

Cardonick looked directly at Whitney and smiled broadly. "So, Doc," he said, "this one's especially for you."

hitney was feeding peanuts to the pigeons in Rittenhouse Square when Schacter caught up with him. "Well, well. I see you're studying ornithology these days," said the detective.

"Yes, well, I find I have quite a bit of free time lately." Whitney rubbed the two-day growth of whiskers on his chin. "How did you know I'd be here?"

"I had one of my men trail you when you left home this morning."

Whitney smiled and continued to feed the birds. "How about that. And I thought I was just being paranoid when I thought I was being followed. Why did you do that?"

"Because I've called you a half dozen times this week and haven't gotten an answer. It was either this or come pounding at your door."

Whitney shrugged his shoulders. "I discontinued my answering service. There didn't seem to be that many messages worth not missing. Sorry."

"The truth of the matter is that I'm worried about you. You look like hell. You're turning yourself into a recluse."

Schacter grabbed one of Whitney's peanuts. He shelled it and tossed it toward the rear of the flock, near a runt that hadn't been able to muscle its way to the food.

"Thomas, is there anything I can do?"

Whitney shook his head. Schacter rested his hand on his friend's shoulder, but Whitney pulled away and continued feeding the pigeons.

Schacter sighed and stood up. "Gotta go now, Thomas. Let me know if you want me for anything."

"You could kill him," murmured Whitney as the detective began to walk away.

"What was that?"

Whitney looked directly at him for the first time. "I know this sounds crazy, Stan, but I feel like Cardonick had this whole thing planned from the beginning. Like he was out to get me in the worst possible way."

Schacter decided not to reveal that he'd begun to wonder the same thing. He didn't want to say anything until he was sure. "Forget it. You were just in the wrong place at the wrong time. He made monkeys out of us all—you, me, his lawyer, the jury. He's probably making one out of Reverend Isaac, too. Unless you buy all this born-again crap."

"I'm not sure what to believe anymore, Stan. Really, I'm not."

Schacter walked to the corner of 19th and Walnut streets and got into a squad car that had been waiting for him. *I know this sounds crazy, but I feel like Cardonick had this whole thing planned from the beginning.* Schacter had begun of late to have similar suspicions. But when Whitney said those words, the detective realized just how ridiculous the whole idea was.

Denise Cardonick twisted the ends of her hair nervously. "I'm supposed to be at work now. I told my boss I didn't feel well and he said I should go home early. I didn't want to tell anyone where I was really going. I just hope Gordon doesn't decide to call me at work. If he knew I was here there's no telling what he might do."

"Yeah, well, let's just keep this our little secret, then," said Schacter.

"It happened yesterday. I was using this new vacuum cleaner Gordon bought me, one of those fancy self-propelled models with all the attachments. He's been buying me lots of things lately. That bar job is paying him real well."

Schacter raised his eyebrows. He made a notation on his desk appointment blotter.

"Anyway," she continued, "I guess I got carried away with it. I started vacuuming things I've never cleaned before. I took off the heating duct covers and vacuumed the vents. Then I vacuumed out the top section of Gordon's piano, where the strings and the hammers are. And then I opened up the bottom section of the piano, down near the pedals." She fumbled nervously in her handbag. She pulled out an envelope and passed it to the detective. "And that's where I found this."

Inside the envelope were four newspaper clippings, slightly yellowed with age. The articles were about various criminal trials that had taken place in the Philadelphia area. In each instance the defendant had pleaded not guilty by reason of insanity. Thomas Whitney had testified at all the trials. Whitney's name had been underlined in red ink—presumably by Cardonick—whenever it appeared in the articles.

The detective grunted. "Interesting, but why did you bring them to me?"

"I don't know. Gordon must have collected these while he was at Littleton, since I know Dr. Whitney has been on a leave of absence and hasn't testified in court since Gordon was released. I got scared when I found them. I really don't know why. Maybe it's because they were hidden so carefully. I kept asking myself, 'Why would Gordon save these, and why would he hide them in the piano?'"

Schacter pretended to yawn. He, too, was curious about the clippings. He didn't want to appear too interested, though. If he did, she might feel obliged to tell Cardonick what she'd found and to whom she'd shown it. The detective copied the names of the four defendants named in the articles.

He handed the envelope to her. "Thank you, Mrs. Cardonick. I'll let you know if I think of anything. In the meantime I wouldn't worry too much about these if I were you. And, like I said, we'll just keep this visit secret between you and me."

After she left, Schacter reviewed the four names he'd written. *Sharon Goldman. Alvin Toggler. Carl Denton. Andrea Oliphant.* He remembered their cases vaguely, even though he hadn't been involved with any of them. Something Denise had said didn't fit in quite right, but he couldn't tell what that something might be.

Suddenly he understood what was wrong. *Gordon must have collected these while he was at Littleton.* That couldn't have happened, Schacter realized. All four cases had been tried in 1982, *before* Cardonick was arrested. Months before the Christmas Eve killings, Gordon Cardonick was collecting newspaper articles about the doctor who eventually would evaluate him.

He remembered what he'd said to Fuller Bloomberg. *Everything means something. The trick is trying to figure out what that "something" is.*

Schacter received a call from a clerk at the Department of Social Services. "I haven't gotten hold yet of that report you asked for," she said. "The one on Gordon Green from 1969. I have my assistant digging through the files in our warehouse, but we've got a lot of other pressing business here, as I'm sure you can appreciate." She sounded mildly irritated.

Schacter sighed. "Any idea when you'll have it?"

"We're almost done searching through Dr. Foley's papers. I guess we could get it to you in a week or so."

"Dr. Foley?"

"Yes. Cynthia Foley. She was the psychiatrist who wrote the report. Didn't you know that?"

"Yes, yes, of course," lied Schacter. Suddenly there was no great need to read it. "Thanks for trying. Just send it along when you find it."

So Whitney hadn't done the DSS evaluation of young Gordon Green. Schacter wasn't terribly surprised. The idea that there might have been an earlier connection between Whitney and Cardonick became increasingly preposterous the longer he thought about it.

But there was still the unsolved matter of the clippings Cardonick's wife had shown him: Why had the killer collected them *before* his arrest on Christmas Eve?

Schacter discussed the matter with Rienzi. "Of course, I'm sure you've already thought of this," the lieutenant said with know-it-all smugness, "but he could still have collected them *after* the killings. You'd be surprised how many people keep old newspapers in their garages. Maybe Cardonick got hold of those articles recently to satisfy some morbid curiosity about Dr. Whitney."

Rienzi was right, the captain mused. Hell, for all Schacter knew, Denise Cardonick could have collected the clippings herself and pretended to find them inside her husband's piano. That made as much sense as any other explanation he could come up with.

Whitney had gone nearly forty-eight hours without sleep. Bolstered by an occasional amphetamine, he'd walked around the neighborhood a bit, listened to recordings of all nine Beethoven symphonies, and watched portions of a telethon for some obscure disease whose name he couldn't remember.

All day long he'd moved about restlessly, never able to sit in one place for more than a few minutes. He seemed to have boundless energy: he scrubbed and mopped his kitchen floor—carelessly, but at great length; he rearranged all the books in his library, first by subject, then by author. At first the energized feeling was pleasant, but by late afternoon his nerves were jangling uncontrollably. He felt as though his body would never catch up with itself.

A single letter arrived in the mail. He recognized the printing on the envelope.

October 17, 1983

Dear Thomas,

When I was a youngster, the other children loved to frolic in the summer. But while they were swimming and playing ball, I was involved in more solitary pursuits. Did you know that a red ant, when cut in half, becomes two separate creatures, each moving about in its own direction? Did you know that the rays of the August sun, when focused into a pinpoint through the lens of a magnifying glass, ignite a spider in seven seconds? Did you know that the tip of a hat pin, when carefully inserted into the base of a tadpole's skull, causes its four little legs to spring suddenly to full extension?

My friends loved the summer. But I was just killing time (ha-ha), waiting for the days to grow shorter. I lived for the return of standard time. For me, turning the clock back marked the real beginning of winter. And I loved the winter. It always reminded me of death.

I used to roam the city streets in the dark. I hunted stray cats and killed them. Watching them die always gave me a hard-on, and I felt quite close to my victims as they died. At first that confused me. But then I realized that hate and love are really quite close to each other on the map of human emotions. They're not opposites. They're each the opposite of indifference. Even murder can be an act of love.

The slower my victims' deaths were, the more complete my satisfaction. Once I sealed shut a trash can with my prey inside, then pressed my ear against it and listened to the cat's ever-weakening attempts to scratch itself out of the death cylinder. Another time I impaled a cat through its paw on a wrought-iron fence, then watched it struggle for an hour until it collapsed from the cold and the loss of blood.

Torture has always been dear to me.

I've treasured our relationship, Thomas. Knowing that I've added in some small way to your suffering fills my soul with joy. But the time has come to complete our little cat-and-mouse game. I hear you scratching on the death cylinder. I smell your sweat as you search frantically for a way out.

But death is the only way out, Thomas. Either you choose the time and place or I will. And, as you know by now, I prefer the slow kill.

Your dear friend,
The Phoenix

P.S. How is your lovely wife, Allison? Please give her my regards when you see her.

The bottom of the letter was marked by the bloodied pawprint of a cat.

*   *   *

Sometime after nightfall Whitney took a Valium and tried to relax. He tried to sit motionless in an easy chair in his den, but his fingers and toes kept dancing in spite of himself.

The quiet hum of the fluorescent kitchen light seemed to grow louder and louder until it was exploding inside his head. He leapt up and turned it off.

He sat down again, and immediately became disturbed by the thought that he was at a terrible disadvantage: He couldn't see anything in the darkness outside his windows, but anyone out there could see him clearly if they wished to. He walked through the entire house pulling down shades and venetian blinds.

He returned to his chair and tried to shut off all thought. It was an impossible task. After a while the Valium took over, and the thoughts came more slowly. He recalled reading somewhere that telephones could be wired to pick up sound in a room and broadcast it elsewhere. He wondered if anyone was listening to him at that moment, then tried to dismiss the idea as ridiculous. He was still considering the notion when the phone rang.

He answered it on the fourth ring. He said nothing.

The caller hesitated. "Hello? Thomas, are you there?"

"Who is this?"

"Thomas, it's Percy Osborne. Are you all right? Your voice sounds a little strange."

Whitney took a deep breath. "Yes, I'm fine, Percy. I was just trying to catch up on this month's psychiatric journals. I guess I lost track of the time. What time is it, anyway?"

"It's almost eleven. I'm sorry to call so late, but I just got off the phone with Senator Ouimette, the one who's sponsoring that bill abolishing the insanity defense. His committee is going to begin hearings next month, right around Thanksgiving, and you're going to be subpoenaed to testify. I'm afraid the senator is looking to publicly rip apart a proponent of the insanity defense. I tried to convince him to call on me, but—"

"But I make a much fatter target."

Osborne was silent for a moment. "I'm sorry, Thomas. I wanted you to hear it from me first. Thought it might make things a little easier for you."

Whitney sighed. "Sounds like it'll be a real circus, with me as the main attraction."

After he finished talking with Osborne, Whitney walked up to his bedroom. Soon afterward his front doorbell rang. He put on his robe, walked downstairs, and looked through the peephole in the door. He saw no one.

"Yes? Who is it?" There was no reply. "Who's there? Hello?"

He went back upstairs. Moments later he heard the crashing of glass and a loud thud. The noise came from his living room, directly below the bedroom. He looked out his bedroom window. He thought he saw a dark-clothed figure dashing down his front path toward the street.

He went downstairs and threw open the drapes. The rock had shattered two windowpanes. The drapes had stopped their forward motion, and the rock had dropped harmlessly to the floor.

There was a piece of paper attached to it with string. Whitney untied the paper and read:

> Thomas—
> Hand-delivered present outside front door. Hope you like it.
>   The Phoenix

Whitney unlocked the rolltop desk in the corner of the room and pulled out his handgun. It had been months since he fired it, since the last time Schacter took him to the police practice range. It shook in his tired, frightened hand.

He opened the door. A large cat lay motionless on the front stoop. A knife had been plunged deep into the creature's heart. The blood was beginning to congeal in the animal's matted hair.

Whitney slammed the door shut and stood in the middle of the living room. A sudden gust of air blew into the room through the hole in the window.

The phone in his den rang. He let it ring ten times, fifteen times, twenty times.

He picked up the receiver and held it to his ear without speaking. He heard the sound of a cat howling.

He screamed into the phone so loudly that his throat and chest began to ache. A voice on the other end began to laugh maniacally.

Whitney aimed his pistol into the telephone and squeezed the trigger.

The emergency call came in to Schacter's home during Johnny Carson's monologue. The detective threw a raincoat over his pajamas, attached the portable flashing blue light to the top of his Plymouth, and sped toward Chestnut Hill. He reached Whitney's home in a record eight minutes.

Two uniformed officers stood near their cruiser outside Whitney's front door. "Captain Schacter?" asked one of them when the detective arrived.

Schacter flashed his police identification. The young man whistled admiringly. "Whew, you sure got here fast. I'm Mazza, the one who called you. I thought that was the safest thing to do."

"Yes, good job, Mazza. How many gunshots were there?"

"Well, sir, one of the neighbors called the station a little after eleven. She said that first she heard something that sounded like glass breaking, like maybe someone was trying to bust into Dr. Whitney's house. Then a minute or two later she heard a gunshot. We did a once-over of the exterior. No signs of forced entry, but someone obviously threw something through that window over there." The officer directed his flashlight to the broken panes.

Schacter grunted.

"Then we found this, Captain." Mazza shined his light on the dead cat. "It's a fresh kill. The body feels pretty warm. Then someone inside the house asked us what we wanted. When I identified myself he said he didn't call for the police, that we should go away.

"I told him about the neighbor's report, and he said there wasn't any problem. He came to the front window and pulled open the curtains, and he said, 'See—there's nothing wrong.' It was Dr. Whitney. I recognized him from the news stories.

"I said we'd like to come in anyway just to check and make sure everything was okay. But he looked at me kind of strange. He wouldn't let us inside. I didn't want to make a bad situation worse by barging in, so I called the station. Lieutenant Costello said this guy is a friend of yours, and he said we should try to get you out here to talk to him."

Schacter pounded on the front door. "Thomas! Thomas, it's me, Stanley. I want to talk to you. Will you open the door?" There was no reply. "Thomas, damn it, it's fifteen degrees out here, and I'm in nothing but my pajamas and raincoat. Let me in!"

The dead-bolt lock snapped and the doorknob turned slowly. The door opened a quarter of the way. Schacter slipped inside.

He followed Whitney into the living room. The psychiatrist slumped against the rolltop desk, breathing heavily and cradling his head in his arms. "Did you see the cat?"

Schacter nodded his head. "Any idea where it came from?"

Whitney handed him the letter. The detective read it and set it down on the coffee table. He noticed Whitney's pill vials. "Your neighbor heard glass breaking and a gunshot."

Whitney told him about the rock. "I picked up my handgun when I heard the noise. It discharged accidentally."

"Uh-huh." The detective gathered up the pill containers and slipped them into his pocket.

"Hey!" exclaimed the psychiatrist. "What are you doing? You can't do that."

"Sue me. Call a cop if you want to. I'll be right back."

Schacter walked outside and spoke to the two patrolmen. He instructed them to remove the knife from the cat, have it checked for fingerprints, and dispose of the animal. He told them to arrange for a patrol car to keep watch on Whitney's house for the rest of the night.

When he returned to the living room he found Whitney stretched out on the sofa with his eyes half closed. Schacter read the letter again and replaced it in its envelope. And then he noticed the postmark. "Do you know anyone in Atlantic City?"

Whitney was too tired to respond with anything more than a guttural noise. Schacter interpreted that as a negative reply.

"Huh. All the other letters came from Philadelphia," said the detective, rubbing his chin pensively. "This one came from Atlantic City."

"Atlantic City," mumbled Whitney. "The Elephant Hotel." He fell into a heavy sleep.

In Whitney's dream, the young woman sat in a folding chair on the Atlantic City beach. It was midday, summer, and the sun was shining brightly, yet there was no one else there.

"You always arrive early for your appointment," said Whitney.

"Yes," she replied.

As always, Whitney was struck by the woman's ethereal beauty. He was especially fond of her eyes. One of them was green, the other blue. The green eye was warm and inviting, and it seemed to beckon him. But the blue eye was cold and distant. The woman gazed out across the ocean, searching for something that Whitney could neither see nor understand.

"It's nice to see that one of you is on time," said Whitney. He knew he shouldn't take sides, but he couldn't help himself in this case. "Do you know where he is?"

The woman gestured toward the boardwalk and its gambling casinos.

Whitney stood near the roulette table. "She's down by the ocean," he said to the man next to him. "We've been waiting for you."

"Fuck off," the man said. "I'll be there when I feel like it. I'm only here because the court made me come. Otherwise, I'd never agree to it."

"We never agree on anything, Doctor," the woman said as the three of them sat inside the dingy office.

"I know," replied Whitney. "Maybe that's what attracted the two of you to each other in the first place." He sat at his lopsided desk; Freud's *Psychopathology of Everyday Life* substituted for its missing leg.

"Let's start at the beginning," said Whitney. "Tell me about your first date."

Music filled the small, steamy room. The melody was dominated by strings, in three-quarter time, with a vaguely French flavor.

The man began to sing: "We met at nine."

"We met at eight," she corrected him.

"I was on time."

"No, you were late."

"Ah, yes," sang the man. "I remember it well."

The sound of the music mixed with the noise from the city traffic outside the office. Whitney couldn't take it any longer. He held a conch shell to his ear, and he lost himself in the imagined sound of the ocean's roar.

He was on the beach again, naked and alone. A howling cat, blood dripping from its paws, ran in a circle around him. He shot the cat, but two more bleeding cats appeared in its place. He shot again, and again, and again. There were more and more cats. They scratched at his legs. His blood mixed with theirs. He began to howl.

The melody ran through Whitney's head all morning, but he could only remember the first five lyric lines:

> We met at nine.
> We met at eight.
> I was on time.
> No, you were late.
> Ah, yes! I remember it well.

It was the same tune that had preoccupied him once before, around the time of Cardonick's trial. What was the name of that movie, the one with Maurice Chevalier? Later in the morning he remembered: *Gigi*. What a peculiar name, he thought. *Gigi*.

He watched a television game show that was interchangeable with any of a dozen other such programs. Two chubby housewives and an army corporal were competing for the weekly grand prize. Off-camera, the announcer's voice droned on; it was identical to the voices on all the other shows. Whitney didn't really pay much attention until the announcer listed the prizes that the winner would receive. "... from American Tourister. And to help you break in your new luggage, a getaway weekend for two in fabulous, exciting Atlantic City! Yes, that's right, we'll fly you and that special someone to America's Playground. You'll stay at the luxurious Resorts International Hotel, where you'll..."

Atlantic City. The woman with one green eye, one blue. The tiny office that opened directly onto the noise and bustle of the city. Disconnected pieces of a puzzle, they began to lock into position alongside one another in his mind.

Whitney dashed to his basement, to the pile of boxes at its farthest end. He rummaged through them for the papers that so many years earlier sat in that lopsided desk in the dingy little office. An hour passed, then another. In the very last folder he found what he was looking for.

Gigi. Atlantic City. It all made perfect sense to him now. The realization was so powerful that his hands began to shake as if a thousand volts of electricity were passing through them.

He carried the folder upstairs and placed it with the latest letter from the Phoenix. He stared at the stack of papers for several minutes, until a wide smile crept slowly across his face.

I know who you are, you son of a bitch, he thought. *I know who you are.*

Marsella sat in a well-padded reclining chair in his den. A tall, muscular, somewhat effeminate man stood next to him. The tall man wore skintight slacks and T-shirt and was manicuring Marsella's left hand.

Marsella gave a phony smile to the visitor seated on his sofa. "Can I interest you in a manicure, Captain Shinkler?"

"Schacter," corrected his visitor. "No, thanks."

"Schacter," Marsella repeated. "Sorry about that. Anyway, George here is excellent. The secret is in the cuticles. People who do nails well are a dime a dozen, but George is an absolute artist when it comes to cuticles. You're sure you wouldn't like to give it a try? My treat, of course."

Schacter shook his head.

"Very well." Marsella sighed. "I must say, I find your visit here very unusual. When the police want to talk with me, they usually look for me at my bar."

"And how often do police come looking for you?"

"Captain Shankler—"

"Schacter," said the detective.

"Sorry." Marsella smiled coldly once again. "Captain, I'm a law-abiding man. But the police do come to the bar now and then. You know—the occasional complaint from a neighbor about a noisy patron. Or sometimes one of my customers runs out on his wife, and she sends the cops around to look for him. And of course, there's the annual solicitation for the police charities. But, like I said, I'm surprised to see you come to my house to do business."

Schacter grunted. "I came here because the matter I want to discuss is personal."

"Personal?"

"Yes," said Schacter. "It involves your son."

Marsella was confused. "My son? But I don't... What do you mean?"

"Your son. The one with the, uh, problem. You know—the one you wanted to hire Fuller Bloomberg to represent."

Marsella's body tensed. The change was barely perceptible, but it was enough to make his hand twitch involuntarily, causing the manicurist's artistic fingers to draw a bit of blood from one of Marsella's cuticles.

"Ouch!"

"I'm so sorry, Mr. Marsella."

"Be careful, damn it!" Marsella glanced at Schacter, then turned back to the manicurist with contrived politeness. "No problem, George. Just a little nick."

"Would you like me to get a Band-Aid, sir?"

"No, there's no need. You're finished with this hand, so why don't you take a break? Go into the kitchen and ask Geraldine to make you some lunch."

"Yes, sir." The manicurist left and shut the door behind him.

Marsella eyed his visitor suspiciously. "Suppose you tell me what this is all about."

"Ah," sighed Schacter as he leaned back and propped his feet on Marsella's coffee table. "Kids, kids, kids. What can a father do? You work yourself to the bone to give them a decent home, and still they break your heart every time. I'm a father myself, and it just about kills me when I see a boy from a nice family get into trouble with drugs. What exactly was it with your son? Marijuana? Amphetamines? Cocaine?"

Marsella drummed his fingers on the arm of his chair. "I don't have a son. But I suppose you know that, don't you?"

"Yes. And I also know that you've been looking for a very special envelope." The detective pulled a sealed envelope from his breast pocket and placed it on the coffee table.

Marsella leaned forward in his chair. His eyes widened as they fixed on the envelope, and for a moment Schacter thought he was going to pounce on it.

"Where did you get that?" asked Marsella.

Schacter smiled. "This?" He unsealed the envelope. Tiny droplets of sweat appeared in the space between Marsella's nose and upper lip.

"I got this out of my desk this morning," continued Schacter. "I needed something to carry my tobacco in." He pulled out a pipe and poured tobacco from the envelope.

Marsella wiped his palms on his pants and stared at his visitor. "Just exactly what do you want, Detective?"

Schacter lit his pipe. "I want to know what makes that envelope worth twenty thousand dollars to you."

"And what if I told you I have no idea what you're talking about?"

"Well, then I guess I'd say you're too smart to think I'd believe that. Besides, I could always bring Bloomberg here to identify you in person. Because when I showed him your picture he had no trouble identifying you as one of the men who came to him looking for the envelope."

"*One* of the men . . . ?"

"Oh," said Schacter. "You thought you were the only one who knew about it. Not so. Hell, I'm beginning to think everyone this side of the Poconos has heard about it. Just what's inside this envelope that makes it so goddamn popular?"

Marsella's eyes narrowed. "You're the detective. You tell me."

"Well, it must have something to do with Gordon Cardonick," said Schacter as he rubbed his chin. "Something you're afraid could fall into the wrong hands—police hands, for example. I figure it's some kind of information that ties him and you together in something that's . . . well, let's just say something that could cause you embarrassment."

"I see. A very interesting theory, Captain. But you said something about other people . . ."

"Ah. Now that's where it gets really interesting. You see, you're not the only one who paid a visit to Bloomberg. Someone else knows about the envelope. He tried to get it from Bloomberg by impersonating one of my men. We don't know who he is, but he seems to want it almost as much as you do."

"So?"

"So maybe this someone else wants to blackmail you. And maybe you'd like to help us get hold of the envelope before he does."

Marsella stood and tossed a small log into the fireplace. "Let's suppose—just for the sake of argument, of course—suppose I did contact this Fillmore Bloombird—"

"Fuller Bloomberg."

"Whatever," said Marsella. "Even if I did contact him, and even if I am looking for this envelope you're talking about—why should I believe that someone else is looking for it, too?"

Schacter sighed. "I guess you'll just have to take my word on that, pal."

Marsella chuckled sarcastically. "Oh, of course. How silly of me. So let's suppose I believe you—again, just for the sake of argument. Why should I help you get hold of this so-called embarrassing envelope?"

Schacter stood and walked over to the fireplace. He stood inches from Marsella's face. "Because I don't give a shit about you," he hissed. "I just want Cardonick. I think you know something that can help me get him. And if you help me get Cardonick, maybe you can get out of this whole thing without too much, uh, embarrassment."

Marsella backed away from Schacter. Neither man spoke for several moments.

The door opened. "Oh, I'm sorry, Mr. Marsella," said the manicurist. "I didn't realize you were still busy."

"That's all right, George. Captain Schacter was just getting ready to leave. I'm sorry I couldn't help you, Captain, but I did find your story very interesting. Imaginative, but interesting. George, please show our guest the way out."

"Don't bother," said Schacter as he headed out of the room. He paused in the doorway and faced Marsella. "I guess I'll just have to find that other guy instead."

T he bartender closed his eyes and
held two fingers against each temple. "Don't tell me," he said. "Ah! I
remember now. Ginger ale, straight up."

Whitney smiled. "Very good. That's exactly right."

"I'll get the hang of this job yet. What was it—about two weeks
ago?"

"Something like that. How's life been treating you, Joe?"

"Oh, can't complain, can't complain."

"You can if you'd like," said Whitney.

The bartender laughed. "What good would that do me? Besides, I'm
the one who's supposed to listen to complaints here. I'll tell you... Damn. I
forget your name."

"Thomas."

"Right. I'll tell you, Thomas. Sometimes I feel like a goddamn
psychoanalyst. You wouldn't believe some of the things people tell me
after they've had a drink or two."

Whitney laughed heartily.

"By the way, what kind of doctor are you?"

"Excuse me?" said Whitney.

"The last time you were here, when Gordon dedicated that song to
you, he called you Doc. So I just assumed you were a doctor. And I was
wondering, what kind are you?"

Whitney thought for a moment. "Retired," he replied.

"Uh-huh." The bartender put Whitney's drink on the counter.
"Anyway, life must be treating you pretty good, Thomas."

"Oh?"

"I mean, I hope you don't mind me saying so, but the last time you were in here you looked awfully low, like maybe you'd just lost your best friend. But you seem in pretty good spirits tonight. Which is it—a lady or a horse?"

Whitney laughed. "No, no—nothing like that. But I finally figured out the solution to a problem that's been bothering me for a long time. So I guess you could say I came here to celebrate."

"Well, what better place to celebrate than in a bar, right?" The bartender gestured toward the piano. "Hey, there's your buddy, getting ready to play."

A few patrons applauded Cardonick as he adjusted his microphone and piano stool. He noticed Whitney almost immediately. "A good friend of mine is here tonight," he said, and he flashed a sinister grin in Whitney's direction. "So I'd like to dedicate my first number to him. Little Anthony and the Imperials recorded it in the early sixties. It's called 'Goin' Out of My Head.'"

Cardonick performed with great spirit, apparently inspired by the opportunity to preen and swagger in front of Whitney. He played several requests, cracked a few jokes, and drew a favorable reaction from his audience. But he seemed oblivious to the crowd's response, so caught up was he in taunting Whitney. Every few minutes Cardonick glanced at his antagonist, arching his back each time and stretching his arms like a vulture strutting victoriously over his prey.

After forty-five minutes Cardonick took a short break. When he returned for his second set he was surprised to see that Whitney was still in the audience.

Cardonick performed a total of three sets, and Whitney stayed the entire time. Two weeks earlier, Whitney had ended his first visit to Marsella's shortly after Cardonick began performing. On that occasion he'd slouched out of the bar, shuffling like a vanquished soldier. But now his spirits were soaring, and Cardonick—like the bartender earlier in the evening—found the change quite striking.

As the evening wore on, Cardonick's enthusiasm for playing faded. But Whitney continued to laugh louder and applaud longer than anyone else. And when Cardonick left the small stage for the third time, Whitney led a small group in shouting for an encore.

The bartender dashed into the back room after Cardonick. "Hey, Gordon, they really dig you out there tonight. They want you to do another number."

261

"Yeah, well, tell them they can blow it out their ass." He grabbed his coat and stormed out of the building.

Cardonick sat up in bed and leaned against the headboard. "Whitney," he murmured.

Denise yawned and opened her eyes. "Did you say something?"

"Nothing important. Go back to sleep."

"How did things go at the bar tonight?"

He stared at her coldly. "Why do you ask?" he snapped.

"I'm just trying to make conversation, that's all. You should try it sometime. I understand lots of married couples do it." She rolled away and faced the wall.

"I can't sleep. I'm going downstairs to watch TV." Cardonick stood and put on his robe. "I wonder what the son of a bitch is trying to prove."

"Who?"

"Whitney. He showed up at Marsella's a couple of weeks ago, and he came back tonight."

"Thomas Whitney? What was he doing there?"

Cardonick noted the attentive tone in her voice. He reached across the bed and grabbed her wrist. He yanked on it and spun her around to face him. "What makes you so damn interested all of a sudden?"

"Ouch!" She pulled herself free and turned away again. "Christ, you're the one who brought it up."

Cardonick put on his slippers and walked downstairs. Denise heard the refrigerator door open and close. The television set blared loudly for several minutes. She remembered the times she'd spent in Whitney's company, and she wondered if he ever thought about her.

She pretended to be asleep when Cardonick returned to bed. He ground his pelvis against her rear as he reached roughly for her breast. Denise held her breath and remained immobile.

Eventually Cardonick wearied of her unresponsiveness and rolled away. Soon his rhythmic breathing indicated he'd fallen asleep.

Denise lay awake for hours, her pillow moistened by tears.

A week later, Whitney was sitting at a table near the piano when Cardonick came out to perform.

As Cardonick began talking to the crowd, Whitney started writing in a small notebook. He scribbled quickly, apparently taking down every word Cardonick said. It reminded Cardonick of their interviews at Littleton.

"Hey, folks," Cardonick said, joking to disguise his uneasiness. "This fella must be trying to steal my jokes. I knew I was funny, but I didn't think I was *that* funny. You want me to talk slower so you don't miss anything, friend?"

Whitney smiled. He kept writing.

"Hey, I got it. He must be a restaurant critic. Uh-oh. Hey, Charlie," Cardonick shouted toward the kitchen. "You better stop using your pecker to mix the salad dressing."

The crowd laughed. Whitney chuckled, too, but he kept writing. He copied the name of each song Cardonick played, and he transcribed everything Cardonick said between songs. Finally Cardonick stopped talking between numbers, and he seemed to play each song louder and faster than the previous one.

"I think I'm coming down with a cold, Joe," Cardonick said to the bartender at the end of his first set of songs. "I guess I'll have to call it a night. Bye."

Cardonick glanced over his shoulder toward Whitney's table. Whitney placed his notebook in his pocket, smiled broadly at Cardonick, and made a thumbs-up gesture.

Cardonick pretended not to notice. He walked quickly out of the room.

The dapper gentleman was sitting at the counter of a Center City coffee shop. Schacter caught him by surprise. "Well, well," said the detective. "If it isn't my old friend, Seymour Dinklemayer."

Dinklemayer spun around on his counter stool. His eyes widened when he saw Schacter. He slipped off the stool and headed for the door. He'd taken only three steps when he bounced into Rienzi. He muttered something under his breath as Rienzi guided him back to the counter. Schacter and Rienzi sat on either side of him.

"Ah," said Schacter. "Nice of you to stay, Seymour. And I believe you've already met Lieutenant Rienzi."

"Hey, how ya doing, Seymour?" said Rienzi, slapping Dinklemayer's back so hard that he almost fell into his piece of cheesecake.

"Please, please, Rienzi," said Schacter. "Let's show a little respect. You'll have to forgive the lieutenant, Seymour. Young folks today don't have enough regard for their elders. Things have changed since you and I were the lieutenant's age, haven't they, Seymour?"

Dinklemayer shifted his eyes back and forth between the two detectives. He sighed deeply and sipped his coffee.

"You should have seen Seymour in the old days, Lieutenant. A veritable master of tumblers and locks. No one could pick his way through a double-gauge Rabson quicker than Seymour. And he could search a room from top to bottom without leaving even a clue that he'd been there. Stamps were his specialty. Stamps and coins. Oh, he'd lift your occasional piece of quality jewelry. But mostly it was stamps and coins, the things that could be sold without being traced to their original owners.

"It was the damnedest thing, Lieutenant. They say Seymour Dinklemayer could burgle people, and that they'd stay burgled for days or weeks without even knowing anything was missing. That's because he only took selected items, never a whole collection. And he never took cash, no matter how much was around, for fear it would tip off the victim that a burglary had taken place."

He rested a friendly arm on Dinklemayer's shoulder. "You know, Seymour," Schacter continued, "nowadays burglars don't care what kind of mess they leave behind. They finish with a place and you'd swear a tornado had hit it. We even had one guy who shit on the floor every time he burgled somebody. You'd better believe that pissed a lot of people off. I'm telling you, Lieutenant, they just don't make them like Seymour Dinklemayer anymore."

Dinklemayer's words were rapid and clipped, like staccato notes on a piano. "All right, Schacter. What do you want? You didn't come here just to talk about old times."

Schacter sighed. "No, unfortunately, I didn't."

"You've got nothing on me. I've been out of the business for years."

"Sure, sure. Of course, the last time I looked it was still against the law to impersonate a police officer."

Dinklemayer grimaced. "I don't have any idea what you're talking about."

"Actually, you did a pretty good job. Bloomberg didn't realize he'd been visited by an impostor until he met the real Rienzi." Schacter smiled at his colleague. "As you can see, Seymour, the resemblance is less than striking."

Dinklemayer looked at Rienzi. The lieutenant grinned at him. Dinklemayer shuddered and looked intently at his coffee.

"You're probably wondering how I figured out it was you," said Schacter. "I showed Bloomberg pictures of all Gordon Cardonick's known associates, people we've been keeping an eye on ever since Cardonick was released. But Bloomberg didn't recognize any of the pictures.

"And then I said to myself, suppose one of these guys hired someone else to impersonate Rienzi? So on a whim I get hold of Clive Burke's payroll tax records, and what do I discover? A part-time typist by the name of S. Dinklemayer."

"That's my sister Sophie, you bastard."

"Yeah, I know. I discovered that when I traced her address. And I discovered something else. She's legally blind, she's arthritic, and she hasn't done any work for Clive Burke in six years."

"So? So Burke sends her a little money each month to help her out. So what?"

"So I figure you're really the S. Dinklemayer he has working for him, and the two of you use your sister as a cover. And sure enough, I flash your picture in front of Bloomberg, and he identifies you in a snap."

Dinklemayer stood up. "I don't need to talk to you until I get in touch with my lawyer."

Rienzi grabbed the man's arm. "Sit down, Dinklemayer," he said, and he lifted the man back onto the stool.

"Tsk, tsk, Seymour," said Schacter. "I'm not here to arrest you. I'm here for a little friendly conversation."

"What do you want?"

Schacter grunted and rubbed his chin. "I want that envelope, Seymour. Burke must've hired you to track it down. I want you to bring it to me instead of him if you find it."

"Why should I do that?"

"You're forgetting, Seymour. There's still that little matter of impersonating a police officer. It'd sure be a shame if Sophie's brother landed back in prison on a rap like that."

Dinklemayer took another bite of cheesecake and washed it down with coffee.

Schacter stood. "You know where to reach me. Think about it, Seymour, but don't think about it for too long. Let's go, Lieutenant."

"See ya, Seymour," said Rienzi. He slapped Dinklemayer on the back once more, and coffee dribbled down the old burglar's chin.

"Gordon is gonna start playing in a few minutes," said the bartender. "He's in the pool room. You want me to let him know you're here?"

"No," said Whitney. "Let's just surprise him. I'll tell you what—do you have a pencil and paper?"

The bartender handed Whitney a notepad and his pen. Whitney scribbled something on it, tore off the top sheet, and folded it in half.

"Here, Joe," he said as he passed two dollars over the counter. "Buy yourself a drink. And when Gordon comes out, tell him his biggest fan requested this song." He gave the paper to the bartender.

"Sure. Hey, there he is now. I'll take it over to him."

Cardonick sat down at the piano and adjusted his stool. The bartender handed the folded paper to him. "Got a request for you, Gordon."

Cardonick read the message out loud. "'The Mickey Mouse Club Theme Song.' What the . . . all right, Joe, who's the comedian?"

"It's your pal over there."

Cardonick glared toward the bar. Whitney met his glance, smiled, and raised his glass in a mock salute.

Cardonick crumpled the paper angrily and stuffed it in the bartender's hand. "Tell the son of a bitch to shove it," he said.

"But, Gordon . . . I don't underst—"

"Get him out of here, Joe. I'll be playing pool. I don't go on until you get him out of here." Cardonick pushed himself back from the piano and walked away.

* * *

"You should try this, Stan," said Whitney. "It'll make you feel ten years younger. I've only been at it for a few weeks, and I can't remember the last time I felt so good."

Schacter stood next to the outdoor track and watched Whitney perform his preliminary stretching exercises. "How far do you run?"

"I started out at about a half mile. I'm up to about a mile and a quarter now." He straightened his legs and spread them apart, and he touched his fingers to the ground several times.

"I don't know, Thomas. I've never seen a serious jogger who looked happy while he was running. Besides, my brother-in-law—the orthopedist—he's really rolling in money these days. Doesn't that tell you anything?"

Whitney laughed, then stopped exercising and turned serious. "Maybe so. But the night I shot my gun off, when they called you to my house—that was the lowest point in my life. I made up my mind to get my ass in gear before it was too late." He rested one leg chest-high against a tree, and leaned in and out as he counted silently.

"Don't get stuck while you're doing that," said Schacter, "or the fire department will have to use the Jaws of Life to rescue you. Anyway, I'm glad you finally managed to get a hold on yourself. I was really getting worried about you."

Whitney placed his hands on his hips and twisted from side to side. "Well, the business with Cardonick really turned things upside down for me."

"I know. Speaking of Cardonick, I hear you've been spending a lot of time at Marsella's, that bar where he works."

"Where did you hear that?"

"I told you, Thomas. We're working on this guy, trying to get something on him for the D.A. I've got undercover men who switch off watching him at the bar. One of them recognized you. What are you, some kind of masochist?"

"Suppose I told you I heard it was a great place to meet women?"

"Suppose I told you to knock off the shit, Thomas. You created a little scene there the other night. They had to ask you to leave."

"The other night? Oh, right. Cardonick requested the pleasure of my absence. The bartender seemed pretty apologetic about the whole thing. He asked me to leave, so I left. What's the problem?"

"I don't want you getting in our way. I want you to stay away from there."

"So, what are you going to do? Arrest me?"

"Don't get sarcastic with me, Thomas."

Whitney touched Schacter's shoulder. "I'm sorry, Stan. Really. You've been a good friend these last couple of months. I don't know what I would've done without you."

The older man was embarrassed by Whitney's show of affection. "Ah, forget it. I guess there's no law against you going to Marsella's, is there? Although I'd feel a lot better if there was one. Listen—Katherine and I want you to come for Thanksgiving dinner next week . . . that is, if you don't kill yourself first trying to become a long-distance runner."

Whitney laughed, then dashed onto the track, his breath turning into clouds of vapor in the chilly November air.

"Why so standoffish, Joe?"

The bartender shrugged his shoulders and continued wiping the counter dry. "I don't know, Thomas. I guess I'm just surprised to see you back again after what happened last week."

"Last week? Oh, you mean Gordon's little temper tantrum. Hell, you know how temperamental these musicians get. It's part of their charm. I certainly don't hold it against you, Joe. You were just doing your job when you asked me to leave. No hard feelings, right?"

"Yeah," the bartender replied hesitantly. "I guess so."

"Terrific." Whitney dropped a five dollar bill on the counter. "A ginger ale for me, Joe. And something for yourself. And would you give this to Gordon when he comes in?" He gave the bartender a sealed envelope.

"Gee, I don't know . . ."

"It's okay, Joe. Really. You could call this something like a peace offering to Gordon."

"Well, he's here already, getting ready to play. You want me to take this to him now?"

Whitney passed him another five dollar bill. "If it's not too much trouble."

The bartender walked to the pool room and handed the envelope to Cardonick. "Your friend Thomas is back again. He asked me to give this to you."

Cardonick ripped open the envelope. "Damn. What the fuck does that son of a bitch want now?" He pulled a piece of paper from the envelope and read silently.

"Another song request?" asked the bartender.

"I'll kill the motherfucker!" Cardonick rushed into the bar. The bartender ran after him.

Cardonick grabbed the lapels of Whitney's sports jacket and spun him around. "Hey, you prick!" he said, and slammed him against the bar. He swung at Whitney with all his might.

The bartender caught Cardonick's fist in midair and brushed it aside as if it were a tiny insect. He wedged himself between the two men and shoved hard to separate them. "That's enough!" He held Cardonick at arm's length. "What the hell is going on between you two, anyway?"

Cardonick snarled at Whitney, the jagged edges of his teeth reflecting the dull light from the bar.

"All right," said the bartender. "It's over. Gordon, back off." He turned toward Whitney. "And you, don't you realize how dangerous this guy is?"

Whitney and Cardonick stood there glowering at each other, neither one moving an inch. After a few moments each took a tentative step backward.

"Okay." The bartender breathed a sigh of relief. "Whatever beef you guys have with each other, as of here and now you're even. Gordon, go cool off before you start to play. And Thomas, I'm going to have to ask you to leave again."

The two men went their respective ways. The bartender bent over and picked up the piece of paper that had made Cardonick so angry. He read the cryptic message on it: G.G.

The caller didn't waste any time with amenities. "Is this Schacter?" he asked.

"No, this is Lieutenant Rienzi."

"Let me talk to Schacter."

"Captain Schacter is out of town on assignment. Is there something I can do for you?"

"Yeah. I want you to take a message." The voice became louder and more insistent. "Tell Schacter to get his buddy Whitney off my back! I'm sick and tired of that guy hassling me. I know you cops are putting him up to it. So all of you had better leave me the fuck alone or there's gonna be trouble! You got it, cop?"

"Who are you?"

"Who am I?" the caller shouted. "You know who the fuck I am! This is Gordon Cardonick, you asshole! And this is my last warning. Good-bye."

The train ride from Philadelphia to New York City lasted two hours. Schacter used the time to review the facts of the case.

Elliot Sharman, the University of Pennsylvania student whom Cardonick had killed, was a drug dealer. Cardonick testified to that at his recommitment hearing, and Schacter's investigation confirmed it. Apparently the Ivy League junior was supplementing his generous allowance by supplying his classmates with marijuana and cocaine.

Schacter still didn't know the identity of the man who paid Cardonick to murder Elliot Sharman. The detective had exhausted his list of informants, and nobody knew of anyone named Cazzy. *Nobody except Cardonick,* he thought.

One thing was certain: Cardonick had been spending a considerable amount of money. There were the donations to Reverend Isaac's church, the new sports car, the payoffs on old credit card balances, and the advance payment on their mortgage principal. Schacter assumed Cardonick was still receiving money from Cazzy, and that in return he was protecting his benefactor from the police.

Schacter supposed that one of the six drug dealers Cardonick had contacted was Cazzy. Robert Marsella and Clive Burke were the prime suspects. Fuller Bloomberg had identified Marsella as the one who tried to buy the mysterious envelope for twenty thousand dollars. And it was Seymour Dinklemayer, working for Burke, who masqueraded as Rienzi. But Marsella and Burke couldn't both be Cazzy, so why were both of them so interested in that envelope? For now, it was just one more riddle for Schacter to solve.

The taxi driver navigated with the reckless abandon of one who had mastered the cardinal rules of Manhattan driving: the horn takes precedence over the brake, and a yellow light means you should accelerate to avoid the red. "Pretty fancy area, eh, pal?" he said when they reached the East Side brownstone that was Schacter's destination. "Nixon used to live around the corner. People were pissed as hell to see old Tricky Dick move in. But let me tell you, they were sorry to see him go. This was the safest neighborhood in the city when he was living here. Them Secret Service guys don't take no shit." Schacter nodded his agreement as he paid his fare. He slammed the car door behind him, walked up the steps, and rang the bell.

A butler opened the door. "Yes, sir," he said after Schacter identified himself. "Miss Champeau is expecting you. Please come in." The butler led him through the marble-inlaid foyer to the library. "Captain Stanley Schacter here to see you, miss."

"Yes, thank you, Horace. Please come in, Captain Schacter." Marilyn Champeau, girlfriend of the late Elliot Sharman, sat quietly on a couch on the far side of the room. Her dark, arrow-straight hair was closely cropped. She was pale and thin, and she hardly looked like someone who'd spent the last few months in California.

Before Schacter had a chance to sit, the doors of the library opened once more. They were joined by a regal-looking man with a leather attaché case. "How do you do, Captain Schacter. I'm Martin Putnam, Miss Champeau's attorney."

"He means he's my father's lawyer, don't you, Mr. Putnam?"

"Representing your interests, my dear," he replied.

"My father wanted to be present," she explained to Schacter, "but I was dead set against it. The only way I could get him to agree to stay away was by letting Mr. Putnam come. I hope you don't mind."

"No, of course not," said the detective. This was a criminal investigation, and Putnam looked more like the stocks-and-bonds type of lawyer. Schacter hoped the man wouldn't intrude too much into the conversation.

"I suppose you want to talk about Elliot, don't you, Captain?"

"Yes. I'm glad you were at home to answer the phone when I called yesterday. I've been wanting to talk with you for some time now, and your parents didn't seem to know how I might reach you."

She laughed softly. "I know. They probably told you I was traveling."

"As a matter of fact, they did."

"They think they're protecting me. I did travel to England right after the . . . right after Elliot died. My grandmother lives in London. But I've been back in the States since March. I spent some of the time since then at a psychiatric hospital on Long Island, the rest of the time shut up here. So I've been what you might call incommunicado."

She folded and unfolded her hands nervously. Schacter had seen marks before like the ones that dotted her wrists. He wondered how recently she had tried to cut them open.

"Poor Elliot," she sighed. "At least the police caught the man who . . . the man responsible."

Apparently she knew nothing of the more recent developments in the case. Schacter was about to tell her the details, but then he thought better of it. There was no need to upset her unnecessarily. "Actually, Miss Champeau, we believe there may have been more than one person involved. That's why I wanted to interview you."

The news took her by surprise. "But . . . yes, of course, but I—"

Putnam interrupted her. "Marilyn, let me remind you that you're under no obligation to speak with this gentleman. This isn't even his jurisdiction."

"That's all right, Mr. Putnam," she replied. "I'm sure the captain doesn't think I had anything to do with . . . with what happened, do you, Captain?"

Schacter smiled gently. "No, of course not. I'm just hoping that you might have some information that can help us find the person we're looking for."

"But I don't see how..."

The detective continued. "Miss Champeau, we know Elliot was selling drugs. Our information on that is pretty solid. Did you know he was involved in that kind of activity?"

Marilyn lowered her eyes. She nodded without speaking.

"Marilyn," said Putnam, "you're treading on dangerous ground here. You could leave yourself open for—"

It was Schacter's turn to interrupt. "Please, Miss Champeau. I'm not here to harm you. I'm only interested in making sure whoever was involved in Elliot's murder gets the punishment they deserve."

Tears formed in her eyes. She reached for a tissue and blew her nose. "It's all right, Mr. Putnam. I'm sorry, Captain Schacter. Please go on."

"We believe Elliot purchased a large amount of cocaine shortly before his death. We're looking for the person who sold it to him."

She chuckled sardonically. "He got burned."

"Excuse me?"

"Burned. Isn't that what you call it when you get cheated in a drug transaction?"

"Yes, it is. How did he get burned?"

"The week before Christmas, Elliot bought an ounce of cocaine—at least he thought it was cocaine—for five thousand dollars. He bought it from someone he had dealt with once or twice before."

"Did you go with him?"

She nodded. "I waited in the Burger King while Elliot and the other man did their business in the car. Anyway, it turned out to be bad stuff, more baking soda than cocaine. Elliot broke it down into grams, and the first couple of people he sold them to, friends of ours, said the stuff was no good. Elliot called the seller and demanded his money back. The seller said, sure, no problem, just bring me the stuff back. That's where Elliot was going when he...when he..."

She burst into tears. "I told him not to go. He didn't need the money that badly. I even offered to lend him some. I told him he was getting in over his head by meeting with this guy again. We fought about it. That's why I didn't go with him."

Schacter watched sadly as the young woman cried. Putnam seemed more embarrassed than anything else; clearly, he was not used to comforting people.

"Miss Champeau," said the detective. "We think the person who sold him those drugs was involved in the murder. Did Elliot ever mention the man's name?"

274

She blew her nose again. "Just a first name. Gary or Cary—something like that."

"How about Cazzy?" asked Schacter. "Could that have been it?"

"Maybe. I don't know. I really can't remember. I'm sorry."

"You said you went with him when he purchased the drugs. Were you able to see the man he bought them from?"

"Sort of, but it was dark."

"Do you think you'd recognize the person if you saw him again?"

She shrugged her shoulders. "I might. I don't know."

Schacter could barely contain his excitement. "Miss Champeau, I have some pictures to show you. I want you to look at each one carefully and tell me if you see the man who met Elliot that night in the parking lot."

He spread two dozen photographs on the table in front of her. Some of the people were principals in the case, and others were decoys.

Marilyn studied the pictures. She eliminated them one at a time, turning each photo facedown in the process. First she rejected a picture of Julius Erving. "Not this one," she said. "He wasn't black." She disqualified seven other pictures of black and Hispanic men. One by one she turned over most of the others, including all six of Schacter's suspects: Robert Marsella, Clive Burke, and the four other drug dealers Cardonick had been involved with.

She stared at the remaining two pictures for what seemed like an eternity. Finally she returned one of them to Schacter. "This man is too old," she said. It was Vice-President George Bush.

She held the last picture up in front of her face. "I'm not sure. I wouldn't swear to it, but I think this is him. This is your Cazzy."

She turned the photo around so Schacter could see it. It was a picture of Gordon Cardonick.

Whitney had thought about it over and over again. He was sure he'd finally figured it out.

A few nights earlier he had recorded the tape outside the firehouse in his neighborhood. It provided just the effect he wanted: the sound of sirens gradually fading away as the emergency vehicles drove off.

Standing in the pay phone outside the corner convenience store, Whitney could see Cardonick's house halfway down the block. He checked his wristwatch. *Ten minutes before six.* He switched on his portable tape recorder, slipped the necessary coins into the phone, and called Cardonick.

He held the phone several inches away from his mouth and shouted into it. He thought this would heighten the sense of urgency in his voice, as well as help to disguise it.

"Mr. Cardonick?"

"Yes. Who is this?"

"Mr. Cardonick, this is Sergeant Gladding of the Philadelphia Police."

"Listen, you bast—"

"Sir, there's been a serious automobile accident. Your mother-in-law and your daughter are being taken by ambulance to Northeast Hospital." Whitney turned his face away and shouted even louder. "I have the father on the phone right now." That was a nice authentic touch, he told himself. "Mr. Cardonick, can you get to the hospital yourself, or would you like me to send a police car to pick you up? Sir?"

Cardonick hesitated for just a moment. "No, no. I'll get there as soon as I can." He hung up.

Seconds later Whitney watched as Cardonick ran from his front door, started the motor of his new sports car, and blasted down the street toward the hospital.

He checked his watch again. *Exactly six o'clock.* He estimated that it would take Cardonick five minutes to reach the hospital, at least five minutes to realize there had been no accident, and another five minutes to return home. *More than enough time.*

He walked briskly to Cardonick's house. He turned the front door-knob. It was locked. He inserted a credit card into the crevice between the door and the doorjamb. The trick had worked in any number of detective novels he had read, but it didn't work for him. He pushed his shoulder against the door. It refused to budge.

A teenage girl walked by with a small terrier. She paused by a tree at the curb while her dog relieved himself. Whitney smiled nervously at her. He ran his hands through all of his pockets as if he were searching for a misplaced house key. Beads of sweat formed on his forehead in spite of the autumn chill.

The girl and her dog moved on. Whitney wrapped his right hand in a handkerchief and punched through a small windowpane near the top of the door. He reached for the lock on the inside of the door. He came up at least a foot short.

He lifted his right leg up in the air and aimed it at a spot just above the doorknob. Leaning back on his left foot, he lunged forward and planted his foot flat against the spot he had selected. The door opened an inch; a second kick opened it completely.

The living room was cluttered with several unopened cartons. Apparently Cardonick had just bought a state-of-the-art stereo system. Whitney scanned the room for the object of his hunt, the one he had read about in Cardonick's hospital chart. Whitney felt certain that the object would occupy a prominent position in the house, and he was sure he would recognize it as soon as he found it.

He looked unsuccessfully in the living room, dining room, and kitchen, then upstairs in the bedrooms. He dashed back down the stairs and then into the basement.

There were several empty cartons strewn around the room. Two microphones and an array of expensive-looking recording equipment were pushed over to one side of the room. Cardonick's piano sat on the other side.

There it is. A chill ran through Whitney when he saw the framed photograph on top of the old upright. He lifted it into his hands. She was even more beautiful than he remembered.

Whitney read the inscription: *I love you. Remember me always.* It was Valerie Green, Cardonick's mother, the woman with one green eye and one blue eye.

He took a pair of scissors and a razor blade from his pocket. He removed the photo from its frame, cut it into dozens of tiny pieces, and spread them across the keyboard of Cardonick's piano.

Whitney closed his eyes and slid the blade across the fleshy part of his left palm. Squeezing the palm with his right hand, he dripped a trail of blood over the pieces of Cardonick's prized souvenir.

"Please, sir, try to settle down." The emergency room receptionist was afraid the man might become violent. She looked around to see if there were any police in the vicinity.

"Settle down?" Cardonick screamed. "What do you mean, 'settle down'? First you tell me they're not here yet, and now you tell me you don't even have any record of an accident report."

She backed her chair away slowly. She tried to remain calm and even in her tone, but her voice began to shake out of fear. "I'm sure there's been some sort of mistake, sir. I'll just be a minute."

She returned with a hospital security guard. "What's the problem, bud?" the guard asked menacingly.

"What's the problem?" Cardonick repeated. He struggled to retain control. "I received a call from the police saying my daughter was in an accident. The ambulance was supposed to bring her here."

"Yeah, right, that's what the lady here just told me. I just checked with the police, and they don't show any such accident. Sorry, bud. Looks like someone's playing some kind of joke on you. Not a very funny one, either."

Some kind of joke, thought Cardonick. He ran to the pay phone in the hospital lobby and dialed his mother-in-law's number.

"Hello," she said.

The wave of sudden relief nearly forced him off his feet. For the first time in his life, he was glad to hear her voice.

"Hello," she repeated. "Who is this?"

He hung up without speaking and ran to his car. *Whitney!*

Cardonick sounded out of breath when he answered the phone. "Hello?"

278

"This is Whitney. I'm at Marsella's. I think I left something on your piano. Would you mind bringing it with you when you come?"

"You son of a—"

"Come on, now. Be a pal. Run downstairs to your piano and see if I left something on it."

Cardonick laid down the phone receiver and went down to the basement. A minute later Whitney heard him screaming at the top of his lungs. "You motherfucker! I'll kill you!"

Perfect, thought Whitney. *I'm waiting.*

48

Schacter stopped by the police station on his way home from the train depot. Rienzi told him about the telephone call from Cardonick.

Schacter grunted. "He sounds pretty agitated, doesn't he?"

"Yes, sir. I think he's heading off the deep end. I don't care what anybody says—I think the guy is nuts."

"Maybe," said Schacter as he rubbed his chin. "Maybe not."

"How did things go in New York? Did you find out anything from the girl?"

Schacter smiled. "Well, I think I know who Cazzy is. She made a tentative ID from one of the pictures I showed her."

"Wait, don't tell me. It's Clive Burke, isn't it?"

Schacter shook his head.

"Marsella?"

Schacter shook his head again.

Rienzi furrowed his brow. "If it's not Burke, and it's not Marsella . . . Holy shit! Don't tell me it's Seymour Dinklemayer. I didn't think he was the sort who'd get involved with murder."

"No," laughed Schacter. "It wasn't Seymour."

"Hell, I don't know. Don't just stand there. Which one did she pick? Who is he?"

"Meet the mysterious and elusive Cazzy," Schacter said as he dropped Cardonick's picture on the table with a flourish.

Rienzi's jaw dropped open. "What the fuck . . . I don't get it."

"Gordon Cardonick and Elliot Sharman were involved in a drug transaction," explained Schacter. "The deal went sour, so Cardonick

280

killed Sharman. Plain and simple. No Cazzy—unless Cardonick used that name himself. No mystery person paying Cardonick to murder Sharman."

"But I still don't understand. What about the five thousand dollars Cardonick had in his safe deposit box?"

"He got it from Sharman. Cardonick sold him an ounce of cocaine for five thousand dollars. It turned out to be crap. Sharman complained, so Cardonick agreed to meet with him and return the money. But Cardonick had no intention of doing that. He kept the money, and he killed Sharman on his way to the meeting."

"But the license number that was in the safe deposit box with the money..."

"They turned their drug deal in a parking lot. Cardonick probably wrote the number to help him find Sharman's car. Lucky for him, he stuck the number in with the money when he put it in the safe deposit box. It sure came in handy when he produced it in court. All he had to do then was make up the story about Cazzy and the murder contract."

"Well, I'll be damned." Rienzi stared dumbfoundedly at Cardonick's picture for several moments. "Where does this leave us?"

"If we can show that there was never any murder contract, then it means Cardonick was lying when he talked about it at his recommitment hearing in September. I'll get hold of the D.A. and the chief in the morning. If they give me the okay, I'll pick Cardonick up and book him for perjury."

Rienzi smiled. "I'd love to see that asshole's face when you read him his rights."

"Yeah. In the meantime, maybe we'll get lucky. If he's half as hopped-up as he sounded when he called you earlier," joked Schacter, "maybe he'll go out and kill a few more people tonight. Then we can really nail him to the wall."

"Great."

"Rest up, Lieutenant. It may be a pretty busy day tomorrow. And you should wear a nice suit tomorrow, one that'll look good when the television reporters come to interview us."

Rienzi laughed. "Yes, sir. Good night. Oh, I almost forgot. This came for you while you were in New York." He handed Schacter a large sealed folder. "A messenger from the Department of Social Services brought it over this afternoon."

Schacter went upstairs to his office and opened the folder. Inside was a copy of Dr. Foley's 1969 evaluation of Cardonick, the one that figured in the DSS decision to remove the boy from his home.

The detective read:

DEPARTMENT OF SOCIAL SERVICES
Cynthia Foley, M.D.

Name: Green, Gordon [Gigi]
Date of birth: April 3, 1956
Date of report: November 15, 1969

Reason for referral

Gordon Green, age thirteen, is the only child of Richard and Valerie Green from Northeast Philadelphia. The boy goes by the nickname Gigi, which was given to him by his mother, and which represents his first and last initials (G.G.).

Gigi was referred to the DSS by his junior high school counselor. According to her, the boy arrived at school one day in October with bruises on his arms, legs, and back. Gigi told the counselor that the bruises resulted from a beating by his father. He told her that he has suffered severe beatings for approximately two years, "ever since the old man stopped beating up my mother and started hitting me instead."

This is the second DSS evaluation of the child and his family. In 1967 his elementary school principal insisted that the Greens have Gigi examined by a psychiatrist. The boy had been caught several times fighting with peers and teasing pets in the neighborhood. At that time his parents were planning to divorce. A DSS psychiatrist examined the boy and his parents. As a result of the DSS evaluation they entered family counseling, which they apparently discontinued after three or four sessions. However, the couple did not go through with the divorce.

Behavior during interviews

Gigi was interviewed on three occasions. At first he was reluctant to talk with me. He stated that he hates psychiatrists. Apparently, he blames the DSS doctor who evaluated him in 1967 for the fact that his mother did not divorce his father. He feels that if the divorce had gone through, he would not have had to endure his father's beatings these past two years.

At the beginning of our first meeting Gigi drew a picture of the

282

psychiatrist who interviewed him in 1967. Then he held it up and stabbed it several times with his pencil. "I want him to die," he said. Then he ran underneath my desk and said, "Don't let him get me." (All of this was, no doubt, a symbolic expression of his anger toward and fear of his father.) Only when I assured Gigi that the other psychiatrist no longer works here was he willing to come out from his hiding place.

There was a link between Cardonick and Whitney after all. Schacter was certain of it now, even though Dr. Foley's report never mentioned Whitney by name.

It was too late in the day to call DSS to verify the identity of that first psychiatrist. The detective dialed Whitney's number, hoping his friend would remember, but there was no answer.

Schacter wondered if Denise Cardonick had ever heard her husband talk about that 1967 evaluation. He tried reaching her at work. Her employer, a Mr. Jason, informed Schacter that she had already left for the day. "She went to her mother's house for dinner, Captain. I think I have the number here someplace..."

"Denise will be down in a minute, Captain Schacter. She's helping Jennifer wash up for dinner. Can I get you something to drink?"

"No, thank you, Mrs. Boudreau."

"It's Gordon again, isn't it?"

"Ma'am?"

"He's in trouble again, isn't he? I swear, what will it take to make Denise realize she's better off without him? Do you have children, Captain?"

"Pardon?"

"Children never listen, do they? I should probably lie and try to convince my daughter how much I like Gordon. Then maybe she'd get rid of him, before it's too late."

"I'm sure Captain Schacter isn't interested in gossip, Mother," Denise said as she and Jennifer walked downstairs. "Good evening, Captain."

"Hello, Mrs. Cardonick. I'm sorry to trouble you like this. I wonder if I could have a minute of your time."

"Of course. Mother, would you take Jennifer into the kitchen while I talk with the captain?"

Jennifer ran up to Schacter before her grandmother could grab her hand. "Are you a policeman?"

Schacter leaned over and smiled at her. "I sure am, honey."

She frowned. "My daddy says the police stink."

"Jennifer!" shouted Denise. "Captain Schacter is a very nice man. He's Mommy's friend. I want you to tell him you're sorry right now."

The little girl looked at the ground sheepishly. "I'm sorry." She held out her box of saltwater taffy as a peace offering. "Here. You can have one of these."

"Oh, boy," he said, his eyes open wide with exaggerated enthusiasm. "My favorite kind." He unwrapped a piece of the candy and dropped it in his mouth. "I really like saltwater taffy. When I was your age, I used to buy big boxes every summer on the boardwalk."

"My daddy bought them for me in Atlantic City."

"Isn't that nice." It took a moment for her remark to register. Schacter stopped in the middle of his chewing. His eyes grew narrow and the smile disappeared from his face. "When was he in Atlantic City?"

The girl was frightened by the detective's sudden coolness. She rushed across the room and buried her face in Denise's skirt.

"Oh, Jennifer. Don't be so silly. Tell Captain Schacter about our nice trip." Denise turned toward the detective. "Gordon took us to Atlantic City last month. We had a lovely time, didn't we, Jennifer?"

Schacter had a notion which, had it occurred some other time, he might have dismissed as ridiculous. But it had been a day for shocking realizations. Perhaps there was one more in store.

He swallowed the candy and stared at Denise. "Did he mail any letters?"

"Did he . . . huh?"

"Your husband," Schacter said loudly. "Did he mail any letters from Atlantic City?"

"No . . . I don't know . . ."

"What difference does that make, Captain?" asked Denise's mother.

His voice trembled as he spoke. "Phoenix . . . Mrs. Cardonick, does the name Phoenix mean anything to you?"

She sensed the urgency in Schacter's voice, and she wrung her hands nervously. "It's in New Mexico, isn't it? I think it's the state capital."

"Arizona, Denise," said her mother disapprovingly.

Denise frowned. "I'm sorry, Captain. I was never very good at geography."

Schacter's mind reeled as he tried to fit together the pieces of an intricate puzzle. He was still struggling with the realization that Cardonick might, indeed, be Cazzy. And now he wondered: *Was Cardonick also the Phoenix all along?*

It seemed too incredible to be true. And yet he was certain Cardonick and Whitney had met years earlier—the DSS report convinced him of that—and that the meeting had filled Cardonick with the rage of a killer.

And then there were the newspaper clippings, the ones Denise had found in Cardonick's piano. Skeptical earlier, now Schacter was convinced: Cardonick stalked Whitney for a year *before* the Christmas Eve murders.

The Phoenix was wickedly manipulative, a master of psychological assassination—just like Cardonick.

Schacter had to warn Whitney. The Phoenix had threatened his friend with death. And Whitney had been pushing Cardonick hard, not realizing how long and how deeply the man had been hating him, not suspecting that Cardonick and the Phoenix might be one and the same. And judging from Cardonick's call to Rienzi that day, the killer was reaching his breaking point.

Schacter rushed to the telephone and dialed Whitney's number. There was no answer.

"Is your husband playing at Marsella's bar tonight?" he asked.

"Yes, he is."

Schacter was out the door without another word. He stuck the magnetic flashing light onto the roof of his car. His tires squealed as he pulled away quickly from the curb.

"This is Detective Captain Stanley Schacter," he barked into his two-way radio. "Send all available units to Marsella's bar at the corner of Cottman and Brinkley." He paused, then added reluctantly: "Possible homicide in progress."

Whitney, you pigheaded son of a bitch! I warned you to stay away from that bar!

The evening was young. There were only a few patrons in Marsella's bar.

Whitney was sitting at a small table in the corner. He was sweating profusely.

He was waiting for Cardonick.

He reached inside his sports jacket and fingered the two-inch barrel of his thirty-eight caliber Colt Detective Special. All five chambers were ready to go, and he tightened his grip on the handle.

He'd never shot anyone. Now, after all those years at Littleton—years of vicarious participation in scores of brutal scenes—Whitney was poised on the threshold of the ultimate act: the taking of a human life.

Whitney stared intently at the rear door, the door Cardonick always used. His pulse was racing; he could almost hear his heart beat. His throat and mouth were parched, but he didn't dare divert his attention to the ginger ale on the table in front of him.

"Something wrong with your drink, sir?" asked the waitress.

"Hmm? Oh, no, Bonnie. Everything is fine. Thanks."

Whitney remembered the story the bartender had told him on his first visit to Marsella's, the story about Bonnie wanting to go to Atlantic City with Cardonick. It was a story of no seeming importance, something he wasn't even aware he'd tucked away into the back of his mind, until he heard Schacter say, "All the other letters came from Philadelphia. This one came from Atlantic City."

And the dream he had that night unlocked the mystery for him. The woman with a green eye and a blue eye was Valerie Green, Cardonick's mother. And Whitney and Cardonick had met before, years earlier.

After an evaluation, Whitney had suggested that the boy's parents enter marriage counseling. He met with the couple two or three times, but soon they stopped keeping their appointments. Two years later the father was jailed for abusing young Gordon, the boy was taken from his mother, and Valerie Green killed herself out of grief.

Cardonick was the Phoenix—Whitney was certain of that—and the last letter from the Phoenix an unmistakable death threat.

He tried to imagine how it would be. Cardonick would rush at him, gun in hand. But Whitney was prepared. He would reach into his jacket, extract the Colt Detective Special, and pump the trigger until the bullet chamber was empty. *And everyone would call it self-defense.*

He hunched over the table, never taking his eye off the rear door. The sound of blood pulsing through his temples reverberated in his skull. He wiped his clammy palm on the edge of the tablecloth, then returned it to the handgun. Slowly he began pulling the weapon out of his jacket pocket, first one inch, then another, then—

Whump. The blow caught him by surprise. It pushed him down into his chair and held him there. Whitney saw the hairy, muscled hand on his shoulder and stared up into the most sinister face he'd ever seen.

"Is this the guy, boss?"

"I do believe it is. Check his wallet, Eddie. Let's find out for sure."

The hairy man reached inside Whitney's back pants pocket. "Here it is, Mr. Marsella."

Marsella opened the billfold. "Very good, Eddie. Uh-huh—Dr. Thomas Whitney. Well, well. I've heard quite a bit about you, Doctor."

"Yeah," snickered the hairy man, "quite a bit."

"Quiet, Eddie. We wouldn't want the doctor to think we're inhospitable. But I guess he knows us better than that. I understand you've been our guest quite often, haven't you, Doctor?"

Whitney started to shake. Any minute now, Cardonick would blaze into the room. The psychiatrist felt the sweat pouring down his forehead and into his eyes. They burned, but the hairy man's grasp prevented him from rubbing them.

"Hey, you." Eddie tightened his hands around Whitney's arms. "Mr. Marsella asked you a question."

"What?" said Whitney. He could barely hear his own voice.

"Well, Doctor, my piano player tells me you've been coming here a little too often to suit him." Marsella shrugged his shoulders. "Musicians—

287

what can you do? Still, I want to keep Gordon happy. Search him, Eddie."

The hairy man plucked Whitney off the chair and threw him face-forward against the wall. He ran his hands through Whitney's pockets while the waitress and bartender watched in silence. He wrapped his paw around the handgun and yanked it out of Whitney's jacket.

Whitney's heart beat so feverishly that he could feel it pounding against the inside of his rib cage.

Marsella fondled the weapon. "Well, well. What have we here? Looks like a concealed weapon to me. What does it look like to you, Eddie?"

There was a large gap between the hairy man's two front teeth when he smiled. "Looks like a concealed weapon to me, too, boss."

"Tsk. Tsk. I wonder if the doctor has a license to carry concealed weapons. You know, Doctor, guns and bars don't mix very well. Even Eddie isn't allowed to carry a gun in here, are you, Eddie?"

"Uh-uh, boss. You want me to throw him out?"

"No, we'll let the police handle this one. They tend to take a dim view of this sort of thing. Keep our guest company, Eddie. I'll telephone the police from my office." He called to the waitress. "Bonnie, another ginger ale for my friend here. On the house." Marsella left.

Whitney eyed the rear door, the one leading to the pool room and Marsella's office, the one he was sure Cardonick would come through within seconds. His pulse was racing so fast it took his breath away. He turned to the hairy man. "Listen, you've got to understand—"

"Shut up. Don't try to confuse me." The man twisted Whitney's arm until pain shot through his entire upper body.

Seconds seemed to stretch endlessly, and he could only hear the sound of his breathing. He saw a police cruiser come to an abrupt halt outside the tavern. A blue light swirled around the room in perfect synchronicity with his heartbeat. Now a second blue light poured through the window and circled inside the tavern. And still he could not move . . .

The first gunshot came from beyond the rear door. It echoed off the walls of the enclosed corridor. All movement in the bar ceased for a fraction of a second. Whitney heard the dull thud of a body hitting the floor in the corridor.

Cardonick exploded into the bar, his pistol smoking at his side. He paused for the smallest instant, saw Whitney, then charged forward like a lunatic beast.

The waitress screamed. The hairy man flipped the table up and dove behind it. Cardonick howled wildly, too crazed to utter an intelligible word.

Whitney screamed "No!" and turned to run toward the blue police lights. Schacter was running from his car toward the tavern. The two friends locked eyes for an instant through the window.

Whitney heard one shot, then another. The pain was white-hot. It seared through his back and bludgeoned him to the floor. His body jerked as if under someone else's control, rolling him onto his back.

The door was open and Schacter was shouting something at him, but Whitney heard only his own erratic breathing. The scene froze and then evaporated like a movie-screen fadeout.

A final, deafening shot rang out.

50

The older Schacter got, the younger the hospital's doctors seemed. The bearded, ponytailed man in a physician's smock found the detective in the hallway outside the intensive care unit. "Captain, I'm Wally Kolb, the surgeon who performed the operation. Are you here to place him under arrest?"

Schacter grimaced. "How is he, Doctor?"

"About as well as can be expected. The bullet missed his heart by about an inch, and his lung by even less. He lost a lot of blood."

The surgeon handed Schacter a small plastic bag. "This is for you. The bullet split when it lodged against his rib cage. We got the whole thing in these two chunks here."

"Thank you." Schacter pocketed the bag. "Well, Doctor—"

"Please," interrupted the surgeon. "Call me Wally."

The young man's informality was disconcerting. Schacter preferred doctors to be older and more reserved.

"Well," the detective continued, "what do you think? Will he make it?"

"Yes, he'll make it. He won't be kicking any field goals in the near future, but he should have a relatively straightforward recovery."

"Can I see him now?"

"I can let you have ten minutes with him. If you don't mind a nurse being present, that is."

"No, of course not. Thank you, Doctor."

"Please," replied the surgeon as he led Schacter toward the restricted area, "call me Wally."

The nurse sat unobtrusively with a magazine in the corner of the room as Schacter approached the bed. He paused a moment to control his anger and said, "You didn't really think you'd get away with it, did you?"

Whitney opened his eyes. He stared blankly at his visitor for a moment, then smiled weakly. He looked at the intravenous tubes sticking out of his arm and shuddered.

"I told you to stay away from that goddamn bar. You got lucky, Thomas."

Whitney's voice was hoarse and feeble. It hardly sounded like his own. "What . . . what about Cardonick?"

"Dead."

Whitney closed his eyes and breathed deeply. "How?"

"The bartender." Schacter smiled grimly. "I told you once before, Thomas. We had undercover men watching Cardonick at Marsella's. The bartender was one of ours."

The nurse leaned forward, trying to hear the conversation without appearing to be eavesdropping.

Schacter said, "When I looked through the window, I saw you hit the ground. Then I heard another shot. I was sure you were dead. But it was the bartender shooting Cardonick."

Whitney sighed. "Pretty fortunate for me."

"Uh-huh. But Marsella wasn't quite so lucky. Cardonick killed him with one shot. Marsella had a handgun—a Colt Detective Special—but he didn't have time to use it. I figure he was just in the wrong place at the wrong time. Cardonick was coming after you. And he's been coming after you for a long time."

Whitney looked away and sighed.

"What's the matter, Thomas? You look uneasy all of a sudden."

"I guess I just don't know what you mean, Stan."

"What I mean is this: I think Cardonick and the Phoenix were one and the same person."

Whitney whistled softly through his teeth. "That's incredible," he said. "I don't know if I can believe that."

Schacter grunted, rubbed his chin, and told Whitney about Dr. Foley's 1969 DSS report and her mention of an earlier evaluation. "Think back, Thomas. In 1967, an eleven-year-old boy. Do you remember examining Gordon Green?"

Whitney closed his eyes as if he were searching his memory. "Hell, Stan, that's so long ago. I've done thousands of evaluations since then."

"See if this helps you. He went by a pretty unusual nickname back then. Gigi."

"Gigi?" Whitney furrowed his brow. "Sorry, Stan. I'm drawing a blank on that one. That's a girl's name, isn't it? Like in the movie?"

"Yeah, well, no matter. I'll get a copy of that 'sixty-seven report tomorrow. And I'll bet you dollars to doughnuts your signature is on the bottom of it."

The surgeon stepped into the room. "Captain Schacter, you're going to have to leave now. I don't want my patient to get exhausted."

"Just a couple of minutes more. What do you say, Wally?"

The surgeon turned to his nurse. She nodded her head to indicate that everything was under control. "All right, Captain. A few more minutes." He left the door ajar.

Whitney shook his head. "I just don't know if I can buy your theory. That's more than sixteen years ago. A hell of a long time to carry a grudge, don't you think?"

The detective told Whitney about the newspaper clippings Denise had discovered. "I don't think we'll ever know the whole story, now that Cardonick is dead. But I figure he saw you on the grounds of Littleton the first time he went there. That must have jogged his memory. Then, after he got out on parole, he started keeping track of you. It turned into some kind of obsession."

"And that's when I started getting letters from the Phoenix."

"Exactly. And when he got arrested for the Christmas Eve killings a year later—while he was waiting for you to begin your evaluation of him—he figured out a way to bring you down."

"Wouldn't it have been simpler for him just to kill me?"

"When?"

"After he got out of Littleton the first time. Or the second time, for that matter."

"Yeah, well, what can you say about a guy who would torture kittens to death? He obviously liked watching his victims squirm. I think he enjoyed sticking the blade in slowly and then twisting it."

Whitney's face contorted in sudden pain. "Did they get the bullet?"

Schacter smiled and displayed the plastic bag. "You can have it as a souvenir after the boys at the lab match it up with Cardonick's pistol. Just a formality at this point. Then we can close the book on this case once and for all. The press should get a hell of a lot of mileage out of this one. But this time, I have a feeling you're gonna come out smelling like a rose."

"Really?"

"Yeah. You see, one of the emergency room assistants recognized Cardonick when they carried his body in. Turns out Cardonick was here at the hospital earlier this evening, about twenty minutes before he shot you. He had some crazy idea about his daughter being in danger. They thought he was out of his mind, and they also thought he might get violent. They called the police, but Cardonick was gone before anything could come of it. When the press gets hold of that, they'll think you were right about him all along on the Christmas Eve killings."

"Not guilty by reason of insanity," said Whitney.

"Yeah. But if Cardonick was really as smart as he thought he was, he'd never have come after you, and no one would ever have thought to look at him again. He almost got away with murder."

Whitney smiled and closed his eyes and turned away.

The surgeon returned. "I'm sorry, Captain. I can't let you stay any longer."

"Sure thing," he replied. He patted Whitney's leg and walked toward the door.

Schacter paused in the doorway and turned around to face Whitney. "Thomas," he called.

"Yes?"

The detective stared silently at his friend, as if he were struggling to place the final pieces in a huge puzzle.

"What is it, Stan?"

Schacter's eyes narrowed. "You wouldn't happen to know anything about this, would you?"

"About what, Stan?"

He stared at Whitney, examining his face carefully. "About that 1967 report. About Cardonick being the Phoenix."

"But...but, Stan," stammered Whitney. "I don't...you know... Hell, Stan. You're the only detective here. I'm just a middle-aged psychiatrist with a damn bullet hole in his back."

The police captain continued to look at Whitney for several seconds. "Yeah, I guess so," Schacter finally said as he turned to leave. "After a day like I've had, your mind can start to play tricks on you."